Nazi-Zombies

The complete collection of stories

By A D Hunt

This book is dedicated to my parents both who have now sadly died, but who were there for me when the (swearword) hit the fan; To my darling wife, Lynette and our children, in age order: - Michael, Eleanor, Jessica and Angela. To my dear friends, who know how hard it is being dyslexic. My Facebook supporter's, those whom I have met, those who I have shared my feelings with and those whom I have fallen out with. (A special mention for J. Also L.H. A.E, D. B and S.K both the American writer and my dear poetry friend in Scotland as well as M.P, oh God I could be here all day! They know who they are. Love to all of them. I would also like to the sincerely thank the publishers who encouraged me to do this. Well that's not true, they said NaziZombies was too short, so I grabbed all my stories and put them together to get over word count. Though I would like to add, that the publishers are great people who work really, really, hard. Bless them to bits, especially you at the back! Come on! Take a bow! Finally, I send a humble sense of gratitude to the creators of "Wolfenstein" without which and whom I would have lost both my sense of humor and the need to fight several years ago: be the light in the darkness

    ADH

A note on the text and a little jumbled bio.

This book in front of you, is 14 years in the making. It comes to you in two parts. Part one is entitled "Nazi-zombies"; this contains "Nazi-zombies" "why I call them NaziZombies" and "NaziZombies: 2 the attack of the Dump". This text is a short satire, written in a "post- truth, Alt fact" style that reflects the age in which we live; where politics and the Aristotelian/Platonic notion for what is termed as "the common good", has been dispelled with, against a need to selfie ourselves to death, while watching endless rubbish on television.

 Part two is entitled "and other animals". This is divided into three sections, Horror, future fantasy and children's stories. It is essentially a collection of texts that I have been working on over the last six to eight years and are also available on my word press blogsite: A.D Hunt author. However, as this is a book format, there are many editorial changes I have made to the stories themselves, thus separating these texts from the on-line blogs.

  One change was the insertion of Dump's mother as opposed to Dump's wife. This is because I found myself in a position of empathy for her. I also had to recognize that satire at its sharpest, cuts deeper, when it is in the memory of the individual. It also changes with the public mood, and can quickly move from being acutely funny, to acutely painful and very unfunny depending upon the circumstances.   I also found some major errors in spelling and punctuation. At first I wanted to keep them in. ZombieNazi's is, I feel, the first Alt fact post truth text. It needs to be spelled badly. I always felt that it was Literature's Punk. A finger well and truly stuck up to the establishment and the prescriptive nature of the publishing industry and the literary critics, who are so self- obsessed with what they consider a good read, that they fail to recognise how the affordance of technology has changed the very essence a text is portrayed.

There is a reason why the old texts have stood the test of time while more modern and post-modern literature is ignored. It is because It does not play well on the theatre of the mind. For it is here, that a book comes alive. At this point, I also would expect you would want me to defend the art of the short story and give some sense of its merit against the novel. To discuss -perhaps- James (swearing) Joyce and Russian (more swearing) formalism, or some witticism in relation to keeping the writing going and how these aspects of writing influenced me. Sorry, no way. The fact is the stories ended. In some cases, the voice of the character simply stopped talking to me, as in NaziZombies, the Long room and Jake. In other cases, I took the text as far as it could possibly go, before the creative juices that inspired the writing simply gave up. In sum, I wrung the idea dry.

My style of writing might seem -to other'-s weak and lack intellectual depth. ("But it's not in POV they cry" well, (swearing) that.) in reply, I don't sit down at the laptop and say "this is what I am going to write" and plan a story from beginning to end, while... aching...over (long pause) every (longer pause) single (a very long pause indeed) word. Though, to my regret I have tried it. However, when I have, nothing comes up and when it does it turns to (swearing); so I stopped writing that way.

I tend to start with one character and take that character into a world, that itself, is morphed through the writing. For me, that's the fun behind it. That is also what makes the ends shocking for me, because even I -the writer- have no idea where the stories are going. This naturally leads to the "why are you a writer" question, especially in an age when writing short stories -like these- have become part of a 50's culture that has now long passed.

In answering this, I must say, you know, I, I don't really know. I have always been a reader of fiction. I especially loved horror stories and thrillers. I read horror - and liked it- because, the end was always bad and that was how I perceived life, then and now. I started writing at an early age and with this came a passion for words and spelling. One of my oldest memories, is sitting in the back seat of our parent's Morris Minor, I think it was, spelling words like "Tyrannosaurus Rex" while my sister did the math. She was and is always good at math. The trouble was -and being honest here- I masked a lot. The dyslexic brain can do that. In fact, I didn't know I had a problem with either reading or writing until I faced a diagnosis of dyslexia from the O.U at 46.

As a prepubescent teen, my first short story was about

an alligator eating people. It went through two drafts; the first, to my perverse delight, made my teacher wince.

The second I received my first commendation, a coveted "A- "as it contained an E.A Poe metaphor that I stole from "The house of Usher". In retrospect and with a degree of English language and literature behind me; I now know I used hyperbole in the first draft of the text. At the time, it was simply fun to watch her wince. That was the only positive thing that happened in five years at an all-boys secondary school. (I shall omit the name.) I left education at 16 with no qualifications, (a c.s.e was/is not a real qualification) mainly because school was vicious, brutal and evil; and I, blandly thinking believed that I could survive in the "real world"

Sadly, I found myself adrift. I was hit with reality of a mid to late 80's Britain where only the elite who "yupped" into their enormous mobile phones could survive, as the factories slowly closed or moved abroad. It is fair to say, that after I left school, I drifted and drank and drifted and drank. My beast -in the darkness- slowly taking hold of me.

I was hit with my first epileptic seizure, after I became a nursing axillary in 1990. This condition has shaped me as an individual and in turn has had an impact upon my writing. Many people just get on with it. I found it impossible. I still do. The fact is, I am not one of those "success" driven people. I haven't sought much from this life, other than to write, have a family and listen to music, occasionally dance, (swearing) have a beer or four, smoke a little weed and late at night, have deep -and what I consider meaningful- conversations about the reality of it all. I didn't know at the time that this led to a liking for philosophy. Truth be told, I had no knowledge of the topic's existence, until I heard the word "valid" used for the first time in 2009. Perhaps that is the problem (…)Perhaps, I've simply wanted to survive and not live life to the full?

Saying that, I've always preferred the inner journey to the outward exploration of the world. This is due to the notion that I perceive this outside world as a pretty horrible, tatty place. Moreover, when it is made neat and tidy, it's usually tidied up by a bunch of super rich psychopath's, who kill the unemployed, the homeless, the mentally ill and-or the disabled; and when they are out of the way, then it's the Jew or the Muslim or the Christian, or any minority that they can think of, because, their vision of neat and tidy, usually leads to enormous buildings dedicated to their wealth and another's less fortunate, less economically supported, suffering.

In my later youth, and then in my early twenties, I used a hell of a lot of notebooks to write in. These were essentially thrown way by my parents because they simply saw scribbling. I lost a lot more work when my ex-partner burned another set at 27, this is work that can never be replaced...I'll leave that sentence hanging.

I lost my position as a nursing auxiliary in 2000, this led to a mental health breakdown in 2001; the fruit of this period of my life is the short story "A tale of the not-so magical garden, the tale of the forget-me-not" During this time I was looked after by my parents. Well, when I say my parent's, it really was my mum, who sought new medication for my ongoing condition.

By 2003 and with a lot of help from a real man of God called Rev (F), I found myself almost stable and in a flat, so I tried to get myself writing and employment again. Though it was hard work. The epilepsy was still uncontrolled and employment was challenging, so it is honest to state that between 2001 to 2004 life was painful. I found myself with a bizarre religious conviction, some of which was because I was lonely, but also it was because of uncontrolled seizures, yet it was more than that. It took a long time for me to recognize a father's love. A lot of this is due to my father, being a police officer was never really at home, and when he was at home, there was a sense of animosity.

We were – and are- two very different people; and the lack of conversation between us, together with the violence I experienced at school didn't help.

So, it became almost destined that the written page and the bottle became a place of both escape and safety. I could be me there and through that feel a sense of freedom. This you will see in texts such as Mr Clay, which is about the freedom of allowing pure imagination and creativity to grow and flow without constraint.

By mid-2004, I met the person who has become my closest friend. Lynette. It was not long after we met that I moved in and with that became directly excluded from the church, which, it has to be said, was to be expected; on the plus side, for first time in my life I became a parent. Being a step father is difficult. To start with You know that this child has no biological connection to you. However, you have to take on the role of father. When that child has a learning challenge, it's even harder. I will not go into details, other than I expected more, from the one person who should have been there but also fully understood the unkindness of men. One thing I have seen is that little boy become a fine young man with a future

By 2005 and the birth of our first daughter there were global signs that things were turning to (swearing). Adverts filled the TV about loans, gold was being sought after in huge amounts, then, as if by magic, the credit crunch (a rubbish BBC gloss to describe the birth of the second great global depression in 2005 (and haven't we been hit by loads of those recently: like bloody Brexit and the Trumpism bigly.)) appeared,   I then decided, that not having any qualification, whatsoever, was simply a (swearing) idea. Our society is a capitalist one, this means, you need coin to make coin. Once you have the coin, then you can do what you want. Look at Donald Trump for that. But if you don't have coin, don't expect the system to help you. It won't. Compared to the old soviet system, where employment and a home is guaranteed by the state, it seems to me this notion of a single free market is well (swearing).

For two years between the birth of Nell and Jessica, I took a long hard look at my life and decided that I had to better myself and through this hopefully our income. So despite the pain (the emotional pain) I recognized the need for an education, However at the age of 35 I was a bit trapped: no money equals no work no work now money so I opted for the only place that would take a person in the benefit prison: The open university.

Here comes a huge question: "Why did it take so long?" Well, to start with I began at the bottom rung, I had to do an induction course into the OU, and then follow-on course, I had to skip a year in 2008, 9 because of various house moves and started again in 2010. Despite that, there was a lot of nappy's, lots of school runs, lots of play with the family, lots of walking, and lots and lots of facing what occurred at (-------------) school.

I must say, that in retrospect, by 2008/9 I was still naïve enough to think that getting a degree might give me the opportunity to find a job that paid enough to keep a roof over our heads. Besides, I was learning. I learned keyboard skills, editing skills, and how to express myself on the paper well. These I thought would help me gain a position as a secretary or a receptionist. The pay would be rubbish, but it would be work and I was obsessed about work.

At the time, the Open University were offering free courses for people on state benefits, the trouble then was, what direction should I take? I had no idea of what course to do. My math was, and still is, well, pretty (swearing, swearing). That being the case, I tried to avoid that. The only thing I knew I could do well was write short stories, so I took a creative writing course, then another creative writing course after that. From here, at about 2010, I was diagnosed by the O.U as having dyslexia and dyspraxia. Which, at the time, made me laugh, as I found myself both an epileptic, dyslexic, a rhyming condition that has shaped my life to that date.

After I received a diploma of higher education in 2011,

I was then convinced, by the OU and by myself that I could take this further and get an honours degree.

I took the challenge and instantly found myself over my head; buried deep in humanities subjects on the nature of art, history, religion and of course English: Where our language came from, where it is going and its influences on culture, through literature; together with the history of the novel and genuine influence on the language we use, before ending with the stylistic approach to literature as well as understanding the creative process though language, and drama.

My head was bursting with new information. It became clear how much I had missed out on because of what occurred at (-------------------) all those years ago...

It was a very difficult time, both emotionally and physically, to start with, I had to consider the influences of religion in a paper during the death of my mother. My dyslexia also kicked in and I found myself writing about how the psychological impact of belief systems has had both a negative and positive impact upon our individuality. (needless to say, I failed that essay with stokes of a pen)

Also in 2012 the UK government had decided to blame the sick and the disabled for being, well, essentially, sick and disabled. Now, wait a minute, I can see it from their position, after all, it was obviously their fault that the credit crunch occurred... wasn't it? After all they sit about all day long, like me doing nothing. It must be them and not the glorious bankers and their sycophantic, sociopathic mates in parliament (who do up their ties, wear business suits and allegedly (swearing) the occasional dead pig or two.) who take money away from people in taxes to keep their coin in line with the tide of hyperinflation and greed. These people are upstanding. They are, we elected them. (I'll leave that sentence hanging.)

So, sigh, coin was removed, we struggled. Coin was given back, this time in my wife's name and we survived. It was at this time I was given a speculative diagnosis of type 2 diabetes, so I could add diabetic to my rhyming diseases, "I'm a poetic, epileptic diabetic dyslexic, see even my conditions rhyme" became a bit of a mantra at home.

The trouble was, to keep up with my studies, and to keep the understanding and new knowledge in my head, I needed brain food. During this phase I took to sniffing rosemary oil and chomping on bags and bags of mini chocolate twirls. This wasn't in any way good for a man in his mid-forties, but I was, for the first time in my life to date, driven to pass something; and pass with honours I did, in 2015.

So here I am, 2 years later an honours degree graduate of English language and literature. "TA DA" Where do I go now? well, I was offered a position to teach English to Chinese children...in China! (lots of swearing and shouting) ok, so that's a no go but here's the nub, I haven't been able to get into teaching here, in the UK either, because to teach I need experience in a class room and I can't get the experience in a class room so I cannot train to teach, maybe you see the cycle.

I went with various agencies for day work but found myself in an endless cycle of traps and (swearing) pigeonholes. I was offered voluntary transcription work at Exeter University that was a disaster and volunteer factory work and with AGE UK. But still no coin. I cannot even get a position at a local recycling plant (see the introduction at the start of Nazi zombies) so depression and finally drinking set in. Perhaps we can now add alcoholic to the list of rhyming conditions? Perhaps it's always been there...

It's fair to say, that things are and have been slowly falling apart. I have physically hit the bottom. This is where I am now, and why you are reading this collection. I hope you enjoy it, find it amusing, occasionally scary with twists and turns. Furthermore, dear reader, thanks so much for buying this. You are helping a family in ways you couldn't possibly imagine. Thanks for stopping by, dear and faithful reader.

Yours A D Hunt

Contents

PART ONE NAZI-ZOMBIES

Nazi-Zombies and Nazi-zombies 2

a post truth reflection on the alt/right and its growth in society.

A note about the text

Nazi zombies and Nazi zombies two came to me in a series of visions from God as I sat there, on the bog, having one of those bowel motions that… No, that is utter bullshit. The truth is, NaziZombies came to me while I was suffering from the most painful bout of depression I have experienced in years. I had just finished my English language and literature degree, (2015, honours 2:2… yeah, I was a bit stunned myself to be honest.) and found myself writing ten job applications a day, and not getting even an interview let alone a reply. One reply I have received is from Devon county council, for a position at the waste and recycling department. It states that "I am not the right material for the position" Naturally, this led me to consider what sort of person Devon county council were looking for in waste management; and why of course I was not the right material for the position. In any case, and for posterity, I have mentally printed it off and put it in a frame in my illusionary office. It hangs on the corner by the doorway. A reminder that in passing through things, life has to get shitty before it gets better.

At about this this time, The UK had its loosely termed "referendum" over the EU, and a certain man whom I cannot name and will not, because I don't want to give the arsehole any credit, was splashed over what has become the state imposed media, telling everyone that this result was "the best thing for the British people." Sadly, with this man's vitriolic and ugly rhetoric, arose hatred, racism and bigotry. I'll leave that sentence hanging.

I then considered that over-all, this man (whom I shall not name) talks utter mindless bullshit, that that if people were honest couldn't really understand. Consider this: - for the last eighty years, the establishment of the UK have been wondering what the EU or Europe was all about. In fact, it has caused such confusion in political circles that the Lisbon treaty (or a UK get of EU/ Europe treaty.) became enshrined in EU law. Ok, that's established premise one. Premise two now follows; if the British establishment have no idea about the EU, how can you, me, a bloke up in Sidwell street or one lone sad Thatcher loving ex stockbroker, would be con man and somehow elected M.E.P have any idea about it? The conclusion logically arrived at is stark. We have no clue either.

However, this man, who shall be nameless does know. He knows more than the establishment does, and -of course we have to believe him.

The fact that he was elected as an M.E.P and then decided not to represent British interests in Europe, and get paid, by the E.U and the rest of us not to do so, for the British people, I might add, left me laughing so hard, I nearly fell on the floor with a heart attack. I simply cannot get my head around this new non-logic. (We now know this non-logic, to be called post-truth, or Alt facts back then it was simply "telly nonsense".)

Then I thought long and hard. What if this insanity over Europe and nationalism itself, was a sort of mental disease? (Like say NaziZombification) it was at the same time, a certain failed corporate businessman began doing precisely the same thing in America, and causing precisely the same backlash. He would rant and shout and all over the TV or on Facebook feeds and there would be similar people, ranting and shouting and talking indecipherable bollocks, I felt a sense of complete dislocation as I watched this deluded dislocated group insanity take people over.
Then the two of them met.

I cannot explain how I felt when I saw that image. It was a mixture of both morbid fascination and black humour. It was a gift from the muse, there is no other word left to define it. Then I started to write.

In writing the text, I found myself with a bit of a problem, especially with the term "Nazi-zombie" as apparently its owned by some American. This bloody mess, led to a prologue being written as an afterthought attached to the middle of the text. If it makes no sense, don't worry about it. I don't, however for conventions sake, I have added it post this note from the NaziZombies and NaziZombies 2. Personally, I must say writing this was utterly cathartic. However now in January 2016 it's become darkly prophetic as the other guy has become president of America. Then I sent both texts to Kindle, who liked it but thought it was too short. So, I stuffed it in here with this little backdrop.

Personally, I loved writing this. I hope you enjoy reading it as much. Also, if it takes off, I will be investing in T--shirts mugs and pens. I might even turn it into a screen play, which is what I feel it should be anyway. When you do see the merchandise, please buy the T-shirt the mug or the pen at Amazon; also, protest silently. Stand in the street, become part of the anti-NaziZombie league, stop watching crap TV and make a bloody difference.

Be the light in the darkness.

AD Hunt.

Nazi-zombies or the rise of the alt/ right and Alt/facts in the UK

The takeover

It's hard to say when it began to fall apart. Some say it began in America during the mid-seventies, when that well-known crook Richard M. Nixon -before he donned his long leather jacket and fled off in his presidential chopper- decided to bring back the notion of the power of the dollar, and something called "the Laffer curve" over the gold standard Some put it down to Thatcher and Reagan and the greed years of the 80's, where the breaking down the nation-state assets was fun; and opting for the stocks and shares and the false notion of market forces held together by mobiles the size of your head, Filofaxes, wine bars, and meetings with large shouldered workaholics; who preferred cocaine and coin, over a fair and equal society. Some put it down to hegemony, caused by companies coalescing like a filthy virus, from small franchises, then companies then conglomerates; and finally, mega corporates, that then strode the world; making profit from the international slave labour market, that in turn, took taxes away from the nation state and into private banks that were -in secret- organised tax havens so that a minority would survive, while the poor were not talked about and quietly slaughtered as their coin was removed.

Some even put it down to a national media bought and owned by three people and whom had an agenda of their own, which was about making themselves richer and more influential than anyone else. Who knows how it began, but it did; and when it did our society fell slowly and silently started to fall apart. It fell apart in drips and drabs, slowly at first, then over the years, it gained greater and greater momentum and while as it fell apart, amongst all this coalescing chaos; people suddenly stopped thinking for themselves and started to eat their own brains.

No one really knows who it was who started that weird craze. I can imagine that it might have been some Etonian boy, who aspired to screw up a country up one day, just possibly after he (allegedly) shoved his rather notably small penis, in the mouth of a roasted pigs head; all slimy and shiny and covered with crackling, one summer afternoon in the 1980s. Or Perhaps it was some unemployed doctor or maybe a dental hygienist, who, after a bitter day at work, took a long hard look at their forehead, one warm late afternoon in July and thought to themselves: now... I wonder what my brain tastes like; and, with a look of delicious desire in their eyes and perhaps with a queer smile upon their wet, shiny, lips, decided   to slowly crack open their own skull, and with a silver spoon in hand, take out selected parts of their temporal lobe. Seasoned –of course- with either honey or perhaps some sea salt for taste

Perhaps, it was some dark, malign, ancient alien species, whom after travelling through the void of space for a millennium, found our little planet of blue and green and thought to itself, "I know, I'll plant this idea in their heads and see what happens, just for a laugh" However, or wherever this idea -of brain eating- cane from it quickly became a secret phenomenon. As I came to understand, this craze was spread by word of mouth. There were secret brain eating parties would take place in hidden locations all over the United Kingdom and Ireland, where groups of people would have their skulls opened and take out selected parts of their brain matter and share it with fellow guests: just for laughs.

However, there was a problem. Essentially The problem was this: people were becoming fucking idiotic. The first reported act of recognized brain eating came after the referendum of 2009; Though the police never fully understood what it was that they had found. A pile undead corpses each of whom had lunatic grins on their faces and blood and brains in their mouths, was prevented from being broadcast, at least on the mainstream media, because one of the corpses found happened to be both chairman of the BBC and on the advisory board of the 1922 committee -as well as a prominent mason- and you can't have a member of the establishment, caught with his pants down eating his own brains can you… its indecent… Anyway, it was hushed up, because the messy non-government at that time, didn't want the public to find out that prominent members of the state, were involved in brain eating. It really wasn't the done thing.

It was 2010 that the NaziZombies began to appear. Though they had been a part of the UK for years. Prior to that the NaziZombies had been -on the whole- forgotten or considered mad; after all, who would listen to a zombie brain eater? Especially a zombie with right wing tendencies. No one. Conversations throughout the 80's ran like a bit like this ordinary people:- "Fuck off you Nazizombie brain eater! Who do you think you're trying to convince with all your talk about "ghghheheyrgdhfhgjghthr" and "ghghhghsuerehehghghg" no one wants to hear that bollocks, so fuck off home an eat your brains in peace."

Stuff like that happened all the time, yet, still their numbers grew. They were invisible and tended to prop up bars and mumble and slur and stagger about and overall, nobody listened, to them, until one NaziZombie brain eater,

Bob Garage, began to appear on the T.V.

He started appearing just after a bizarre helicopter crash, where he was spotted eating the brain of his pilot. Though that part of the story was hushed up. After the crash, for some strange reason Bob became a national hero. Why? No one knew, he just was. He would turn up in strange and bizarre places, like at a pizza hut, and say things like "ffghrrrughnghhs" or "dhgrsuurrghs nnnnsrrdhghhdssshhsh" and people all around him would suddenly appear in the room and applause for no real reason at all.

Then the political establishment would have him on the telly discussing the state of the nation and the now defunct European Union. They would ask him, "well, Bob what do you think of this?" or "what do you think of that Bob" and Bob would say something like "ghsghgsfsfghhurghhughghs" and the commentator would say "well...that's fascinating Bob, you definitely know what you're talking about."

And so this went on until 2016 when the naziZombie takeover began in earnest. It came about because a now well-known brain eating addict and −so rumour had it- that a dead pig shagging- prime minister of the time: the infamous "Dodgy Dave, the pigshagger from Westeros", completely fucked up the world.

He even had the balls to write about it in his memoirs, which he called the "Diary of a dead pig shaggier from Westeros". Then he ran away. His running away is documented in another one of his memoirs called "How to run away and not be seen, a handy political tool, by Dodgy Dave the dead-pig shagger of Westeros. Its available at all bookshops for about a quid and you'll find it next to "fun with Dick and Jayne"

The problem with Dodgy Dave was that he thought that he could stop Bob by giving Bob what he wanted. Can you see the fatal flaw in his thinking there?

The fact was that hardly anyone in the UK actually knew what Bob Garage really wanted at all. Mainly because he talked utter NaziZombie drivel. (see previous grunting sounds) The only people who knew what Bob was talking about were fellow brain eating soon to become NaziZombies. And they all sounded the same. It was a sort of growl of agreement, if you can understand. How the flecking BBC knew what Bob was talking about still amazes me to this day.

Oh, I'm drifting, anyhow, Dave thought he could stop Bob Garage from taking the UK into a national disaster that would be the leaving of the EU. So, Dodgy Dave also a NaziZombie supposedly called Bob's bluff, but, by then, well over half the nation were into brain eating and were becoming NaziZombies so the result was a certainty.

That day was bad. Bob was everywhere going "shgfjsnsghshhshshshshsshhshfj" here and huurhhdghhshsgshsgsdsrsvsjghurgh" there, and all his zombie Nazi mates were on Facebook shouting "hurghghushshsgshshsgshsfhfjsgh" and mindlessly applauding while attacking people in the fecking streets. Skulls were smashed and brains were every-fucking-where. I took to the hills. It was the safest place to be. Me, my wife Rhiannon and my children: Elsie Nonnie and Glan. We had to, it was the safest thing to do. I didn't come back from the hills for twenty years. when we did. The UK was unrecognisable.

what is and how to kill a Nazi-zombie

NaziZombies are not like any other forms of Zombie. Your average zombie, or "undeadite", to give it a posh sounding Latin term, tends to have, as you know, rotten skin, failing organs weak teeth, sunken eyes and a need to devour human flesh. Particularly brains. All of this is controlled by a contagion that rests inside the what is left of their brain. This is where the difference between the zombie and the NaziZombie rests.

Stage one: L.T.V

essentially the disease is a virus. Specifically, a linguistic transferring virus, or an L.T.V for short. The virus is transferred from a host to host, simply by listening to someone who is infected. This is because the virus was found to grow from sound vibrations and impact the brain.

In a process that is still not clearly understood, the brain can interpret the qualities of the sound upon reception of these electric nerve impulses. It was through these electrical nerve impulses, that the disease spread. Firstly, through the compulsion and then the temporal region of the brain. Thus, altering the victim's sense of comprehension, understanding and reality. The higher levels of contagion within the host, the greater the risk of transferring the contagion between both the host body and the next potential victim. The more the victim listens to the host, the greater the contagion is spread. However, this does not work unless the host is in close—ish- proximity to the victim. Therefore, Bob Garage, was so convincing to the hosts on the TV, while, it must be said that pretty much the rest of us watching him say "grrughaaaaarrrggghh" thought he was talking total and utter bollocks.

I only know of one person who was infected by a Bob Garage commentary on TV, and that was my best mate Derhman. But to be fair, he was down the pub and pissed at the time. There was Bob on the TV talking his usual bollocks... the sound was down and the music was thumping out. It was a great crack, then Derhman says to me "You know... that Bob Garage...he makes total sense to me." It was out of the blue and sort of weird, as we never talked politics or religion before. Especially at a pub. You just don't do that. I remember recalling that I said "what the feck are you talking about? The man's a fucking ZombieNazi! He makes as much sense, as slapping sloppy wet dog shite across your face." At which point, three guys who were standing around the bar slowly turned and stared at me; at which point I got the feeling that they didn't like that comment, so I fecked off home. I never saw Derhman again... Sorry...digressing, back to topic

Stage two   Brain-eating.

This is recognized as the compulsion to want to eat your own brains. Now, I know that this might sound a tad impossible due to pain. However, an infected host has a far higher tolerance to pain levels. Essentially What the virus does is deaden pain receptors, by making the person a feckin idiot, thus an infected person could hammer a hole in their head and not feel a fecking thing.

I've seen this... its gross.... It is...honestly... and no, I'm not giving you any examples.

Stage three full on NaziZombification aka the Bob Garage Phase.

This is where the victim is under complete control of the major host. Moreover, the victim needs to listen to more of the hosts words to stay alive. This is because the victim feeds on the hosts words, as a source of nutrients maintaining other organs, and keeping the other individual alive enough to spread the virus but nothing else. The victim tends to start to spread the disease actively by blaming poor people, or mentally ill people, or anyone that's different from the victim for the problems they are having. Like: - "feck I can't get my beer can open! Those feckin' immigrants are fecking with my beer can." You know, stuff like that. Look... I don't talk like that around the kids...this is just between you and me, okay? Then it gets worse. The victim then starts to rant on buses or in pubs about how the foreign immigrant or the bloke without a job is fecking up his or her life. Before long it's any religious denomination.

Finally, this involves going to "EngKip" meetings and listening to speeches by people who are in an advanced stage of NaziZombification. Before too long they are reading Bob's books. Books with such memorable titles as "gurrghughhharrghh". And to be honest, that's all its filled with. Yes, more of that unintelligible gobshite crap. Four hundred and fifty pages of it! A mean, feck. When a person is in a high state of naziZombifiaction then Bob either eats the person or the NaziZombie gets his or her uniform and starts stumbling about looking for people to infect.

How to take out a NaziZombie

The NaziZombie unlike your ordinary zombie, has a very small brain. Pretty much all that is in a NaziZombie skull is that part of the brain at the back of the skull, so, blowing their heads off tends to have no impact upon them at all. However, it does tend to piss them off. They get very violent then. I think it's because they can't infect you as easily. A NaziZombie, when enraged is a difficult beast to take down. This is because though they have no head; however, they can still sense where you are, (no I don't know why either) and they can strangle you and kick too so beware.

I have found that the best way to take out a NaziZombie is to damage the heart through the chest. However, this causes the NaziZombie, to burst into a ball of fire, so banging a stake into the heart is unadvisable. Instead, a good long pole or perhaps a gun, if you can find one is valuable. Another good way to take out a NaziZombie is to dismember it. This is done with a strong sword or a particularly long knife. Remember, that the bones are brittle too, so that when you do take out a NaziZombie stand well clear. Also, and this is a must, never use a hammer. The blows with a hammer can break the bones into fine particles. I have found that the dust itself can carry a form of the Nazi-zombie brain eating part of the virus. it's as if the words have affected the very bones themselves. The most effective way of dealing with the NaziZombie virus is to take out a major host. I found this out two years ago ..I was on an expedition for food. Things were getting short and the winters have been getting worse. I needed supplies, anything really, the kids were hungry and the wife, well, difficult. Anyhow, I was in a small village, looking through what was once a Spar shop for canned goods, when through the broken window of the store front, I saw a large van arrive. It was full of NaziZombies… I can't lie, I was shitting myself. They were slowly getting out of the van, and for some reason known only to them gathering around one NaziZombie in a long black leather overcoat.

I tend to go out fully armed; and have become a good shot. So, despite quaking with fear, I crouched my way to the window. The chief NaziZombie was grunting and growling, fuck knows what. So, I gulped and stood up and shot the fecker as close range in the back. I watched the body suddenly drop. And as it fell all the rest of them burst into flames. It was then I realized two things, to start with I must be totally insane and two: Bob Garage had to be taken out as soon as possible.

How to cope with a loss and possible cure.

I many ways, I know I am one lucky bastard. After all, how many people can say that they are surviving a NaziZombie apocalypse? I Then decided that for one reason or another I must be immune to the virus. But how could I be immune to the virus? could it be that it was because I grew up during the 1980's and had endless shite songs by the likes of Rick Astley "Never going to give you up" or Kylie Minogue "I should be so lucky" running through my head.

From my understanding of how an L.T.V spreads, I think that's partly it. More of that later.

I also think it is because my grandfather, a sea green eyed, partially balding, heavy jawed lapse catholic, and passionate communist from Kilkenny who moved to Edenborough; taught me the best lesson I have ever learned: - that is when people start blaming the less fortunate, or the outsider for their own sad fucked up life, then the real issue is with them, and not the other fellah. "Remember... we are all feckin' immigrants, son. Now be a good boy and pas me, me pint." he used to say... Ahh better days...Oh, I'm rambling again.

I'm rambling, because I don't want to write this part. It's difficult to talk about near loss, especially loss of a loved one, in times like these, especially when the weather is like winter all year and the Nazi-zombies are controlling all forms of media. Well... ok...that's sort of not true as they had control of it before; the Daily Mail was owned by a brain eating NaziZombie for Christ sake. But they have even more now, that's my point. In their world, the Radio, and the big screen are means of communication for the NaziZombie nation. A good example is the six am radio weather report: "Thames dogger, fisher, grughghsrgaarrghh" and don't get me on the fecking today programme on radio four. Sigh, yeah off topic again. I do ramble don't I... My eldest son... Glan ... he went down with the infection six months ago....as I said I am immune to the infection but my kids and wife are not. So, they must take precautions, like cotton wool for the ears and stuff like that. It was, per my calendar, about 217 strikes upon the wall, or thereabouts, since the NaziZombie apocalypse. Snow had been falling for months, making the roads hard to navigate. Glan and I were out on a scavenge in the Essex region at that time. I don't recall the name of the town, but the street names stick in my mind like glue. We were shuttling from house to house to gather in tinned foods and or any supplies we could find. So far, we had managed to gather in quite a few cans of food and some beer.

NaziZombies don't need homes, as they have a hive mind and tend to gather in large stadiums for self-approval, and self-aggrandizement, that being the case, there is no shortage of houses to drop into, which is easy for us, as we tend to be on the move a lot. However, the NaziZombies had taken to constructing big screens and huge speakers, in large open spaces. You know the type of thing, those screens once used as open air cinema, only back then, they were being used to get Bob Garage on stage talking his vile shite thus spreading the virus to those yet uninfected.

I tend to try to remember to carry some cotton wool, so I can plug up Glen's ears, if we are in a heavily controlled NaziZombie region. That, or carry a copy of Rick Astley's greatest hits on a battery operated mp3 player. However, that day, I had a row with Rhiannon about the last food run, so I left home without either. We both saw the screen in Ash park, just off Holloway road, but as there were no NaziZombies about, we thought that the coast was clear.

I didn't know it was a trap. ….The moment we passed fifty feet from the screen, it suddenly burst into life. ….There stood Bob Garage. His eyes flame red, glowed with triumph his mouth, all flabby and wet, wobbled as it undulated as he started to boom out his shite again: "grdughghs, graughughs, guruagurrughhs".
……My face paled as I stared towards Glan. I could see he was transfixed. Then he started to say in that offhand way I heard all those years ago "You know, that Bob Garage is starting to-" ……In a desperation and a pain that only a father can know, I punched him in the face; catching him off guard and knocking him out. I then had to drag him to a terrace house in Holloway road. I kicked down the door, and then dragged him by his arms through the hall and put him on the floor in the front room; just as he started to come around. Suddenly he sat up. His eyes were bulging from his sockets, his mouth open in a huge scream was laced with spittle. "I wanna eat my brain! Da!" he screamed " I wanna eat me brain!" He started to laugh as he started pulling at his hair. I ran about the front room in a dark panic in my stomach, looking for some form of audio equipment.

But the was owned by one of those Ikea fanatics and everything was small and flat and over tidy.

I dithered and ran about the room, not knowing what to do, until I punched Glan in the face again; knocking him out once more. Then I ran upstairs to the bedrooms. One room had a life-size portrait of Bob fucking Garage in it. I think that was the master bedroom. The other was full of crap, the third was beautiful. Nirvana poster's, hippy poster's, spray painted words like FUCK BOB GARAGE! and there, on the floor, amid a pile of notes on sociology was an mp three player.

I put it on. It was Motörhead! I felt my eyes start to bulge from my sockets as I looked through the audio collection and found -whomever it belonged to- guilty little secret: and there thank the Gods it was:- "Kylie Minogue's greatest hits". I ran downstairs, put the ear-buds in Glen's ears, turned the volume up full on the mp3 and blasted "I should be so lucky" into my son's head repeatedly.

Now, I know, many out there will think that in hitting my son like that, and subjecting him to 80's trash music, that I am an utter bastard. Hate me if you want. However, it is the only way I have found of counteracting the virus in its early stages. Long blasts of repetitive bloody awful 80's music, into a subject that is knocked out tends to halt the spread of the virus, and the louder the music, the greater the chance the victim has of being free from it. As this was going on, I went around the house and found enough supplies of canned goods, to keep us going for a week or two. That and some precious bottled water. I sat down and waited.

Those two hours were the longest I have ever known. I looked down at Glan, not knowing if the little boy I held in my arms, 18 years ago, was ever going to be the same boy again, or some vile NaziZombie intent on taking over the world with petty ignorance and brain eating bullshit. As I sat there, I recalled his first steps… his first words: - "Feck you Da" … The way his pale blue eyes shone from his pale face and his ginger hair blowing in the breeze, as Rhiannon and I played catch in the park. I recalled his first day at school, and then passing of his GCSE exams, the year before the nazi-zombifation virus took hold. I cried as I heard my grandpa once more say "Pass me me pint son.

When Glan finally awoke, he rubbed his chin and looked at me. I heard a tap at the window opposite. I looked up and saw a magpie. At the time, I didn't know the significance.

"Da, what happened." So, I told him while he sat there, humming I should be so lucky, lucky, lucky, I should be so lucky in love.

The resistance movement: Meet the guys and the shite plan.

As I said, we moved around a lot; this has a double-edged effect or affect, I didn't know which, it has an impact ok? To start with, there is a lot of naziZombies to kill, which isn't so good. However, on the plus side, there is a chance to meet fellow survivors.

   Begbie was such a survivor. He was a tough Scottish bastard that hated naziZombies from birth. There is a sort of myth about him.   It is said that his first words were "I'm goin' to do you, you fuckin' naziZombie cunt." Which for a child of six months quite a feat and suggests that he was born for greatness. He was also extremely violent at home and this led to him being put into care. Prior the rise of the naziZombies, Begbie was on a downward spiral towards alcoholic oblivion.

   Post the Nazi-zombie event, Begbie became the hero of the resistance. There are stories that are told to this day that say he took out a whole platoon of the NaziZombies, armed only with a long-bladed kitchen knife and Rick Astley's "whenever you need somebody" album.

   Then there is Dark Steve. Dark Steve tends to wear black a lot. He also doesn't say very much accept "yeah" or "no" which means he's hard to get to know. But he is a wiz with anything electrical. It was Dark Steve who managed to get the diesel operated, electricity generator's up and running and in turn got the lathes in the workshop running off staves and the like.   I don't know much more about him. In fact, I have never seen his face.

   Angela Morecombe is a fourteen-year-old who lost her entire family to brain eating NaziZombification. She has the widest and palest blue eyes I have ever seen. She is also a bit moody and sulky, but knows how to throw a javelin; and has learned to break into any shop with ease. She is the unit's case officer. A bright mind with clever fingers too.

   Jordan is a twenty-year-old with a love of all things explosive. His parents managed to survive the onslaught driving off to the hills like we did, surviving is something that we must take for granted these days.   He loves his Bike and is always seen riding about the city cleaving the occasional Nazi-zombie in two usually while listening to tracks by the chemical brothers.

   Jordan also has a very nice strain of cannabis that he has nurtured and grown himself; so, he's always good for a laugh.

   This makes up the core of the resistance, or the people that we have met, while on our travelling. Overall, they are a great bunch of guys' though they are quite argumentative at times; which is why I tend to hang around with them occasionally. We usually have a planned meeting to discuss how we are faring, if we have found any weakness's and what to do about the Nazi- zombies once a month. The last meeting took place at our house, which, never goes down well with Rhiannon; even though they bring the biscuits.

It was a month after I had taken out the patrol and two weeks since Glan's near infection, that the resistance met in our front room to discuss what had been occurring. At that time my understanding of the L.T.V was purely speculative. I knew what worked for me and explained to the group what had happened.

Dark Steve sat there, his face hidden in his black hoodie, next to him was Begbie. Across from him sat Rhiannon, (our other two girls were in bed) Jordan, Glan and Julia sat the far end of the room.

After I had finished giving my thesis, I looked around the room. The silence was deafening.

"So " I began "Have we had a good week?" Another long silence followed.

Dark Steve nodded his head, Begbie looked tired and a bit glum, Julia strained. Jordan was puffing on a Joint, that he passed the Glan. Rhiannon stared at me and I shrugged lamely

"let's get this straight... you've found that listening to shite music has an impact on the virus?" Begbie said incredulously

I nodded. "I see..."

I saw his eyes bulge from his sockets, as he folded his arms across his chest "Rick Astley or Kylie Minogue fuckin' hell! I hate that crap! "

"Hey don't mock the Kylie" said Julie

"-it's not that its crap music" I injected.

"-it's not crap!" Julie spat defiantly.

"You could same about Hawkwind!

Begbie stared coldly at Julie. A heavy silence filled the room.

"Never...mock or deride, the wind in my presence again!" Begbie said angrily.

His words were so powerful we all looked down at the floor, felling as if a headmaster had ranted off to his class. After a while I stated,

"Julie, its, it's not the music, it's the vocal repetition..."

I eased her and she claimed down.

"...In fact, it's any song that has a mildly irritating, or over repetitive vocal chorus, that the listener finds either deeply irritating, annoying or enjoyable.... You know, a song that you can't get out of your head in the morning. It's that, that attacks the virus…. It's as if the song prevents the Bob Garage's words being decoded into the subconscious."

"Does this mean we have to stop killing them?" Begbie sounded tight. His whole life for the last 284 strikes on the wall had been dedicated to the killing of NaziZombies, it had given him a purpose in life. To suddenly change would be hard for him.

"Not necessarily…" I began cautiously, as I didn't want Begbie to leave without getting to the end of the meeting. "

It's a prevention for the virus stop the spread to the brain eating stage. Once that occurs there is no hope for the victim." "Too right! the only good naziZombie is a dead naziZombie Fucking kill em all I say!" Begbie bellowed and everyone else agreed.I then related the incident in the Spar shop.

"So, we, we could take out one chief NaziZombie and loads just, blow up?" Jordan grinned, his eyes glittered with joy.

"yeah" said Dark Steve."

That takes the fuckin fun out o' it" muttered Begbie,

"-Oh go on Begbie, hitting' the big cheese sounds like a luff to me" said Julie.

Dark Steve muttered another yeah, and both Jordan and Glan grinned and giggled in stoned amusement. I could feel Rhiannon's eyes boring into my neck so I looked down and towards the window.

Suddenly a magpie came and settled on the window ledge. It paced outside up and down the window looking in. Glan saw it cautiously and looked away. I stared at it and was about to shoo it off, when Glan suddenly got up went to the window and tapped it sharply.

The bird laughed as it took to flight. I turned back to the room.

"…Well any chance I can get at taking out that Bob fucking Garage I am up for that." Shouted Begbie."

"It might lead to the end of the entire zombie-Nazi hoard" I injected as which point Begbie looked a bit sad.

"oh go on" Rhiannon chided, "I'm sure there will be a few left to kill."

Begbie looked down and blushed a little.

"The problem is getting close enough to Bob Garage so as we are not turned in Nazi-zombies ourselves and want to start eating our own brains and shit" said Jordan and we all agreed.

Unlike before the Nazi-zombie infestation, Bob was always down the pub, or at a restaurant or on TV, making his growling grunting noises and converting most around him into brain eating Nazi-zombies; nowadays he rarely left

Buckingham Palace where he now resided with the Queen and the rest of the Brain eating Nazi-zombie establishment. It was clear, someone or a group of someone's were going to have to break into Buckingham palace and try to take him out.

This, we all agreed was going to be hard, as point one: though many people –over the years- had managed to escape from Buckingham Palace usually naked….not many had managed to get in. Our hope rested in the one grain of factual evidence we had to hand:- Nazi-zombies were as thick as shit; with the memory span of a fish. Oh, sure, there were loads of them, but number's count for nothing, when you have a gang of bright, determined individuals like ourselves, ready to do battle with the NaziZombie hoard no matter the consequences.

We sat down and came up with a sort of plan. Begbie, Glan and I were to climb the fence of Buckingham palace, get around the back of the building, enter though the kitchen, and sneak about the place until we found Bob and then take him out. Meanwhile the others were to cause a commotion outside the palace and force the Nazi-zombies inside to come out and give chase.

To be honest, it was a shite plan. A really shite plan. In fact, it was the worst fucking plan that had ever been invented. In fact if there was sacred place for shite plans to go, this plan would be there, hung high up in a gilded cage, it was as shite as the referendum that started this fecking thing off in the first place. Rhiannon told me it was a shite plan and said that we should wait, however,it was Begbie's plan and I knew, that if I said anything, like the plan was utter cock, he'd kick me head in.

That night, I found sleep hard. For some reason, the magpie earlier that day   kept haunting my mind. I tried to sleep, but when I slept, it would always appear, flying over my head, haunting me. laughing at me with a cold malicious sound of triumph. I woke up with a start.
"What's wrong" Rhiannon groaned,
        "Can't you ever settle down?" I rested back on the pillow and looked up at the ceiling as the dawn slowly encroach upon the day.

A weird meeting at the Mall, just of St James's park

The trip to the heart of London, was a nervous one. We had acquired a large-ish- lorry and filled it up with all of us, and all the equipment we thought we'd need. There was a huge bag of Cotton wool and many speakers of various sizes, that we had gerrymandered to several mp3 players.

A host of batteries, some large swords and large knives, loads of guns, loads of bullets and shotgun shells and a chainsaw or two. Between which sat Glan, the two girls, Angela, Jordan Glen and Dark Steve. I sat in the front of the truck with Begbie and Rhiannon. Rhiannon had elected to drive. She was nervous, and kept flicking her raven hair out of her cornflower blue eyes, between muttering about the city centre fine. Meanwhile Begbie who was next to us in the van said that didn't matter as we were in a nicked van anyway.

"Besides" He retorted "it's post the fucking NaziZombie apocalypse, are you going to pay a fine to? them?"

I must admit I could see the logic in that. The closer we got to London, the denser the zombie-Nazi hoard became.

By the time that we had reached central London, they were every-fuckin-where; all that could be heard were the murmuring growling and grumbling of over one million NaziZombies standing in groups of hundreds along the pavements could be described as louder than our van. However, they were all motionless, as if asleep, so somehow, we managed to make it all the way to Pall Mall. We pulled over at St James park and disembarked. It was night, a dark night, as the moon was new. We moved quietly, so not to wake the Zombie-Nazi's who were around us.

"what's wrong with the fekers" muttered Begbie."Collective consciousness" whispered Angela. They'll all wake up when Bob awakes. He probably can't sense our presence yet.

"Fair snuff" said Begbie, who then dispatched three to keep us warm.

It must be said that the burning of a NaziZombie is really not that nice, There is that stink of burning hair and skin. If the zombie Nazi s fat, it's worse as the organs inside burst out! Recall wanting to heave my guts up as the flames kept us warm.

Despite the fire, it was cold. My fingers were numb and the snow was a good seven to ten inches thick. To keep myself busy I decided to get the equipment ready. It was as I opened the back of the van for the second time, that I heard, in the distance, the galloping of hooves. Both Begbie and I turned around to see what was coming, and there, through the trees could just be seen a man in black leather and furs coming towards, us on a thundering horse

Begbie pulled out his gun and was about to shoot, when he stopped. "No wait." I exclaimed.

The horse stopped and a young man with greasy long raven hair, black eyes, a narrow face and tufts of beard looked towards us

"Winter is here." He said

"I know you...your, your, Jon Snow from Westeros, your canna be here! This is London and WE are facing the NaziZombie infestation!" Go On! fuck off back to Westeros!" I shouted.

"But I have come with my army of..."then he looked around his eyes staring at the great nothingness that was behind him. Yes he was on his own.

" - Oh" he looked down to the snow and kicked it about a bit. "bollocks"!

"Ha ha, yeah, that's right, you're on your own mate, that's what they do there in Westeros; they might bow the knee to your face, but when your back is turned, they'll stab you in it, like the fuckers they are!"

"-a bit like the labour party then" said Angela."-But I have the blessing of the king of Light"

"-Mate, I began "You could have the blessing of the entire planet, however, if George R.R. Martin finds you here, we are in some big shit! One, he could kill us all off just for fun! More importantly HBO will be well pissed off with our God of light, sue us to kingdom come and that will be the end of NaziZombies!

I was about to continue about the continuity of it all, when, from above, we heard this strange and hideous howl. It was as if the sky was filled with daemons. There then followed a sound like the flapping of large leather wings Angela looked up. "Oh fucking hell!

Bright yellow flames suddenly lit up St James park and an explosion was heard. I look to my left and could just see that St Pauls had become a ball of flame. In the yellow orange light,I could see three dragons circling; their leather and fibrous wings taking huge whumps of air. While all around us the ZombieNazis slowly started to stir.

One dragon descended from the heavens and landed heavily. It leant its head forward, and Denerys Stormborn, yes her with the big eyes and the big, well, you know, slowly and seductively started walking towards us.

"Fear not brave men of Britain! I have come to help you with your quest "She said.

"That's a nice piece of arse." Begbie growled like an animal.

"That piece of arse is going to get us into a hell of a lot of trouble!" I started.

"I don't mind that sort of trouble" began Jordan, do you think she'd like a bag of weed to share?"

Rhiannon was looking decidedly pissed off. She was glaring at me, as if it were all my fault. Fer fecks sake, as if

I can control what's going on. The NaziZombies were stirring. Quickly Jon snow hacked one of their heads off.

"Oh fuck no!" I sighed, and buried my head in my hands, as the NaziZombie went to attack him. Begbie finished it off with a lance through its back.

"chopping their heads off only pisses them off" I said. "keep up with the story will ye?"

Jon Muttered sorry as which point Daenerys stared at him acutely.

"Are you the bastard known as Jon Snow, king of the North and from the house Stark?"

He nodded.

She stood her ground thrusting her hips forward.

"I am Daenerys Stormborn from the house Targarian," she boldly proclaimed, "Queen of the South and keeper of the Dragon's! We need to get married and have dirty, slutty sex.

Jon looked down and a seemed a bit awkward.

"It's It's a a bit rushed, isn't it? He began "..Can we at least help our fellow Brothers and sisters fend of the NaziZombie hoard of Great Britain first?

"Oh, err, okay, so don't you want to have sex with me then?

"Errum no, it's Errum, no," Jon Blushed and looked at the ground "no...not that...It's just a bit unexpected that's all.

"Really? oh, come on...surely not..." she giggled gently at that. "Ok, lets help these people out first, then tell me how you feel about it."

"Sure, why not." Jon replied.

"-You lucky, lucky, bastard..." muttered Begbie "...I was only some bit character in Trainspotting.""-Look all of you! Shut the fuck up!" I pleaded. I stared with fear, rising as the zombie Nazi's began to wake up.

"This is supposed to be a serious piece, about the end of the UK, because of a bunch of fecking, fascists NaziZombies taking over the county! It's not about giving away the last series of Game of fucking Thrones!"

Suddenly Tyrion Lannister appeared from behind Daenerys and started to sing Space pants killing off a hoard of Zombie Nazi's at one go

"-Hey, we could do with him. He drinks and knows things." Begbie exclaimed.

"Look, will you all, please, please, please, stop!" I felt exhausted by it all, but I bellowed loud.

Suddenly there was a silence. All eyes turned to me. For the first time, ever, the resistance and its new players stared at me. For the first time, I felt that I was in charge and capable of deciding things. For the first time, in my life

I would have my say. I opened my mouth to speak but then-

"-The way I see it" Rhiannon suddenly exclaimed "is that you..." – she pointed at Denerys," and you" she pointed at Jon, can help with a diversion, while the rest of us break into Buckingham palace...Your majesty?

Both Jon and Daenerys stared at her.

"No, not the fecking useless man! You, woman with the blonde hair, your majesty, we need a dragon to get us into the Palace."

With a nod of her head, Daenerys let a weird call, that sounded like "OI! get down ere now yer buggers," with that one of the dragons flew into the mall and settled down, squashing about twenty slowly waking Nazi-zombies, with its huge feet.

Suddenly Denerys grabbed Jon's hand.

"Come with me your naughty boy." She whispered, as she ran with him over to the waiting dragon in St James park.

Begbie shook his head as he spoke aloud to the back of Jon snow. "You lucky, lucky, lucky, lucky bastard.

"Aye that he is." Replied Tyrion, after all, he managed to survive "the battle of the bastards", did you see that episode? By the way, I thought I was great in Season six. The trouble is people always remember the space pants thing."

"Oh…you were superb. An, don't worry, space pants is our secret weapon. You never know you might make it to the end without dying."

"Really? oh shit. I haven't done a death scene in years. Sorry to see your career has hit a bit of a dry patch lately."

"-Well it's all swings and roundabouts "Began Begbie, as they both started to walk towards the dragon. "Besides I'm in Trainspotting 2 in January."

Within a moment Begbie, Angela, Glan the kids, Rhiannon Tyrion and I were all in the sky, flying on the back of a dragon, in huge sweeping arcs over Buckingham palace, ready to defeat Bob Garage in one last final battle to end the

NaziZombie hoard and save humanity.

The battle for Buckingham palace.

The dragon dropped us off on the top of the palace with a soft grunt. We all got off, and went through the procedure of prepping for a NaziZombie assault.

1. Cotton wool, in the ears, check, also check each other too, to make sure the right amount is inserted. 2. Speakers,

check, make sure your speakers are connected to the MP3 players. And are attached to your outer garments, also make sure that the mp3 attachment is wired correctly. Also, check your friends. Batteries are also important. Make sure the MP3 is fully charged.   3. Weapons: swords out of sheathes, Chainsaws filled with petrol, shotguns filled with cartridges, and belts for extra cartridges correctly attached. Pistols with enough rounds, or lance's well-oiled and sharp. (Nazi-zombies tend to be a bit dry, so a well-oiled lance helps with the penetration; especially if you must take out five at a time.) 4. Motion trackers. Dark Steve invented a means to safely track off the more important Nazi-zombies, as they tend to make their noises at a lower frequency than the troops. This does not have an impact over vision as its over one eye. Finally, when all this is done turn on the mp3 in a synchronized time set.   3...2...1.

We entered through the attic door, and slowly moved down room by room, each of us trying to keep the others back. The NaziZombies were awake now, and trying to get to us, but we had Rick Astley on full blast and there was no way those fuckers were going to take us down without a fight. When one reached Begbie would head-but it, or Dark Steve would grind it with his chainsaw before after Alison shot it in the chest. It was Trevion who hit the first of the second level NaziZombies as his song space pants which he broadcast through a megaphone. This caused it to explode and in turn took out most of the Nazi-zombies on the most of the third floor.

"bloody hell" he muttered.

"good fecking job Tyrion! Keep it up!" yelled Begbie as we fought our way through the flaming corpses that surrounded us.

It's hard to describe the fear one feels in a battle like this. You can see the enemy all around you, with their red eyes and their dried corpse faces. Though you don't understand what they are saying, through their growls or grunts or groans, you fear that you will, because if you do, you know that you too are infected.

It's also hard to explain the sense of weirdness of it all. Here we are in the hub of the monarchy, the hub of the establishment, being attacked by all these NaziZombies, many of whom were well known on the TV news before the Nazi-zombie infestation. I personally shot the NaziZombie Michael Fabricant   in the chest and took out half of the Nazi-zombies around him. Then there was Lord Lord of Lords and Michael Gove. Boy, I tell you that, that felt good. Why is it all these NaziZombies are called Michael?

What hurt was to see my two kiddies involved with this. They would never be the same again. War isn't good. It's not for children. But, in a battle for survival, I couldn't leave them behind. Well maybe I could have left them with the dragon but I wasn't sure how they would fare. Besides, if I fell and was somehow managed to get infected, I would want them to take me out. On a plus, they did manage to take out Theresa May with their bow and arrow's, so, give them something for that.

While, Astley 's "never going to give you up" was playing as loud as we could get it; we fought our way around the palace finally making it to the state rooms tired, weary, soot and blood smeared. We were weary But we were strong we were a team, forged in iron resolved to take on Bob. Garage to the bitter end come what may.

We entered the major state room.

Bob sat on the throne, to his left was Elizabeth and to his right stood Phillip. Personally, I thought that he was a NaziZombie for years, not Bob, but there you go. Bob stood up and began to make his "ghrsughs" and "gsfsrsughs" but it was Glan who spoke.

"why arrear yuzu heeeaaarrere?

We all moved away from Glan. I felt a pang of terror as I looked both towards him and at the huge windows of the main state room, for at the windows were thousands and thousands of eyes... magpie's eyes... staring in on us... their weight slamming against the windows. Their laughter filling the room. I could hear the glass start to crack and splinter under the pressure they were forcing. On the windows.

"I'll ask you again...why arrrrree youuu heeeaaar"

"To get our country back! To get us into a place where we are all given equal rights under a banner of truth honesty and compassion." Said Alison.

"yeah" said Dark Steve.

"Don't you understand yet, your stupid fuckwit!" shouted Begbie "We think you're a vile cunt, that has broken this nation and we want our country back! We don't like you or your stupid market forced economy or your vile Nazi-zombification of our nation! We want to be a nation again! Free from the LIES and the- "

Glan spoke again. I could see the pain written all over his face as the magpies began to chip harder and harder at the windows. Beaks cracked though the glass and mocking laughter could be heard.

"I…. I…. Da! Glan screamed as he shook his body a mass of convulsions. The bullet hit Bob full in the chest. Bob reeled backwards as both the Elizabeth and her Nazi-zombie husband started walking forwards.

Then another door opened and Dave the pig shagger of Westeros stood before us. "you, stupid, stupid Fuck- "he screamed.

But his words were lost as the magpies smashed into the room and began to encircle us. In terror, I knelt to the floor and prayed that it wouldn't be too painful. But then something weird happened. The magpies swirled about us. But they didn't attack us...We felt their feathers but not their beaks, they attacked Elizabeth her zombie-Nazi husband and dodgy Dave. Of Dave, nothing was left at all, except a suit and a tie, neatly done up to the neck of the shirt. Our MP3's became mute leaving silence, as the Magpies left in a flock swirling into the night. And so, we left. We waved farewell to the dragons, Daenerys Jon and Tyrion, and watched them fade into a hazy blip on the horizon from the entrance of Buckingham palace. And then looked at each other. It was over... we were surrounded by flaming bodies...the Nazi-zombie hoard was crushed. It took a while for what could be called normality to return, people who were scared to come outside, slowly started to venture out. But come they did. In the years that followed, Begbie became the new minister of the joint republic of Britain, and reset negotiations with Europe; having to prove to the French that he was up to the job, by nutting, then shooting Le-Pen and burning her carcass on live TV.

It took years to put right the mess the Nazi-zombies left, but I can say, with a hand on my heart, that it was worth it. here are pockets of Nazi-zombies still left. Begbie set about finding them and dispatching them. One: Mark Thatcher is still on the loose. There are rumours that it is in South America somewhere. Overall, we are on the rise... However, America, well that's another story. Trump scares the shit out of us, and he might invade, now we are free.

epilogue how   did the Nazi-zombies rise to power.

 Ok, so now we are left with questions, Why on God's green earth did the Nazi-zombie LTV take over so quickly? Why were Bob Garage's words listened to? why were so many lost to this vicious parasite that led to mass self -indulgent brain eating?

 I put it down to change. People, en-mass fear it. I mean they are really scared of it. They watch the T.V and feel safe that their system is protected...But... If they listen to fear long enough, then they become servants of that fear. They will eat their own brains and –in turn- become servants of a cause that they don't really believe in, yet follow it blindly, without thinking. Our generation. The forty to fifty year olds, who have seen the reality of this fear, can give hope to our children. Fear of change need not be a monster, for change happens, life is like a wild ride where the waves free. God that sounds corny as an ending oh what the feck, I'm Dermot O' Haggarty, if you want to meet me, I'll be at the twisted oak at about 7 pm, cheers.

The end...no not quite.

Epi-prologueamendum why I call them Nazi-zombies and what the feck is going on.

Okay, this is the part I have called the epi-prolougeamendum, where I introduce myself Dermot and explain a bit about this NaziZombie infestation. I know that many people are going to be pissed off by this. To start with, this prologue comes in the wrong place entirely.

I expect many on Facebook page and on the blog, will say, "Hey Dermot, the prologue is at the start of the book! It's not as some(Hail to the chief even though he's such an asshole hail to the chief in a very small handed way; hail to the chief, though he's such a *^&%^$£^&&%$$%$% This is the morning of a brand new day.) weird version of proverbs, shoved in another text for no valid reason at all! You've already ended "NaziZombies" and have started "NaziZombies2 " already Why this now?"

Well, there is a reason for it. To start with, many people in the Facebook world have said "Hey Dermot you're a fecking wingnut, haven't you heard of "Dead Snow" and "ZombieNazi's two" yet? Where have you been. For fecks sake! You can't use that title! "I tend to ignore shit like that... Sometimes. I then received a rather nasty note in my Facebook private in box. Not the usual in box, this is the other one, hidden by the other message box, the one full of men's penis's and or women from Azbeckiststhan, who are single and think that the picture of a flat fish with razor sharp teeth, hiding underneath the sand (My Facebook picture as it is now) is somehow sexy and they want to marry you and have 50 trillion kids, in long drawn out acts of slutty sex. You might not get those sorts of messages…. Well, buried between the promises of undying love, I received a message from Allied Pictures incorporated who basically told me to "Drop the fucking NaziZombie stuff or we will sue you in court for copyright infringement."
When I told them that:-" Hey, I had never heard of your feckin movie at all" They were even more pissed off at that, so they sent copies of the film to me, and then threatened to sue me again, because I had illegally downloaded their film "Dead Snow, " "Dead Snow two" and "Dead Snow the return." due for release in 20168. CE. So, I must come to you now with a bit of prologue.I call them NaziZombies not because they are Nazi's. The alt right as they call themselves don't follow any political ideal at all. They simply make growling noises, tend to stick together and wear similar clothes, and mark their foreheads, to hide

the fact that they have eaten their own brains. In fact, to me, they make no feckin sense at all. Also I have never, ever sat down and had either a valuable argument or decent conversation with what I call NaziZombie. Here is a good example: - I was on the bus to town, just before the Referendum, and next to me was this weird, googly eyed looking guy.

Being friendly, I turned to him and I said: "what a lovely morning." And it was. The sun was shining, the sky, blue, the trees had just bloomed into their early summer green. I noticed a Dove that flew by the window, and with that, a peace descended into my heart. Moreover, I had just had an interview and felt good about myself. The reply was:-
"grughhgughiughururughuehgerengerughhureighierehehghe ueregeherehgiuregreughehgeukipugrughrugrugheregeBobFa ragegrughuegegeuregeuereghiuhegeuregegeregeeuropeisshi truhghguregehehereuererggereghege…." And so, it went on. In fact, it went on for the entire bus trip to town which is about half an hour.

When I started to nod off, being bored by the man's growling noises. Then the fecker nudged me awake and then said aggressively "DEERRMOOT are you lisssteneiggg tttoo meeee!" at which point, thankfully, the bus came to a stop and I got off and I, Well, I ran off to be honest.

I then looked about me. Suddenly I was aware, that people just like that mad fecker on the bus, were everywhere. Oh, not everyone to be sure, but most of the people I saw looked dead, or asleep or were growling making little or no sense at all. To start with I put it down to it being a Monday, after all, Monday is shit for so many reasons. One being that you have to go to that place called work and sit down on your arse with a bunch of people who don't like you and don't want to talk to you, because their lives are more exciting than anything else on the planet; even though they are not, but that's' what people are like

.At the time, I worked at this shop selling phones. The customers would moan that their phones were rubbish, so I would send them next door. I don't know why, as that was a florist: sorry wandering off again. Anyhow, this morning was difficult as everybody who came in looked the same, spoke crap and left in this sort of slow dead style shuffle. What made it worse was the only thing I could understand were the words "Bob Garage is a genius!" For those that don't know, Bob Garage set up this fake political party and spent most of his time on the telly growling zombie crap at people. That is how the disease spreads. So naturally I got into a conversation about how Bob Garage was an utter brain dead bastard; and that he would feck off at any given opportunity; they became enraged and would try to hit me or bight me.

I was fired that day for making the customer's unhappy. As the new zero contract hours meant that I had to hold down about five jobs to pay the mortgage, so I thought, fine, I'll just go to my next job... by the end of the day I was unemployed and unemployable. So, I signed on at an agency or two and they wouldn't hire me either as I didn't sound like this:" grurghrghrurhrgrgrhrurhrgrg" well, being a bit fed up I came home, to my wife and kids, who were not at all happy that I was unemployed, as that meant I would be at home on Facebook all day long worrying about Bob Garage taking over the country. So, that's why I call them NaziZombies not because they are specifically Nazi's or specifically Zombies, but they are in fact very fecking similar to both and I literally have no other means to describe them. So please don't sue me Atlantic films. Now on with Nazi-zombies 2 the rise of the Dump.

Nazi-Zombies 2 the attack of the Dump or the rise of the alt/ right in the USA

Time-lapse

Five years had passed since the last Zombie Nazi threat was crushed. Bob Garage was no more! Begbie had resigned the reins of power to -my now- Ex-wife Rhiannon, who had run off with Begbie's security officer...that was about three years ago... I must say... that pissed me off quite a bit. After all, right under my nose that was... the bloody cheek. There'd be a call from this Brit security officer: -"I must call your wife away on top secret government business, on the orders of Begbie McDonald." He'd say. "Fine" I'd say and tell her and with a quick grin, and a slam of the door off she'd pop for a week or two....Within year, she left me for the fucker.   I mean... the fecking cheek of it.   Anyhow, I had moved into a new flat, which was nice. Glan chose to stay with me until he and his lover Gina found a place of their own. Which was also a relief.

Times were tough, it was true there was plenty of work, I just... lacked the will or the drive. The real difficult thing was entertainment. Big budget movies were no more! Hollywood had been silent for years. Also, there was no face-book or any real internet. Moreover, no fecking torrenting   so I couldn't steal any porn. The fact was, we had been so busy with our own Nazi-zombie infestation, that we hadn't seen what was going on in the States.

Just before and after the referendum of 2016, the U.S.A was having problems with a Nazi-zombie of their own. We had Bob Garage... they had Donald Dump.

Dump was the archetype NaziZombie! He'd appear and people would go fucking mad; either killing each other; or applauding him beating up people in the streets. That or eating people for no fucking reason at all. The Police had to call order. But to be honest, it was hard to see who was the fecking NaziZombie or who wasn't when it came to the Coppers. What made it worse -for the Americans- was how quickly the infection spread. The last images we had before everything went to shit over here, were huge stadiums, filled to the brim with Nazi-zombies growling and grinding and eating each other; I must say, that it was scary to watch. Then, just as our world went belly up, all communication with the United States was lost.

Five years passed, and there was still nothing but rumours. Letters secretly posted about huge Nazi-zombie concentration camps were heard of, but never found. Also, stories were told of places where people were either used as food, or turned into Nazi-zombies. After our success in defeating Bob Garage and his zombie Nazi's the first British republican government got their top boffins onto any data we could get from America.   However, most of it was utter rubbish. Endless re-runs of the Walton's, where the voice of Jon Bob was changed to zombie growling. That or "I love luzi" apparently, a NaziZombie favourite, involving some zombie eating a famous person or two. I Must admit I found the one where Luzi ate Chuck Norris quite amusing. Anyhow, it was that, or images of the fucker Dump endlessly making those nasty NaziZombie noises from his wet fucking drooling lips.

It was easy to see why people were turning on each other. The boffins   conclusion was that this strain of the L.T.V could be more virulent than ours, However, they didn't know. And, to be honest, since Rhiannon left me for that security fucker, I didn't care. I was pissed off with all of them.

Then, about three weeks ago, I got a call from Begbie.

"Hey how's it hanging?" he asked. I was still pissed off with his security secret service agent and told him as much.

"Aye, I am sorry, I am." There was a sort of insincerity in Begbie's voice. He had changed, but I expected that had to do with the power.

"look, can I come over I have something to show you.

"where are you?"

"eerum...just outside your front door."

I opened the front door and there was Begbie, all Armarnied up. Gone was the stubble and the thug look. Instead there was a slicked back clean shaven unrecognizable man. With a fucking Hitachi case... I mean a Hitachi case, he looked like my last parole officer: only in a new suit.

"What do you want?"

"I have something to show you."

Reluctantly I moved aside and let him in.

Begbie came in, and sat down on my crumpled sofa. He opened his suit case and then pulled out a laptop and then opened that too.

"What I must show you is top, fucking secret...got it. No blabbing to no fucker...get it!"

I nodded, as Begbie inserted the memory stick into the laptop. He pressed a couple of keys and the drive came on.

"We got this footage last week. Our spies in the states paid a heavy price for getting it out. Some... were eaten...some went through the process..." he coughed." ...We lost Angela."

"What do you mean?"

Begbie looked down "I mean she fuckin turned. This

L.T.V is a far more virulent than the British version on the virus. Rick Astley, Aha, Duran fucking Duran...even that repetitive Spandau Ballet! Man, it has no effect.

"What about space pants?"

Let's Just say the Dwarf is no more.

I shook my head sadly.

This version of the L.T.V has over a 99% infection rate, we found only compassionate people had a small chance of avoiding infection.   Watch this."

The screen was jumpy, and then blurred. Suddenly it moved into sharp focus. It was a military training camp. Thousands and thousands of American NaziZombies were there, marching about. The low hum of their growling and snarling made me feel sick with fear. Suddenly the image was cut short; and Donald Dump was there. His shitty orange skin was covered with vile green lumps, his eyes were a flaming red his hair well, that was as awful as ever.

"What is this?"

"It's the new C N N news...Dump disbanded CNN after it didn't report the news in a way he liked. "

"ghysrs skkslflhhh" said Dump.

"-they still talk utter bollocks don't they... my fucking god-

"-pay fucking attention."

"gursrrsughshshshs" pause   "guruyughstsyshhhurgh"

At that point Dump got up from behind this desk, (when I say got up, what I mean is that he sort of did this staggering lurch like all fucking NaziZombies do.) As he moved to the left he came to a cardboard map, you know like those old weather maps of the 1970s, only drawn badly and in red crayon. Then with his usual mindless aggression, Dump slap-pointed to a map of Europe. Then he started slapping loads of magnets shaped like planes, planes bomb and missiles onto it...all of which were pointing at one place: the UK.

"The fucker is planning an invasion!" I paused to drink it in "Oh My fucking God!"

"we have to be ready."

"too fucking right. "I agreed " is the Channel Tunnel still working, cause I'm off to France."

"Dermot, I need you...we need you...we need the old gang once more."

"In case you don't know. Angela is now a fucking NaziZombie, oh you do, you told me that!   Dark Steve moved to Morocco with Jordan, Rhiannon left me for your security chief of staff and Glan wants to move to Scotland with his new partner. There are no us, unless you hope to call in the Game of Thrones crew....And we all know what happened to them. They are all fuckin dead. J R R Martin… what a fuckin' bastard."

"Dark Steve, is with me… I have Jordan on a plane from Marrakesh, Rhiannon says she wants a chat with you, and I have a secret weapon. " "Who? What?"

"Pierce Brosnan."

"what? NOO! He's no fucking good! Why not the other Bond? Brosnan is a feckin waste of space!

"Oi, don't you dare dish the Brosnan! He is with us all the way."

I sighed "What's the plan?"

"To take out Dump before he invades … We have the means to get our team to Washington DC and from there, we can break into the Whitehouse and take that Dump down. "

"So Its Buckingham palace all over again? Need I remind you, that we had dragons helping us back then? How are we going to take that Dump out, if we don't have some sort of support?

Begbie looked at me. I could see he was in trouble; He looked down and moody. His blue eyes glazed over a small tear formed. I sighed I was about to nod, and say okay, when Suddenly a strange sound filled the room.

 I looked up. What the fuck is that? "Oh shit, shit, shit! Shit, we're too late!" Begbie said, panic rose in his voice. Come on! Now! Fucking move it!" We both ran outside. Begbie threw me in the back of his open-door limousine; and onto Rhiannon's lap, who told me to feck off.

 "Fucking drive!" Begbie shouted. The car revved up and sped away at a terrifying speed. Outside, the sky was filled with planes. Bombs burst all around us.

I looked up. In the darkness, that was slowly turning to an early fiery golden dawn, I could see planes opening and parachutes deploying. There were American Nazi-zombies falling from the sky. The Invasion of the Dump had just begun.

The drive and the meeting of the five.

 We set off out of London as fast as we could, though the streets and onto the motorway's. Most of the trip, to a secret airbase somewhere in Surrey, was it must be said, quiet and slightly awkward. Rhiannon sat with her arms crossed defiantly looking down. Begbie, kept welsh ragging his waxed hair and attempting to make small talk, which I on the whole I ignored. I was on edge. It wasn't simply the fact that American NaziZombies were falling form the sky and taking over the UK. It was the fact that I hadn't seen either the two girls, since Rhiannon had ran off with the security guard and my life had spiraled into a spiral of ugly self-loathing and regret. I kept opening my mouth to say something, but nothing came out. While the Driver, whose face I couldn't see was swerving all over the road, between broken cars and overturned lorries with superb skill, that was simply stunning. For a while I thought we had the Stig at the wheel.

"Not long now" muttered Begbie. We drove up a narrow winding road, barely big enough for the car. We entered a clearing and drove up to an aerodrome. Thee car skidded to a halt Begbie was the first out, then I then Rhiannon. The trees on the horizon were speckled black against a golden line along a flat horizon and a clear blue sky above. The dawn chorus sang gently. It was a cool morning, bit not crisp, the previous night could have been a nightmare.

The driver got out and the secret service bloke who shagged my ex was standing there.

"you! feck! Begbie why you bring this cunt along!

"It's not what you think" Begbie looked away.

But then the sky was filled with the noise of an approaching plane. It landed by the aerodrome. The plan span and the door opened.

"come on, for fucks sake, we aren't safe yet."

"Where are we going?"

"beyond the wall."

"What? It's full of dead blue zombies and fecking giants and- "

"Not Westeros! Your dumb fuck! Scotland!"

As we bundled into the plane. There sat Dark Steve and Jordan, who were already high. I was on my way too as the THC in the plane melted the nose off my face.

"good morning!" came the dry Scots Irish accent from the pilot. I recognized it straight away. Pierce Brosnan was taking us to Scotland.

"-So you did get him."

"-Don't knock the Bros!" Begbie commanded as the plane circled and took to the sky once more.

I turned to Rhiannon "So… where are the girls?"

"With my parents."

"I see, I see… that's so you!"

"-Well you were never there! You were too busy being you! You were shouting NaziZombie this, an NaziZombie that, meanwhile the girls couldn't bond. Remember! You took that picture of that fecking number plate… what was it now? " MErrrr" an shouted NaziZombie at the top of yer voice!"

"HE WAS A NAZIZOMBIE!"

"NO HE WASN'T! HE HAD A FUCKING STUTTER!"

"GUYS FOR FUCKS SAKE PACK IT IN!" Begbie bellowed

as he took Rhiannon's hand. "

Then it hit me.

"So it was you two after all… Begbie…for Christ sake! For Christ sake! How many beers? How many times did I call you! Shit you make Gove look like a feckin' saint!

I felt betrayed and wounded. The security guard was one thing, I didn't know that cunt, but not my best mate I felt bitterly enraged and wanted to get out of this situation right now.

"We didn't want this to happen." Rhiannon looked down.

I shook my head.

"The things I tried to do for you, the kids, everyone!"

"yeah" Dark Steve said.

"-We should be landing at Scapa Flow in about an hour and a half" Brosnan said over the intercom. Meanwhile, the TV's attached to the back of the seats came on and we saw images of Parachuting American NaziZombies, were cut short by what resembled a decomposing Sarah Palin in some sort of military uniform. She was growling zombie into a loud speaker, while in the background all that could be heard were the growls of murmurs of out of screen NaziZombies. Then the scene went back to London. The streets were being cleansed. Zombies armed with automatic weapons were walking in lines cutting down the citizens as they ran, then injecting the dying with something

"what are they doing?"

"we don't know…" began Jordan. "…We think it's some sort of American Nazi-zombification drug. They don't give it to all the victims. We also haven't got any, to find out what it contains…."

"…American NaziZombies like their guns"

"We managed to catch one at our Scapa flow base…." Begbie took over "…We need to figure out how to kill it."

"-What about transmission?" I was tired. But I needed to get images of my ex-wife and Begbie shagging from my mind.

"-So far, we haven't been affected. I mean the fucker isn't high ranking, He just says Dump, Dump, Dump a lot… If we subject it to Images of Dump, he stands at attention… just rock solid. If we show it pictures of Obama it goes into a rage. We dare not use a Sanders speech…it might be difficult to contain."

I wasn't listening, or at least pretending not to, which would be more accurate. "-We also might have immunity, because of the first influx of the virus." I was thinking aloud.

Begbie nodded. "-we've been thinking that

We examined it under very difficult conditions and found that It's brain had not been eaten; it had, in fact imploded, and somehow...we...we found encrusted brain tissue within the ear.

"Jesus."

yeah... Dump is the catalyst. We know if we take Dump out, then we can stop this hoard."

I stroked my stubble.

"-The bastard will come here." Rhiannon injected

"Yeah..." I began "...his fucking golf course."

I felt the plane slowly begin to descend and looked out of the window.

"We will be landing at Kirkbride naval base soon" began Brosnan."

And then another truth dawned on me.   "I know why you like Brosnan. It was that bond film... "The world is not enough!"

Begbie looked down.

"Yeah, you were good in that. Fuckin ace in-fact. Though Sean Bean does die well."

"Sean Bean always dies. But not like me!"

"sorry." I muttered.

The landing at the airbase

The plane landed at the naval airfield base with ease, we alighted and ran towards one of the many out-buildings. The place was hive of activity. Soldiers and sailors were running about, sirens blasting, mayhem, simply mayhem. As we entered one of the large, office type buildings. Begbie showed his clearance card to a hard-faced sailor who then saluted, and moved to the side, as the six of us entered a lift and descended five floors.

The doors opened to a low ceilinged poorly lit rectangular room, that had at its centre a group of police and army types sitting in deep discussion around a table. We walked towards the table.

"Good morning gentlemen..." came the long drawn out welcome.

I looked around the room, unable to see clearly who it was that was talking to us. I centred on the small screened television that rested on the table.

I stared at it with mixed feelings that riddle me to this day.

Bagpuss sat there, staring out at me; no, I kid you not, there was feckin' bagpuss, all red and white and baggy, that saggy cloth cat looking at us

"I am pleased you got here safely."

"what the fuck is Bagpuss doing here?"

"He's the new weapon of the resistance. Since the last NaziZombie infestation, I felt that we needed someone or something, an AI, that our generation could relate to; so, with help, of course we invented a computer hybrid AI program… together with our Eastern European Confederation allies and we came up with- "

"-fuckin Bagpuss?"   "You would be surprised how many people resonate with him from our generation…" began Begbie "… Originally we thought of Yaffle, but being a teacher, we felt that he might not have the same impact upon our generation…"

"Your, your feckin mad you know that?   "I heeaarrd thaaat…" Bagpuss said

"…. But being an A.I with…"
"-fuckin hell…"
"-an Ai tuned into the Dump soundwave we can- "
"-I loved that show! We can build It we can mend it; we can fix it we can wash it like new, new. new!"
"Heeley pay attention!" Bagpuss interrupted.
"Listen mate, Bagpuss can hear all that Nazi-zombie, braindead waffle; and turn it into sounds we can understand. We have, in Bagpuss, our own enigma machine."
"- but you need a conduit."
"Yep and we have one…." Began Rhiannon, he came to us freely about three weeks ago. We thought he was a deep infiltration NaziZombie operative. It turns out he is a resistance fighter, fighting against the NAziZombies That's how e knew they were planning to invade. What we didn't know was when."
I looked around the table, wondering who the fuck these soldiers were.
"Don't worry about those guys yet; the big surprise is the conduit, come with me.
Jordan, Dark Steve and I followed Rhiannon and Begbie into a side room. in the middle of that room lit up with white halogen bulbs within a plexi-glass box, within the box stood
"-Arnold Swarzenegger?
"-We call it the infiltrator."
"-I bet you do."
"-look, this is serious…the NaziZombies are real, Dump is real! We have to stop this!"
"Yeah the Infiltrator…Poor bastard."
The naziZombiefied Swarzenegger stared out at us, though his dead red flaming eyes. It kept saying "Dump…Duuuump Duuummmp" repeatedly. It's' face was pale and the skin, drawn tight round the nose. Its hair was white. I could see crusty grey brain matter around it's ears
"It seems that the infiltrator has links directly to Dump,

so it can communicate. Bagpuss has walled up the send signal but we can still receive information from Dump and all chief NaziZombies across the UK... We know that there is a plan and it's got something to do with his Golf club.

"Well I said that-" I snapped.

"-Yes, but it's about proof. What if we had all gone there and he didn't show.

"-It's Donald Dump, it's been a NaziZombie from birth of course it's predictable."

"I loved the Terminator" said Dark Steve.

"We all turned to Dark Steve. There was a long pause before Begbie said: "Shut up Dark Steve."

We returned to the other room and met the officials gathered there.

There was Major Major, Chief constable Ima Bastard, General Fosworth guffaw protein fart , Admiral Seaworthy as fuck and Chief air Marshall Tally, Bally-Hoe.

They all sat at the table looking up at us.

"So" began Begbie "Chief Constable Bastard, what is the police presence on the ground like?"

"I can confirm that I am in touch with most of the forces of the North of England.

"-Is that your real name? Bastard?" I asked.

"Yes, I come from a long line of Bastard's, there has been a bastard in her majesties police force, since the time of its inception."

"That I don't deny." I replied

"Major Major, and General Fosworth w-what is the status of the Army?" Asked Rhiannon.

"We, we, have five battalions here, ready for deployment. However, we are waiting for, for Admiral seaworthy as fuck to get his ships ready."

"-I can't... "injected Admiral seaworthy as fuck, "I simply can't...there's no time...Besides Dodgy Dave the piggy of Westeros sold our Fleet to India. We have one ship...Boaty McBoatface.... So, to get the troops across the-"

"-look stop now, just fucking stop! Boaty Mcfucking boatface? I liked the Chief constable bastard, but bringing fucking Boaty along is simply not on. It's not funny and it does not work.

"It's the only line I have." Said Seaworthy as fuck.

Begbie stared at me.

"Are you okay?"

"What do you mean?"

"Are you having one of those episodes again?"

"Piss off."

"We'll use the submarines, get what we can of the fleet together." Said seaworthy as fuck

"Good work Gentlemen." Begbie nodded.

As we left the room I wondering why I was there, as Begbie, muttered something under his breath and about artistic license and pish poor writing under his breath.

The Plan is sort of made but then

it didn't take long for Begbie and I to come to some sort of plan. Well, saying that it did. A bit. Mainly because I was still pissed off with him for shagging my ex-wife, which you must understand must be expected. Anyhow, via the infiltrator, we had found out that the Dump was going to be in Aberdeen in the next week. It didn't take us long to see why. It was where he had built his shite golf course.

At the time, many thought it bizarre; after all, who builds a golf course outside Aberdeen? The winds alone there are awful for ball direction. But as it was Dump, it was assumed that the man was mad enough to ignore the reality of physics. He did after all have his own form of alternate truth and alternate facts, that were real to him…just not real to any normal person.

The problem was technology, we were in the post net age. All we had were a couple of old copies of an old brochure advertising the course, describing it, giving list of all those who had played there, followed by a load of NaziZombie drivel, that was impossible to read. Since then Begbie had sent over a few surveillance drones over the links to get a lay of the land so to speak…It was crap…many top golfers refused to go there when it opened. In fact, only NaziZombies like the infiltrator and Stallone aka the bone cruncher, were ever seen there; and when they were there, they were not playing much golf; they were just wandering mindlessly about in awful neon orange and green V neck jumpers and slacks, stomping about in typical NaziZombie fashion, shouting a lot of unintelligible nonsense.

I recall that as we sat there pondering over this tatty piece of paper There was something in the wording of his introduction of the pamphlet that bothered us: "links land".

I thought about the fist NaziZombie problem here, then I thought about Dump and how he had always been in the public eye, in one way or another. Then the veil was lifted. This invasion by the Dump had been planned for years in advance. Even prior the NaziZombie collapse in the UK. It became clear to us that Dump's plans to invade Europe with his own version/brand of the NaziZombie virus, had been put on hold during our outbreak. Now that was contained, he had the chance to revive his plans and attack once more. The problem was, at the time, we didn't know how advanced Dumps plans were. Europe had suffered terribly at the hands of the Dump, the resistance had learned that huge tracts of land hand been bombed to make bigger and bigger golf courses. Belgium – for instance- was already one huge golf course. France was already half completed. There also was another problem: the growing accounts of missing Aberdonians. To start with nobody knew that people were going missing at all. Until it was too late.

'We are picking up some weird electromagnetic readings coming from the links...' began Jordan in a mist of weed smoke; 'I mean really weird...look.'

We all stared into the monitor screen and noticed the compass was not reading true north.

'The heat levels are unusual too.' Begbie muttered, 'Do we know what's causing that?'

'well, it could be due to the microclimate.'

'- we are talking about Aberdeen here...' Rhiannon sighed

The Camera picked out a couple of NaziZombies wandering about. The lower grounds of the club house.

'Close up?' Begbie murmured.

The screen zoomed in.   At first sight, it was obvious that these were not a-typical NaziZombies. They had the orange skin and faded toupee's to be expected of the American version of the virus and their clothing was crass even for golfer's, but there was something else about them that seemed strange. Something that, to be honest, I couldn't put my finger on...observing them, they seemed to be pretending to take golf strokes without using any form of golf club. I have to say, it was very weird indeed.

'I think it's Dump's advanced guards...' began Jordan, '...At one time, they might have been CIA or FBI officer's.

'Now they just wander about trying to fit in.' Rhiannon reported between puffs of her e-cigarette.

'-If the advanced guard is on the links now, then perhaps, we can assume tha- '

I was cut short as Dump appeared. I felt an icy hand grab at my stomach, as I saw that he was holding the hand of-

'-Angela. The bastard has Angela, what is he doing.

He lifted their hands up together.

'You mean Angela and Dump are?'

I didn't want to think about it.   Angela being fondled by that fucking NaziZombie made my skin crawl.

'So, this is what we do!' Begbie took command

'We get on that fucking golf course! we get Angela back and we kill that fucker Dump, before he turns the rest of the UK into his own fucking private hotel and golf club. The army are on our side. We also have Brosnan.'

'Why is he so important?'

'He just fucking is! OKAY!'

Suddenly sirens screamed and an intercom message came though.

'Hostiles we have hostiles! Coming in low.' Majo Major announced nasally.

We turned on the outside surveillance camera's

The sky was filled with helicopters.

'My god it's like apocalypse now!' I cried.

'Air mobile! Come on, we have to move!' Begbie yelled and the group of us re-entered the main hall, and followed the chiefs of staff up to ground level. We ran onto the airfield and saw our soldiers and sailors take up perimeters, their guns clicked into position as the Ride of the Valkyries boomed from speakers overhead.

There was the sound of helicopters, and more. There was a sound of someone talking NaziZombie! "ghghghghghghgndhdbgmgkgkglfjdgdhfjgkglgjfdbfjgkhlhglfkfjd gcb"

'The bastards are coming out of the rising sun, with the south Westerly wind! the virus! It's spreading! Come on!"

We ran to take cover, desperately shoving in cotton wool into ours ears as quickly as possible. Many of our men who were not quick enough became NaziZombies immediately; I saw Chief Inspector Bastard's brains, explode from his ears, leaving streaks of gore and matted brain tissue all over his shoulders and the ground. With a sudden thrust, I staved him in the chest, and avoided the flames, just as Rear Admiral Seaworthy as Fuck screamed. I turned just to see him bend double in pain, grabbing hold of his ears. There was sudden slurping popping sound as his brains slipped over his fingers.

'O fuck me!' I screamed as Dark Steve staved him in the chest.

Then the bombs began to fall. Yellow flame lit up the horizon; as the helicopters span in low; shouting out Nazi zombie Dump slogans before dropping bombs

We fought our way to the far side of the perimeter fence and the waiting car that would take us to Aberdeen. I got inside. The other's followed.

'You know where to go!' Shouted Begbie as the car sped away. Only then did I realise that it was Pierce Brosnan.

'Why are you here.' I asked

'It's a secret.' Came the reply.

'Oh yeah, that' fine coming from the man who played the worst secret agent in history. I mean James Bond, say the name and you know what's going to happen next.

'Oh, that's not fair…by the end Roger Moore, really was far worse than I. Especially in the later films such as Moonraker.'

'Aye, but to be fair, when they stuck to the texts, such as

the man with the golden gun, he was better tha-'

'Fer fucks sake, just drive!' Bellowed Rhiannon 'we've got to get to the links before Dump leaves.

With a wry smile Brosnan put his foot to the floor, as the VW, campervan for that was what we were bundled into, chugged off along the narrow winding road towards Aberdeen.

Aberdeen.

The trip in the campervan was difficult. I kept wanting to ask Brosnan about his career, while Begbie was getting annoyed that we were not going fast enough. It also didn't help that Jordan was on his fifth joint and the van was filled with THC... Aberdeen... it sounds eerie on the tongue. I visited it prior the zombieNazi invasion and it was a strange place even then: alien and scary. The weirdest thing about the city, back then, was its desolation. Aberdeen was never known for its night life; a fish and chip shop that sold the battered Mars bar and a wine bar were the main attractions even before the first Nazi zombie invasion; but that day it was twice as desolate than before.

Not even the birds sang as we made our way up to the 'bridge of Dom' that had been renamed the Bridge of doom, in wild graffiti letters. I know, there are the pedantic out there, saying why are you crossing the Bridge of Dom, your just after a cheap laugh and are out to take the piss out of Aberdeen. That Is very unfair and untrue. The fact is we got lost, that's because we all got stoned, on Jordan's weed; This led to Brosnan spending a good half hour raiding the desolate shops for crisps, pizza and munchie food. It also meant, we went around the whole of the bloody city just trying to find a way to the fucking golf course.

When we finally hit the A90, I couldn't believe my eyes. Every 90 years stood a poster of Dump's mother promoting social values.

"I just want to be the people's princess" said one

"Didn't Di-"

"Yep" said Begbie.

"I have a dream" said another.

'Hey didn't Martin Luther king say that?'

'Unofficially, yes...' Began Jordan. 'But...according to sources the new texts in schools is the Dump book of history, so now it's Dump's mum who said it. In fact, she has been recorded as saying every positive thing that mankind has ever said."

'"Give me your poor and your huddled masses," Dump's mum said that!'

'No, she didn't! that's what was once written on the Statue

of liberty, until Dump had spray painted the words "Fuck off you immigrants. Especially Mexicans and Muslims!" Followed by "my Great Grandfather was a Scot, my grandfather was a Scot so I am a Scot too, so feck off yer twats unless you got money!"

'I think the world's goon' fucking arse up, if you ask me. Begbie muttered.

'She hasn't said that yet. 'muttered Dark Steve. We all stared at Dark Steve, whose face was hidden under his black hoodie, wafts of THC smoke bellowed from the hood.

'You gotta remember...' he spoke laconically '...that she is an immigrant with a thick accent, who plagiarizes just about everyone, especially colored women, and is ravenously leered at in the stadiums full of pasty faced fucking NaziZombies who think that colored people and immigrants are destroying the world.'

'That's profound Dark Steve.' I said with awe.

'Yeah... I nicked it from Facebook.'

We drove past another poster with her on. This time the words "blessed are the rich for they pay enough to enter the kingdom of heaven.'

'Is she parodying Jesus now? Is nothing sacred?' I shook my head sadly

'No parody mate: pure NaziZombie Dumpism." Jordan said sadly

The fact that I could read it all bothered me... It meant that I was infected. Though I think the THC helped to stem the infection to a lesser degree...

'You have to understand...' Jordan continued.'...this virus is contagious...It starts with one sad, old bugger muttering about the, the price of fish and becomes like open warfare about immigration and why the immigrants are the problem the next.'. I have to admit I gad to agree with him.

Aberdeen was a shit hole. Even the chip shops were closed. We passed a looted Asda that had posters promoting Dumps' his golf links all over it.

'Jesus. You'd think that people would have caught on.'

'You have to understand,' Began Begbie 'that everything that made the west tick once came out of Aberdeen. Oil, linen, Sky satellite TV call centers... all from here... then the oil dried up, the sky broke and the linen came from Pakistan...so they turned to Dump. And his golf course.

'Not long now.' Muttered Brosnan, who pulled the VW up close to a long and extremely high barbed wire fence. Beyond that stood a thick line of trees. A pale light of a searchlight combed over the tops of the branches that were picked out in white before night returned once more.

We all got out of the campervan. well, when I say, "got out" we sort of mumbled stuff and stretched our legs a bit.

'This is the perimeter fence of the Links, beyond this barbed wire and the trees are search lights and the largest gathering of American NaziZombies this side of the Atlantic. It's not going to be easy. But if we pick our targets well, we might get to the wolf's lair before the dawn rises…. ok Brosnan, you know what to do.

'Wolfs Lair?' I looked at Begbie sardonically.

'my code word for it.'

With a swift wave of his hand Brosnan disappeared along the side of the fence and into the gloom.

'Where the fuck is he going?'

'That's classified.' Said Begbie, who began looking along the fence with a shielded torch. After about five minutes he gave a sigh of relief.

'Dark Steve! Jordan. Here '

Rhiannon and I watched as Dark Steve took off his backpack and removed a small laptop. Within a second or two of typing in some command's both Jordan and Dark Steve said ok.

With a wry grin on his face, Begbie started cutting the fence.

While I began wondering what on earth was Pearce Brosnan doing with us at all.

The Links part 1

As an aside, I must say, right now, that I fucking hate golf! I come from a long line of golfing hater's, from Oscar Wilde who called this vile pass-time, the "ruin of a long walk", to Jaspar Carrot who equated the ball followers on BBC T.V to world war two searchlight operatives… "where is the ball??? Is it to the right? Is it to the left…no…no…we seem to have lost it in the ball in the sky…"

Why on earth people must hit a ball with a stick to get the bloody thing in a hole, when all they need do is drop it in while carrying it in their pocket, defies me. How this bizarre pass-time, (because it is no way a fecking sport) began, is also obscure; rooted in ancient myth and ancient(ier) legend. Most people consider that "early golf" began in the Netherlands, during the middle ages. No doubt by some vile aristocrat, who thought that aiming a ball at a poor person's head while they were running away was " a Jolly Good Sport eh?"

"Modern Golf", is considered as a Scottish invention; the first documented "game" being mentioned is in the Scottish parliament and recorded during 1457, where King James the 1st, no doubt realizing the dangers of the "sport" promptly banned it with immediate effect. But that never stopped the vile game from spreading. Many now conclude that the birth of the NaziZombie virus can be directly related to Golf, as uncontrolled thought's that relate to bigoted ideas, spread easy when a person is distracted by hitting a ball with a club into the air.

Moreover, there is a fascinating correlation between golf and periods of extreme poverty. By the 1920's in the states alone, there were more 1,100 "clubs" across America, however ww2 and the end of the first NaziZombie hoard, nearly also nearly killed off the game completely; despite that, like a sleeping dragon, it came back to popularity in the post war and the post-modern era. What Golf does, is that it takes huge amounts of land that were open to people to walk on and -basically- enjoy and turn them into secret underground headquarters' for NaziZombies. Up qo the fences. Then men or women, in bizarre uniforms and poor taste in slacks, and V necked sweaters roam about shouting "urheghegehereheghearghsgsrghhharrrgh" which is probably NaziZombie for "fuck off or you will be eaten."

The club houses themselves are named after famous NaziZombies in history, who enjoyed being bigoted arseholes right up to the end. St Andrew being one. At one time, it was only only men who could roll up their left trouser leg just above the knee and quote from the NaziZombie bible "gurreghehegreregeiehegeghhh" could enter. This very slowly changed over time, as the male members realized that their wives were as indoctrinated as they were themselves when it came to this bizarre pass-time.

Dump knew this of course, which was why he established "the Dump's links" a place that before its construction, was once noted for its natural beauty and scientific interest. Which was why he bought it and in the space of two years, wrecked, re-organized and fenced it off from the rest of the country. Gone were the ancient natural sand dunes and the rare grasslands. Instead, behind huge fences rose shitty lawns with sandpits; where stumbling Nazi-zombies, mindlessly wandered about in some form of stupefaction, protecting the surface from the secret terrors that slither and writhe, like hideous lingering worms, beneath. Something that we found out later to our cost.

Getting though the perimeter fence was tough, but not as tough as sneaking through the wooded "rough" (and there is another thing, why call the area off the course rough? Its NATURE, in all her glory, not some lawn for Je-us sake) the place was chocked with the hoard. Red eyes glared from along the patches of mowed grass, searchlights filled the sky and scoured the tree while the NaziZombies were murmuring "Dump...Dump...Dump..." is some sort of rhythmic chant, It added both to the surreal nature of what was happening and the horrifying realities of what would happen if only one of us was caught.

I for one I kept thinking about how the dragons came in our hour of need. This time I knew that we were on our own. I could feel my heart thump heavily in my chest; while we made sort of bird calling noises to keep the hoard from finding us.

Then it happened. Helicopters filled the sky. I was terrified
thinking that this was the bunch from the naval base. But it wasn't. For I saw Begbie stand up and say

'Good on yer Brosnan!'

Suddenly the sky was filled with hundreds of ninja warriors, who fell from long ropes down into the Nazi zombie hoard. Guns rattled off and swords slashed as the NaziZombies began to fall to the ground, their bodies either popping like melons, or being engulfed in flames.

'You know these guys are trained to peak performance.' Began Begbie 'They slam bricks into their groin as a pass-time.'

'No!' I looked shocked

'It's fecking true. I've seen 'em train.'

Brosnan, his face stern was holding a flame thrower, he let off bursts of yellow flame from the weapon as he fought his way to our position.

He almost didn't make it, as two came charging at him from behind, but just in time, he turned and burned them off to paper.

'I'd knew you'd not let me down.' Said Begbie, his voice rich with satisfaction as he slapped Brosnan on the back.

'Well, once a Bond, always a Bond...' Brosnan began'...besides Connery said never, ever, ever, ever again.'

We bitterly fought our way forward over the links, killing the NaziZombie hoard around us; our Ninja warriors fighting by our side. It was as we made it to the club house, that bad fortune started to overcome us. We had almost reached the rear entrance, when all of a sudden, upon the balcony of the building, Dump appeared. Having picked up a weapon I raised it and took a shot. It bounced off. There was a protective dome surrounded the building.

'It's his ego defense mechanism.' Shouted Rhiannon, over the screams of the battle. 'How are we ever going to break that?'

Then suddenly, there was a strange guttural quaking sound. We all looked at dark Steve, who said nothing. Then we knew it was the ground. The middle of the links course slowly descended and out of the pit came a weapon that we feared would seal our fate. A life-sized replica of Dumps mother... over fifty feet tall, using the most lethal weapon in the Nazi zombie armory...the over worked cliché

The links part 2

If there is one thing worse than Vogon poetry, it is the Robotic cliché. This technology developed out of semiotics; led to something humanity had never expected. A weapon of devastating proportions. Entire populations of cities were laid waste by this devastating literature device. Men, women and children would attempt to flee as phrases' like "tip of the iceberg" and "all things being equal" were boomed out of enormous speakers to shatter limb's, crush organs and sever arteries. It was the united nations who, just after the first use of the weapon declared the use of robotic cliché illegal and a weapon of mass destruction.

However, that didn't stop Dump from stockpiling them. What we didn't know that on every one of Dumps courses all around the world the giant replica robots of Dumps mother were slowly coming out of the ground and beginning an act of genocide never seen on the earth before.

This was because Dump had specifically chosen each site for his links specifically for the transmission of cliché all over the world; thus, causing a vibrational tonal effect, and destabilising the magnetic field that in turn began destroying the planet's eco system. All of which he attempted to do to make way for Trumps new hotel complexes on Mars and the moon. This we found out a little later.

As the robot arose from the links, I felt that the end had come. How could we break through the ego Dome and the Cliché' monster, on a golf course filled with NaziZombies?

Of course, Brosnan and the ball breaking Ninja's were helping, but I felt, that at that time, resistance was futile.

With a ferocity, I had never seen before, the sky above the links began to fill with rolling clouds, that that twisted and spiraled, as the cliché robot began to speak

"Live and learn" the robot bellowed from its mouth. Lightening began to fill the sky and hit the ego dome, within which, Dump stood waving like some deluded lunatic and with each strike the dome shrank a little.

'Avoid like the plague' Bellowed the robot taking out fifty ninja that were climbing the robot at the time. The cloud cover became heavy and a rising wind began to twist the trees.

'Age before beauty' the Robot boomed and the wind began to howl. Lighting ripped the sky and finally burst through the ego dome.

We then charged into the club house taking out three of the Dump guards with our weapons, who burst into flame.

'Alive and kicking' boomed the robot again just as we managed to cover our ears, as Begbie kicked in the glass window that led to the hallway of the club house.

From the relative safety of inside the club house we would see how will the sky had become. Dark rolling clouds broiled overhead; while along the course and into the middle-distance trees were cracking wildly and being uprooted then thrown like children's toys across a room.

'what the fuck is going on?

'It's the fucking end of the world!'

Rhiannon got to her knees, her wide eyes were filled with fear.

The door at the far end of the hall opened and Dump staggered in. His eyes a grey flame.

'YOU THINK THAT YOU COULD STOP ME? NO ONE CAN STOP ME! IM KING OF THE WORLD! BOW DOWN AND WORSHIP YOUR GOD!'

'YOUR NO GOD!' bellowed Begbie, 'YOU'RE A CHEAP TRICK! A CON! A JOKE! YOU ONLY GOT INTO POWER BECAUSE YOU BRIBED YOUR WAY IN!'

'YOU CAN'T PROVE THAT!' snarled Dump who fired an electricity bolt from his hand hitting Begbie full in the chest and sending him flying across the room.

'BEGBIE!' Rhiannon and I screamed and ran to him; as Dump slowly walked forward; greed hate and determination written all over his grey flaky face and fiery fury shone from his flaming red eyes. Jordan took a couple of shots and was then lifted into the air while Dark Steve fled the room.

We knelt by Begbie and tried to comfort him. There was huge blackened scar on his chest. I could see that he was barely breathing.

We called his name and held him as Dump laughed menacingly.

We could feel his fettered breath as he made is way towards us.

Then a bright light filled the room. Almost blinding us. What followed was something we that we didn't expect at all.

It was the beginning of the French national anthem.

Begbie looked up at me, with tired pain riddled, yet hope filled eyes. 'is it? Could it be?'

Then followed the song:

'Love, love love!'

Dump screamed and howled in pain as the roof of the club house began to snap, crack, twist and crumble into dust, to spiral upwards into the light.

'There's nothing you can do that can't be done, there's

nothing you can't sing that can't be sung, nothing you can say but your can learn how to play the game, it's easy…'

Outside the zombie-Nazi's began to violently shake and fall to the ground, while Dumps' secret service agents burst into flames. Dump screamed, unable to move.

'Nothing that you can make that can't be made, no one that you can save that can't be saved, nothing you can do, but to learn how to be you in time, it's easy….'

The wind stopped blowing and the song filled the air.

'All you need is love' the NaziZombies began to falter around the ground. 'All you need is love' Their bodies quaked lifted and exploded 'all you need is love, 'then many of them caught fire as the cliché robot exploded. 'love love, love is all you need. '

Many of the black robed ninjas began dancing as the song continued into its instrumental break continued.

Dark Steve suddenly came in to the wrecked building with Brosnan; and Dump, who couldn't move but simply kept shouting hate, was weakening his hold on Jordan. Finally, with a gasp Jordan was free and ran to help us get Begbie outside. We were one hundred feet from the golf house as the song reached its second verse; then the club house slowly crumbled away leaving Dump alone and surrounded by a strange purple light. His impenetrable ego force-field.

The song became louder filling the sky 'Nothing you can know that isn't known, nothing you can't see that isn't shown. Nowhere you can be that isn't where your meant to be…it's easy.'

'All you need is love, all you need is love, all you need is love, love, love is all you need. 'what was left of the Nazi-zombies were being driven towards the flaming broken robot in the center of the links; who then began to throw themselves into the flames

'All you need is lobe (altogether now) all you need is love (everybody) all you need is love, love, love is all you need. And at this point the clouds around the bright light above began to spin slowly as Love is all you need began to be sung faster and faster. Dump screamed and held his head as the dome around him burst. He screamed in bestial fury as the words reached their pinnacle. He pushed his hands over his face as he was lifted.

Then out of the light came, John Lennon dressed in a yellow T-shirt, dark stripped trousers and a corduroy jacked and next to him came George Harrison, in a Denim jacket shirt and jeans.

'Well I'll be f- 'I started to say

'-Now now.' Said George.

'-But you're….so heaven is real?

Lennon looked at Harrison and they both giggled.

'Nah, but there's something going on back here and it's a laugh…he coughed; 'but when we saw what was going on, on earth, we had to do something…so we thought we'd put a stop to it. Aint that right George.

'Sure is John.'

Lennon and Harrison looked at dump as he bellowed from inside his sphere.

'Nazi-zombies are easy to get rid of.' Lennon quipped 'If you break their ego, they soon crash to the floor and dissolve.'

With that Lennon pulled a pin out from inside his brown corduroy jacket. Dump looked at the pin in terror. Lennon pushed the pin into the bubble. It burst, and with that Dump began to slowly dissolve into a wriggling, slithering worm onto the lawn of the links.

From out of his Denim Jacket, George pulled out a small vial and a pair of tweezers

'Careful now George, don't let-

'-Ahh don't you go on so.'

Carefully George picked up the little worm; put it in the vial and sealed it with a cork bung.

They both sighed with satisfaction

'Is that it?

' for this cycle yep.'

'no more NaziZombies?'

'Well every thousand odd years or so, some mad person comes along to made a mess of things…but this is it for now.'

I turned away from John Lennon and knelt beside Begbie. I told him that it was over, that finally it was all over. But Begbie couldn't hear me. His eyes were glazed.

I looked back to Lennon and Harrison and saw Begbie with them.

'It's up to you now kiddo,' Begbie said as they all went up into the spiraling clouds together, as the final words of love is all you need she loves you yeah, yeah, yeah, dwindled into the night.

Rhiannon, Jordan, Dark Steve, Broson, a couple of hundred Ninja and I were left in the near dark standing in a broken golf links by the flames of the rotting corpses of Nazi zombies.

'That bastard Begbie… he always gets' the better death scene.' Muttered Brosnan. We looked at each other, then gagged on the smell of decomposing flesh.

Six months have passed since the fight at the links. Most of it feels like a surreal dream; yet the world feels like a better place now. Occasionally Begbie comes into my dreams; usually to ask how Rhiannon is.

I look at her picture in the paper. She is running for Prime minister now and her new husband is, yes Brosnan…well…I can't complain, not everyone can say that they have an ex-James Bond as a step in law can they.

part two: the other animals.

The Long room.

For L. without whom...

Cold Creek, New England 1984

The loss of Innocence... history teaches us, that it is has and has always been a painful process. It also teaches us, as individuals, that people, who we put in a position of prominence in our lives are not who or what they seem to be, and through that, life, in all its beauty and wonder can also be a cause of great heartache and pain. Despite giving us an inner strength to continue. I was fourteen at the time, and when it was over, I would never be the same again.

What occurred took place in the space of two years, between the winter of Nineteen hundred and twenty-two and nineteen hundred and twenty-three. The day it came to a head was an early afternoon; church had been over an hour or two, but the whole street was there, standing or sitting in their respected places. The men wearing their stiff black suits with white shirts and black ties. The women wearing their paisley pattern thin flannelette dresses, with the obligatory pinafore, in varied shades of the colors green or brown, around their tight waists. They wore them as a symbol; proof of not only of their identity, but also as a statement to their men. "We are in charge", these aged pinafores silently proclaimed and none of them men of theirs ever denied it.

We were never related to the street, but since we needed a fellowship, for our move from Harlem New York, had left us bereft of kith and kin, they had become our extended family. Though, I must admit that Daddy didn't exactly approve. But Daddy had no faith.

By the Long rooms double doors, stood Aunt Bessie, a stern looking, pencil thin lady in her late fifties. Opposite her, and sittin' in the only rocker that the old house had, sat her husband who everybody affectionately called Uncle Silas.

They were like chalk and cheese -Silas and Bessie- for he was a rounding bald man with a huge smile that never seemed to leave his face and that showed a thousand teeth, all shiny and white that shone outward against the gloom of the room. Next to Aunt Bessie, sat Aunt Masie, Bessie's sister; she was just as thin and just as stern looking, but with her arms crossed, I could see that she was nursing a private pain. Then there was Douglas, with his wife Elspeth, with her two elder boys, Drew and Sam, finally next to Uncle Silas, stood Uncle Frank; out of all of them, I felt the closest to Uncle Frank, even though, I, prior to this incident, adored Uncle Silas.

Unfortunately, I did not expect the crowded chatty front room suddenly turn silent as I entered. I started feeling awkward, so I turned and stared towards the fire where Uncle Silas sat. As usual, Uncle always had the right words for every situation. He turned toward me and said. "Good child, Your Daddy still got a lot of living' to do, and just coz you see the dead, don't mean that he has. You got admit it child the shines on you..."I looked at Uncle Frank and he smiled down at me. Don't worry child, I heard him say inside me, things are going to be fine. I must say his kind words soothed my nerves somewhat. You just shine as bright as you can. He said.

I knew all about the shine, 'cause I'd been blessed with it. Most folks around here call it the shine. To explain it to someone else is hard, another way of looking at it, is seeing the hidden things of this world. It's sort of like seeing the future or the past, or –if you lose someone special and lose them badly- you can see who it was who did it. Or what happened. You can also see those who've moved on; and sometimes that's a blessing, but sometimes it aint. Some people shine so bright that they can talk to others likeminded without even opening their mouths. Some shine so bright, those that live in the dark want to drain you dry...that's when it gets scary

From what I've been told, the shine-goes way back; as far back as far as even Uncle Silas can remember and he's as old as time itself. I remember, he told me, that the shine was well known in the homeland. He said that those who had it were thought to be sacred: "the keeper of the keys" or so he called them. I remember how he told me too: in hushed tones. He made it sound like all those who were blessed with the shine were keepers of a sacred law and the protectors of the peace, I think it was 'cause they could see why folks did the things they did... and stop something bad from happening, like a murder or a war...something like that anyway... He also said that this was something that I should not tell folks outside the street about; 'cause as he put it "folk outside of the street would not understand, and would become scared, as most folks fear things that they don't understand." I wasn't exactly sure what Uncle Silas meant by that; but he said don't breathe a word, and it was fine with me. After all, I'm good at keeping secrets. So I stood there, looking around the long room, wondering why they had me here and wondering what would happen next.

From the Diary of Clarise Winslow 1923 time dates omitted.

There are times when I wonder why God, in his kindness, mercy and infinite love, had chosen me for such a gift. I think that it has something to do with my mom, 'cause once, at school, there was an incident between Lucy Cricket and me. Lucy Cricket and I never got on that well; she was pointy nosed, blond haired, blue eyed an vain with it too, mainly as she lived on the other side of town -or liked to think she did- if you know what I mean; anyways, she always talked down to me, or was plain nasty. Despite it all I took what she threw at me, till early spring, last year, just before everything happened.

    I was in the playground, during lunch, when Lucy pushed me over. At first there was shock, then, I remember getting a feeling, deep inside me, like I was as hot as embers on a coal fire, and at the same time, I simply thought about crushing her little white piggy nose. Within a second of thinking it, rich, near black blood, began gushing out from her nose and down her white linin school dress. Well, Lucy began hollering' and all the other children began hollering' too; I had just managed to stand up, when Mr Crawford, the English teacher, came running over to see if Lucy was hurt.

    I remember saying' over and repeatedly that I had not touched her. But Mr Crawford just gave me the cold eye and said that "folks like mine could not be trusted." He said that he "knew my mom" and that "...if Alice and I were blood kin to that witch, then we would be as damned as her on judgement day." That hurt deeply, but I just looked down, just as uncle Silas told me to, would do no good complaining' no how.

    Later that day, after I got home, Mom asked me why I was all upset. I recall that stare she gave me with her huge almond eyes before she suddenly spoke without opening her mouth. Lucy Cricket was a crock of fool. The words said. An with that came an image of Lucy Cricket dressed as a clown.

    I took a step back and Mom smiled warmly.

 'I saw what happened.' She said gently, don't tell your Pa, he'll get all flustered and all. So, for a year it was our secret.

    Then Mom passed on... the street turned up to help Dad, but he never trusted the street that much, so despite their care and kindness, we–that bein' Alice and I- watched on, as our dear dad begin to crumble. I recall that from that point on, he began to walk with a slight stoop, he also worked all the time, so the street took both Alice and I on, helping us with our homework making meals for us, babysitting, stuff like that.

To start with Both Alice and I too hurt and hurt bad 'cause I missed my Mom so, but then a month after mom's passing, Alice came to my room at night and told me that she had seen Mom, that she was alright. At the time I hated them both for that. But not for long, 'cause Mom came to me a week later and told me that she had been in pain a long time, (with something called cancer -though I don't know what a cancer is and how it could take my mom from me.) and now the pain had gone.

To begin with –when I saw her- my mom, I mean- I got scared. But, soon after, the fear passed and in its place, peace grew. Eventually Mom went away to be with Jesus. But, before she went, she told me something, she said "look after your Pa, 'cause he is going to need you soon."   It is said that twins even twins that are not alike, share a bond. From experience, I know this to be true. Alice was always the brighter and the prettier out of the two of us, she was also the bolder of the two of us so I was always in her shadow. I was never as close to her than the day she passed and that was one of the strangest days that I can remember. I remember… It was just before Christmas 22, that I had the vision. Outside the street had a special - almost magical- feel about it. The air was thick with the thought of snow; people exhaled a dragon's breath of steam into the cold air and both the roast chestnut sellers and the hot dog stands were glowing with rich red coal light and fuming with broiling heat, thus gathering a small crowd of tired hungry shoppers, as they made their way home in the clear ice blue cold of this crisp, late evening sky.

The city governors had also just put up the celebration lights; so, from every telegraph pole a string of multi-coloured bulbs and bunting criss-crossed the road in a ragged diamond shape. I remember seeing all this and more.

I remember seeing Alice walking home from house group; wearing her thick black and white check long coat, carrying her huge black leather bound bible in her gloved left hand; I could even see the tips of her long flowing auburn hair beneath her white woolen cap, whishing about her cheeks, as she made her way through the crowds.

The snow began to fall in thick heavy clumps along the sidewalk, to gather in the corners where only snow could grow, as she made her way home. O saw her as she passed the side alley that cut the street in half. In summer months, the alley was a short cut we used to get into the city Centre. During the cold winter months, no one dared go down there. The alley was darkness, no light ever shone there, not for a moment.

The dark from the alley was complete. Then, the dark vanished, and I saw two white lights like a pair of silver eyes glisten as a snarling demon appeared. I can still see its face, all twisted and burning with hate. Its leather dead skin cracked and scabbed with savage cuts. The eyes burning… forever burning with revenge, cruelty and savage delight. Suddenly It leaped out of the darkness, and charged for Alice. With a savage fury it slid, like a fiery snake, out of the darkness, its body covered in scales and flame red, its eyes a blazing fire, with its huge three fingered talons, it knocked her to the ground, then under its hideous claw, crushed her skull instantly; before suddenly disappearing into the nigh

I say it was strange for a reason. The reason being is that week I was taken ill with a brain fever, and God's witness that's what I dreamt; down to the last detail. It took a week to recover from my sickness and when I did and told Dad the dream, I also saw the strain' and pain on his face as he slowly took my hand and told me Alice was gone. I recall his face, large and oval, his close-cropped Brown hair and his almond eyes riddled with love and pain. If he was not heartbroken before, he sure looked it now.

I should 'a been heartbroken too, and, if it were not for the shine, I know I would 'a been… things could have been so different. But the shine helped me stay together. In fact, it did more than keep me together, it kept Alice and I in touch with each other, even after her funeral. That was the only reason I did not go plain crazy, and that was the reason why Daddy finally turned away from the street.

Daddy was surprised when I didn't cry like he did; but I was a good girl and I didn't want to upset Uncle Silas. So, I kept Alice's visits a secret. Uncle Silas said not to tell Dad because he said that Dad was "a man born outside of our ways and ignorant of the ancient teachings." I nodded and smiled at Uncle Silas as he told me this one day after church. So…I kept my mouth shut

But one day Alice came and began telling me something about Jared, well, I tried to listen, but I didn't get it all, she seemed a little fainter that day, so I asked her to speak up a bit, not knowing that Dad had come through the door and had been listening to our conversation.

Daddy asked me what I was doing' and I clammed my mouth tight as I could get it. But Daddy got cross and he said sternly that "If I didn't tell this instant then he would tan my brown behind and send me to bed with no supper… Well… I didn't want a tanning, so I told him… no, not everything, just the Alice stuff and Mom coming to tell me that I had to look after him.

As I told him, daddy's face changed. I could feel the hurt

within him build up to the surface... I saw other faces too... strange, hideous enraged faces pulling up out of him and coming out of the walls around and behind him. They were screaming at each other and at Dad too. They were familiar, but too scary to look at for long, and then Daddy smiled, and asked me where these ideas had come from. I then mentioned Uncle Silas, and the other members of the street.

At that Dad's face changed once more. He grabbed my hand roughly and dragged me out of the door of my room, down the stairs and out of the front door. I felt his iron like grip on my wrist. I kept pleading Daddy, don't hurt me, but he was in another place 'cause he didn't hear a word I was saying, as we crossed the street and entered Uncle Silas's house.

We then burst into the long room. The long room was poorly lit by three large oil lamps scattered about the room and the large fire burning in the hearth. Strange shadows flickered on the walls like people dancing. I could hear old voices from long ago whisper around us. Uncle Silas was sitting by the fire in his rocker as my Dad crossed the wooden floor and then the thick red rug.

"My daughter..." He began crossly. "Said that the dead talk to her... she said that you have encouraged this... she said she had some kind of connection to Alice and to Abigail..."

"-Take it easy son." Began Uncle Silas. His voice calm and persuasive.

"-Don't call me that!" My Daddy bellowed. I could see he was shaking. "Don't you dare call me that! I am not your son any more than my children are your uncles and aunts!" I became scared. I hated it when Daddy was cross it hurt me so

"We are all brothers and sisters in the eyes of God." Said Uncle Silas calmly.

"GOD?" Daddy became so angry I wanted to leave the room and pee.

"What has God done to me? He has taken my wife and one of my children, the only things that were ever precious to me... He's taken them AND I HATE HIM FOR IT!"

I could see the pain in Uncle Silas face, I saw the sadness on the face of Uncle Frank face too and I wanted to cry.

"I ask one thing... Just, just one thing... stay away from my family... all of you... Just stay away... You're all about the Devil's business... and I... my family and I... want nothing more to do with you... do you understand? Stay away from us!" and with that, he dragged me home.

That would have been the end of it, if it were not for Alice.

Daddy was at home a lot more after that, which was nice 'cause I had been having bad dreams about Alice, the trouble was I could not remember them when I woke. One night must have been very bad. I woke to see Daddy staring down upon me with the strangest look upon his face.

I asked him what was wrong, and he suddenly smiled and said, "Nothing dear, now go to sleep." The next day at school I heard through the grapevine that Jared went missing. At the time it meant nothing, till I was picked up by Uncle Silas from the nurse at school, who then brought me, for one final time to the Long Room.

* * *

"That's enough," Inserted Aunt Bessie urgently. "We aint here to listen to you put on so...we need to hear from your shine. We need to know what happed last night." and with that she opened her purse and pulled out a soiled rag. I knew that the rag had belonged to Jared. For I recognized the shirt it had come from, despite the bloodstain.

I Knew what they wanted. They wanted me to touch the rag and see within. Silas was getting on and they knew I shone the brightest in the room. I didn't want to do this, the thought of it made me sick to my stomach, and scared me, though at the time I didn't know why. I looked towards Bessie and I saw in her dark eyes a look of desperation, a need to know the truth, they screamed at me from hollow pits.

"Who took him Clarice, who took my boy from me?" She said her voice almost a whisper.

"My Boy..." Her words still cause a lump in my throat, but not through grief; for her "boy" for was no boy at all. He was a man... the worst kind of man too.

I had known Jared since our move. I had put up with his jibes in the schoolroom, and fled his gangling shadow when I had seen it coming' down the hall during lunch. Alice was always the stronger of the two of us; she always put him in his place. I was grateful to God when he finally quit school to get a job working with Mr Gregson who owned the baker shop on the corner of third and ninth, but we still had to put up with his ranking language when he used to see me and Alice walk home, hand in hand. No... He was no friend of ours but that day in November, he just disappeared, vanished like a specter on the night of Halloween just before the dawn. All that could be found, so I was told, was this bloody rag, and not much else. So, I took the bloody rag in my hand. What else could I have done? I only wish I hadn't.

Suddenly it became dark, then light once more and Alice was standing next to me. Next to her stood Mom and then Uncle Frank.

Its Ok Alice mouthed at me, don't be afraid; nothing you see is going to hurt you. I simply nodded and at that; Uncle Frank and Mom smiled too.

I could see Jared walking – I guessed- home. the lights that shone from above made the sidewalk glow. At that time, I couldn't hear a sound, but that could be because it was the way that Alice and the others wanted me to see. Then, out of the darkness, I could hear something… foot falls… slow and steady, keeping pace with Jared. Now Jared either must of heard something' or felt something', cause he began to act scared, his eyes were wider and he even began walking' a little faster, But the footsteps kept pace and began to get faster too.

Then, out of the darkness, I could make out a figure. It was blurry, out of focus, but I could see that it was a man. Jared must have seen this too because now he was running. Then dived down the same ally where Alice had died a year previously.

The blurred man followed. He had something in his right hand. It shone in the lamp light. It was a thin, long bladed knife. Jared screamed out, but only once. The blurred man was in a frenzy of silent violence. He made no sound. Not even a breath, as he stabbed and stabbed and stabbed Jared again and again and again.

I saw the keen bladed knife puncture the skin of the throat. Then bury deep. It was pulled out. A fountain of blood began to gush out in a wide ark, splattering across the man's brown suit and then soak into the dirty water, the broken stones and the dog shit of the alley floor. The blurred man became quite calm. I saw him delicately put the knife into his jacket pocket and then watched shocked, as he dragged the limp blood splattered body down the alley to the nearest sewer cover. I Knew Jared, he might have been gangly, but he was no lightweight either. I heard the Blurred man grunt and groan under the dead weight that he carried before him. I saw the shirt rip and the piece of cloth get left in the ally. I saw the blurred man slip once or twice, as the water and the blood from the body mixed amongst the old stones. I heard I heard Jared's shoes crunch as he slid along the road and watched as the man whose face I could not see then, scrambled around in the trash, desperate to look for something. He seemed upset at first, but then he became calm once more, as he pulled out a jemmy. He opened the sewer and pushed the body into it. Then resealed the sewer once more. Then he picked up a bag that was next to the Jemmy, pulled it open and pulled out a large long black coat. He put it on. Heavy rain began to fall, washing the blood away from the cobblestones and into the open drain by the side of the buildings, as the blurred man began to slowly walk away.

All the time I ached inside. For there was something about the knife and the brown suit that I recognized, but for some reason could not place; as the man made his way out of the ally and out onto the street. Alice suddenly spoke... "You see, and yet you are blind... you know yet you do not want to understand." Her voice shimmered like a waterfall

Alice, what do you mean?

She pointed slowly towards the blurred man, who began to turn into someone I knew, but could not bear to see.

I came back to the long room with a start, to find that my nose was bleeding. I could feel the whole room staring at me anxiously.

"Oh...Daddy" I said, my voice was barely a whisper "Why did you do it?"

Uncle Silas looked at me with eyes of love and said not a word till I was cleaned up.

"So... child'" He asked gently. "You see who it was? You know what happened to Jared?"

Behind me, I could hear Maize say, "Did you hear that? She said "Oh, Daddy", she said it.

Another voice shut her up.

I nodded and looked down at the rich red rug, hoping against hope that I could bury myself in it and run away. Uncle Silas smiled and placed a comforting hand upon my shoulder. It's alright child, I heard him say silently, it's alright. I felt weak at the knees and then fell forward, and then I remember nothing' till the sun was up.

* * *

When I came too, I found myself in a strange blue, white room with a high and decorated ceiling. I saw Uncle Silas standing over me. He looked deep into my eyes.

"Now... don't be scared girl, you know that we look after our own, we always have and we always do. Believe me child, there aint no lawman coming here fo you or your daddy."

I looked up at him and found myself squeezing my hands tight as I could do, a nervous habit, so Daddy said... Daddy

"Did you see your Daddy child? Was it him?"

I nodded slowly, as tears began to build. I felt a pin prick a stab of pain then I must have fallen asleep again, 'cause when I woke the room was not blue but white. I turned to my left and saw that the curtains were blue.

I got up out of bed and made my out of the room. When I entered the hall, I realized that I was still at Uncle Silas and Aunt Bessie's home. Slowly and as silently as I could, I made my way down the stairs. I could hear shouting coming from the long room but I could see that the heavy doors were closed; so, I slowly I began to creep past it. I had reached half way to the front door, when That burst open and Maize appeared in the doorway.

"Now Where you think you going chil?" she asked.

"Nowhere." I lied, badly.

She smiled and put a firm hand upon my shoulder and led me back into the long room. When I entered, I heard the words "He'll come here when he knows we have hi- "

I had never seen the long room so crowded, it looked like the whole street had turned up this time; and they all stared at me like a hawk watching it's prey.

"Am I a prisoner here?" I asked.

Uncle Silas smiled once more, and then laughed. "Oh, no, child you can leave... once your Daddy arrives." And when those words left Uncle Silas's mouth, I realized that though he might be smiling on the outside, there was something else inside him; and that was not smiling at all... no not one little bit.

It was then I became real scared... more scared than I have ever been in my life before. I looked to my left and saw Uncle Frank. He looked sadly at Silas, then he came over to where I was standing and he whispered me a little secret. I looked down and tried not to let on what had happened.

"My Daddy was right about you! you are about the Devil's business. You use the old ways to justify yourselves, but you use it for your own aims." I said crossly, hiding my fear as best I could.

"That's not true Clarice." Said Betty sternly. "We stick to our own, that's all, we do nothing... nothing that's not been handed down in the law." I could hear the anger in her voice. "Jared was one of our own, an we want Justice."

"Is it Justice that you want?" I heard a voice coming from behind me. I turned around and saw Daddy standing in the doorway.

"Oh Daddy!" I screamed, and tried to wrestle myself free from the iron grip of Maize.

"LET HER GO!" He bellowed. The power of his voice filled the room. It rustled the red velvet curtains and made the yellow-papered walls shake.

Instantly I felt the hand lift from my shoulder so I ran into his arms.

But, within a second, of being in his arms Frank touched my mind's eye and I was back into the alley once more. Only this time it was Christmas, and I was behind the wheel of a truck...Jared, was I and I was Jared. I was looking at the woman who I loved and who had spurned me, I was feeling jealous, a jealous rage filled by raged faces that came out of the dark shadows and filled the cab of the truck and waited... I Jared waited for the moment for her to pass. I Jared felt my foot upon the accelerator and saw Alice, her arms out-stretched, screaming NOOOO!

I opened my eyes and looked back into the room. I looked at Maize, Betty, Silas and Douglas.

Now... said Uncle Frank, listen to me, and repeat exactly what I say.

I obeyed.

"My Dad took Jared's life, because Jared took Alice's... Now, Maize, if that is too much to bear, then there is nothing more I can give you. If you live by the old ways you would know and would accept the law regarding the payment for taking a life. This man worked within the ancient law. He took the life using the ancient ways, and to save pain he removed the body to a suitable place of rest. All this is accepted by the ancient law... If there is a case for..." I paused as I didn't understand Uncle Frank clearly at this point "r...r... rest...It...u... ton... then please make your case. Otherwise... be still."

Silence filled the long room, then slowly one at a time the people began to leave. All knowing that some greater than I had spoken and I was simply the conduit.

When it was Just Daddy, Uncle Silas and me, Uncle Silas began to laugh. He laughed so deeply I thought that the room would cave in. "Good child... it appears that you have a spiritual advocate... may I ask... is he bout six feet tall, wearing a deep green suit and fedora hat? Does he have a small white goatee beard.

I was stunned; he had described Uncle Frank to a tee. I nodded slowly.

"Uncle Frank."

"Now... did "Uncle Frank" tell you a secret?" Asked Silas.

I nodded. Silas bent closer, "Now, Child, whisper it in my ear."

"But he told me not to say." I said to Silas, feeling upset that I had to choose between the two oldest grand-pappy men in my life.

Silas nodded "I don't think he'd mind..." he said quietly, "not if it's only between you and me."

So, I whispered in Uncle Silas's ear... what did I tell him? Oh, no! you can't trap me like that! like I've already said, I'm good at keeping secrets.

Cold Creek, New England, 1984

Well, that's my story. I grew up and moved, married well

and had a daughter who married a fine man called Daniel Holleran, they had twins too. One died, naturally the other, Daniel junior, went on to became a fine chef an he has the Shine about him too I cannot recall how many conversations we used to have without ever opening our mouths. he works in some fancy hotel on the outskirts of Colorado. Don't ask me its name, I forget stuff like that now... that's me done... but come by any time you like... and next time bring some nice fruit cake.

The Cobbe house

The Cobbe house, for that is still how it is known to many of the folk of Bridgeton, New Jersey, rested on the top of St Joseph's hill, by what is now known as Franklin Drive. It stood separate from most of the other houses in town; as if cut off and estranged from society. It stood upon a rocky outcrop of a hill, whose vantage point, overlooked pretty much most of the town but its shadow, for cast one it did, came mainly down to the cross roads of West Commerce street, Atlantic Street and the lake with an air of something preternaturally uncanny. I recall that many of the people of the town wouldn't look up at it; and still many avoid the place where It once stood to this day. They prefer to look down, or the other way, as if to avoid direct eye contact with the place. If you ask them why, there is never an answer, just a vague glisten from the eye and an awkward scanty smile, from closed, near pursed lips.

Nevertheless, it was always enticing, for young children's furtive imagination's; as many, myself included, wondered along the long winding track, that led to the large, overtly gothic, black painted, rusted, wrought iron gates; that were locked -tight shut- with a heavy chain, and a heavier bolt; that existed, perhaps, for two reasons: - one, to stop people getting in… and two: - perhaps… just perhaps…to stop something from inside getting out.

My memory of the house rests both objectively, and deeply personally painful. Objectively, my understanding of the Cobbe house, comes through the direct evidence, that relates to the extensive and painfully detailed research, that my Uncle: - a Mr. Douglas Freemantle- whom, at one time, happened to be the town's local chemist, had conducted over many, many years.

He was a thick whiskered, bespectacled dry skinned and rather wiry man, as I recall him to be -whom, it must be said- also volunteered at the local museum as an amateur historian and researcher of some renown. He was also a man both of extreme intellect and careful observation; yet had the gentlest of heart, and a wry sense of humor, that, due to his sudden death some ten years ago now, has left me bereft of humor in these latter years of my life.

Subjectively, the Cobbe house has tainted me deeply in ways that will never leave and despite all that has happened, despite believing now that it's all finally over, my nights will be forever restless.

In looking at the history of the property, one must begin in the year 1756, when a Mr. Samuel Cobbe and his family of five children: - Delores, Stephen, Marcus, Stephen Junior and Eleanor, or Nell together with his demure wife, Alice Cobbe; moved into the town, from Boston, with dreams of turning the money he had made from trading with the East India tea company, into land acquisition and property. This is seen clearly in many of the correspondences that he made between his wife and the property partners, of the autumn of the preceding year.

It is also fair to state, that during the construction of the said property, soon to become known as the Cobbe house, that while his family lived in rather cramped accommodation in the Centre of town, nothing of note, or perhaps I should say nothing that might be considered as disturbing occurred.

It was only after the construction of the property and the first death of Stephen Junior, in the summer of 1777, whilst being taken to town by cart and pony on the hilly wooded track from the house to town, that luck began to change for the Cobbe family. For not long after, in 1778, both Delores and Marcus succumbed to what was called on their death certificates as "a wasting disease".

In 1779, Mr. Cobbe senior himself lost his life though a sudden and inexplicable heart attack caused by unknown factors, what was also written on the death certificate was the look of terror and pain frozen on his features during the inquest, inferring that the poor man had literally died of fright. His death left a tired and drawn looking Alice to look after baby Nell, upon whom she doted on, and Stephen Cobbe. Whom was now the only male heir to the estate.

After Nell's sudden unexpected and terrible death in the winter of 1781, Alice, now a broken woman, lost her sanity, and was, with help from the servants, supported in the upper attic rooms of the property. Though Samuel senior's income at the time of his death was quite large, it dwindled quickly; as money needed to tend to the upkeep of Alice, and the property ate into the family fortune. Stephen jr, took to working wherever he could to maintain her mother within the safety of the house that she refused to leave, yet was, when looking at Stephen's letters to the local doctors at the time, was "in abject fear of."

Yet, despite his best efforts, he failed to keep many of the staff for longer than a month at a time. Many left for undisclosed reasons. Some left due to the "strange and poisonous odor" that tended to fill certain room's such as "the cellar and the servant's quarters" on the below floor. Yet nothing could be found to trace the smell, that one servant stated "seemed to leak through the floorboards and the foundations themselves."

Finally, and tragically, Alice "succumbed to her

madness". She was found by her most faithful servant, an Abigail Freemantle, hanging by her neck, from a tightly wrapped bedsheet, from one of the roof beam's in the spring morning of 1783. How she could have reached it has never fully been understood.

Despite renovations that cost Stephen what was left of his father's income; only outside parties, from half way across the country would be interested in wanting to buy the property and even then, all of those, on hearing of the loss of fortune in relation to the Cobbe's, were then suddenly disinclined to consider taking on a property that had, as they saw it, "dark connotations associated with it."

It was not long after this, in the late autumn of 1785, that Stephen himself disappeared. No one knew where he went. Some say he went mad himself, other's that he went abroad. In truth, no one knew. However, many of the towns local folk have said that whatever moved into that house in the summer of 1777, has never truly left. Strange and spectral images were seen at the windows and at one time a "queere fluttering" was reported to have been heard about the place.

In the end, the most hardened of people, with little imagination and   the most cynical of outlook, concluded that such sounds and images were the work of local smuggler's, who tended to bring shipments from the Cohansey River. (as Bridgeton was briefly known as "Cohansey Township") as they possibly considered that the house's unique position: - overlooking the Tumbling Dam Lake, now called Sunset Lake, near the northern boundary of the city, led to it being ideal for many nefarious individuals, to use the property for distribution of untaxed goods.

It was briefly owned in 1886, by the Berwick family, who came from Wisconsin, though there is little direct or indirect evidence, in relation to their ownership of the property, other than the paying for, and the construction and installation of, the high wall, the brick pillars and the heavy wrought iron gates that after a fall in in the year 1923.

Finally, there was no reason as to why, after so many years, that the house itself should remain so intact. After all, nature has always reclaimed what human beings have dared to put upon the landscape. Yet here, upon that hill, the house remained for many years untouched. Nothing, not even poison Ivy, claimed the dry dirt earth around the house. It was as if...as if...dare I say, nature herself, had shunned this place, and would have forever done so, if it were not for what occurred

My first experience of the property began as a young child, in the late spring of 1923. I was, at that time, a thin and impressionable youth; with a very fertile imagination, that, dare I say, led me into trouble more than one occasion. Unlike many people of the town, I would look up St Joseph's hill and stare at the house, with a sort of dread fascination whose square black windows seemed, at least to me, have an unearthly dead glare about them.

Before that spring day, my friends and I would, on dares, reach those heavy iron gates of the house, along the narrow tree lined winding track and tenderly touch the cold rusted iron with our hot, hot hands and shout excitedly about how "Mad Alice would come and get you!" for stories never die in a small town. Earlier in the late spring of the year 1923 a terrible storm had buffeted the town; leading to, amongst other things, the collapse of the old iron gates of the derelict property; so, it was, with trepidation and a degree of excitement, that the four of us, Tony, Cerci, Nell and I -Drew Sanderson- stood, for the very first time in our short lives, in front of the full shadow of the Cobbe House.

***

There were the four of us: Tony Cerci, Nell and I. Bound by childhood passions, a small town's street's and, at that time, schooling. By the time of the great storm of the spring of nineteen hundred and twenty-three; the five of us had reached that age where both curiosity and independence flourished in equal measure and where play, though not yet fully discarded, was both frowned upon and secretly enjoyed in equal measure.

In this age, we would explore, either the Cohansey river as it rolled, raged, churned and splashed its way through the town's gully, cutting it in two; or fish then swim in the Tumbling Dam Lake as I recall it was called back then.

Summer's in Bridgeton were long warm and riddled with mystery. Whether it involved going up to the Cobbe house on a dare, or to swim the river or the lake or to peddle ice creams from Mr. Dawlish, for a buck or two, given in turn and in kind, by a gentle eye.

Cerci Middlestone, was my next-door neighbor. She was –at that time- 12 Years of age with thick auburn hair, I recall her long lashes over wide eyes cornflower blue eyes and freckles, over a slightly small and narrow nose; and a long, yet square chin. Being thirteen myself at the time, I was slowly becoming aware of that unique species of human known as "girls" and found myself shyly taken by her beauty and her presence.

Her father Mr. Jeremy Middlestone, worked at the bank from morning to late, forcing her mother, (whom I only knew as Mrs Middlestone, because her austere frown from her thin face narrow line drawn lips and her over crossed arms; making her very fearful and unapproachable.) to stay at home, cook and clean.

Her best Friend was Eleanor Kirkbride, or Nell, as she liked to be called. Nell was 12; a narrow-faced sea green eyed, blonde haired girl with an upturned nose and a smattering of freckles. Unlike the rest of us, who lived along Rhode street, she lived three streets away in Briar street, in what was part of "poor town" I didn't know her parents.

Anthony Sables, or Tony, was my best friend.   He was a large boy for his age that being the same as mine, 12, though he was born in the month of October on all hallows eve. He had curly, chestnut brown hair and wide set hazel eyes that glittered with constant humor. His father, Donald Sables owned the bakery in town and would always hand out a donut or two to for us, as part payment for a position as delivery boys.

Finally, there is I, Drew Sanderson. Not much is left of that boy of so many years ago, he had Blonde hair and brown to green narrow eyes in wide sockets. A long nose and a narrow mouth over a strong jaw and pointed chin, giving the boy I am looking at, in a faded picture in front of me an impish grin. There are many things that I would have liked to tell that young boy right now. But I doubt that he would have ever listened to me anyway, so I will just look back with soft tears.

That was us, known around the school as "the flunky club" A name given to us as we tended to not fit in with the other children of our age. Before I continue, there is something else about the flunky club that set us apart from the other kids. There was a reason as to why we didn't fit in. We could share things. Things that most kids couldn't share with others. We knew things too; things that we simply shouldn't know. Things that are hard to explain to other's.

For instance, when Nell trapped her foot in the river in the fall of 1921, Both Tony and I heard her scream and ran to help her. Even though no one else could hear her. When in the winter of 1922, Tony found himself trapped in the well on Parson's farm, he called out; it was Cerci, Nell and I who somehow knew where he was, ans managed to find him and get him home, much to his parents -and the towns- thanks. Even when Circe was in trouble with the school Bully Stephen Brinks; who wanted to do something to her, down the alley behind the picture house; all three of us could hear her cry and were there to protect her.

We were always there for each other and always knew what we were thinking... to a degree... we could partition our minds and have secret thoughts, but overall, we had a collective mind that we simply called "sharing" mainly because that is was what it was like. We could share one another's thoughts, feelings and emotions without even uttering a single word. It's hard to explain something like this to someone who does not, nor has not experienced it. So, it was no co-incidence that what happened, happened the way it did. What worried us, was why?

I recall it was the last summer before we were to be split. Cerci had been told she was to go a fashionable new middle school twenty miles away; Nell's parents were moving away too as neither the mother or the father could find work; while at the time I thought Tony and I were destined to go to Bridgeton middle; I didn't know that this was the last time we would see each other for a great many years.

The Cobbe house changed everything. it was one of those defining moments, that comes along once or maybe twice in life. An occurrence that itself, act's as a fulcrum, to send people in directions that perhaps they didn't expect. I must say, if we had known where it would lead, we would never have entered that damned house. For it is one thing to stand by the gates of a knowingly forbidden place and look on with pulse racing. It is altogether another, to cross that threshold, as we did in the summer of nineteen hundred and twenty-three, to immerse ourselves in that...that dreadful place. Yet how were we to know? On our first close inspection of the house, the myths and the fears change, from the fearful to the fantastical and finally to the banal. Those ancient crumbling walls, take on a less spectral and terrifying notion and become a castle, the windows battlement's where Knights battle dragons for the hands of princesses; or copper's chase robber's around a stash of treasure hidden by pirates for hundreds of years, until all our energies were spent and we saw the house for what it was: a ruin. The Cobbe's were gone. Their story a myth. This was simply an old house left to rot away.

The house itself was south facing, so a warm glowing sun, shone through the cracked and splintered windows onto the bleached peeling paper on the walls, and the arched doorway, whose wooden door, had fallen outward, onto the crumbling brick steps. In our collective mind's eye, it took on the gate entrance to a castle. The house itself was two stories high with a high round, or perhaps, eye like window on the left gable, as well as two dormer windows equidistant apart. The outside walls were plaster over stone and many of the top floor windows were narrow and gothic in design, the ground floor had four sets of large narrow windows either side of the arched doorway creating a hollow space, where the wind howled through in hisses.

Another thing that needs to be mentioned was at that time, when the four of us chose to venture upon the grounds, we knew very little about the history of the house. My Uncle preferring to keep his research to himself, and away from the minds of children whom at that age, would exaggerate this rather ugly and tragic place. I recalled we ran around the outside kicking up the dust and the dead grass and whooping and cheering at our success as having managed to, at least on one level, face our fears, knowing that, in the end, there was nothing here to be afraid of. After all what loves the dark; tends to stay in the dark.

It was one thing to play about the grounds of the large grey rotting house; and another to take that step inside. After an hour or two of exploring the unkempt garden, playing on the chain swing at the rear of the property and throwing stones down the brick well, that ended with a distant PLUNK we then turned our attention to the cavernous front door and the darkness within.

The first thing I recall was the unusual smell, sour and musty and altogether unpleasant. Our footsteps creaked on the decayed boards with each step we took. The main hall was large and dilapidated, pictures of long dead men and women, damp and encrusted, hung loosely in rotting wooden frames; the dark green painted wall's bubbled with huge round patches of black damp in the corner's that spread in circles, while in the near dark, plump, well fed spiders, teased their webs, with over-long wiry fibrous legs.

The floor was riddled with a strange, glistening white fungi, that was distorted into shapes that seemed -to me- like the twisted forms of men and women; and the smell coming from this was nauseous to say the least. In the near dark, they seemed to glow with a pale, blueish tint that was both exiting, and at the same time disturbing.

'I think we should go' said Cerci, as she slowly took my hand. I being just as afraid, but not wanting to show it, smiled into her cornflower eyes and tightened my grip.

'Whatever was here, has long passed.' I began. There is nothing to be afraid of.'

'No!' Nell interrupted. 'It's sleeping…can't you feel it?'

The trouble was we could feel it…all of us, yet no one spoke of it in our minds. This was -in retrospect- our greatest mistake.

I heard a sudden scratch to the left and started; back as a large fat rat, about the same size a fully-grown cat, suddenly scuttled into the darkness. In the dim light, I could see its feral eyes glistening as it stared at me. Suddenly Tony howled. He leaped on my back. We both fell to the dusty, grimy floor. I screamed with a wrestle turned to face him. My fist drawn back

'Enough!'

'Oh come on durtbag!' He giggled, and soon we were laughing once more

We avoided the basement as the stench was so foul; so, we went from room after room, ending up in an attic, that was filled with dried cracked boxes full of old broken toys, and rattling spinning wheels that were decomposing into something both evil and to me, utterly alien

It was Nell who found the hand mirror. She picked it up and began to play with it, gently stoking her hair.

'Look at me, Queen Nell, lady of the manor.'

Suddenly she shrieked.

The mirror was thrown to the floor.

I turned to her. Tony who was next to her began to comfort her, as she started to chough; before becoming hysterical

'It's in th- walls in the walls the WALLS!... they're...they're moving!

We looked and saw nothing. With a nervous hand, I picked up the ornate mirror and considered It and seeing nothing but my reflection, I put it down.

Cerci then said that it was time to go, and on the whole I believed her. It was as we started to leave that I saw Tony pick up a small tin soldier that he had found and let him put it in his pocket. At the time, I thought nothing of it. I only wish I had the foresight to tell him to put it back. Then it happened...the walls moved. Slowly at first, as if a cold breeze has blown through the room. Then then they moved faster. In and out...in and out... like slow and regular breathing. Suddenly there rose a hollow knocking sound a knock...knock...knock... as if someone, or something was wanting to come in. The knocking became louder and louder and louder. Without thinking we turned from that attic room and fled from the house as fast as we could.

I recall running, out of that damned house. Down the narrow woodland path and onward to the safety of home. Looking back, perhaps we should have laughed when we reached the friendly lights of town. But Nell was still shaken and I... I was utterly terrified.

It was early evening when we were in sight of home. The sun was a huge oval orange ball on the horizon and streaks of iron colored orange and crimson cloud streaked across it. I looked down into Bridgeton at the valley beneath and the tall trees that rose up like black spears in the evening. In the near light, I looked to my right and at Tony, who was looking down at the toy soldier he had picked up from the attic space. It was small, about an half an inch tall; painted red and black with a sliver face that was hard to see. It was standing at attention. Its rifle pointed upward its legs set apart. The large black hat: domed.

'you, shouldn't have- 'I began. Feeling unnerved.

'-I know...but...I've always wanted one.' Came the downcast reply.

I was going to persist, perhaps, with hind sight, I should have done. Part of me wanted to throw the thing into the woods and be done with this whole, horrible business. Instead, and despite myself, I shrugged and put my hands in my trouser, pockets. I looked behind me to see Cerci, who was still holding Nell's hand as we reached the corner of Prospect and Briar street; where we said fare well, and went our separate ways.

Nell, turned left and down the hill, towards Briar. Cerci, Tony and I right towards Prospect. When in the sight of home, Cerci pecked my cheek and then ran off, leaving Tony and I.

Tony giggled a little at that, but said nothing. I blushed as I saw her run up the steps and through her door with a bang.

'--Tony...' The soldier was bothering me, bothering me. Like an itch I couldn't scratch; a darkness had pervaded my heart. A sense of something ominous; that I could not put my finger on felt ominously close.

'...Do you really want that thing... its- '

'-It's mine an' I ain't parting- 'He spat. Then he charged off towards his house on the corner of Prospect, three doors down and just in sight from where I lived.

'Okay... well' I called out after him. I received no reply. I stood there, alone, looking at his back as he turned into his house and out of sight. The night began to reveal stars, a shooting star streaked out overhead. A golden moon was seen glittering through the trees at the top of the road. The evening was full of crickets and bullfrogs croaking to be heard. I didn't know that would be the last night of peace I was to have for nearly thirty years.

That night I did not sleep well. The dreams were the most vivid that I have ever experienced. Even now, despite the thirty years that have lapsed since that fateful night, even now, those images wrestle with me still. The reality of them, even down to the sensations I felt; which is why I am speaking in the present tense. I am standing in the attic space of the Cobbe house, in front of that door.

The knocking sound becomes louder and louder until it becomes a boom. Then the door handle is turned, slowly carefully as if what is behind it cannot grasp the handle properly. Then the door violently swings inward to reveal utter darkness. But there is something in the darkness. I can just about make it out. I hear its slithering and its knocking. It is calling me in. Into the dark. Its voice is like that of a small child. Yet... there is something malign in it. Something inhuman and evil. It wants me to come and play. Despite myself, despite screaming NO I find myself being drawn to the dark. To the noise and the voice, I hear it calling me, calling me ever onward. The doorway looms closer. I can smell something ugly decaying, like wet rotten meat left to bake in the sun. I hold onto the door frame. I scream.

I then woke up. Only to think I do, to find myself in a huge four poster bed. I am not alone. There is something next to me in the bed. Whatever it is, it is still...unmoving...I am repulsed by the shape that is so still. I cannot be assured that it even breathes. I feel the weight of the linen. It ties me down to the bed. I cannot move. I feel my breathing begin to feel constrained. Then it grabs for me.

Then I am on the path towards the Cobbe house. I see it looming through the trees of the narrow path to my left. I feel the dampness of the soil beneath my feet. I turn to run, but I cannot. The ground grabs at my feet. I feel it turn into fingers. The fingers to hands the hands on wild unearthly arms. I hear a pony and trap coming, but there is no pony or trap. I hear the clacking of a whip. The pulling on of reigns, but there is nothing there. Nothing other than the feeling of being dragged down into the earth by hands that grip me tighter and tighter still. I feel I am being suffocated. That there is something, something above me. Something pale with yellow fiery slit snake like eyes that wants to feed on me, and carry on feeding on me for eternity.

***

When I finally awoke, time and voices rippled through me. I felt Nell's nervousness, and Circe's fear. I tried to reach Tony but there was nothing. Just a huge black wall. I tried to press though it, but it was impossible. It was as if Tony had deliberately blocked us out.

I felt drained of strength and weak to my knees. I arose from my sweaty bed and with a great pain walked across the floorboard's and greeted that warm sunny morning in July. I looked out of my window to see Cerci sitting by her window opposite mine and looking very drawn and pale as if she was very ill.

I called out for her and asked if she was okay. She smiled weakly and began saying that she had had terrible dreams about the Cobbe house, the door in the attic and something inside...in the dark. I considered her beautiful eyes, and smiled weakly back. she seemed so sick pale and drawn. I held back on my story at the time. I simply mentioned that she looked wan.

'Have you seen yourself?'

I went to the mirror on my chest of draws and stared at a pale faced a pale sickly looking young boy. It was then that I heard a scream coming from up the street. My heart leapt as I knew it was Tony.

I ran through the hall down the stairs, and out of the front door, in my nightgown Cerci followed me out at the same time. She stood on her veranda. We stared at each other, each realizing that something was wrong. I looked up to where Tony lived and saw Mrs Sables burst out of the front door and scream as she ran down the road pleading for a doctor. In an instant Both Cerci and I ran up to her. She was in her own nightgown that was soaked in blood and babbling something about Tony. Then she ran past us and up the street.

We charged up to Tony's front door and tried to get in. But Mr. Sables wouldn't let us. He just kept saying please stay away, in pleads He stood there looking tearful and in shock His grey eyes wide, his moustache damp. Sweat fell in heavy pearls from his shining balding head.

From inside the house, all we could hear were Tony's constant screaming and then what sounded like grown up adult maniacal laughter. Mr Sables paled at hearing that, then bellowed 'Just go HOME!'.

He slammed the door on us; We turned away, just as both the Doctor and the Sheriff arrived, who then told us to leave. So, we both sat down on my parent's porch looking sadly and fearfully towards the Sable's place.

Fifteen minutes later Nell arrived, also looking as pale as the two of us. She too recalled her dream with the exact detail as I have already described. It was clear that all three of us had had the same dream. The only difference was Tony…something, we knew not what, had happened to Tony, Something terrible. It was then that I recalled the tin soldier that he picked up, and my concern

'Perhaps that was the key.' Circe remarked.

'But it's such a small thing.'

'-From a dark house… nothing good came from there.'

We knew wat we had to do. We felt the command whispered to us, from we know not where. We held each other's hands, and we began sharing, thinking that our combined effort might break down the wall each of us saw inside our minds.

In our minds eye, we saw the wall. It was huge and made of black bricks. We called out to Tony and as we did so, the bricks started to come down, one at a time. I could feel a surge of energy within me, something that I nor Nell or Cerci had felt before. The wall began to crumble away, faster and faster. As the final bricks fell away, we saw it.

It, for there was no other word to describe what we saw, glared at us. It had human features, yet it was not human in any way I could describe. There was a corruption about its wild unkempt hair, the green eyes viscously bright twinkled, its hands had nails that resembled razors while sharpened teeth, yellow and rotten, shone from wide set drooling lips. It was clear that it wanted to harm us all of us. I had no doubt that it was very same thing I saw in my dream that morning

'little puppets…little puppets…' there was a singing jingle it its high pitched voice. 'Imm coming forrr YOU!' it screamed savagely as it reached out towards us. We each screamed and let go of each other's hands. The wall returned.

'Tony's behind the wall. It has him it has him what are we going to do?'

 I was mute. A dark colored hospital van came up the road and stopped outside Tony's house. Two men in white shirts and trousers alighted from either door and walked into the house. Minutes seem to pass, though it felt like a forever. Then both the men in white came out of the house writhing between them was Tony. But a Tony that I simply didn't recognize. His hair had turned from the curly brown to a bleached white, his skin pale and sunken, his eyes wild. He was screaming at the top of his lungs with the voice of someone that clearly was not his, as the two men put him into the van and then slammed the door

The van drove away. The street was silent again. And the morning sun had risen just a little bit higher.

I didn't see Tony again for nearly thirty years.   Between then and our final meeting, I recall our friendship, with affection; for we were more like brother's that friends. His eyes and his smile bring back happy more innocent memories. Memories that are not bound to that damn house or hideous thing that resided there. What followed has never left me. It led me to meeting Tony at The Arkham asylum for the mentally insane, led me back to my old home town of Bridgeton of the last meeting of the flunky club and that damned house that has haunted my life from that day to this. I think of Cerci with such fondness, for she was my first real love. Though I never shared it with her. In retrospect, I should have done, and for that I will always feel like half a man. Unable to be honest with my true feelings.   There was a moment, just after the van left that morning, when once again we held our hands tightly. We both saw it and felt it. For the words were shared between us in our minds. Yet, it never went further than that tender touch of hands between us.

later that day, we found out what had happened. Tony had entered his baby brother's room and smothered him with a pillow. His mother tried to pull him off, but he was too strong. He was shouting in a language that might have been French or something similar, and attacked his mother scratching at her neck as he tried to bite her. she screamed and defended herself, but found he had the strength of a fully-grown man, not the 12-year-old boy that he was.

It took Mr Sables an age to hold him down and tie up his wrists and legs to stop him from hurting anyone else, even himself. while his mother then ran into the street to get both the sheriff and the doctor.

The doctor on examining him said that he had no idea what had happened in the night, and considered calling the local Catholic priest as he was so changed, he felt that he might provide some solace. In the end the call was made to Arkham Asylum and the van was called. Tony was taken away and put into the care of the Asylum indefinitely; as he was a danger to himself and others about him. Mr. Sables said later that day and officially in the public record of the event later, written down in the Bridgeton Chronicle, and relating to the court case over the death of the little baby boy. That it was clear that his son had "changed forever, into someone or something unrecognizable.

It was not long after the incident that Mr and Mrs Sables moved away and the incident itself, though not forgotten became part of the history of the town. it was personally hard to hear of "Crazy Sables" spoken in the same breath as "Mad Alice" especially as I had known Tony before what had happened, seen that carefree, smile and the sideways grin that always touched the border of cynicism... The reality was nobody, other than Nell Cerci and I knew how or perhaps why it happened; even though the toy soldier was hard to accept as a catalyst. I know better now... though I wish, to my heart that I did not. For those dreams haunt me still; they have led me to become a coward and not face fears that rise and oppress me, for in the dark, and in the half light, when I awake, I always see that odd little furtive deformed creature slow slink from my bedroom around the corner and disappear into the mists of twilight. An inhabitant both dream world and the dark, it waits to prey upon me, dragging me through my darkest fears to feed upon my anxiety

For many years post this tragic event Bridgeton became a prison and a place of fear. People usually children would go missing, and despite the best efforts of the police no bodies were ever recovered. It was as if they were simply stolen in the night; and despite my best efforts to persuade the police to check the Cobbe house, no one bothered to enter it ever. Over the years, I aged and became sick with fear; terrified to open my mouth as with hideous regularity a child would disappear.

people are like batteries storing energy both positive and negative as electrical pulses stimulate the brain If you can accept that, then Places are like battery chargers. They absorb and discharge what happens inside them. Consider if you will sacred spaces like Churches where there has been a lot of peace. if a person enters these buildings they feel or sense that energy. The same exists in a primary school. Which is full of strong energy

Conversely, if a place experienced pain and sorrow, then the place is negatively charged. The Cobbe house and Arkham are negatively charged places. This charge has an impact not only upon the building, but on the people, that inhabit it over time. Moreover, it attracts those who resonate with that charge. Be they living or dead.

Arkham with its looming towers and gothic walls, was such a place. Inside, its greasy white tiles and dirt floor, said more about how the world tolerates the mentally unwell than anything else. I went from corridor after corridor, room after room, each filled with men or women strapped to beds, or tied in jackets. The smell, of too many people, unwashed and uncared for, living in their own fecal matter was both disheartening and disturbing. If this was the age of enlightenment in mental health treatment, then that age had yet to come to this terrible place.

The moment I entered his room, I sensed an oppression that I couldn't put my finger on.

Tony was in a narrow white greasy tiled room. Blinds or shutters were pulled on the right-hand wall making the room more of a dark grey than a white. The linen on the bed hadn't been changed. It stank. Lice and other vermin crawled over the sheets, while cockroaches scurried in the corners of the room.

I saw Tony lying on his bed. His white hair was long and unkempt, his face under his heavy beard, podgy his teeth yellow stained and broken.

'Of course, he must be sedated...' began the orderly, a large bald headed, heavy jawed man in a white suit. '...in the last week, he took out the eye of one of the other inmates.'

'I see.'

'Doctor Jarvis will see you...if you would like... he knows the case well.'

I shook my head.

Tony stared up at the ceiling. Saying nothing. His eyes glazed. His fist clenched.

'He cannot feed himself...both his hands are tight fists.'
He has something in his hand, but we cannot pry it open. '

I sat down next to Tony, I felt a lump in my throat. Guilt had kept me away. Guilt and fear. I hated myself as I sat there.

'Both his parents are dead now.'

'I. I'm sorry. Dear friend... I am so sorry...'

Memories of Mr. Sables went through my mind. A youth now lost, as it is with time. Then thoughts of the two of us playing. Running swimming ice creams bicycle rides newspaper deliveries... I put my hand on top of Tony's clenched fist.

Then, from within the room, a light came on. The orderly suddenly turned and I too looked towards the entrance of the room where the light switch was located. To note that the switch a large flipper switch in a rounded mount had, without physical influences, somehow pushed itself down into the on position. Slowly, sense of oppression began to lift and the room became somehow brighter all round.

The orderly stepped towards the door, preferring the dark than the light the room began to fill with.

Tony then sighed and from a twisted face of red that then faded to yellow, he slipped from this world, opening his hands for the first time in thirty long years.

I looked at the puncture wounds, where his over long nails had cut deep into his palms. Then Looked at what he held in his hand.

The flesh on the palm was white and greasy, it stank with putrefaction. Yet I could just make out something that had been so tightly squeezed for so long the thing was almost embedded into the palm itself. With a little effort managed to pull it out. It fell into my hand with a wet slurping sound.

For the first time in thirty years I held that damned toy soldier in my hand.

Having met Tony last week, and experienced the uncanny while at that terrible hospital; I became determined to find both Circe and Nell; and for one last time, go to the Cobbe house, to face this once and for all.

I became increasingly resolute as I felt increasingly under attack from a source that I could not see, but felt that was all around me. Moreover, that tin soldier being in my home-made things incredibly difficult; to the point that I thought about going alone to face, what needed to be faced. Yet, the more I thought of that, the more I felt utterly terrified to do so.

Moreover, the dreams that I had experienced lately are getting harder and harder to fight against. The dark place where I go at night, is unlike anything that I have experienced before. It's like our world, in as much as it has all the same roads and streets in it. Only it's twisted, no… corrupted…into something hideously alien. Some buildings glow with a white phosphorous light, some are whirlpools of darkness; It's like I am trudge walking, in a liquid of dark green half-light, where floats these strange luminescent spheres, that have the appearance of jellyfish, yet are not jellyfish but consume each other with a ferocity that is hard to put into words; but also there rest hideous and violent thing's that must have been human once, that roam in the shadow's and are terrifyingly impossible to describe; for fear of losing my sanity.

Every morning I wake up feeling more and more drained, while that damned tin soldier always seems to find its way back by my bedside, no matter where I place it. Last night I put it in my Uncle's safe downstairs. This morning, again, it is there on my bedside cabinet staring at me with its cold face. I am starting to see features in it now, so grotesque and malign; I scream awake when I open my eyes.

I decided to go to the library and conduct a little private research on the subject and found something remarkable.

I came across something called "Banging" pronounced with the nasal inflection /nj/ common to the region as in "banjing" from south east Asia, to be exact from the island chain of the Philippines. It was an ethnographic study carried out by a well-known researcher, who shall not be named, (as it bears little relevance to this text.)who discovered that Many of the Hmong people of the islands, believe that a sudden and unexpected death is due to malevolent supernatural forces. Specifically, that of a child whom has died both suddenly and unexpectedly and who can literally drain the "life force" out of its chosen host.

Symptoms of this disease, though some would also call it an attack include a sudden wasting away of the body in the physical realm; as the dream state becomes ever more powerful. The loss of motor control reflexes and a creeping insanity as the individual begins to lose control of what "reality" or his or her sense of what this is. Of course, I can accept that everyone's notion of what is real, differs from individual to individual; however, it is this sense of being in touch and touching, that is lost. I am finding myself at a loss to explain, what is going on. I look in the mirror and see this half me, with sunken glittering eyes, wrinkled skin and drawn self and know that IT is trying to kill me; yet I cannot explain it to another person without sounding insane myself.

More recently this rather frightening wasting away has been shown by scientific studies to be virtually identical to

"Bragada syndrome", which is well-described in medical literature as a cause of sudden cardiac death, in association with a violent stimulation of the Pineal gland of the brain; which is most stimulated during sleep...the point is, what has occurred and what is occurring has led me to the personal conviction that something evil, unhuman and deeply malevolent, drove my dearest friend insane. It took his life and is trying to do the same thing again: to me. In our nativity as children, we called it "it"; but perhaps a better name would be a dream stalker, for it's as if I am being literally haunted, chased or driven to death in my dreams. I am writing thins down, knowing inside how insane it sounds. But it is more than insane.

Due to my uncle's long connection to historical research, and since his rather tragic and unexpected death last year; I, being one of his beneficiaries, I have managed to gain excess to his extensive archive, that he kept in his dusty, dry, many shelved oak lines apartment's, close to the town library.

In mulling over the many papers found there, I uncovered a link both to this region of the world and the Cobbe property. Per the document's, Mr. Cobbe employed a pair of female servants from the Philippines, whose names were Chona and Lualhati Ocampo. Whether this happens to be their names or not is questionable, as it is the names given under the registry of transfer from London and Malaca on the ship Tiberius, notable in that that it took the occasionally, profitable though very difficult route around Cape Horn; for both the purchase of Copra, oil and slaves, stopping at the Rhode Island port as or when necessary.

From the start the Ocampo's found life in this town of Bridgeton difficult to say the least. There is recorded through local church gossip that became associated with the house and specifically in relation to the Ocampo's, in as much as their form of Protestantism, was far too strict and specifically, their prayers were not "uttered at the proper time or directed towards the proper object"; all of which led to grave speculations in relation to the sisters who became shunned by the townsfolk when they came from the Thatched house into town for any necessary items.

During my research of these documents, and five years before the house and the town became afflicted with trouble's, Chona, was found to be pregnant. A male child, of notable mixed race origin, was born and duly named "Andrew Cobbe". This led to speculations about who was the father of the child? It seems, through inference of the available recorded data, that the child must have belonged to Mr. Cobbe senior himself, who also tried, but with little effect to press upon his physician some problems or bizarre malady with Andrew's health, that were not being fully addressed.

This Andrew, was recorded as being a sickly boy from birth; Yet, though there is a register of his birth, there is no register of his death. He, like Chona and Lualhati mysteriously disappeared precisely one calendar month, before the death of the first Cobbe child on the narrow road to the house.

The tragedy's that followed the Cobbe family then overshadow the disappearance of the Ocampo's whom, though were considered as being the cause of the problems associated with the Cobbe family are never discussed in any form of direct evidence found in the form of local correspondences to date.

Armed with this new information, and with the loss of Tony I sought out Nell and Cerci, in the hope that we could exorcize the house and rid ourselves of whatever malevolent form of creature that had infested the house; and fed off the Cobbe's and the rest of us.

In many ways Nell, Cerci and I had drifted apart. Nell, having moved to New York was living in the Brooklyn region of the city and the bridge close to Heart Crane's muse. She had become quite a celebrity, and was making many eyes turn on Broadway. Not so for Circe whom from her last correspondence was struggling with a child Called Daniel. When I spoke to Nell, about the death of Tony, she was already in tears about it

***

My life since the day Tony was taken hadn't been easy. After a medical discharge from the Army due to Temporal lobe epilepsy, I found it harder and harder to find work. In fact, the older I became, the tougher it got. I felt as if IT was controlling the strings of my life, setting me up for a fall at every convenient turn. I met my own wife Delores, a raven-haired cornflower eyed Circe in every way but name, just after my discharge when I found myself a working at the Bridgeton library. We both had three little girls all of whom were precocious and adorable. However, after 9 year years, it became clear that things between Delores and I began to frazzle out; I couldn't seem to keep a job and she was annoyed at my illness.

We became distant and finally settled for a divorce three years ago. I get to the see the kids – occasionally-. her new lover is a man called Todd Foster, a slick haired "snake oiled salesman" whom I found loathsome, when I first met him. All chin and muscle, however, she was happy and that was all that mattered; So, I ended up at home, officially washed up at thirty-five, with no direction, except that Damned house with my two dearest friends' both of whom would be facing up to the that damned thing that has caused so much pain to our collective lives.

The phone call with Nell was difficult for many reasons. To start with, I knew her partner Steve Donovan from high school. He was a science major and a relentless bully, who had, on one occasion beaten me to the ground, when I refused to move out of the way for him.   recall him as being a tall and semi muscular man, with a strong jaw, narrow cheeks, a wide mouth and flat nose; a man who found people like me an annoyance, and a hindrance to those whom he considered unintelligent enough to grab his concept of the world.

Nell had bloomed from the scrawny 12-year-old from Briar Street. Her narrow features had taken on an almost angelic quality; the once greasy blond strait hair had become wavy. Money and determination had done the rest to shape our Nell into Eleanor Quint. The actress and the up and coming movie star.

They had met in the last year of Bridgeton High. She had fallen for his intellect, over his, if the irony can be stated, his natural charm; and they moved in together not long after Nell having attained a scholarship at the prestigious New York academy for performing arts. It was here that her talent for register and method acting had won her a lot of notoriety and this, in turn, led to roles in some major Broadway shows. Whereas, Steve, per Nell, struggled with the life of academia. Reading between Nell's words, I could hear that he had become an embittered drunk, who was both possessive and manipulative

When I called her, and told her about Tony I could hear her cry.

'Was he...

'He wasn't the Tony we knew... the man in that bed...' I gulped a bit at the memory, 'I simply couldn't recognize him.'

'It's funny...' she began, 'I, I felt him go....no... I saw him... the little boy... Steve had stormed out after...well, another row... I, I was sitting on the bed, confused... I, I wanted to call you, just to have a chat, a real chat like we used to. But, but it's not easy with Steve. I looked up and there, in the corner of the room was Tony. The little boy... he stared at me, and he said that everything was going to be okay now, and I wasn't to worry any more...I did like him so. I always had...' Sallow laughter 'My first crush, they say it never leaves, and it hasn't... will not.'

I gulped back a bit. 'Tony wasn't the same man.'

'You have the toy soldier' Her voice sounded cold;

authoritarian. As if in command. I hadn't mentioned it; and was going to, but I was cut off.

'Steve's back. I must go. Tony said that we must return it... I'll be on the 17:20 train and should be in Bridgeton by 18:45. We can talk more then. Ring Cerci'

The phone line went dead.

Cerci had had far less luck, though her beauty had remained, life had not been kind to her; aging her prematurely. Her first marriage to a realtor called Johnny Smits, to a tall gangly man I recalled, from Bridgeton High had ended when she found that he was having an affair with his boss: the wealthy Marty Freeman. She had suspected that Johnny wasn't into girls from the start, but she was in love with him and their marriage did produce a boy Daniel. However Daniel had learning problems and had been diagnosed with autism early on; and though Johnny had promised to stand by her, she felt that living a lie over something else wasn't going to work. Her second marriage to a large man with heavy jowls: Brendon Davey. Brendon was the local barkeep in Shepherdson, a town five miles from Bridgeton. It was a marriage that had led to an abortion as he didn't want "another spastic child to have to pay out for."

She stayed with him more out of necessity and need over love, as it seemed that his love for her was rather with her father's money than herself; and as soon as that had dried up: so had his affection for her. Finally, for Cerci, Love in its emotional sense had died as soon as it became apparent that he had a stronger attachment to his porn collection; whom he seemed to prefer, than using his manhood in the proper way, for the proper reasons.

For Cerci, this had become, yet again, another marriage of convenience. However, this time, the roles were reversed. Moreover, this time it was a marriage that was more about keeping a roof over her and Daniel's head, than about commitment to each other. I called her directly after I spoke to Nell.

'So Tony's finally at peace.' She sounded relieved.

'Yeah.' I began. I was nervous as I still was fond of Circe, even though time and space had displaced us.

I explained the account at Arkham, the soldier and Nell's decision to meet up later that evening. On hearing about Nell, Circe's voice lifted.

'That's it then. I haven't seen Nell in a month of Saturday's, there's so much to do, pack a bag or two and I need somewhere for Daniel to go I must have somewhere for Daniel go I can't expect him to come along it would be so good to meet up once more. Even if it is to go up to that damned house that has caused so much pain.' I mentioned that mother and father, though in their sixties would be able to and with that I heard a sigh of satisfaction.

'It…it would be nice to see you again.' I said nervously, still feeling like that awkward child of so many years ago. At that Circi became defensive and quiet.

'Yes, but we know, that can never happen.' She said flatly.

The reason it could never be was due to a dream; a dream we both shared the night Tony turned insane. We both had found ourselves in the dark world, where IT lived. We were outside the Cobbe house and…it was there, in the shadows of the trees, watching us. We could feel it's red eyes glaring hotly and maliciously at us.

'You're so easy to spot when your together' it rasped, its pale face shone and its read hair swirled about his head. 'I don't need feeding now, but I will come and I will feed. I WILL FEED!'

'You don't scare me!' I yelled at it. And it laughed cruelly back.

"Time is such a bitch? DON'T YOU THINK?'

Cerci took a step backwards.

'YEAH AND BOY AM I GOING TO MESS WITH YOU BEAUTY!' he sneered.

I held her hand and in that touch, something happened, we both began to glow with this white swirling light. Eyes form the shadows began to glow, teeth ever-sharp glistened with saliva. Talons curled in the weird light.

'Ahh…look everyone, THEY are in LOVE!' It laughed 'Love gets you KILLED HERE SWEETIE!' Its voice was venomous and cruel.

We took a step back; as It walked through the trees. Its malformed bulbous head shone in the pale light. Its hideous features twisted with rage and torment.

'First I will devour Tony…then I will come for you…dear Peter… then Circe and finally Nell, whom I will savor the taste of.' He walked slowly forward. 'One at a time…One at a time… I will eat you…one at a time.' All around him, voices began to laugh cruelly and eyes slit and alien stared out.

Cerci wriggled free of my hand, turned and ran. I followed her. But I couldn't reach her. All I could hear were her words: 'I don't love you Peter I don't love you Peter, oh Peter Dear Peter I don't love you at all.'

I woke up and found myself utterly exhausted. I staggered from my bed and went to the mirror. I looked even more pale than before. I went to my bedroom window and saw Circe sitting on her bed, her knees drawn up under her nightgown.

I called and called, but she never came.

'its' just a dream!' the words came out hollow 'It can't hurt us!'

Circe got up and looked at me.

'That's not true and you know it Drew'

With that the window closed; and Summer was over forever.

***

Bridgeton train station never deserved the name. It was built in 1864, and was partially torn down 100 hundred years later, as the main line had been moved a mile of so east. As I stood there and looked up, it was clear that it was in decline. It could be best described as an iron bridge platform; unprotecting anyone from the elements, save for a single, tired looking yellow painted, wooden shack, that had a red painted roof; both of which were peeling and in need desperate need of attention.

The shack stood on the left-hand side of the platform, which in turn straddled the river; and divided the town. The raised platform led to two flights of wooden steps, that descended in a zig-zag fashion from the bridge platform down to the ground level, that clicked and clacked from over use towards the narrow ticket office, where a tired looking, pug nosed, round faced, grey walrus mustachioed ticket collector, stood, plucking at the tickets that were given to him; and at the same time shouted out, though bellowed would be more accurate, where the next train was coming from, or going to, in his broad New England accent.

I recall that the September sun hung low in the sky that day. It shimmered like an angry ball between folds of Iron clouds; giving no heat. A cold north easterly whipped the commuters as they made their way down to the ground in undulating waves.

I then saw Nell like a bird of paradise full of colour, flighty and light amid the mass of beige hat's and the grey or black coats of the early evening, fighting against a writhing sea of bland humanity, as it battled and desperately fought for freedom through a single green gate in front of me.

As I saw her and waved. For a second she didn't see me, and in that second I could admire how beautiful she had become. Her hair bobbed around her now elfin features, her sea green eyes, wide open full of life and glittering with excitement were astonishing. I felt my mouth dry and a stirring that I didn't expect. Then she saw me she gave an impish grin and like a bird darted between grey masses who looked tired and weary from life's cruel jokes.

I came to the collector who made no register of my

appearance. Then as Nell handed her ticket over; he grabbed her hand and held it in a vice like grip.

'You think that you can defeat ME?' the collector spat; his eyes wide.

Nell, tried to pull away from his grip but he held her hand tighter.

'Every little thought...every little dream...I'm here, there and everywhere in-between.'

I went to take her hand; it was clear that the dark land was spreading. Nell looked visibly shaken.

'You didn't defeat me twenty years ago! A you AINT GONNA DO IT NOW!' the words were forced on arcs of putrid smelling spittle, that riddled the evening air. Then suddenly he let go and was himself again.

I took Nell's arm, who looked decidedly shaken.

'It's going to get worse.' I muttered

She gave a side nod, and then grinned again.

'so where's Circe?'

I expect at Repperton's its the only bar left in town.'

Repperton's looked more like a shack from the outside that a bar. Inside, despite that Elvis Presley's "Heartbreak hotel" was booming from the Juke box; it was clear that Epperson's had seen better days, it's wooden veneered walls were need a polish from the collection of dust that had gathered in the nooks. The ceiling, had yellowed with tobacco stain. The bar was to the left of the entrance, and to the right and in the half-light inglenooks with tables set into them, gave the impression of life. Only the stools along the bar made from oak and plumped up with horse hair, and covered with a mixture of black horsehair and pink cotton shone as if new. The place was rich with the smell of old tobacco and beer.

I saw Circe within the far side inglenook straight away. She smiled sadly down and away from me, yet still raised her hand. I noticed that even in the half light of the bar, she was wearing far too much makeup I didn't realize why until we moved closer and noted the puffiness of her features. I was going to say something, then Nell squeezed my arm, and our minds, as they used to do left images, that need not be discussed here, but can be inferred. Next to her, sat a tall gangly looking boy with a narrow face; whose eyes were fixed on the table in front of him. We walked over and greeted each other warmly.

'This is Daniel' said Circe.

'it's nice to meet you Daniel.' Nell spoke warmly and held out her hand.

Daniel looked down and rocked slightly.

'It's a new environment and a little loud for him.' Replied Circe, as we settled in the seats around the table.

Behind me the entrance to the bar slammed open and a man I barely recognized came in.

However, he recognized us right away.

'Well. if it isn't the flunky club, gathered for one last meeting I bet.' Stephen Brinks drawled from sneering lips. Nell smiled.

'It's nice to know that we're still remembered.' Her words were terse, which with sarcasm and an intonation that sounded like an insult. It was clear she was talking to him as if he was a child.

Stephen who failed to see the comment, drawled on.

'look here, Circe had a child…. looks like an idiot to me.'

'Ayah, but I don' don' bleed in the bowl when I dump. Dump dump.'

Stephen's face paled a bit at Daniel's remark.

'-Man got little time left to breath here.' Daniel retorted as he rocked.

'Daniel!' Circe snapped as Stephen looked at the table we sat at and sneered.

'Flunky club, was all you were an' all you be.' The he turned on me.

'I'm going to wait for you outside and finish the job off.' he spat with varmint; and in the half-light of the bar his glassy eyes glittered with rage. It again had come.

'Who's the boy? Seems he needs my special touch? Perhaps I'll come to him first and – '

'Enough!' Circe leapt up from her chair. 'I'm sick of you! you hear me! Sick of all you've done here! We are coming for you!'

It smiled though Stephen's eyes coldly. Its presence filled the room. Light's in the bar dimmed. The music slowed to an ugly drawl. Its eyes took hold of Stephen. They glittered with hate.

'Looking forward to it dearie!' it hissed as it turned.

Then suddenly the music sped up the lights returned. Stephen had vanished.

We sat there staring at each other, not knowing what to say. Grabbing small comfort from the images we shared to each other; while Daniel kept singing ''it's all over now.'

We arose and then left the bar and took to walking up towards my parent's place on Prospect hill.

I was nervous as we left Repperton's. I kept feeling that Brinks would be there, waiting in the shadows, or standing in the car park. His fists in tight balls, his eyes, feverously glittering, shaking for violence. He wasn't of course. It, for need of a better word, had a habit of using people, then discarding them as it saw fit; so, I relaxed a little as we took the narrow path at the rear of Repperton's then left along Sligo street, and past the narrow wooden houses that made up this area of town.

I hadn't left Bridgeton; so perhaps I had become blinded, at least to a degree, as to that present state of the town. However, Nell and Circe both in lampoon cartoon images -together with Daniel's contribution that, it must be said, made us all laugh- shared images of broken toys damaged doll's houses and rickety train sets.

At first I was embarrassed and slightly ashamed to admit that the town I loved had fallen into such decline. But in the end, I had to admit it. For It was true, there was a slow, though formless, decay occurring in Bridgeton.

Businesses' that should have flourished; such as the iron foundry and the sawmill were on the brink of folding and floundering. One document, published in the "Bridgeton Gazette" discussed how the timber produced here "wasn't strong enough" or "too brittle" for use. Another relating to the foundry, stated that the metal ingots were "not of the right quality"; thus, leading to a layoff of 1/3rd of the town's workforce.

But that wasn't all. Families who moved here, hardly stayed for anytime at all anymore; people left giving no real reason, other than a sense of feeling "unwelcome" thus leaving the overall population of the town increasingly both elderly and infirm, as they simply were too old, or too tired to go through the process of relocation.

The high street itself also reflected this change, becoming increasingly artisan and selective. Most of the major retailers had moved five miles out of town public houses and churches became abandoned and people became increasingly isolated; and the rail line was becoming increasingly intermittent. I had to face it, the town was dying.

With this fresh eye given by Circe, Nell and Daniel, I saw the houses we past in a new light. The lawns were overgrown. The windows needed cleaning, the rooves were missing the occasional tile; hedges were overgrown and unkempt, all of which, in this slow growing twilight, led me to shudder. I had to face the reality. It was taking control of the town. I thought about the Cobbe house and I shuddered, locking the image away so no one could share it.

Finally, Nell broke the silence.

'yes, it does all seems more dilapidated than I remember it...' she sighed a little as we as we walked towards prospect street, her blonde hair blowing in the westerly. Circe smiled wanly.

'Dagger's n a dirt road' muttered Daniel, as we walked in the slowly encroaching night. We turned the corner and there was a tractor with a crane attachment by the old Sables place. With a sign outside the house that registered it for demolition. Circe then looked up to the end of the street at her old home.

'It seems smaller somehow.'

'We were smaller then; perspectives change.' I sighed.

I pushed open the old wire door and then the front door and stood in the oak lined hall, of my parent's home. Then made my way to the pale green painted kitchen at the rear.

'where your folks?' Nell asked

'Mum passed away two years ago... Dad, found the house a hard upkeep. I took it on an' rent some of the larger rooms to boarders. I tend to stay at my old Uncles house, but, there is little space for all of us. This house pays for his stay at Bridgeton General... after his stoke... he found life...painful. There's no one here at the present...it fills up more in the summer months; an' I have bookings for next year paid in so...though I am running at a loss, it's not a huge loss an' the bank's good, but-'

I put the coffee on the stove as we all sat in the kitchen around the long green tiled table.

With a faltering hand, I felt inside my jacket pocket and slowly pulled out the soldier. I placed it in the Centre of the table and as we all sat down and stared at it, I finally explained where my research had led to.

'So...it's a child?'

I nodded at Circe, 'it's a child that.... Has...suffered badly and, and-'

Nell looked down and away.

'-I felt...I felt that I let Tony down, we were his friends.'

'-The Tony we knew was stolen from us by this thing. The sleepless nights, the endless dreams, I don't know why I haven't gone insane...but I don't know what to do. My Uncle wasn't an exorcist, he was a a historian, a chemist. Science was his God...'

'I I think if we all hadn't moved when we did-' But Nell was cut short.

Suddenly, the kitchen draws all around the room were violently being pulled open of their own volition one at a time. They fell to the floor witch a crash. The light overhead began to dim.

Daniel began to mutter and rock as the overhead light slowly began to spin.

'tickitytockityticketytockitybangbangBANG'

The only empty chair in the room opposite me suddenly pulled back, and a presence began to fill the room.

We held each other's hands across the table and the rattling began to subside; but a cool, breeze and hard laughter began to fill the room.

Then as quickly as it started it trailed off.

I looked around the room nervously. My heart thumping

sickly in my chest.

'Butterfly's' 'Daniel sang; and a moment later, through soft swirls of incandescent light, the most colorful butterflies, that I had ever seen suddenly burst into the room and began to dance about us. In gentle flapping circles, they flew up to the ceiling, then they swooped down once more; and when they touched the walls, and then went through the walls, they returned once more; leaving sparkles of bubbling golden green light; that popped in an ethereal spectral mist. Daniel giggled happily as the fragrance of summer filled that near winter kitchen.

'This place is silly' Daniel giggled.

We all looked at Daniel with awe; unable to fully understand what was happening; or at least having the words at our disposal to comprehend the beauty and wonder that shone about us.

Then Daniel took command, his voice sounded different, older more sure.

'WE need to go the Cellar…he's buried in the cellar, with the other's…we need to free him an, an' cleanse the town.' All the while Daniel was looking mesmerized at the butterflies that flew about him.

I Looked at Circe and a slow tear formed in her eye.

'Daddy goorrn Daddy gorrn' Daniel sang as the butterflies touched us filling us with peace.

'He's a beautiful boy.'

'Yes.' Circe shone considering my eyes; and for a second that lasted a lifetime, I felt the closest I have ever been to love.

One by one the butterflies slowly slipped back into a spectral mist. I looked down at the toy soldier, now finally resolved.

That cold late September night; must be the most ingrained into my memory. It had been raining the day before, so the path had become a quagmire of rutted animal tracks, that clung to our shoes, and numbed our feet. Our coats, though wrapped about us, failed to keep out the encroaching blue winter chill, that tainted our faces in the half-light. On my back, I carried a rucksack that contained gasoline in coke bottles stuffed with rags, in my pocket a Ronson lighter and that damned toy soldier. Nell and Circe each carried a spade tied to their backs on s ling made of string. I knew we were prepared. Despite that, there was a growing sense of dark foreboding within all of us, as we made our way up the steep incline that led to the plateau that looked over the town.

Our torches shone a dim yellow light, that concealed more than it revealed. Trees took on a spectral presence and seemed to turn towards us, the knots of unformed limbs, were peeling back to become lidless yellow eyes that stared towards us with alien, unnatural hostility. Strange noises and stranger odors, like that of decay, crawled out of the darkness; and tried to enfold us with lank feelers over our faces, that gave us all shudders. It was trying to push us away. That in-itself spurred us on.

It was as we were in sight of the house that the first incident occurred. A horse and cart were heard. The sound became louder and louder; then the scream's started. We looked all around us for where the sound was coming from. In the spinning torch light, I saw Circe's strained face, her eyes on stalks as the screaming became louder and louder. Nell grabbed my arm. Even Daniel who seemed the less aware or perhaps more so, than the rest of us, even he, at one point, put his hands over his ears. To stop the screaming Then it suddenly stopped.

The silence was numb and more terrifying than the noise that preceded it   We are in for it now, I thought and slowly took the lead.

'These are images... things that have been... trapped by, by that dark entity.'

I pointed the flashlight towards the house that, in the darkness loomed ugly and threatening.   It was true. Time was dislocated here, fractured by something bigger than ourselves.   It took us fifteen minutes to reach the front door of the house; and for the first time, I began to think how utterly insane this was. We should have waited until the morning, when the light of day, would have put all such thoughts to rest. Instead here we were on the cusp of night entering our childhood fears.

The open door of the decaying house looked more akin to a cavernous mouth than ever. Strange murmuring's and scuttling's were heard inside. I felt my hands involuntarily start shake as I stood there. Yet, Daniel was the least afraid of all of us. I still recall how he stood there, in the direct beam of the flashlight, his shadow reflecting off the walls... seemed, at least to me, to offer some form of protection. I didn't see it. Nell did, and she screamed. Some form of shape. A feeler or a leg of something huge and monstrous, grabbed hold of his waist. In a second he had been violently sucked into the night of the house. Circe screamed and charged in. We all followed. Yet He was nowhere to be seen. With grim resolution, we fought our way down that narrow hall, down the stairs and into the cellar, that stank with such putrefaction, that it's hard to describe.

'Daniel!' screamed Circe, pleading at the darkness. 'Let him go! you fuck!'

Yet nothing was heard, save a faint flapping sound from

above. I felt feelers on my neck, I didn't want to look up, to train the torch upon what was roaming the room, above our heads. Instead I fought to find the place where in this darkness the end of all this. In the left corner of the room, there grew some form of matted fungi, which reflected a pale blue tint when not under the light of the torch. Next to it, not facing us, but kneeling on the dirt floor was Daniel. I took the toy soldier from my pocket and threw it towards him and onto the fungi, that, with a slithering hiss wrapped itself around it. It was then that I saw, within that fungal mass, the corruption of a human child. I suddenly slithered down into the dirt. Circe screamed and ran for Daniel, yet something above him, suddenly threw her backwards across the room with a violent thwack.

It hissed malevolently, wrapping a tendril around the neck of Daniel.

Daniel let out a chocking Mum. Nell threw me the spade upon her back and dived to help Circe as it flapped its chitin wings as it lifted itself just off the ground. Daniel's feet hung an inch off the ground.

With Desperation and in the half light of my thrown I dug down, then putting the torch onto the hole clawed at the ground fighting off the feelers that were pulling at me. Eventually I reached the slithering huddled mass and cut into it with my spade, slamming into it again and again. The thing burst and a hideous s liquid sputtered out all over my hands like warm coffee. Then I took off my rucksack and with a shaking hand lit and threw the first of my incendiaries into the pit. A burst of flame curled up. There was a hiss and hideous scream. I didn't dare look, I just pulled Daniel aside, as Nell pulled a limp Circe from the floor and up the stairs.   I carried Daniel outside and put him of the ground. Then went back to help Nell and Circe. When finally, we were all free, I lit and threw the other three incendiaries into the gaping hole of the mouth of the house. Flames curled up the walls and out of the gaping vacant windows. Cracking the beams and turning the night sky into a pale orange hue. Then came the most chilling of all things. For above the house, an eclipse of moths slowly circled. They danced in the flames. Many burned, with hideously human cries. Daniel who had slowly come around shouted 'look' and as he did so, the moths faded into ashes as the house burned to the ground.

That was all six months ago. Since then, many look up to the plateau where the Cobbe house once stood. People are coming back to Bridgeton and, once or twice, when I look that way, I see a little more growth coming back to that once poisonous hill. However, whenever I see a moth…I

cannot help but shudder. As for the flunky club? Well, Nell
has moved into movies; while Circe, took Daniel west. I get
the occasional letter; and I? well I...I am left with my
memories, that occasionally, just occasionally mind you,
spill out into my dreams.

Whistle on the wind

Josh rubbed his three-day stubble and tiredly turned towards Lyn. Who smiled coldly. The kids were being noisy and the traffic was heavy. A combination always made her nervous. It led a to a tell. A slight shake of her tousled blonde hair and that smile, which hid her boiling rage. On days like this he wished he could drive. But years of epileptic seizures had closed a door to that. In the back seat of their marine Seat Ibiza, Eleanor 10, Jessica 8 and A.J 6 were bored and painfully showing it.

'Are we there yet' called Eleanor

'-No not yet.' Josh replied.

'-Ouch!' blurted out Jess

'-Eleanor leave your sister alone!' Came Lyn's retort.

-'DAAAD! She's pinching me. AJ protested

'Eleanor!'

'Kids keep the noise down.'

Giggles laughter, screams.

'Come on now girls, mummy is trying to drive.' Josh sighed.

They stopped the car at the old priory. It was a pre-arranged decision to stop here for a picnic, before returning home to Exeter, after the weekend at his once best man, Steve and his wife Pauline's rambling home in Plymouth. Mainly as it was a handy place to let the kids remove some of their energy, in what had been already been an arduous journey and a terrible weekend.

Josh desperately wanted to forget the weekend and especially those silent messages which passed between Lyn and Steve, that became painfully obvious and personally embarrassing after two bottles of wine.

It was a sultry early afternoon. The sky had thick rolling, dark clumpy cloud that threatened rain. The overgrown grass blew wildly about   the wooden fences and the foreground of the abbey; whose   dark corners, broken arches and tumbledown buildings made of ancient grey stone mixed with the rich red rock of Devon. Stood out against the sky. As he walked about taking the scene in with his Canon Desi, clicking here, pausing to set a frame there; Josh felt a nausea grow. He felt it as strange stabbing in the back of his neck, as if unseen eyes, bloated with a loathing of living things, gazed with cold indifference from the very rock itself.

The nausea increased. Signs of a seizure. He mediated the feelings of anxiety down. This is a ruin. There is nothing out of the ordinary. Its energy is in the stone and the stone is old. The dizziness peaked and then ebbed, a dark tide slid back.

'Look Dad'

It was A.J, her green eyes shone with the delight of pushing boundaries, as she scaled the wall. She had her mother's beauty and his love of excitement. Still

'AJ get down!'

Giggle. 'come and get me!

'Come on girls, its food time.' called Lyn.

Two girls came scrambling out of the shadows of the abbey, as the one in front of him clambered down the rough grey-stone wall.

Eleanor came over to the blanket

'Look what I've found.'

Two tiny hands covered with slimy mud, red clay and sand were open, palms up to reveal in the clinging clay a long narrow tube. The trinity as he sometimes called them, instantly began bickering.

'What's that?'

'Dunno.'

'Give it to me!

'No! it's mine!'

'It's not fair!'

'Girls please!'

Lyn rummaged in her handbag for the wet wipes. Always there for the emergencies.

'You can't eat with hands like that. '

The muddy tube being all things dirty to Lyn, was thrown in the long grass by the fence. Josh put down the camera on corner of the blanket and then walked towards where the muddy tube had been discarded. He picked it up and as he did, his curiosity slowly grew. The encrusted tube was about five inches long. It glinted with an azure stain in the rich near burgundy slimy red clay. Josh casually walked back to the blanket and picked up the plastic packet of wet wipes already almost empty, due to three mucky little girls and their ferocious appetite for adventure. Carefully he began to remove the clay.

'Josh put it down- 'sigh

'-but it's actually quite' –

'-Daaaad, it's probably got dog poo on it- 'Jess blurted

'-Errgehh! Daddy picking up!' AJ squealed

'Eleanor touched it first!'

'Just leave me alone!' Eleanor barked.

'EL EN ORR!' Jess and AJ howled at the top of their voices

Oh, god kids!

It cleaned up well. It was about five inches in diameter,

made of bronze, or brass, he couldn't tell, but then he wasn't a metallurgist. He was an unemployed father   of three, with a condition that restricted his employment and a degree, that, if he had the ambition, (which right now, he confessed to himself he had little of.) he could turn into something valuable.

'The writing's familiar-'

'-Darling, just put it down.'

He noted that Lyn had that awkward face he recognised. He glanced at her, smiled, slightly, and looked down again. Desperately trying not to hear the tiredness in her voice. Knowing and fearing the distance between them.

'-It has some Anglo-Saxon runes on it.'

The soft sweet smelling wipes finally removed the wet clay in a smear across the tube. Through the mud, tiny indentations could be seen. There were runes and they were Anglo Saxon. He was certain of it. He recalled during the Dane law, that began around   638 CE, many practices were exchanged, the writing of runes was one of them. The Anglo Saxon Runic alphabet, differed from the Viking in many respects. Some of this was due to accent a dialect differences between locations; making the runic system exchangeable to a point.

The letters stood out Cael e.g. h..ae w...ill c...y..me. ...Cal ende hae will cyme... call and he will come... Fascinating he thought

There were also three tiny holes near the bottom of the tube. Taking his pen knife from his pocket he began to slowly remove the wet soil from within the tube. Red muddy water suddenly spilled out onto the blanket.

'Josh!' That sigh again.

With a little difficulty, he removed the rest of mud clearing it completely.

'Darling, please put that thing down. 'she sounded as if she was talking to a child. She always did.

'-It's a, a whistle I think.'

'-Or some old tat some other tourist dropped while climbing the walls. Darling, you dig something up, Eleanor copies you. '

'-She has a love of historical finds.'

Lyn gave her stare to Josh. The stare that Josh new too well. The stare that said don't be an arse and be realistic

'-Have you seen any jobs lately?'

'-Nothing.'

'-You're not looking hard enough. Seven years you have been working towards that bloody degree. Now you have it, start making some money.'

Josh looked down and away from the kids. Lyn had said that in front of them deliberately.

'-Why don't   you look for work.'

'-We've been there Josh. For Christs sake, don't be an arse.'

'What's an arse Daddy?' AJ looked up innocently.

Josh walked away. He found Eleanor at his side a moment later.

'I love you Daddy.'

'I love you too p-.' He was going to say pumpkin, but changed his mind, as she was recently diagnosed as having Asperger syndrome   Ergo she would not understand a metaphor. She never would. A sad lump formed in his throat. Then he faked a grin and looked at this their eldest daughter with love.

'Tell me... where did you find it?'

Eleanor smiled and led Josh to the western wall.

'Just down their Dad.' She said quietly.

'Dad, why is Mummy like that?'

Mummy is worried that there isn't enough money to keep us in our home Mummy hates daddy Mummy has met Steve and thinks he' s better fuck It happens. Josh's eyes became strained.

'It's nothing to worry about darling.'

The words sounded empty in his voice, Josh knew that Eleanor was smart enough to pick up on it

'So where exactly did you find it?'

She pointed down at the base of the wall.

Both looked at the hole recently uncovered by the weekend rain. Feeling a little nervous and not knowing why, Josh put his hand into the earth and felt something hard and narrow. He pulled at it. With a soft plop the earth released its secret. It was the topper most part of a human skeletal finger

'That settles it, put it back. It's some piece of history that belonged to that old dead body. Leave it alone. Her words were even more shocking by the ferocity of the sound

Jess looked at the whistle.

'Mummy's right. We should leave it here. '

'I think we should take it to the museum in Exeter.' Josh tried to persuade

Lyn gave Josh a hard stare.

Here we go again no dammit on this I stand 'I am taking this back home; I am going to properly clean it and when we get home I am going to take it to Exeter museum. That's that!'

Lyn looked at Josh. Her now mirthless eyes glittered with contempt.

'Fair enough.' came her terse reply.

'Can I see daddy? AJ asked.

Josh passed her the little whistle.

AJ thought about it, playing with the little whistle in her tiny fingers. Then she put her mouth to one end and blew. The sound it made was ethereal. A whisper on the wind, Josh thought absently. The sound was captivating and yet distant; and in its sound, something seemed to wake. Josh shook his head

Lyn stared at AJ and then at Josh with anger.

'That's so fucking you isn't it! Christ, you let them do anything! How do you know that this whistle, or whatever it is, doesn't have some, weird shit on it?

'-You can't keep them bottled up for-'

' -or something! The germs are everywhere!

'-what the hell is wrong with you?'

'-It was next to a fucking corpse!'

-Jesus Lyn! I'm sorry!'

'-Be a fucking parent Josh for Christ's sake!'

'-What the-

'-I'm I'm sick of being the grown up around here Josh! Sick of it!'

She looked away.

Silence settled around the picnic blanket, as Josh held back the tears and the rage.

The drive home was in silence, as was the rest of the night, where only Lyn could be heard giggling into her I-phone.

When bed came, it was full of wild dark horses

Josh heard a scream. He arose and walked to the communal bedroom that the three girls shared. AJ was kneeling in her cabin bed. Her hands were over her eyes, screaming in hysterical wails. He walked towards her and tried to hold her, but she wrestled in his arms and fought him off. He took a step back

'She's still in the dream.

Then she pulled her tiny hands away from her face with forceful movements, as if someone or something, was stopping her

Then she stared towards him.

'Why did you let me touch it Dad? 'Her voice was low dark and malevolent. Her eyes were lost cold black sockets

Josh awoke screaming.

That morning AJ came into bed with them.

'I had a bad dream daddy.'

'Darling what happened?' he waited for the reply

'At the broken place there was something there a dark thing it chased me and I couldn't get away.' Her voice came in soft sobs.

Lyn moaned low.

'Come on let's get up.' He whispered.

An hour later over a summery breakfast, Josh spoke to Lyn.

'You're right. I'm, I'm going to the museum today to see what's there. Lyn smiled warmly at him.

'I can be a bitch sometimes.'

He could hear the sadness in her voice, but   the sincerity was not there; and he knew that would never come back. Trust had been broken.

It was mid-morning by the time he finally met with the staff of the Royal Albert Memorial Museum. He had already been waiting half an hour, so he decided to avoid the issue of work and show the find instead.

'Fascinating, fascinating and and where   did you find it?' asked the plump sweaty little man, who greeted him with an officious plum weighted voice.

'Plympton Priory.'

'-yes yes, a fascinating find, and close to where a body was found you say? 'There was a long pause. 'You do know the story...about the   Priory? Large boggle eyes stared into his own over the top of polished spectacles.

'No.'

'Well I am surprised... I thought that everyone knew.'

Josh held back his sense of mirthless derision.

'The priory was once run by an abbot of, let's say, a questionable faith. His practices...they were...err...frowned upon. It's said that he ...'

Josh nodded in the right places, but overall found the man vacuous and full of his own words: in fact, a complete bore.

'...incidentally You were right about the runic alphabet. It is Anglo Saxon not Viking... the fact that it was found at the abbey infers that it might be part of an older treasure...I'm not sure what the words themselves mean. "Cal ended have wile cyme." Sounds very, MR James. Of course, the word Cyme also refers   to a claim so the owner is owned by the action of calling on "Hai" whomever, or whatever "He.... a" might be.   Umm I wonder... Can we, have it? His puffy ruddy   face was flushed with excitement.

At that point Josh felt odd. There was something in the curator's face that troubled him. Or was it his own desire to keep this treasure? He felt a strange sense of attachment to the whistle no he didn't want to part with it. That was that. Josh gave his best fake smile.

'I'll think about it.' He said.

Nods followed farewells as Josh left.

That night when both Josh and Lyn were about to go to bed themselves terrifying screams were heard coming from the girl's bedroom.

Both Lyn and Josh ran up the stairs. They reached the door and Josh tried to open it. But it was held fast. He slammed against it.

'Open the door!' Ordered Lyn

'I can't' it's not moving.'

'JOSH!

MUMMY! DADDY! HELP! DADDY! MUMMY!

Josh slammed into the door. Once. Nothing happened. Twice. Again, nothing. The third and the fourth time nothing. The screams were getting louder and louder. They could hear things smashing loudly around the room.

With a final viscous kick, Josh   smashed the door open and they both fell into the room, to see three duvets slowly begin to wrap about their children's necks. the room howled and screamed with unseen violence; as they fought against the duvet's that were themselves forming into hideous half formed faces.

He fought and grappled AJ free and pushed her out of the room. Then he grabbed Jess and Lyn pulled Eleanor free, carrying her as they staggered down the stairs. They entered the front room. While behind them, the bedroom was howling.

'Is everyone okay?'

Lyn looked helplessly up towards Josh, who was holding Eleanor tightly. He could see that she was barely breathing.

She's not waking Josh!   SHE'S NOT WAKING!'

Josh stared down his green eyes bulging from his tired sockets.

There was a burning sensation in his pocket. He pulled the whistle out. It hit the floor. Only then did he know what to do.

They drove to the priory on dark open roads carrying out a step of blind faith. When they finally arrived at the ruins Josh took little time in replacing the whistle where he found it, in the hope that if he did so, then Eleanor would wake.

With trepidation in his heart, he walked back to the car and towards a ruddy sunrise.

My name is Jake

Hi, my name is Jake and no I'm not telling you anything else about me. Though I would agree -to a point- that when people come to visit, I tend to... how can I put it, not to make them feel very welcome. Whether it's in how I slam a door; or close a cupboard, or stomp about the floorboards Displaying my anger has been...how can I put it...not too difficult for me.

In many ways, I don't want to be understood or figured out. I don't want my daemons put to rest. I am very happy with them hanging about thank you very much. But there is also the sense of the perverse in what I do. I want people to hate me, to fear me. I want people to go and think, never again. I enjoy trapping people in games and love to see their pale faces as I scream at them.

Some people now want to analyze me. They want to put me under the spotlight and try to figure out why I do...what I do... to those I say, fair enough, give it your best shot. But one thing is for certain you will never get to me. Ever.

Steven Peter's and his family tried to get to me. They wanted me so much at first, and made me feel welcome. Yet, then they started talking down to me when I started acting up; and I never like that ever; after all I do have a sense of pride, I need to be recognized! I NEED TO BE RESPECTED! Sorry... a a little rage bomb there... I tend to let them off occasionally.

In the end, I had to do away with Steven Peters and his sorry family. They annoyed me too much. Sighing here, moaning there, getting people in to to try to understand me! I DON'T NEED THAT! I DON'T NEED THAT AT ALL! so... I had to settle the score

Now...it's not easy settling any score. After all, I am not a murderer... well... not an intentional one... I, I don't seek vengeance, I simply ask that, when you do see me, you respect me and you respect my sense of self; after all It's not easy being me. It's not... no one understands. Ever. I guess now, you are wondering what on earth did you do to settle your score with the Peter's family? I can imagine you are thinking all sorts of nasty stuff. How I came through the front door screaming like a madman; a felling axe in my hand. How I with hysterical laughter took to carving up Peter's his near to do wife and his children with a HACK JACK HACK HIGGARTY SPLAT, hee hee-hee... Well I didn't. I am not like that. I am an artist. I pick my moments carefully. I choose the most vulnerable, the most loved, and... I...twist them. Oh, not all at once you understand... after all, it's better when there is a little thought behind it, don't you agree? Oh, of course you do. I think you will agree with me that there is nothing better than twisting the knife or turning the screw just that little bit, to see what happens, when the person goes over the edge... Perhaps you think I am cruel. A soulless being. I disagree I have feelings, I do. I do... I do do do! I FUCKING DO

Now you have me all upset. If you carry on like that, I'll not talk to you any-more. You see...You must understand, that I am an artist. I work slowly, and methodically. There is purpose in my action's.... I take pride in that. Many don't see that; they simply don't understand me at all.

So how do I start things off? Well, most of the time I do this by simply moving things about. This is something that I enjoy. Nothing gets me giggling more, than watching the mice run the course of the trap. Scurrying here, muttering there, running about, getting increasingly hysterical because "I know damn well that I put the (insert any precious desperately needed object) down here!"   Where are your key's? glasses? The TV remote. Nowadays, it's more fun than ever. Knocking out the wife or the internet for an hour or two; and then watching them turn it off, or on, fiddling with the lead, and finding it unplugged. It is simply me ...being funny. Oh come on, where is your sense of humor?

Then I turn the key a little. I increase the hostility by whispering in people's ears, stuff that they don't normally think. Notions and feeling's that the mice never understand. Then I sit back and catch them.   "Big Brother" yeah, they get their ideas from me. I send them letters about who to put with whom and what to say to press that button and watch them squir

Now I know you're thinking... you're thinking. You're thinking what a bastard. How utterly cruel. But you see you must understand me, and my history. Many don't want to know me. The truth is I push people away, because I was unloved and feel unloved and want people to understand... to love me for who I am...hehehehehehe. I bet you nearly fell for that one. I bet!

I do get attracted to people though. Take Mrs Peter's. Fiona... I mean mmm, now she's a beauty, a real looker, beautiful green eyes. It's the eyes for me, every, all the time... I just fall in love or deep lust, I donno which the moment that I make contact... chestnut close cropped hair with a well-formed body that made me feel alll all electricalll. I mean the sparks were there from day one.

Once I caught her in the bathroom, sudsing herself in the shower... I watched has she slowly rubbed the gel into her skin, teasing her buds, and ... well... I wanted to join in so so much... then Peter's came in and he spoiled it, I might as well have watched porn hub, over Old Peter's shoulder for all the fun I get nowadays! I will say, in my day I was well bigger than he was, ever. where was I? oh yeah sorry wandering...After the stuff goes missing and the voices, then comes the dreams. Perhaps, this is where I show my real self? Hell, no! fuck that! No, I use all sorts of weird things, floating in their heads. Peter's had a thing for his secretary...why when Mrs Peter's, Fiona, was simply gorgeous, I don't know. Anyway, I get into Peter's head and have the secretary get all juicy on him... you know what I mean. Then I turn the secretary into one of my mates, usually the one who likes using surgical implements... and watch the fucker wake up screaming. Seriously, that is such fucking fun. Once I think he nearly caught me. well I was about too long torturing the fucker, when he woke, and caught a glimpse of my red hair and pale face as I made it to the door. He told Mrs Peter's about that. She laughed at him. Which made my day. Yes, sleep deprivation is a major tool at my disposal. Especially with kids. The Brats piss me off, but hey they are so vulnerable...You get the kids ratty after two weeks of dreams, and the mice forget that I am even there. Boy do the sparks fly. Old' Mr. Peter's blames Mr's Peter's the kids blame each other. The anger rises. Heaven Yeah! Feeding time; and boy do we feed.... Then comes the real fun.

Then I start moving things about. Sometimes, in front of them. Most of the time not. It's now I tend to get more attention to myself. I must say, at this point, I cannot help it. I can't. It's like, wanting to be a part of the game again. Connecting with the mice in the cage; makes me think of...other times... better times...TIME'S I DON'T WANT TO TALK ABOUT!... another rage bomb...sorry... sometimes life gets to me, you know? It's tough. So, the stuff goes flying and the mice bring in other mice with machines to poke and prod me and piss me off. So, I tell, them to go. It got like that with the Peter's. I had enough of their bitching, OK OK I know I caused it, but there comes a time when you must cut the cord and say goodbye. I became annoyed with Old Peter's three weeks ago. I don't know what happened. Maybe it was because he started getting all loved up with Fiona...anyway. I decided I had had enough of them, so I got up, and started slamming all the doors and shouting. Fiona, she screamed. So, I pinned her to the bed. and stopped her from breathing... Old' Peter's, he tried to stop me, so I threw that fucker across the room. Then threw their precious walnut veneered 1930's cabinet on top of him. Knocking the bastard out.

The brats heard the banging, so I locked them in their room and used a toy clown in their little wardrobe to stare at them menacingly. I crawled out and scared the little fuckers big time heheheheheh. Then I turned on the water taps and the gas and the TV and the internet. on the laptop showing Fiona what dirty old Peters had been glopping off to, while his wife had been at work. She didn't get that message though. Fiona screamed and leapt from the bed, pulling the cabinet of her husband yelling at me to "fuck off and leave her family alone!" That's when I came out and fully revealed myself to her... She saw me standing over her bed. I saw her face all knot up in terror and she screaked as she looked away. Gosh, I mean I know I'm no looker but that's just unfair.

She dragged her hubby from the room pulled him down the stairs with a colobbbidy clobbidy club and had him by the front door, while I kept chucking stuff about! I was well annoyed now. That and sexually horny. It's not very often that I do reveal myself, but when I do I WANT MORE THAN A FUCKING SCREAM!

Then came the two kids. The brats were wailing and wailing and I was well pissed off at their noise. I mean not at their fear, but the racket was deafening. So reluctantly, I opened the door and let her in. She carried the little fucker's down the stairs and then they all began to scratch at the front door... damaging the paintwork! I mean... come on! I know they wanted out. I could read their minds... but I wasn't ready for that...yet.... I need respect! I am a being that commands it! So, I slammed all the doors one at a time. I started up in the attic by lifting the attic door and up and slamming it down hard enough to splinter the hinges. Then the first floor. Smashing and punching hole after hole on each door as I passed. Then I came down the stairs smashing the boards one at a time with a SMASH CRUNCH SMASH! I WANTED THEM TO KNOW HOW PISSED OFF I WAS! heehaw it's all fun

Then I stood at the far end of the hall, by the basement door. I DON'T LIKE THE BASEMENT! I NEVER GO INTO THE BASEMENT AND IF YOU GO THERE I WILL GET YOU! I WILL RIP YOUR MIND OUT! I stood there. And walked towards them and just before I reached them, the front door opens and with a screaming howl I threw them into the street, slamming the door behind them. Now... I am alone again...

People don't like me very much... but then again, I don't like people much either. They scare me. They say they want to help me to reach the light...but I don't want the light. I don't want the dark either... I just want to be here, in this space and given respect and...maybe... left alone.... I know what I don't want. I don't want anyone to go into the basement and find me...but then again, maybe I do... maybe I am insane? I do think I am insane sometimes... or maybe it's them...those voices in the cellar... calling, calling calling... maybe I am the only sane one in this neighborhood? Maybe I just need to be forgotten and left to my world...alone

The Cupboard

The front door key felt heavy in my hand, as I pulled it from my pocket and slowly inserted it. There was a near silent click, as the well-oiled lock turned. Then, from along the narrow open passage, a heavy breeze came from behind. It allowed the front door to open inward slowly with a croaking wail. I recall that I paused before I entered... I paused... and I inhaled...

The flat stank... But it had more than that fetid odour of boiled cabbage, or that sweet and sour onion stench, which came from aged bodies, long neglected. I dismissed some images that came to mind, as a cold shudder went along my spine. Behind me, I heard the increased volume of a drum and bass track. It distracted me. Nervously I turned and looked down over the balcony, to see three youths; one in a white, shell-suit and a baseball cap; the other two in navy jackets and baggies. They were laughing and pushing against each other, as they made their way across the open square of the estates' Greenfield.

I felt myself relax, as the music began to fade into the distance. Then, feeling a little distant and dizzy, I turned back to the flat entrance once more. I paused again, hiding from myself...hiding from those thoughts I wished I never had, before I decided to come here. But, here I was, at nine in the morning, on a very damp day in August; standing at the entrance of my late parents flat, with an ice-cold heart. The bravest I could manage. And, like many an errant knight; I came armed... but only with some fresh paint, a roller set, a mop, a bucket, some flash detergent and a roll of black bags... all within a collection of pale brown, crusty, cardboard boxes. For I was determined to have this ruin turned into something a little more livable.

I shook my head. This wasn't the first time I had been here, but it was the first since the flat came into my possession; so perhaps that affected the way I looked at it. I was saddened by the fact that the flat hadn't changed much in twenty years. It's' pale blue walls had a little more grime. The carpet, I recall, was once rich ochre...now it seemed like a dirty brown sea; interspersed with islands of mouldy food scraps, age cracked, hand rolled, cigarette butts, next to spindle like ash or tiny dots of black melted carpet, which had the appearance of star constellations amongst the clouds of long neglected, brown beer stains.

I avoided turning right to go into the larger bedroom, I wasn't ready for that yet. Instead I turned left and entered the front room.

I found myself looking in the grimy full length mirror upon the opposite wall and noticed a sour faced, overweight man in his late forties; with close cropped hair, some baggy ill, fitting t-shirt and combat trousers stare back at me. Instantly I looked away...back across the room, towards the black velvet, three-seated sofa. It had a caved in look from apathetic overuse and rested opposite grey, green lump of a television.

I recall that Mum and Dad had bought that bloody thing the day we moved here. I even remember watching the Nelson Mandela concert on it. We moved here in nineteen eighty-seven. Back then, it had been part of a new housing development project. I know...If she had lived...she would have hated what it had turned into. But three years after we moved here, she died... From then on, it was just him and me...him and me...

I came back here, partly to take on my inheritance. But mostly to dig out with a heavy chisel, some of my most painful memories of my childhood. They seemed to hang about both me and these shadow aged walls, like black rotten, teeth, in a pair of red swollen gums. They needed to be dealt with, and if I had to do it, so much the better.

I chose to start with the lime green coloured galley kitchen. For, next to the bathroom, it was the most disgusting room in the flat. With a bitter sigh, I began by emptying out the occasionally age dusted, but, mostly greasy utensils from the long neglected, cabinets. However, two hours later, the room started to look and to feel a little better. I was almost done when, out of the corner of my eye and saw a cupboard.

I hadn't meant to forget the cupboard. To start with I thought I supposed it had been a Freudian slip. But that didn't ring quite right inside me. I looked around the kitchen... the cabinets, walls and floor between both that cupboard and I were clean. There was simply no reason for me to forget it. I looked again and became of the opinion that the cupboard itself was wrong... What I mean is there was something about it that didn't look... or feel... right.

To start with, I put it down to the fact that it came out of the wall at a peculiar angle; it was high resting in the top left hand corner, at an angle of about 45 degrees from the wall...but even that didn't quite ring true inside me. Eventually, I had to face a truly terrible truth that rested deep within me... I knew... I simply knew... without a shadow of doubt in my heart... that this corner box cupboard hadn't existed prior to the moment that I had rested my eyes upon it less than five minutes previously.

Slowly I walked across the room, feeling somehow, a little out of myself; separate and off kilter to the world. I could feel my heart thump, thump, clod-thump within me. And as it began to beat faster, all about me the room began to get colder and colder and colder still...until, as my hand reached out towards the cupboard door. I could see the whispers of my breath curl away from me.

I recall that had no idea what I'd find. So, with anxiety building within me, I nervously and very slowly opened the door. There rested a mug sitting there all alone. On a black, damp stained, wooden shelf. As I stared at it, agonizing memories come flooding back, with the intensity of a thousand needles pushing deep into each pore of my skin.

The mug...his mug.... He always drank out of that bloody thing... that, aged grey white, cracked mug with that awful multi shaded green leaf pattern...the stain of black tea around the inner rim, that never came off no matter how many times I put the thing in the sink

'But I had thrown this away...' I found myself saying aloud as I felt I felt the walls tighten. '...I had thrown this way the day he died...' I told myself again and again and again.

The mug...the handle cracked and loose fitting...like a dead and half rotten bones desperately needing to be ripped out... dead and rotten...even now I can see it... just resting there, in the middle of the bottom shelf of that cupboard... and in the pattern staring at me...dead and rotten...his face leered...

The official report into my fathers' death is thus...He died –peacefully- in his sleep seven weeks ago...the gas of his grimy duel hob stove having been left on. He was found, with his mug by his bedside, by the carer who looked after him on alternative days...an old man, white haired, toothless, unshaven and unkempt...there was a lengthy investigation, but after two weeks, the county coroner recorded a death by misadventure. So, that was that. A week later his body was cremated; no one came to pay their respects, and at the end of what was a cold winters' day, I put the ashes in the bin.

But then I started to have dreams...he kept coming in the night...looking at me...pointing at me...calling me a murderer...scraping his long nails against the walls of my bedroom...tapping his hands upon my wardrobe...whispering foul things in my ear... it took me seven months to face it... seven months of foul disordered dreams, seven months of private agony, before I decided to return here and finally get the job done.

That's what led me back to the flat... But As I opened the

cupboard door and saw the mug it all came back with a savage scream...how I had put enough of his sleeping draft in that mug to knock him out in almost half an hour...how I had waited until he was asleep, then after pulling the cooker away from the wall, I attached a large hose to the gas pipe, ran the hose under the door, into his bedroom and then blocked up the air holes around the hose as best I could; before walking back to the kitchen to put the gas on...I recall I paused...then I slowly opened the valve... how I had left till six in the morning, then, upon my return, how I turned the gas off, removed the rags from beneath the doorway, re-fixed the gas-pipe to the cooker, wound up the extension Hose I brought with me; before opening the door, going back to the cooker and turning it on. Then I left once more. I was home in less than fifteen minutes. I had killed him but he had killed me first... and it was all around that mug...

That mug...that mug...that man...he hurt me...he...did things...but I waited...I waited...oh how I waited...it's a sin to kill but is it a sin to seek justice? I tried to forget what he did to me... but it wouldn't go away...no tears, no amount of scrubbing can clean my mind, nothing rids me of those memories of him...touching me... and that cup...as it shone its' reflection brightly in the afternoon light though the glass frame of the garden shed... as he and I were together on the allotment...

there...there...there...there...his ghost strokes my hand so gently...so very gently...

A gathering of crows

'...The dream is a dark lagniappe. The crows are in flight.
There are hundreds of them...hundreds of them...flying in a
circle It's early...early in the morning...or evening... I can't be
sure of which... the, the, cloud is touched with gold and
steel. I see their three lobed eyes blink with slick greasy
ease... their dark wings stretch out...causing the wind
between the feathers to sound susurrus... The crows touch
the cloud...Misty...grey...cold...the cloud is swirled into
evanescent spirals that ripple at the wing tips.... the cloud
become darker...heavy...then heavier... weighed by cosmic
elemental pressure... A minute raindrop -lighter than air-
takes shape.... It begins to swell...It silently falls with other
drops...through clouds to hurtle towards the ground...I follow
it down. Down.   Down. Faster and faster.... I see the
village – Bridgeton- from a very high point. All the slate
rooves... the hills... The gnarled oak trees... The stone
walls.... all there in minute detail...I, I follow the rain drop....
It falls down... as a tear from God...down... until, until it
touches my cheek.'

   '-And, you awake screaming?
   '-yes.'
   '-interesting...'
 - 'it's been the same dream now for months. I fall and
I...I-'
   '... listen...you've been under a lot of anxiety of late. The
death of your brother- '
   '-What's that go to do with it? That, that was two years
ago...I'm I'm dealing with that- '
   '-Be honest, you've not let him go.'
 '- he is, was, my, my brother, I love... loved him.
   They sat in the musty oak veneered and book filled
vestry. A room that naturally doubled up as Father
Douglas's study.   The sun came in feathers through the
arched lead- lined window that was behind where Dawn sat,
leaning forward. Her hands pressed together, her creased
face, wrought with lines of anxiety. Dust particles floated as
the grey cloud gave way to yellow morning sunlight. They
swam lighter than air before they dissolved into the dark
once more. The pale ochre turned to dark earth, with the
turning of a spade. Father Douglas solemnly stared at Dawn
from his red leather wingback chair. His large oval, opal
eyes glistened.

   Dawn watched Father Douglas carefully. She noted that

his partially bald head had a trace of sweat; and that for the third time in half an hour, he looked as if he was on the verge of saying something. His lips were parted, almost trembling. Words were being fought against with a shake of his head, that reminded Dawn of an attempt to defend oneself against an angry wasp in late summer.

She chose to release the situation from him.

'I, I have to admit father...' the word "father "clawed at Dawn's throat. 'I... I That I think you're   right... I, I haven't let Davey   go...He was, is my little brother an, and I...'

'- it's understandable....' Dawn received comfort in the gentle sounds of Father Douglas's voice. '...The loss of a loved one takes time...Sometimes it never really leaves.'

'-I know father...' She faltered again as she stared into his eyes. '...You've been a huge help since, his, his.' a tear formed.

Father Douglas got up from the chair, he reached for her and hugged her gently. 'There, there, there... there.'   His old voice sounded cracked, tired yet kind.

They released slowly.

In penumbra, from the lead-lined window, Father Douglas McIntyre Brooded at Dawn's back as she left the tiny church of St Andrews and walked down the path towards church Street. His eyes narrowed as the grandfather clock, in the left-hand corner of the room, ticked the seconds off in dark regularity

Dawn left the small church. She covered her fetching thick chestnut, tousled hair, with the hood of her black fur-lined winter coat. Her sharp clicking shoes, becoming a resonating echo down the narrow concrete path.

How long had it been? Two years, yes two years since Davey's sudden death. His body found in his attic bedroom. No trace of a weapon... nothing found.... Not a fingerprint nor a footprint...despite the blood.... The blood.

She remembered the day too well. The phone call...the police... going to the Mortuary, in Exeter, to view the corpse. His face.... his handsome, youthful, face. Broken. Savaged. Dented with vile, viscous the filled blows. What caused that hate? Why? Davey was an innocent.

She blocked that image. She didn't want to see that dead face. She wanted to see Davey, as she remembered him. The bright cornflower eyes, the brown scraggly mop of hair on top. The pointed chin and the narrow nose beneath. The wry smile or that cheeky grin. White teeth. Smiles and laughter...Yes...Smiles and laughter. Then there was a return of loss and the sudden stab of heartache that came with it.

His loss brought the end to her family. She was all alone. Alone with nothing but the dry crusty church; and the crumbling faces of the   parishioners for company. Most of whom, it had to be said, or, at least considered, were unable to try to resolve, either her anger or her frustration. No, she corrected herself, there were two. Father Douglas, who had listened, given support and occasionally prayed with her and, of course, Dorothea…Doretha…Why hadn't she mentioned Dorothea to Father Douglas? after all, it was her funeral today.

Dorothea's cracked face and tired eyes shone. Another pang came. As she walked towards the village shops, her forest green eyes with their own crow's feet, became misty. Perhaps …perhaps I'm afraid to…. Though that's silly…She looked at her watch. 10:35… time enough for a tea in the Cake house before the funeral-

There was a sudden very loud rasping "Caw". A Crow suddenly flew past her head. Its wings clipped her hood. The sudden sound brought her out of herself. She looked up, absorbing the scene. She shuddered violently. The sky was becoming dark with storm and something else… Crows had slowly begun to gather.

"The cake house" can only be described as artisan. Away went the 60's style greasy joe, after the old "Bridgeton Café" owners moved to Exeter -or so she had heard via the village gossip-. Now the old place had a late Victorian feel. The newly added arched windows had a selection of pastries and breads next to a large heavy oak counter. The old greasy cream walls had been painted with a mixture of Chartreuse and olive green; also, the tired, chipped plastic counter at the back had been removed to make way for more tables. Instead, rough wooden steps at the back of the café, ascended into the secret recesses where, behind a newly painted white door, the new owners could be heard clattering cups and plates to fill their orders. In short, Dawn approved. Besides the tea was very nice and so was the Carrot Cake. She forked off a corner of the crumbling cake onto her stainless-steel fork, and tasted the morsel. A slight twinge of pleasure filled her mouth and then her stomach.

'-Are year going' to Doretha's funeral? I 'ear the' 'ole village will be there'

The voice caught her off guard. It was Elizabeth Ackerson, though Dawn recalled she liked to be called "Dizzy" due to her liking for wine at Three Arms. She had the ruddy face to prove it.

Dawn smiled and looked down into her cup of steaming earl grey. 'yes…yes, I intend to.'

'-Thud's going' to be a huge wake at the' Arms if your coming?'

'-I might…it, it depends.'

Dizzy stared at her. The word "depends" were perceived

as a look of bewilderment upon her round face, who'd not like to go to the Arms?   To defend herself from the onslaught that would inevitably infer, if she refused, Dawn quickly added: 'I, I have a distant cousin   coming for tea. He has some information about Davey... so ...he... said.'   It was a lie. But convincing enough to sound true.

   Dizzy looked sadly down. There was a clatter of plates and a murmur of voices. 'Losing' Davey was tough for us all. Many o' us looked to him, fir, year know...Even though I'm new, Davey helped me with' his ways.... Worse than losing a doctor that.' With a sad smile Dizzy stood to leave. 'Well, I best be going', got a mountain to do a 'fore funeral.'

   As she rose, there was a sudden sharp clatter, crash and a hideous screech at the window.   The clientele stared towards the front of the shop; just as the middle pane exploded inwards

   Glass splinters shattered and scattered.
 The cake house became silent. People stared in disbelief A crow stood in the broken window frame. The   narrow beak bobbed, the wings   flapped aggressively.   It Cawed, raising its head as it did so.   Another Crow came, Then another, and another.

   They stood there. Looking in at the people sitting at their tables aggressively claiming their demesne; their heads motionless. Their three lobed eyes black blinking, greasy grey black. All three stared directly at Dawn.

   Then suddenly they rose. One at a time, they circled inside the shop. Flying low, scratching at the heads of the clientele as they did so. Cutting the soft skin with their razor sharp talons. With a squeal, Dizzy ducked, as one attacked her hair. While another went for an old gentleman sitting by the entrance; as the third, once it had completed its circuit, stood on the counter staring at Dawn. Blinking its black eyes. Then they flew out, one at a time and were gone.

   The following silence was numbing.
   '-Me god's' said one.
    '-That be bad. Said another.
    A third silently wept in shock.
   'I'm   sorry I have to go.' Dawn said to nervously to nobody. She stumbled as she made her way out of the buzzing room and onto the high street. She looked up at the slow gathering dark clouds, and the   truculent rustling of feathers that was gathering in the wind. Slowly she crossed the high street and followed   the old red wall as it descended and then rose a sharply into middle distance; where the medieval block tower of St Andrews church, and the fingers of the old yew trees could be glimpsed.

   In the gathering storm, the assemblage of mourners,

wrapped black against the rain, seemed to her, disembodied the darkening light. Everything began to unravel into unreality. Suddenly, a westerly tore down the street, making the trees rustle and the gathering crows call out in rasping CAW's; and as they called out. Suddenly, for no reason that she could fathom, Dorothea appeared in her mind.   -I have some news, some news about Davey… listen, listen, Dawn Listen!' Dawn fought against the image; thrusting it from her mind. 'Come on Dawn! Hold it together!' The words failed to work. She had reached the church now and with that a deeper anxiety began to fester inside her.

   During the summer, these haphazard heaps of fragmented stone, ravaged and twisted by age, had almost been lost amongst the tall pointed brown stalks of the wild grasses. They had become home to blue winged butterflies and the plump bumble bees, whom floated about them with spectral abandon; around the shadows of the ancient gnarled and twisted oak tree's, who with their lush green leaves, looked down upon the stones with kind friendly faces. Their branches, open arms, giving the appearance protection to this now long departed congregation.

   However, in the dark, brought about by the season's change, and the strangeness of the day, came the twisted things. The old stones were now riddled with Verdigris. They were homes to plump shiny hairless spiders; whose over-long spindling legs took a careful stroke, over the aged copper bold fronted letters; or covered the stone creases, with gossamer, to hide the names of interred. Leaving, in their stead, pale pearls of moisture gathering in tiny cold blue droplets.

    While the naked trees, broken backed and saw toothed, heaved as they leaned over; ready for revenge…It was as if… Dawn thought… as if… the long-interred dead had come to welcome her dear, dear, dead friend, with both savage triumph and hideous laughter.

   She looked down as she made her way towards the heavy faced pall-bearers, around the finely polished rose-wood casket. Looking towards her right, she saw Father Douglas who –after greeting a couple of the mourners- slowly began to limp towards her, across the brown damp grass.   There was a sharp screeching sound followed by a 'click, click' and a rasping reaching 'Caw…caw.' It made her jump and look around. Upon one of the aged grave-stones rested another crow. Only this was the biggest that she had ever seen. it's' sinewy, scaled three toed talons, made a nerve-shredding gravelly scraping sound, as it extended its long pointed claws upon the crumbling stone for support. It let out another rasping 'Caw'; as it aggressively bobbed its head, then stretched and throbbed its large shiny black wings in a sudden sharp move. It made her jump back a little. The crow called out once more; and from above, came a reply.

She looked up to see another crow, just as huge as the first, slowly curl down from the grey spectral sky, to settle upon another of the broken grey-brown stones directly in front of her. Then another and another and another. They stared at the growing congregation blackly. Their eyes, a black pale glistening slick, flicked up once... twice... then slowly one final time, to stare with alien malign intensity.

Dawn felt nervous. They're looking at me... I know it...I can feel their cold eyes burning into me. . It's' as if they're absorbing me...I don' want to be absorbed... taken   by these creatures.

'I'm not one of you!' The desperate words fell from her mouth as a bitter, half meant, prayer. She shuddered, as the creatures stared. Then, came an answer from their cold, dark world. A world that she could almost touch; for the crows called out in unison and they were calling out to her. 'Dawn Shaw... Dawn Shaw... CAW' click, click, 'CAW, CAW... CAW!'

She could feel the world begin to sink in upon her, as she heard her name again and again and again. So, she buried herself into the darkly dressed congregation around her. A steady drumming rain, fell upon the casket with the staccato of a rat, tat tat, that was then hidden by rumbling thunder, that she felt flow right through her. The drumming, the murmurs' cawing of the crows. The tapping of the coffin lid. She searched herself for an answer. One eventually came. But not from her.

'Murder...' he word was whispered by Dorothea week ago. 'Murder... they say, though the police cannot prove it. They think it's-'

She suddenly spins violently back towards the on-coming crowd, to again see the face of Father Douglas who was standing before her.

'Are you okay Dawn?'

'-Yes... yes...' Dawn smiled and looked down. 'It's, it's the bird's.'

'-I... I didn't know that you suffered from Ornithophobia...' came the mild reply; and as an aside he con 'It's called a murder you know.' At that he chuckled to himself.

'-What is?'

'-why a gathering of Crows. It's a murder... not an apt setting for a churchyard really.'

He stared down at Dawn gently. His moist oval eyes glistening '...Rather...' but he didn't finish what he was saying. Instead he simply looked down, his aged face, pensive, before he changed the topic.

'-you and Dorothea were friends?'

'- Yes...' she faltered and looked down, as a tear began to form. '... We were very close. I was the last one to- '

'Oh, you were? I, I didn't know that. Yes. we never-

'But he was suddenly cut short. As suddenly out of the gloom came a wail like that of a small child. The congregation stared up. Suddenly a huge black object plummeted from the broiling sky. The congregation stepped back aghast as a huge crow slammed into the coffin lid with a violent thud. The crowd moved away from the coffin as the black beast lay prone. Its eyes gouged out. Its wings outstretched. Its head twisted over its wing in a dark parody of the Christ himself. It lay motionless upon the green wreath and the coffin lid. Its blood, dark steaming out as it streamed from the dead bird, which slid down like slow treacle towards the open grave. For a moment, there was silence. Even the crows had stopped cawing. Then with the strength of some unseen and terrible force; the crow began to move, and, as a harbinger, it blindly lifted itself and flew directly at Dawn's face. Dawn gasped and held back a scream, as the blind bloody crow caught her hood. Father Douglas slammed the bird away with a strike of his hand, just as Dawn started to fall just as Father Douglas reached for her and held her in his arms.

The world twisted away from underneath her feet. She wasn't at the churchyard any more. She was at Davey's two room flat, just above the old Butchers place. Everything was in stark detail. The flowery yellow mottled wallpaper was peeling at the roof join; where black mottled damp patches had started to spread. The red linin curtains were pulled away from the window, to bring sunlight in There was a smell of patchouli oil, to cover the heavier smell of cannabis resin.   On a little table by the door, Ash from an incense stick holder, blended with the overflowing ash in the tray. Along the wall in front of here rested the bed its dirty linen, yet to be washed. Then there were the bookshelves. The little room was filled with books. Books on healing, on magic and the occult. Books scattered on the floor.   Books piled up on the window shelf, books on nature and on herbs. Books. Books. Books.   The other smell here, the strongest of all, was that of an old library.

It was then that she saw, that she was not herself. She had different hands...older hands... a man's hands. And in one of those hands rested a small rubber handled hammer. She was hot. Burning up. She could feel the clammy sense of exertion. She, he, was holding the hammer, tightly. She could feel him. Smell him. But she couldn't see him. She was looking through his eyes into this room. Moreover; she was powerless. Unable to move. Unable to think. It was like being at the cinema. Only more immersive. The monster was in charge. Then the images became kaleidoscopic. Slamming buffeting into one another. Davey moving away. Davey screaming. Davey being pushed to the floor. Davey shouting NO! NO! PLEASE GODS NO! Davey's head suddenly cracking open like an old walnut. Each blow was heard as a hard-cracking crunch as the hammer   slammed down into his skull. Once. Twice. Three times. She screamed but was mute. She could Just to stare at the broken corpse of her brother that rested at her feet.

Suddenly the tiny attic window exploded inward and the huge crow from the coffin returned.   It stood on the window shelf. Looking deep into Dawn's eyes. She was frozen solidly staring. From the centre of the crow's head, the feathers slowly peeled away to reveal a final terrifying third eye. The eye became larger and larger and larger. Somehow, she didn't know how, she turned away to see her reflection in the mirror on the dresser behind her.

But she didn't see herself.

It was Father Douglas who glared back at her. Douglas her friend. His face a mask of murderous rage. His hands soaked in warm blood. His eyes, wide and as black as midnight. Suddenly and with a savage yell he reached out for her.   NO!

There was darkness and in the darkness, she could sense swirl of black wings. Then a burst of iridescent colour, dazzling to her eyes. The world twisted away once more, then returned. Only this time, she was back in St Andrews Churchyard... only it wasn't winter.... The sky had a strange golden hue. She felt a gentle summer breeze on the nape of her neck. Butterflies darted about the stems of grass as plump bumble bees, rich with pollen bobbed about. The air was clear. Light was everywhere. It even emanated from the old grave stones. More importantly, there was Davey. Davey smiling, Davey reaching out and in her arms, once more...The Davey she knew and loved.

'-Oh Davey... my little one. Davey... Davey come here.'

And he did come. He reached her and gave her a hug and held her tight. Then he took a step back.

'-You're going wake up soon Dawn... but it's okay... you hear me... its' okay.' Dawn smiled and stroked his face. He smiled once, the glint in his eyes shining and then he was gone; turned into a glitter of mist, lost upon the warm summer breeze. That sped up into the golden apple of the sun.

Then there was darkness and then pain. When she came

around she found herself in the warm surroundings of the church hall. Father Douglas was standing just a few feet from her.

'So…your back…' He began gently. '… You know you gave everybody quite a scare…'

Dawn tried not to look nervous. she lay there as he continued '…If it wasn't for the fact that I know of your condition- '

'-Condition?'

'-Epilepsy…' He smiled gently. Reassuringly, like an old father. An old friend.

'- But…I, I don't have epilepsy.'

'Oh, my dear, but you do. You had a very nasty seizure just now. I expect its' because of the loss and the stress of it all. Seizures can happen at any time you know…' he smiled distantly, '…I've seen it before…' he looked down; and away from her. '…in another parish.' The voice slipped. It became dark. Apprehensive. Then he smiled; before kneeling beside her a tick flicked his right eye.

'You spoke… just now…'

'-Did I?'

'Yes…' he said gently as slowly knelt closer; his face slowly turning menacing. '…you kept calling out Davey's name… 'as he knelt next to her, '…I didn't know you shared his faith…' he stroked her hair. 'It was the crows that gave it away you see… the gathering of crows.' He smiled. His lips wet. Spittle curled down the left side of his mouth, in a line of drool. 'I had to get you inside, away from the crowds, people will talk you know, and   I can't have that…' he smiled. '…people talking… it's not proper. It's not proper at all.

She stared at him, knowing with a sense of fatality, the reality of her vision. Her face became a blank mask before she replied

'Why did you do it?

'-Do what?'

'Kill him… kill Davey… why…?' Betrayal crumbled out of her face.

'-I, I didn't kill Davey…' he began his eyes gentle, serene, his jowls giving him the appearance of an aged baby. '…My dear… I saved him… I saved him from himself. It was an act of kindness… the best thing in fact'

'-what, what about Dorothea?' Was that an act of kindness too?

'Poor Dorothea…' Douglas shook his head sadly. 'She had a stroke, bought about by years and years of sustained alcohol abuse. She fell and that was that… Old people die you know…It's a sad reality.' As he spoke Douglas came closer and closer to Dawn as she lay prone on the floor. He knelt by her side.

Slowly she tried to get to her feet, but Douglas pinned her down in almost a vice-like grip 'It's sad...you see... I thought you, you were different... From him...from Davey.... I thought that you... held to the true faith...' His eyes became mirthless and malign. '...But now...' his hands became heavy upon her, as his voice began to growl '... I have to save you, from the same fate as him.' With trembling fingers, he stretched out with his hands. They surrounded Dawns' throat. He began to tighten. To squeeze. As he squeezed, he bellowed with spittle spouting from his lips: - 'THOU SHALT NOT SUFFER A WITCH TO LIVE!'

***

In the sky above the tiny hall where the priest knelt clutching at Dawn's throat, for one final time the crows began to gather. They rose as one single entity into storm riddled sky ; a huge spiral that swirled about itself in frightening ecstasy. Their wings, as black fingers outstretched out upon the rising wind, that hissed and sighed in slow soft whispered measures.

Together as one they circled above the hall and then above the old village, higher and higher up into the wild mists of the rolling clouds above they flew. Hidden, within the mists of the clouds, in sweeps they flew in a circle and as they flew within the circle, raindrops began to form and then to fall. And as their made rain fell, the crows knew that it was time to depart; So, from this a silent sacred unknown pilgrimage, they left. Some flew to the north, some to the south, some to the east. Leaving a chosen few to fly to the west; carrying with them the souls of both Davey and Dawn, to the ancient land of the elder Gods, and where, so it is said, that the sun and the moon embrace

Cyclops

"...the cyclops makes monsters of us all" Roy Braithwaite
(taken from a taped recording made by his Niece Geraldine
Braithwaite 1987)

You- you know the story of, of the Odyssey?   The book is a
favourite o' mine ever since I read it as a child. One o' my
favourite parts in the book, then an' now, is the story of the
Cyclops. You know, 'ow, ow he'd poked that titan in the
eye? "Oo's done that?" bellows the Cyclops! His face all, all
red, wit' blood, his mouth an open 'ole wit' tombstone teeth.
Oh, 'ow he shouts wit' gusto. Spittle fillin 'is beard   as 'e
staggers about scratching his, his fingers 'gains'' the dirt
walls of the cave. "I'll have you yet!"   He stomps
    "I 'ave" shouts the brave Odysseus. "An' what's your
name then?"   Bellows the blinded Titan. "My name..."
Odysseus shouts: "...is no man!" ...So off the Cyclops goes...
blindly staggering' about in pain, bewailing that: "No man
has taken me eye out." As a child, the Cyclops terrified me.
He'd be there, under me bed wanting to eat me bones up,
as I grew up I put such childish things away. I started to
see the funny side o' it. 'Ow the titan shouted to his mates,
or   replied "No man? oo did it then?" But then the great
war came an' that brought the cyclops back.   Yer see...I
know the cyclops is real... I know... for I saw 'im... I saw 'im
at Fromelle. An for me Fromelle changed everything. Yer
see, I I also fell in love.
    My War? What was it like? What do you mean? How I
felt when war broke out? Or later?
     For me, the outbreak of hostilities was a, was a bit of a-
blank. I know it sounds funny to say it like, but it's' true. I
was 18 at the time yer see, so I didn't think much about it,
at the start. I was a prim an' proper clerk for a cloth
manufacturer back then. To me, the thought of signing up
was... well it was, was simply a 'oliday away from the daily
grind...made doubly exiting' as I was going' away with me
pals. The realization of it...well... that was a little different.
     The thin' that stounds out now, as I look back at it,
were the smells; for war 'as a a smell all its own...There was
the, the smell of unwashed men: a sour stink, made worse
by suffering and fear. Then there was the smell of that itchy
and, it 'as to be said, mostly damp woolen green-khaki
uniform. Add to this the, the stench of ammonia; made
worse by the rats, the shit. There was the stench of trench-
foot: Just rotting limbs in wet leather boots. The, the
stench of bad breath of loose teeth in rotting gums, and of

vinegar and bicarbonate of soda.

Most of all, there is the smell unique to war: the smell of blood, blood swirlin' in cold stagnant water. It was a smell hard to, to, put into words. I know that i'll never forget it.

Then there were the sights. I doubt I will ever forget the, the cuts; in the soil whose tops were weighted with' sandbags, whose sides were shored up with slowly rusting corrugated iron and; an' whose floor was made up of busted, planks of broken wood. Whose bottom was Constantly filled with' a line of muddy water, no matter the season.

The green, brown dugouts were deep too We were like moles there, scurrying' around in the near dark warming ourselves as best we could around candles in the dark, where black frost bitten hands and noses glowed in the soft yellow candlelight. All of that I witnessed, and more...But... there is an impression like, that we spent our entire time buried wit bombin' That's simply not so. It was, however erratic, we could 'ave been there for as short as a day or as long as a week, depending upon bombardment. The trenches worked, if you can call it that, on a rotation basis yer see. So, the trenches themselves weren't our 'ome's, as such, that were our tents, a quarter mile back, However, we were on permanent alert, in case the enemy breeched our defensive line

To best describe it, is like saying' we 'ad either days or 'ours of sheer bloody terror, followed by days or 'hours of sleep if your luck was in, or days of blinding boredom, or duties if not. No, it wasn't all doom a gloom, as the poets as Owen and McRae, would 'ave you believe. Fun was to be 'ad away from the trenches...fun and love... But, but that's not to say, that, that their words weren't true, they were...they were.

My battalion? I was in the 61st regiment, 2nd west Midland brigade- based from Dudley, a town situated in the heart of the Black Country. A place I'm proud to call me 'ome. See that picture there? That's us. the fella in the middle of the front row? That's me... I, I joined my regiment through the "Pals" connected to me position at the factory. At that time, the biggest "Pal", the one who we all looked to at the start of it all, was Harry Pendleton... but...but... you know... it's funny how people an friendship's change...'ow real faces shine, when the Cyclops rises.

Before the war, I envied Harry Pendleton... The light in his forest green eyes, his confidence... on good days...in my mind's eye...I still, still see that Harry, jaunting down Blackheath high street. His, his straw boater, sat on his head, set at that quirky angle, to hide that ginger crop, we all knew he hated so much. I remember his shaped moustache, above those sardonic thin lips...That's on good days...On the bad days....when I can 'ear the blasting bombs, I don't see that confident man. I see 'ow the cyclops remade Harry. How it had paled his, his skin; drawn it; mottled, muddied and sunken it. I see 'ow the confidence had gone, 'ow his cornflower eyes seemed to stand out, near feral, nervously glittering' in near buried dark sockets. Right now, I can see 'im as he stands by the ladder, quaking.... waiting...waiting of' the whistle to take us over the top. So, as your see, the poets were right, men, you see, they don't want to die. Not for something' that they don't believe in, and by the end, not many men believed in it anymore. On either side. On those days' I also think of Jack. It helps your see.

See that fella there? that's Jack...Yep... Jack Wattyl his name was.... Jack... I never met a man like that 'afore or since... 'eye, never was a part of us pals were Jack. Jack was what 'arry called "an add on" ... I recall 'ow 'arry used to mock his tatty clothes an' his background. Yer see, Harry coming from a middle-class background, used to think 'ee was something of a man of the world, and that meant he 'ad a-a dis-dis-dislike of the likes of Jack from the start.

At 'ome, Jack battled from job to job. Unwanted 'an unwelcome. Disowned. Many were the times ee'd ask if I know of any positions at the mill goin' I did try once or twice. But 'arry...ee'd made it clear that 'ee wasn't welcome. An I, I was too full of Harry to know the difference. You see Jacks, Jacks face? In the picture? All rat like? You know, narrow, with a pointed nose an' thin narrow lips? He doesn't look like much, but 'ee was a gentleman, Though the picture doesn't show it. Underneath that cap, 'ee also 'ad thick mound of glossy wavy coal black 'air, the pic doesn't show host forest green eyes that seemed always this side of weary. Not mirthless... or sneaky... just weary. That was Jack. The home lad.....Its funny, you knpw...The Cyclops made Jack. For jack knew a truth about the war, He knew that it made us all equal. There were no airs o' graces in the trenches. Just us men a fear an' the bombs. I got to knew 'im really well in the end and by that in a friendlier way; of' ee saved my life yer see.

It Tow-er, the last week of the Somme, an it was as close to Hell as I had seen with these eyes. For a full week, we were under heavy bombardment, wit' no relief. Day and night, the shells came upon us. Our dugouts crumbled under it. They would fall flat on top 'o us and we'd have to dig ourselves, and our comrades out. Once or twice that week, we'd find them. Their mouths and noses clogged with dirt, their skin sallow in the half light. suffocated. That or...or smashed to a pulp.

By the end of that week, we were near hysterical. Fights broke out, as we fought like the fuckin' rats to get away. I recall fists and fingers scratching' into my face, as we tried to get out. Then in came the C.O. and the sergeant His face. raw red. His eyes near out of their sockets. He shot twice into the air. At which one of us leapt at him. Though ee was bayoneted by the sergeant. Then The C.O shot two men at point blank range I the head. The bullets crumpled their skulls. Blood burst out.

We would have turned on that bastard, were it not for that fuckin' sergeant, whose machine gun was pointed at us. We all took a step back. Both guns were trained on us. I felt the tension rise. If anyone raised a rifle, we would be shot or for the firing squad. We simply stood there. Facing each other as the real enemy, as the bombs rained down upon us on the ground shook. I don't know 'ow long we stood there like that. It could 'ave been a minute or a few second's. Time is fluid in situations like that.

Then there was a huge "whump" in sound, followed by a numbing. My ears popped and the ground slid under me feet....The darkness... The silence...the numbness ... at first it was tranquil.... But as time moved on I realized I was conscious and I couldn't breathe. ... I couldn't breathe...there...was...this...oppressive weight I felt ...I felt...like I had died and gone to Hell. Fingers reached for me. Talons clawed, Then, suddenly, I was pulled back an' then air, stinking foul air, filled my lungs... an as my vision cleared there was Jack grinning.

'No Blighty wound on you then, sad that.' He quipped.

We hugged. That was the first time... I felt...like...like I was reborn. I never forgot that

***

I first found out that Jack had an "operation" as he called it, about a month later during one of our rest furloughs from the front line. I had just finished my lunch, which was "soup" though it were poor meat that formed a rubbery magma in my mouth; it blended sickly with the rice and pasta, with the cooked potatoes, that blended together to this thin gruel; that was insipid and lacked any vitamins or decent vegetables for that matter.

I have to say here, that It was only after it ended I heard

'ow the distribution of food to the front-line canteens was a joke...simply because of the huge task in hand. Yer see, word never, or rarely, got back to the kitchens about troop advancement, this was since it was supposedly secret. This meant that the supplies intended for a certain detachment, would only reach their destination after that detachment had departed. So many did without food at all, this led to a huge black market in food distribution...Yer, well, anyway, I, I sat in the mess tent, pouring' over which o' me tabs, I was goin to smoke, when jack, -'oo was sitting across from me- asks me if I want a pack of players. Fags in the trenches were rationed, so if you liked a smoke and couldn't keep control of your ration, you were fooked. I remember looking' at the large stubs a thinking' well I'm fooked. I I looked up an' I must 'ave had a face on me, as Jack simply smiled.

An hour later we were 'bout a quarter- mile away, sitting almost out of full sight of the dirt track road that led to the front

I remember It was a warm clear day an I was on lookout, faking' rest, with my back leaning' on a, a large part blasted flint walled barn. The doors, I remember, that they had red paint which was, was peeling off and blistering' off revealing the, the pale sun bleached wood underneath. In the distance, I could hear the thumping' of the shells and to my right, I could just make out between the green line avenue of majestic trees, the clumping thump of soldiers an' horse trotting' or marching' either towards the bombs or away from them...T'was a Thump...thump...thump like a heavy heartbeat

We were sitting there Jack to the left to me, wit' this this big bag he was carrying'. I 'ad finished my second to last stub an' was crumbling the fag into the dry grass an dirt. I watched the blue smoke curl up from the green grass as I stubbed the tab out. Churning the earth an with it feeling a sharp pain rise up me arm as the orange embers of the fag burnt me thumb

'What you think about all this then?' He knew what I was thinking

'The war?' he quipped. 'Ee grinned at that; then sighed as 'ee lay back, propping' his feet up on the knapsack 'ee'd brought wit' him. His soft green eyes shone as he rubbed his two-day stubble. Then Ee took off his cap and welsh ragged his oily black hair. His narrow jaw an long nose glistened in the early afternoon light.

'Well, there's money to be made, an when it's all over
   '-yer think it will be? Over I mean?'
   '-One day sure.
   '-Yer think, it be a different world? A better one?'

'Won't be the same! That's true enough. No more Kings. The Russians revolted, that's good for the likes of us. If we can do the' same?'

I smiled, closing my eyes, feelin' the warmth o the sun onme face imagining' him starin' into me, wit his huge green beautiful eyes... Yes...I did think, that, at that moment, there could be a better world.

'It was a moment like no other, for or since. I stared at him feeling elated scared exited and a host of other feeling's I had never felt towards another man before.

'I'd like a world where we could be free to love.

I recall there was a pause then, I felt my tongue heavy as expectation rose in me. The feeling's that rose, scared me. My words blundered on.

'I I never what that, what I mean is I- '

Jack giggled, his voice gentle. '-forget it'

I still recall that burning fag. I recall 'ow the blue smoke came from the green grass in spirals, as the brown dried tobacco an' the blue grey ash, an' what was left of the white paper disintegrated into the soil. I felt the sun bake me legs... it shone just over the tree line

'I just wanted to say- 'but me words were cut short as I felt someone standing' in me light.

I looked up an opened an eye, to see what was goin' on an' there stood this youngish lad with a nasty scar down his right cheek.

Jack gets up then an ee say's "Keep an eye out Roy" then, then he shakes this lads hand and says

'So what you go to trade

'-Managed to get a nice scotch from the officer's mess.'

Jack smiles that smile

'-What you you, you w-want for it?' stammered out Scarface.

'The usual.' Was Jack's dry sounding' reply.

'-Fuck off!' Scarface retorts his vowels rich and deep. 'You fuckin' know how hard it is to peddle that? If I am caught-

'-You're not, not back at the front for a, another couple of days, an, from what I hear- "Jack's grin was what I remember then

'-yeah? Good aunt that like you Jack. Bending' over for favours.

'-You got to do what you got to do to survive.

Scarface looked sullen then.

'-come on don't be cunt.' Jack grinned and flashed a small bottle of something' from the bag 'ee 'ad.

Scarface, sighed at that and shrugged his shoulders 'Four cartons.'

'-Three' Jack came back quickly. I smiled

Scarface looked up at the sky and then gave a small nod before taking Jacks fag; then silently took a drag, to sign the deal.

'Stay here.' Jack says. Then both men went inside the old flint barn and out of sight; an I kept me head down, faking' sleep, ready to move if I see an officer. Tension grew in every second. Yer see, if we were caught then it would be field punishment number one. Which would mean being staked out in no-man's land till yer bought it.

Once or twice, I saw an officer look. But none came over. Five minutes. Ten. Fifteen passed. I was getting nervous; I can tell you. Finally, an with much relief, the man with the scar and then Jack came out of the barn, without the bag.

Jack 'ad his wiry smile on his narrow face and a light shone in his eyes. He chucked me a pack of players that I nervously stuff into my tunic pocket

'That's for standing duty.' He said, as we made our way back along to the field entrance towards the men an' the horses stomping up the dirt

'-What's that all about then?

'Stashing up for a rainy day.' Was all ee said, as we put our 'ear's down an' joined the battle-weary lines 'evading back to barracks.

That night, when all was quiet, I felt a tap on my shoulder. I woke a turned to see Jack smiling' at me.

'I've got something' for yer.' He said gently. A win' 'hat ee gave me a letter.

'If anything,' 'appends to me, you must open this. But not before.'

With that, he gently kissed my forehead, a slipped into the night once more. I held that letter tightly in my hand, till morning' came.

$$***$$

If the Cyclops had taken a human form, amongst us, it would have taken the shape of Sargent Brennagan. Brennagan was both a crook and a bastard in equal measure. So much so, that it t'was hard to know when one ended and other began. I told you of how 'ee treated us during the last week of the Somme? Well,'ee, like I survived that, though 'ee never trusted me again. Unlike that fuckin C.O.

Brennagan 'ad this gruff, cracked voice, that burst out of his wide mouth, that contained these black and green teeth. His cheeks were ruddy and his sapphire eyes, which were widely set a had this permanent gaze of contempt, glittering from them. It was clear that ee 'ated everyone below 'im, less there was cut in it for 'im.

Three weeks 'ad passed since the flint Barn trade off. An we were both slurpin' our tea. He slowly passed me a letter under the table, which I took, just as Brennagan came into the tent.

'-Gentlemen, he began as ee scowled at us 'You lads... have been given a special assignment.' There was a viscous grin on his face
Us sir?' I was always polite to my superior officers.

Yes, you...laddie.' He hissed. 'you're to go to Fromelle, there is a commanding officer, a Major Sweet, you are to support the Major in' doing what the officer tells you to do...ARE WE CLEAR?'

We stood up and saluted; and with, with his viscous stare bearing on our backs, he watched us as we made our way to Fromelle. I recall it was a 'ot day, made even 'otter by the uniforms we wore, but, that walk, well, we coulda' been on 'oliday. We walked slowly; the seeds of the long ochre grass were blown' in the wind. The summer trees rustled, knocking out the, the sound o' the near distant artillery shells.

The air was full of nutmeg...funny that. The odd things that come to mind from solong ago, why I could smell nutmeg,I shallnever know, but I could that day.

'What's that letter you gave me for.' I say.

'It's a surprise.' He grinned, as he looked down.

I stared at his profile. Unsure what to say or do. This letter was a new twist to our friendship...which...was had become more than that, I must say.

We were, I am not ashamed to say, very fond of each other by then. Twas the Cyclops that brought us together, I was sure of it, an together, we were going to come out of it. I was sure in the knowledge of that too.
 But this letter... It was like stating he feared the worst.

'You can't say that...Say that you're goin' to die.'

'-It's just in case.'

 - 'I'll be there for you.'

Ee took my hand gently. And in that I felt conflict and strength in equal measure.

'I know you.' He said gently

With that I smiled.

An hour later, we were on the outskirts of Fromelle.

$$***$$

There isn't much to Fromelle, its really just This this line of trees, towards an old farmstead. Oaks and birches slide off towards the west. The odd painted house with large windows, like you might see in an early Van Gogh By the time we reached the place, the sun was a huge orange ball that that settled in the dusk. But even in the dim light, I could see in front of us, a huge pile of bodies.

The men …the bodies…were not only from our side…they were Germans Turkish too… All men…all equal… ranked like ourselves…The pile was three feet high…. and ten feet across I had never before or since, seen so many dead in one place before.

Major Sweet didn't smile or shake our hands. His voice carried the, the veneer of the aristocracy, that, in the recent months I 'ad come to loathe. Yet, there was something else in this man.

'Bury them here!' his spoke tartly. 'There is to be no trace of them? do you understand?

He stared at us. His skin ruddy, his amber eyes smarting. I could see that he hated this, place. Moreover, hated to do this, hated everything about this and most of all he, he hated ordering' us to do it.

'Sir, why are- '

'-That's classified.' The reply was stark

'-But- 'Jack's face paled.

'-If you fail, or refuse, you will be shot and added to the pile. Do you Understand? DO YOU UNDERSTAND!'

I still remember 'ow ee bellowed that out. This was fear talking' nowt else.

What had happened here and why was this being done? We never knew, and to this day I still don't know. All I knew was that we 'ad no choice… we dug…We dug and we dug and we dug.

I recall the heavy weight of the spade in my hand and the blisters that burst that soon became callouses; an as the, the night drew in, the cold. The bitter cold. Around us were the dead. The brave dead. Piled up, like, like stiff dolls. The English khaki, the German blue grey, French Blue Serge, they were all rounds us. then I stared at their faces…Their odd faces, the alien looking' skin… everything piled up…piled up like stacks of rotten meat, that the flies spat on to liquefy munch and fuck on. But that, that, that didn't scare me. I'd seen bodies. What scared me were the eyes. Or, the lack of them.

Hundreds of men, from all sides of this terrible war, lying in an unknown grave with empty sockets, an amongst the corpses were…their ghosts…. I could feel them tug at me, pull on me, drag on me, breathe into my heart and want to scream into my ears. I felt their skinless fingers scratch my hands and felt them tug at me feet as I lifted the corpses bloody and broken and placed them into this newly dig shallow grave. What could have taken so many lives from both sides and to do this to them?

T'was then that I realised a half truth. A terrible monster

had done this did this. Not men. T'was   the Cyclops, from
under my bed, finally getting his revenge against Odysseus
all those centuries ago. I could feel his presence and see his
single furious eye in the moonlight; oppressively baring
down on me. His teeth -tombstones. His drool, at the sight
of this feast filling his thick pubic beard rich wit spittle and
blood as ee feasted upon the souls around us.

   I heard mocking' in the skies and looking' up I
remember seeing' that though the moonlit cloud the
fingers of crow's wings, circling, circling, circling' overhead.
They call it a murder of crows.

   Silently We dug and we dug, we carried and we carried
we stood over and we bowed our heads. How did they all
end up here? All alone hundreds of miles from home
Separated from their families and friends? These empty
eyed people? Perhaps better men than me will be able to
put a reason to it. I see simply war. There was no good or
bad, or right or wrong, or an us or a them. It was the
Cyclops.

   It was total night when we 'd finished. I was numb with
the cold. Numb with the task and sick to my stomach. In
the light of a yellow lamp I looked at Jack an ee looked at
me

   Our faces were stark.

   We both thought it, and our eyes welled with the
immensity of it. Then, we did something that I am not
ashamed of. We kissed.   We reached for each other and
kissed long and hard. We hugged and held each other,
needing each other, but not wanting each other. Right
there and then, during all this death I fell in love. I fell in
love with him.

 A month later Jack died no man's land.

   I was behind him. I saw through my gas mask amid the
exploding' shells, the cracking soil and the pale of ghosts
faces. I saw   his body buckle and break as the bullets from
the German machine gun cut into him. But in my mind's
eye,o r I think it were, Its hard to say... I...I saw' im...I saw
the Cyclops, he stood over the enemy trench, his half
naked form wet with sweat and rain...his pubic dark beard
wet wit spittle an wit the blood of the men ee was ripping it
bits...while his eye was the most terrifying thing of all... 'twer
huge large and singular... staring out at, at me through the
mist of the battlefiled with hate and venom. Its veins
distended as it glistened, while from its tombstone mouth.
An It roared! It bellowed! It screamed. I looked away,
terrified at the sight, wanting this eternity to be over. Then
I saw Jack... I saw Jack run his body dartin' 'and divin' as
slow explosions ripped the earth around us...Then it

happened... I gasped and raged as I saw his body buckle and then and there I realized the truth of those men in that unmarked grave. This war was never going to end and if it did, it would not end with a victor. This was a killing field. A means to an end. A cull of innocents. I screamed as the shells went off around me I mud and blood slapped my face We were fodder for them!

   I vaguely recall that I charged over to Jack as bullets flew about me. I screamed my silence through my mask; as I fought through the barbs of wire. Then there was darkness, darkness and a dizzy thumping sound in my head. I thought that I was going to die, I felt separate; a distance from myself. Then I, I awoke in a field hospital, a mile from the front

   To my right a nurse, I'll never know her name, was tending my wounds. On the other side of me was the Captain from the burying detail. He looked down at me, and with a tear in his eye and he smiled.

   '-You got your Blighty wound. 'was all he said. Then he walked away. So, they brought me home. That was all of twenty years ago today. I hear they are calling it the "the war to end all wars" now perhaps it will be, though something tells me, it's the tip of the iceberg. For my solace, I have the letter that Jack gave me. Inside the contents read thus:-

   My dearest Roy,

What I must say, you already know. Our love, that can bear no name, will be forever in my heart. Know, that I loved you from the start, and protected you when and where I could. I fear that without me, you might be lost in some hideous action. However, if you manage to survive this terrible war, or end up with a Blighty wound, before you leave for home, go to the old flint barn, you remember it? and look under the wooden boards in the right-hand corner....There is a chest. Its contents are for you. Use them wisely and well.

My love for you always and forever,

your Jack x

   The ironic thing is that I never managed to read the letter, until I was on the boat, on the way home. I've thought about saving for a ticket to get back and find that old barn. Though I get a feeling that a certain Londoner has made his mark upon it Harry Pendleton and I managed to survive... but ee is the only one of our old pals that has. I hear from him in letters and the occasional post card. He wants to meet up. But I doubt I will. After all, I hate those bloody boater hats.

A cold October evening

As I return to the broken porch broken porch on this wild October evening, the old farmhouse, rests with its grey peeling wooden walls and its crumbing out-buildings, yet it looks alien to me. Even though the memories of this place haunt my soul. I look away from the congealed litter, stuffed in the corners by the wind. I look between cracked wooden floorboards, to see the dirt beneath. I stare up and look through the blistered and buckled ceiling of the veranda, up into the house, into the dark of the attic.   I seek sanity. It is an act of desperation. An over ambitious method, that's never worked. The ghost riddled memories crowd upon me, in a cycle of terrifying repetition again and again and again.

On the horizon, whey colored clouds roll over. They ripple over and upon each other, into an envelope of broiling darkness that gathers overhead. Across to my left, along the dark dirt road, that starts by the broken picket gate; I can see the yellow tape close to where I parked my car. "There and no further" the taped line states, with words that even after ten years working with the local cop's I never want to read.

To the right, slowly swaying along the edge of the dark dirt road, stands the large old oak trees. The wild wind whipping, has stripped them of their leaves; their branches are bare. Taught, like old spider's limbs. They groan with the sound of old twisted rope and whisper with menacing hints, discordantly played against the ice rain, that lashes against the dirty and partially broken window panes, with a dark, hollow, drumming. In the growing twilight, their grey bark is full of wrinkled shadow's, making faces, twisted with age and some fathomless cruelty. They slowly turn towards me.

Then I become aware of a strange scratching sound. I look to where the sound was coming from. Though I can't be sure, I feel, deep in my gut, that, whatever it is, it's coming from behind the old barn door. I turn towards the barn. The scratching gnawing sound happens again. Only this time I hear something else; something that sounds disquietingly like the mirthless giggle of a little child. I feel my heart begin to thump heavily in my chest. I take a cautious step forward. There's a clatter. A howl. A low moan. A sudden snapping, cracking of something heavy, stamping hard upon old dried cord-wood.

I pause and hold my breath.

'Hello? Is anyone there?'

I can hear the subtle quake in my voice. I want to call

out his name. But, but, I dare not, dare not speak. I start to shake; as I feel my nerves begin to shred. so, I tried to think about happy times, how once the sun shone warmly and how we four happy children -all boys- ran amongst these farm buildings. The images don't stay. They flee into the shadow. I hear the padding and then the slapping of retreating feet. Once again, my nerves begin to get the better of me.

I stare at the old barn door. Not taking my eyes off it. Seconds pass.

The world becomes dizzy. Colour spots fly in front of my eyes.

Then there is a sudden explosion of noise. I shout a squeal as my   heart rises into my mouth. Suddenly a form; someone... or... something, almost half formed -moving far too quick to get an accurate description- darts from the left, through open broken doorway, then back into the deep dark recesses of the crumbling barn.

I try to take another step. But my feet are frozen solid to the spot. There's something there... I can feel it... feel it's' malevolence staring directly at me. Its hostile animal eyes, full of hate burning into me...chilling me to the bone. I stare, Stare, Stare.

'Mr Freeman?'

I jump at the sound of a voice and suddenly turn.

'Mr Freeman?' this time her voice her voice sounded a little cautious.

'Yes... Richard Marcus Freeman... 'I stare at the petite woman in the tight-fitting grey and navy dress that reveals the right amount of cleavage and calf to keep my interest; so, I smile warmly. She looks about twenty, almost half my age. '...but you can call me Marcus...and you must be... Ms Atherton?' I smile and reach out, with an unsteady right hand.

She takes my hand gently. She feels warm to the touch.

'Mrs Dianna Atherton...'

'Pleased to meet you.' I nod. Her hair is platinum, the color that Munroe wore so well; and it suites her too.

I smile and hold here her eyes for far too long. They're large, round and forest green. A   thought is contained.   A secret touch.

She takes an uncertain step up onto the porch and walks by me, leaving the delicate scent of Channel No 5 in the air as she passes. She walks towards the crumbing entrance.

As she reaches the door, she turns and smiles   then she blushes slightly as she looked away. Pulling her white handbag, that hung from her left wrist, closer to her midriff, before examining the deadbolt.

'I I understand that you were sent here, to Boston, from

,from New York?

I nod.

'Personally I wouldn't have called you in, but, but I've come to understand that you have an "expertise" that, that Detective Sullivan considers useful…'

Her voice sounds direct, forcing me to be more open with her than I want to be. I also hear the cynical slant on the word expertise and try not to let it bother me. But it does.

Yes…' I replied, feeling awkward '…We worked together-

'-yes, yes, he told me, the Etherton case in '63?'

'-He told you?'

My mind went elsewhere. Deep   into a brown, dirty cellar, cluttered with gritty magazines and filled with terror. A pale blue chair, and a man slumped in the chair smiling at me with dead eyes. The black barrelled revolver   pointing directly at my face, and the words "Time to die mother-fucker!" shouted at me in a voice that rolled its way through me like a freight train

I could feel myself shake a little.

'It's supposed to be a-

'Yes, yes, a black file…' her voice sounds strained as she fights with the dead-lock placed on the door. '… Sullivan's an old Hump F- friend. He recommended you when I called him, after I was set up as the investigating officer, once we found… ahh.' it is a sigh of satisfaction as the deadlock slips back, with a thick click '-what we found.'

I heard the mirthless laugher once more, I can't help myself. I turn to stare towards the barn once more; feeling the nape of my neck begin to tingle.

'Well… you better Follow me. '

She pulls a switch-blade from her white handbag, to slice the hidden seal of yellow tape I had seen so many times before. Then after putting   the knife away. There appears a flash light. Its clicked on, before the door is pulled fully open with a slow creak.

Despite the strong smell of corruption, the hall brought back happy memories, of old metal trucks being pushed along black and white tiles, their tippers full of dust and rocks, while the scent of acid sweet lemonade and rich fruity laughter came from the kitchen.

Time slips back as we almost collide.

'Watch your step!'

I look down and take a step back.

The naked body is large. Its yellowing skin is distended abound the abdomen which slowly slithers, writhes and undulates, giving the disturbing appearance of being alive. But…It is alive with those that feed off the dead.   The throat had been ripped out, almost to the point of decapitation. The left side of the face, the nose and the lower jaw, have been gnawed away by a...a...a wild animal...where... where the eyes should have been being...are... two cavernous holes. Glistening maggots slowly writhe, while plump black flies, with large red eyes, angrily buzz in sharp darts about the room.

The smell of death becomes terrifyingly oppressive. My heart thuds sickly in my chest. I want to retch. Nuzzled vomit and bile rises water fills my throat. I gag it back.

Dianna places some Vicks under the nose and along the tip of her top lip. She then gave the small container to me.

'-We received a phone call at, at about four this morning, from a, a person unknown, stating there was - and I directly quote from the call "a cadaver found in suspicious circumstances at the Morrison farm." Cadaver, who says that? Anyhow, two patrol officers found this, taped it up and called it in. I was called out here with Sullivan hour or two ago, he suggested that I call you.... The rest you know.

'You seem to be taking this rather well.' Noting her objectivity.

'My father was a butcher; I'm used to slabs of meat. Rotten or otherwise. 'What do you make of that? Dianna pointed with her torch towards the far hall wall.

Written in blood, were the words Mors! Nex! Angelus Mortis!'it means-

'-I know what it means.' My words are sharp, ice riddles me.

'Look...' I hear strain in her voice, '...when Sullivan told me what happened, I couldn't believe it, I I really couldn't. But, but when he showed me the file-

'-A file you're not meant to see.'

'-You know, I couldn't have bothered...what did you have planned today? Another trip to the Rehab centre? The Church you go to? Even the employment exchange? If you can do what he says you can do-

'There's only one reason that you'd call me. There's only one reason that Sullivan would have even mentioned me at all, and that's because there have been others... Have there been? Other's?'

Dianna tries to talk but falters. She's rolled out of the way.

I can tell you by simply looking in this room that there have been at least another five, all the same M.O, throat gouged, left to bleed out and all   called three weeks after the crime; where were they?   all of them circling this place. Like reference points on a map. I I also bet you can't find any finger prints, foot prints or any fucking thing to suggest that another person has been here. Then there are the words...' I point at the Latin, '...written on the wall.'

She stares at me, I can see she's pissed, but I've had enough, yes she's sexy, but she's a condescending bitch that needs to know what she's up against

'What you want me to do is connect the pieces for you. You want me to...to connect with him... You want me find out what happened. But even if you do know, what I know, you couldn't arrest the killer, because there's no evidence to support your case. You are floundering in the fucking dark with no means of support. But you want this case because of what it will mean for your reputation. What you don't know, or seem to care about, the collateral. How I feel when I do this. I'll tell you something else for free. I was born here. I lived here, in this house, with my family and I know, to a fine holy fuck that if I do this for you, you wouldn't want to know the answer, because the answer will break your soul.

 I kneel by the cadaver, shake my head, and rest my hand just above the undulating chest.

The world begins to spin. Memories collide, explode into half seen images. The four of us in patchwork images of burnt film. Their names Tommy, Steve, Glen. I. Smiles, laughter. I skip in circles in the farm garden, Mum smiling, Dad smiling. A light in the sky, a light so bright that it almost blinds. Mum screaming. My Dad, his face all bloody his eyes wild with fear and hate. Tommy, Glenn Steve lying in a pile. My legs running, running, running in the dark. Cars, I fall. Cars driving almost over me. Lights burning bright and then: laughter, cold, cruel laughter. A hand …scarred…nails like hooks, skin like wet leather, black, black swollen lidless eyes, millions of teeth   in drooling lips Snapping. Coming out at me grasping, scraping. A hot foetid hungry breath longing for my flesh. I feel myself scream.

 I open my eyes, and roughly wipe the tears that are smarting my vision with the arm of my jacket.

A heavy sad sigh fills the air. 'His name, his name was, was Terrance Brangan, he was forty-five years old; he was a father of three girls and a step father to one boy… he was in love with his wife, but he was bored an' looking elsewhere for sexual excitement. He cheated in his mind, but not with his body, he was depressed because his mother died in January, and he had just lost his job at the tannery in Lulworth twenty miles away… he had no other means to support his family…he, he was a, a sad, lonely man, that didn't know the good he was doing… was enough to please the God he feared.' That's the body here.

Dianna looks at me. Her eyes were open wide.

'you want to know the killer? You can't catch the killer. He's going to trap you here, in this place with me, for all eternity... You laugh? You don't know time... twenty years ago, something came here.... it took my mum, dad and brother's.... It made me run.... The police thought my dad went mad, and he did, sort-of... But what that... thing left me with, was a gift. And what a gift... The gift of being able to see the last thoughts of the dead. It's not a blessing... it's a curse... and the thing that gave it to me is here...in the barn.... But you have to understand...' I feel a sad smile curl on my lips, 'That We can' t reason with it, trap it or even kill it.'

I hear the thumping sound from the barn. It's getting louder and louder. I hear steps upon veranda. Hard low hollow breathing. I don't bother to turn. To stare. I stand immobile. Smiling. I see Dianna pull out her gun. She fires twice. She screams. I feel a cold gnarled hard hand upon my shoulder and I begin to laugh hysterically, as I return to the broken porch on this wild October evening...

The old farmhouse, with its grey peeling wooden walls and its crumbing out-buildings, looks alien to me. Yet, the memories of this place haunt my soul. I look away from the congealed litter, stuffed in the corners by the wind. I look between cracked wooden floorboards, to see the dirt beneath. I stare up and look through the blistered and buckled ceiling of the veranda, up into the house, Into the dark of the attic. I seek sanity. It is an act of desperation; an over tried method, that has never worked. The ghost riddled memories crowd upon me in a cycle of terrifying repetition, again and again and again.

A strange case of dismemberment

The evidence lay strewn in tatters across the tarmac path. Bits of it were being blown by a sharp westerly breeze, that rattled the brittle trees to a hiss. Detective Inspector Raven was the first to arrive upon the scene. Through his long years of experience, he paced the ground; analysing the evidence to hand; and noting the warm blood. Evidence to support the fact that If this was a murder, then the suspect could still be in the area. Not long after he arrived came Detective Sergeant Crow.

'Glad to see you here Crow. Now...what do you make of it?'

Crow kept his distance; unsure as to how he should react.
There has definitely been an assault carried out sir...The blood alone-   -Yes yes! but look around! What do you see.

'Houses sir?'

'precisely. And not one of these homes called in any activity, or heard anything untoward. Don't you think that's rather odd?'

'Sir, I simply received a message to meet you here. I don't know the background of the case at all.'

'- Ahh I see... well, this is all I know, we received a call on the wire, from someone anonymous, though we traced call to someone near Barley Lane...' Raven nodded to the line of houses to his left and just behind where Crow stood. '...a little after half past seven this morning. The call informed us that an attack had occurred in Sylvan Heights...here... I came here first and saw this, and you arrived a little later. In sum... I am in the dark as much as you are... However, there is plenty of evidence to support the fact that a particularly vicious attack has occurred...Note the blood upon the path. The scratch lines in the concrete and the amount of-

'-Yes, sir I see it. it's quite disturbing.'

'But no body Crow! Not one part of the body is found!'

'Then someone must have carried it off.'

But carrying a body with all these houses around...

'You think that there might be more than one accomplice sir?'

'Yes Crow I do!'

Slowly, Raven began to gather the evidence together. While Crow and two other officers patrolled the area for other signs of violence.

They did not have to look far. A little over one hundred

feet away down a side alley, of wooden fences the rest of the dismembered corpse was found.

The body lay twisted and misshapen. Spread out as if lying on a wooden cross. The head lay twisted at a hideous angle; and one of its' eyes had been gouged out. That lay glistening wet in the late morning sun, a few inches from the cadaver's head. The feet had been gnawed at, as had one leg.

The stomach   had been ripped open and its liver and lungs had been torn free.

'Sir. Called Crow, you better come quick.'

 Raven appeared a moment later.

'-My gods! it's only a young un.' Said one officer.

Raven turned to Crow.

'It's another one. The same MO! look!'

'-How...how are we going to tell the parents?'

'-whoever did this was an animal!' said another officer.

'I agree...' Raven's eye glistened misty. '...we need to identify the body and then contact the relatives. But keep this quiet! Whatever it is is still here in the area.

'How can you tell?

'Look Crow.'

 Crow saw steam slowly rise from the dead body.

'ETD five hours ago. We know the other evidence occurred two hours ago, so who, or whatever did this, is still in the area. Crow get other officers! I want a perimeter set up. If anyone sees anything, call me straight away! Also, don't let anyone out of this area know what's going on! We have to contain the region and maintain a low profile.'

'I know a Curtis Magpie, who lives in the block over there Crow nodded to the block of flats to the far end of the estate.

'Go and check him out and see what he knows!' Muttered Raven

Within five minutes Crow had cornered Magpie as he was coming out if the flats.

'Oi Magpie!'

 'Get out of it Crow! I'm going' straight!'

'You stay where you are!'

Magpie was about to take off, when Crow knocked him down and sent him flying across the parking lot.

'God's you needn't do that. I pay my taxes I don't hurt no-one!'

'There's a fucking kid dismembered just not five hundred feet from where you live Magpie!'

'I didn't do it! I never hurt kids!'

'Nah, you're just a thieving git!'

'got a make an honest living.'

'what you know about honesty.'

'More than you Crow!'

'yeah! Where were you at six thirty this morning?'

'-taking a dump yer filth!'

Crow leaned on magpie forcing him to the ground. They faced each other, their eyes full of hostility and cold blooded murder

'-Don't give me that.' Crow ratcheted

Another officer appeared, then another, then a third.

Magpie backed down.

'I …I was in my room ask the wife ask the wife I saw nothing! I head a scream is all. I howl that sent a shudder through me, but… I saw nothing' Nothing!'

Crow took a step back. Then he nodded his head as Magpie shot off.

'If you hear anything, anything at all…' but the call fell on deaf ears, as Magpie was fast out of sight.

That's the world today no one sees anything, anything at all…

'Crow! Come here!'

Crow heard Raven shout and came as soon as he could. He could see Inspector Raven and three other officers at the top of the alley by a large bin shed. They were staring at something upon the ground.

'What you found?'

Raven took a step back to reveal a huge print in the dirt.

'Is that what I think it is?'

'There is only one creature alive known to do that.' Replied Raven.

Raven turned to see a hideous single slit eye, peer though the wooden fence toward him. A dark growl followed. Crow saw it next and leapt to the right as a dark furry talon suddenly ripped through a hole in the fence. Both Raven and Crow managed to get clear as the creature took the fence in one huge leap, and then with its body low its eyes full of malign fury, its long lips pulled back over razor sharp teeth, it snarled as it began to prepare for the attack once more. It leaped into the air, its talons slashing, its hideous howl sent shudders down the backs of the officers. One officer managed to get away, while another wasn't so lucky. Its sharp teeth clamped down with savage fury upon the officer's leg who then cried out in pain.

Crow and some of his other officers circled and then attacked the creature one at a time, fending off the monster with savage blows; until the beast hissed and with a scream fled down the alley over the fence and out of sight.

Crow came to the injured officer and called it in; while Raven cautiously descended the path that the monster took down the alley. He came back a moment later.

'The beast has entered one of the houses. Right now, there is nothing we can do....I don't know...fucking human's keeping beasts like that should be a crime....Crow call in the medical team and get the word out. No bird is safe in this area until the beast is dealt with!

With that, Raven took off to headquarters; after all he had to find the parents of the baby Pidgeon. After that, no bird song was heard in Sylvan Heights that day or for the rest of the week, while the beast lay in its basket, slowly purring itself to sleep

Home world

Space is a dark numb silent place, that is peppered with trillions of billions of millions of dots of light, that are streaking outward in spiral of tears, within an unfathomable black mass.

Space is void, numb and mute. Space is deaf and voiceless. Space is the sacred home of the old gods; yet hostile and violent to life. Exposure leads to blood boiling in freezing veins that violently undulate, before bursting and cracking apart; exsanguinating spores of blood-ice crystals, into the darkness from every single pore of exposed skin. Eyes crystalize, expand then then pop with no sound at all.

Space is an eternal sea of vacuum; yet space is not empty. Space is filled with dust and balls of gas and matter that might, if the conditions are right, build life. If there is any sound in space, it comes from within.

Ships of space don't come out of the dark. They are part of the dark. Therefore, they are only seen in part. They don't rust, as there is no oxygen. However, depending upon their age, they are pitted and dented; broken by bits of rock debris, which over time, collide into them. They are also riddled with Nano-sized holes, as meteors, impossible to see, puncture their sides, regularly.

Although the Excelsior is fifteen years of age, this, when analysing space craft, is old. She -for her captain has personified her thus- moves silently, sluggishly, ploughing heavily within this eternal sea.   Her throbbing ion thrusters, which circle the craft equidistantly along her midriff, are blue balls of pressurized gas , they push her onward in this numb mute blackness called the evernight; however, they make at least part of her, glow a pale blue in the darkness.

Within the very functional cramped control room of the Excelsior, a song is playing over a pair of portable cracked and muffled speakers. It is a song sung by a choir, possibly of hundreds. The tune is backed by applause, as it is sung in praise:

'-There's an Earth-err waiting on the ground, He'd like to come and meet us, and fill us with his sound. There's an Earth-err waiting on the ground, He's told us not to blow it, because he knows it will come around, He told me Let the children lose it, Let the children use it, Let all the children boogie...' and while the song plays, a woman, whose name and title is flight Officer Patricia Jennings second class, is partially seen through the green, red and blue lights, of luminous buttons and semi- holographic screens, that surround him.   She is twenty-eight years of age. Though she looks older; as her pale pinched skin seems grey; her large brown eyes are buried deep in her skull sockets. She is gaunt, pinched thin due to poor diet and space sickness: a malady she caught three sectors ago. Her oily grey-green, single zip jump suit hangs off her making her look more masculine than feminine; yet her bright attractive eyes glitter with mirth as she tunelessly whistles along to the song while tapping buttons and scanning screens.

Jennings stares at one of the many consoles along the far wall.   She stares deeply: unblinking. A look of concern causes brown wiry lines to fester upon her forehead. She moves to another console. She touches another button. The she stares deeply. Her eyes shine as her face lit by lines of white: a reflection from the screen. She slowly stops whistling and wonder forces her to stroke her square jaw she moves from her jaw to massage something under her jump suit. It rests on a partially seen metallic chain around her neck.

In the background the song continues. In its orchestral chorus, many voices are heard singing in jubilation for this unknown man and this unknown place. The rhythmic clapping is hypnotic to her ears. Jennings appears distant: not in control.   In this state, her fingers stroke over and then engage the "all hands" intercom button.

The whole ship then shudders with: 'I had to phone someone so I picked on you Hey, that's far out so you heard him too! Switch on the TV we may pick him up on channel two, Look out your window I can see his light, If we can sparkle he may land tonight, Don't tell your poppa or he'll get us locked up in fright...'

Jennings was interrupted from her trance like state by Captain Wallace's voice, who blasts into her ear via the chat headset.

The voice is decidedly hostile.

'Jennings!' a short pause 'Jennings's!' another pause 'JENNINGS! This is your captain! Y' know...the poor fucking idiot that pays you to do your fucking job!   Now shut mother fucking Earther crap off! Now Jennings! Fr Steller's sake! I'm trying to sleep! Jennings! Jennings! I'm... I'm warning you! Jennings! I'm I'm fu-cking warning you! Jennings! JENNINGS! If you, you don't shut that that shit off, right, right fucking NOW! I'm coming up there, an' I swear to the stars, I will come up there, I will come up there Jennings an' will use your fucking arse to seal that fucking coolant leak! Are we clear! Jennings, are we Fucking clear! JENNINGS!'

'-Sir!' The song went off.

***

Captain Peter Wallace, officer first class, (who also has the emerald star for bravery.) is brown eyed, dark skinned and very, very bearded. He is in his cabin, looking up at the wires of bunk above; tracing the lines with his pupils. Right now, he cannot sleep and he's pissed off about it.

Time has passed and Wallace has tried everything, to sleep. He had even tried masturbation. However not even that helped; especially as the semen spurted then floated out of reach, before he could tissue it away. That Earther song is the final straw. He lay there imagining pushing Jennings out into space without a suit on, or decapitating her in a lift malfunction, or crushing her by-

'Captain...Captain Wallace... sir?' there was an awkward pause. '...sir.'

'What is it Jennings!' Snapped Wallace.

Jennings used to the cold dismissive tone, replied in the official voice of respect given between a subordinate and a commanding officer; however, Jennings was certain that sooner, rather than later, she would snap. 'Sir...could you come to control... please. Sir.'

Shit, thought Wallace.

He rubbed his tight curled grey hair in frustration. Two back to back twelve hour shifts and completed six hyper jumps with a partially working bosun drive an just when I manage to shut down just when my eyes close I get woken up by fucking Earther music and a fuck knows what.

'Is it Important?' He asked coolly his voice stretched tight; visceral. Dangerous.

'Sir...it's... better if you simply come.'

***

Wallace hates Jennings. He hates her because she smiles a lot. He hates her because she always played those hymnals and sings them badly. But most of all, he hates Jennings because Jennings is a believer... one of those who called themselves "Earther's".

Earthers! Even the name sounded crap. They believed, so Wallace had heard, that they were THE chosen people; that their descendants had come from some fuckin' mythical planet called "Earth" I mean, for fucks sake, what sort of name is that? You might as well call the planet "Barry "or "Dave" or something equally stupid. Of course, a planet has fucking earth. It was a joke. A sick joke to starve the poor out of air credits; Yet, this loony cult had found influence on the corporate board of the mining colonies, who -at the same time- supplied the raw elements needed to sustain vital life support on the planets of Cygnus 3; It was this that hurt like a space blister. Not the stupid fucking songs. The songs he could live with... occasionally.... It was the enforced control that Wallace loathed. Control that Jennings and those who were like him had over the rights of the less fortunate.

He sat up and once more, out of an unconscious anxiety habit, pulled his hand through his tight curled fading to grey hair. He looked, with a warm sense of affection on his face, towards the image he had put up on the opposite wall, forgetting, in that moment that he placed it there to hide a particularly nasty stain caused by a decompression malfunction two tours ago.

Death was part of life in space. The two embrace like old lovers.

The image Wallace stared at was of the excelsior when she was commissioned: and boy, he thought, was she beautiful. A long tube like structure all white and pristine. Dent less and glittering. His eyes warmed as he recalled that the ship was once the pride of their fleet. Their computer Ai, known as Chamberlain, was the most expensive ever commissioned.

Time is a bastard though. Time had ripped into Chamberlain's circuits and organic cluster brain. Time and the inability to pay for upgrades, had, after 15 years of service, led to hideous accident.

Chamberlain malfunctioned and opened the wrong door. In computer terms, it was a simple switch malfunction. However, this switch malfunction led to the pulverization of three of his best hands who had just taken off their suits, after finishing an external cleaning duty.

It had taken four crew two double shifts over planned leave to clean the mess up; and in that time, the report had been sent and the verdict of the council had confirmed. Both Chamberlain and the excelsior were to be mothballed: broken down for parts; while the captain, though recognized as not responsible, was also to be retired from active duty.

He hoped both he and Jennings might be able to get the ship to dry dock and that nothing would go so drastically wrong as to have to wake him up once more. But now...well it could be nothing, a fault with the containment system on level four. It had happened before. Jennings, despite being a wanker and an Earther to boot, was still a fairly competent at her position. She wouldn't call him up to the control room without a valid reason.

Slowly, Wallace sighs, as he stands, his magnetic boots keeping him on the floor; he clinks and clanks his way out of his cabin and along the stained walls of the corridor to the only working service tube on his level. Let's hope it's the containment system in the lower decks he mused as the tube lift lurched to life.

***

Jennings hates Wallace, but for very opposite reasons, than Wallace hates Jennings.

Jennings hates Wallace because she regards Wallace as having no hope and Wallace is willing to almost evangelically share this hopelessness with anyone, anywhere he can.

She also hates Wallace because Wallace had, since his first shift on board the Excelsior, Wallace had made her life next to unbearable. The puzzle was why Wallace had chosen her for this last trip. That made no sense. Unless, of course it was to throw more bile, before his retirement from active duty.

She recalls the words of Wallace as he left the control room 12 hours previously: "I don't want to be disturbed! You understand me? You are not to call me unless it's absolutely fucking Critical!" At which Jennings thought hail hamburger and said "sir" laconically.

As the shift wore on, Jennings had become bored. Since the decommissioning of Excelsior, and the removal of most of the crew, her job consisted of looking at greasy old green computer screens, adjusting the dial to the particle flow of the Bosun drive, as it gradually fed on the particles it needed to prepare for the next star-jump; as well as scan for possible collisions, with larger bodies of rock which were, in this sector of space, fortunately very few and far between. It was mind numbing, tedious and at the same time intricate enough, to the point that one mistake, might be a threat to the ship and –her- present two-man crew.

As she sat there, sullenly looking at the grey green screens, she recalled the interview for the position of officer second class.

In those days, Jennings looked immaculate, and very attractive, even though she said it herself. Her close cropped blonde hair suited her square jaw and her wide set eyes and full wet lips.

The blue and grey steel uniform with gold epaulettes was pressed and shone, and curved in nicely. In sum, she looked, believed and felt herself attractive and even though she was perhaps ashamed to admit it, very hot and damn cool.

She stood stiffly at attention as the door behind, hissed

and then out of her field of vision, slowly curled open.

She desperately tried to hide the shock she felt as Space commander Wallace, first class and owner of the emerald star for gallantry first class, slowly and rather drunkenly, staggered into the room.

Wallace was unshaven and unkempt in appearance. His flight jacket was covered with stains. Moreover, she could smell that he stank of diesel juice, which meant as far as she was concerned that he had a huge drink problem, and that meant he was unreliable. It was only as the interview came to a close, that she knew she would be in for a rough tour of duty.

'I see here, from your data cube...' Wallace, sneered, his eyes glittered with maliciousness as he spoke in a vindictive drawl '...that you...you... are an Earther?" the condescending weight on the last word sounded insulting to her ears. She didn't flinch.

'Yes.' She replied awkwardly, sensing a blush of embarrassment rise in her cheeks.

'I see...' His words were drawn out drunk. The air became thick in a weighted pause as Wallace stared Jennings down. Then Wallace continued
...I'll be frank with you... I don't much like you. I, I don't like the way you... you look an' I definitely don't like what you believe...'however... by law, the captain of a star-ship must take at least one of your kind on board.

Jennings squeezed her jaw together, as Wallace glowered vindictively. At the stare Jennings gulped nervously. She wanted to leave the room and vomit up her breakfast. But she held her ground. She focused her eyes at the far end of the room; as she tried to hide her emotions. yet, inside, she was blistering with pain.

She felt a drip of nervous sweat trickle down the side of her neck as she   felt Wallace's eyes glower into her, looking for a sign of weakness, any weakness at all.   The pause was long. She felt it last forever.

'I ask one thing...' Wallace continued as he sneered'...don't try to convert me or the crew! If you do...' Wallace smiled but his eyes bore into Jennings with glittering fury. He stepped closer and closer towards her until their faces were less than an inch apart. She could taste the sourness of the booze on his breath at the back of her throat. She tightened her hands into fists and dug her nails into the palms of her hands. The skin gave way. A tingle of pain shot up her arm. She tried not to grimace. A small sarcastic smile touched the corner of her mouthWallace barely noticed. He spoke coolly and, Jennings thought, terrifyingly benign, 'If you do.... I'll blow you into deep space.' The words were whispered as Wallace smiled.

She knew then, that he meant it. Her heart jumped. She felt that she was looking into an abyss. However, she simply nodded and gave a brisk salute as Wallace, with a drunken dismissive wave, left the room.

The whole experience had left her feeling upset, frustrated and alienated. Now with this first tour almost over and on a duty, that involved dry docking Wallace's own ship, she looked weary. The uniform had gone, and she was alone with the largest cynic in the tri-colony for company. She shook his head, as an image of blowing Wallace out into deep space entered her mind. That would teach the fucktard a lesson. Yes that would-

A smile appears on Jennings face as the control room door curls open and Wallace enters the room.

'There something funny?'

'-Yes sir.'

'-Now what would that be?'

'- Sir, Blowing you into space... sir.'

Wallace stared at Jennings. '-You're a cunt... you know that?'

'-Yes sir and so are you! Sir!'

Wallace grinned. 'Going' to make a spacer out of you yet. Despite your   earther crap.'

Jennings looked down and away.

'So why am I here? It better be fucking valid; I shit you not.'

'There's... something errs, bouncing off the err... forward scanner... Sir.'

Wallace walked over to the main screen, and stared into the holographic monitor. Their faces shone gold green in the semi darkness of the room.

Wallace scratched his head If Chamberlain was on line, things would have been so very different, but....

'I wonder what that is.' He found himself saying to no-one in-particular, and checked himself... it's true he thought, out here in the void, the loneliness could be so destructive. His mind wandered once more, as he saw the blip appear in the top half of the screen; as a matter of routine he automatically went through the failsafe procedure. When that proved negative, his mind raced.

Jennings smiled. '-it's not an asteroid the chemical elements are far too ordered; there are far too many metal composites in the structure; it could be... '

'-it could be a Delphic scout; they have been seen this far out...but there's no organic components in the scan and Delphic designs always have organic composites within its structure.'

Wallace became worried. The Delphi were a warrior spacer breed. They had claims over the ore planetoids, so they said; and this led to minor skirmishes from time to time, if they attacked the ship would blow at one attack.

'I', I'm waiting for the I C U to send a detailed projected Image.

There was a beep as the image corrector for unidentified objects began to make an image on the main screen at the far end of the room.

First a circle...then a dish, then an antenna... then a huge box like object, with legs projecting off it.

'what in the four cells is that?' Wallace stammered.

'It's reading as a structure of alien design. Not recognized by either the planetoids or the known races.

It looks like a probe... But it's not Delphic? Could it be a trap? They have been known to trap ships but not this far into known Cygnus territory

The image was complete.

'Oh my...Oh my Earth!'

Wallace sneered at Jennings.

'What is it?

'Hope.' replied Jennings, her voice almost a whisper.

'What do you mean?' Asked Wallace testily.

Jennings braced herself for the attack before she continued.

'What you are looking at...' she pointed to the screen nervously, hardly containing her excitement, '...is, is what we call... the sacred key... look...'

From around her neck, Jennings produced something that Wallace thought was incredibly delicate. It was a golden dish attached to a cube, with three long antennae stretching out from it in three directions. Wallace stares at the metallic object around Jennings neck; then he looks at the screen. Then he looks back again. They were similar. No, they were the almost same.

'We, We get this when we become Earther's... we believe it it is the hope... according to the ancient-'

'-You mean the ramblings of that senile old fucktard spacer Westernhope? He was put in prison for being a fucking loony you know!'

'- it, it contains a sacred key...' she gulped air nervously awaiting Wallace's bitter tirade

'the way...the way to Earth.'

Wallace looked at the view screen and then again at the necklace. My Sweet stars, he thought, Could it actually be true?

'You can't expect me to believe that that we have found some fucking ancient Earth artefact...can you..?' He tried not to hide his mirth or the rising anxiety, that was breaking the wall of cynicism within him.

'Sir...' Began Jennings, '...all I know is this... ' she raised her necklace to show Wallace. '...this is called the voyager, and that satellite out there... sir...it's the same!' Wallace hears the crescendo of excitement in Jennings voice. At that moment, he wanted to punch her very hard in the face. Wallace started shaking his head from, side to side.

'Can, can you deny your eyes?'

'Oh oh, oh just just JUST FUCK OFF JENNINGS! I, I, I don't need this an' I don't don't fucking need you! Its' easy for you isn't' it!' Life is so fucking easy! so easy and controlled! 'He takes step towards her and almost raises a fist. Then he manages to gain control and lowers it. '...Life's not like that! Fuckin' wake up! It it just isn't!'

He sadly and painfully turns away to leave the control room, with his head lowered, his shoulders slumped. Then he turns back and in what Jennings thought as an after-thought, mutters:

'Joss make sure you get the thing stowed safely.'

As Wallace slowly leaves the control room. Jennings looks at the image on the monitor screen. Yes it is that simple it is. She thought happily. As she begins to engage the tractor beam.

*

Slowly the Excelsior's front airlock opens and the ancient craft is brought on board. Then, as the pressure was increased, the soundless silence ended.

With excitement building in her heart, Jennings makes her way from the control room to the front air lock hanger. She looks through the window to see the probe resting on the hanger floor. The door hisses and starts to curl open; though Jennings is through the door before its completes its cycle.

The ship is a lot larger than she expected it to be. However, its main antennae are damaged bent, no doubt, by collisions. With nervous eyes she glances all over the craft, looking for the promised key. Her heart leaps when he sees a gold disc. The promise from the founder! With her heart racing she climbs the structure reaches for it, and pulls it off the ancient ship.

***

Wallace is sitting on the floor in the computer room. His knees are drawn up and his head is bowed. The dimly lit room which hums and hisses. It is a mass of brown wires and blue holes in the walls where glossy tubes pulse light into glossy organic cubes that are placed in even intervals around the circular room. Now, they   fluctuate in pulses of light that glow between soft green and purple.

There is a dry musty smell of corrosion and burnt electrical connectors. It's a smell that Wallace feels comfortable with. In the middle of the room is a blue circle. With his nerves torn to shreds, he gives the activation code and then says

'Chamberlain...'

The circle in the middle of the room glows with a blue light. Slowly a face begins to form.

'What is it, son?'

'I...I'm scared.'

'What of?

 'of?' a pause.

'Of of facing that the earthers might be real and there is a place for us to live and grow without being trapped within husking crafts that are breaking down of hating and of hurting Jennings because he was right all along of of of

'-of...being wrong.' Wallace stammers.

'-Is finding earth so bad?'

'-What, what do you mean?'

'Cygnus is dying. Resources are being used up. The people are dying.

Wallace stared into the face of Chamberlain, whose lines creased around the eyes. In the soft blue light created for the hologram they appear wet. Chamberlain's voice crumbles into segments. 'People need air. The colonies have faced being ripped apart by the the Delphi and other races, who see us as as a threat. Therefore, the council look to the religious movement of the earthers... it gives   the colonies something to hold on to.

'So Earth could be our only hope?'

'Or... it could be our greatest fear.'

Wallace looks up to Chamberlain. His eyes glistening with tears.

The communicator in Wallace's ear starts to ring.

'What is, is it Jennings?'

'Sir...I've found it.'her voice is exuberant

'-What?'

'-Sir I've found earth. I know where it is. I've plotted its possible course from the disc. I haven't got the equations for the bosun drive yet but I know where to-

'-What disc?'

 '-The disc that we were told is on the craft that that would lead us back to earth!'

Wallace instantly thinks more Earther crap. Yet he pauses in his reply.

'-Ok, ok. So there is a disc and this disc has information on it. Ok ok, have you put the relevant data into the computer yet?

Chamberlain lights up. His eyes are aglow; it's as if even he has found something to believe in.

'Just doing it now sir.'

Carell, the little turd is determined isn't she.

'-Don't you think that finding where we were from is worth the effort?' Wallace asks over Jennings shouting about only needing one three pulse jump; and that they have enough particles for the trip.

'-Can the bosun handle the trip, or will be blasted into the four vectors?'

The question is weighted.

Wallace knows that Chamberlain could do the equations however if he does, then he could lose more of his precious memory. In other words, this could be a one-way trip. Chamberlain smiles sadly.

'I can't promise son. The system is weak. I could easily put us in the middle of a sun.'

Well that's lifted my confidence.

'-Ok, ok…' Wallace scratches his beard as he gets up to leave. Chamberlain sadly smiles, before he dissipates back into the gloom from where he came.

***

The control room is brighter now that Wallace has re engaged Chamberlain. The greasy unwashed walls are green grey, more of the hard ware tubes are seen. The metallic floor dirty and greasy. Their faces seem green blue in the circle of lights in the control room. Wallace walks from the lift to see Jennings excitedly looking at a gold metallic disc in her hands. Wallace sees that she is oblivious to her surroundings. Only the dice matters. Only the disc and earth.

'-It has music too; would you like to listen to it?'

-No I'd rather vomit'okay, lets listen.'

The gold plaque has a small port. Jennings feeds a wire into the plaque and then into a console. A moment later, a hideous warped sound that makes Wallace and Jennings grimace begins to fill the ship.

'-What the Carell is that?'

'-its earth music.

'-Its its its fucking awful!'

Jennings looks upset, her face is flushed, as she panics over the console. Touching buttons changes nothing. The sound makes Wallace hold his ears in pain.

'-for frack's sake get that shit off!'

Jennings presses a button on the room is silent once more.

'-I'll run it through encryption analysis' comes the voice of Chamberlain.

'-Sir? Chamberlain's higher functions are supposed to be-

'   -how do you expect to work out the equations for the bosun drive? Manually? Do you know how long that would take? Its uncharted space isn't it?

Jennings looked down and away.

Thought so.

'-whether we like it or not, if we are going to go to earth, we must engage the boson; so, we need Chamberlain. It's either that, or dry dock; and if we go there, then we will lose the opportunity to go to earth, because, you know, you know, as well as as I, that this information will be passed onto some other gobshite from the council...Now... do you want to go to Earth or not?'

Jennings face starts to go red.

'yeah, thought so.'

It took Chamberlain half an hour to make the equation. In that half hour Both Jennings and Wallace sat opposite each other in the canteen, drinking the last of the Diesel Juice.

'What do you think, we'll find when we get there?'

'I I don't know? Perhaps what was left of us, perhaps a garden?'

'Why do you think we lost contact?'

'The books tell us that we lost contact, nothing more. Look aren't you curious?

-'Of course I am.

'-Then why the questions? Why doubt the books?'

'-because humans ask questions, that's what makes us survive. That's what gives us strength. We ask questions and seek solutions. We reach out, we investigate, we analyse...We don't rely on blind faith to get us through.'

'But without faith, what are we?'

Wallace scratches his chin.

'Better off.'

'Hah, that's a lie. You have a faith. You see the stars and our ability to survive as something noble. You don't want to think that where we came from and, from that, who we are is relevant to our, our-.

'Souls?'

'Perhaps.

'-That's untrue. '

'-Is it?'

'-I'm I'm a a realist...'

'You sound hollow.'

'-I have the right to believe what I like.'

'-and I don't? Do you know what we believe in? Have you even thought about it? '

'-Well, what do you believe in?'

'-History. '

'-that's not an answer! That's fracking obtuse.

'We believe that where we came from holds the key to our survival here: in space. It's our home! We won't be cut off scratching out solar gems or for nuggets of air.'

'Earth is, was a myth... it has no significance. We have to live in the now, for if we don't we die and our- '

'you know, I was like you once. I went through the corps training program. I came top of the ethics class.'

'-then why become an Earther? Why give all that up?'

'-because I wanted to believe in something greater-.'

'-captain Wallace, I have computed the bosun fold to Earth; ready to fold in T minus fifteen seconds and counting.

Their faces paled.

'You ready for this?'

'Fuck you! Sir!'

Wallace grinned savagely. I bet you are. They took the empty seats scattered about the room. The seats slid forward and up.

Outside was the void... Wallace thought the void that...oh fuck it.

'5 ... 4...3... bosun engine start.'

Here we go. Wallace grimaces as he holds the sides of his seat. ... 2'

The ship begins to shake violently. Wallace sees Jennings slide in and out of focus. Wallace starts to heave. His head pounds. Jennings screams and doubles over as the ship creaks and buckles in noises that deafen.

1...co-ordinates set... preparing for jump.

There is a pause that lasts forever as time and space slow down. Jjjjjj- Uuuuuu-Mmmmmm-Pppppp

Light blasts, out in waves of emitted energy. There is a huge pulse of X-rays. The space where the Excelsior once was being now empty.

Wallace awakes feeling hungover. He vomits. A trickle of blood comes from the corner of his mouth.

'Captain Wallace? Are you here sir?'

It was Chamberlain.

'Is Jennings?'

'Patricia Jennings officer first class, is still asleep. We are in orbit and approximately 91.6 million m's from the nearest star-

'have you seen it? Is it there?'

'You mean earth?'

'Yes. 'I have.'

'What's it like?'

'you will see for yourself in three H's from now.'

Jennings stirred.

For the first time in months he saw something wonderful in Jennings. He wanted to touch her, kiss her. He wanted to-

Jennings smiled. 'Did we make it'?

'Yes' Said Wallace gently, as he stared at her, his eyes glistening with tears, 'I think we possibly did.

Mr. ClaY

"...and behold, a great red dragon having seven heads and ten horns, and on his heads were seven diadems... his tail swept away a third of the stars of heaven, and threw them to the earth" (Rev. 12:3-4) KJV.

Coldharbour on an early November morning: A bitter place. The houses of the village have black slate roofs specked green with bloated deep green lichen that have been sliced by knives of salt. Saw toothed and defiant they stand, showing the finger to the wild rolling ocean that incessantly surges, together with the wailing winds that in a wild tempestuous marriage of abuse, batter the slate rocks of coast. The winds with the accumulations of parental pressures also bring on the thunderous gold, white and pig iron of the Cumulonimbus that ever threaten and then bring on with violent shouts onto the streets of hard and heavy rain.

The narrow-cobbled streets glisten wet, each stone is corner filled with plash from the night before. They reflect the storm from above that is disturbed stillicidium. This road writhes, like a smooth black snake; down the steep deep green of the hill, the rutted cliff of west-point where the lighthouse stands. Its tall tower shines a steady beam of light against the storm fueled sky; and beyond that, standing upon the tip of the cliff and looking down with unearthly judgement upon the village is the old grey keep: its green and black high stone walls are caught by the sun as it slowly creeps above the timeless horizon of the wild sea, while in its shade the standing stone circle of the oracle, its keeper awaiting the call, looks down from the windows of the old keep, the eye is black and three lobed, it turns away from the light and hides in the gloom away from the shattered windows that also glint with what could be seen within the mind's eye as utter maleficence.

The road moves down and around; through the village to the left and then to the port side of the harbour and its entrance: the quay and then then away out of the harbour entrance and off to the empty endless timeless sea, that froths and foams in surges of cream green and gold.

The fisherman's quay reeks of rotten fish carcass. The smell clings to the air, and rises about the town in ghostly gusts that slam into and around the half-filled battered wooden boxes that are piled haphazardly within the awning of the corrugated iron roofed transit shed.

To the right of the cottages and beside the transit shed stands the black painted walls of old ship Inn. Its owner:

Alexander Drake now stands in the doorway. His square chin is a mask of dark stubble, his pale blue eyes are glazed with wild fury and his bald head glistens with sweat. His burly arms rest crossing over his belly that ale, rum, hard cheese and harder bread have extended. His breathing is hard as he stares out at the slow gathering on the dock; feeling the weight of his watch in his trouser pocket as it slowly ticks, ticks, ticks.

Behind him, near and in penumbra, stands his wife: Judith. About her withdraw face wild hair trailed her large dark eyes dart a flighty stare at the action taking place upon the quay, while also chasing the shadow of a low skimming gull. Her full lips are bitten back by her gapped front teeth, almost seen, as she watches the crowd gather as the three boats slowly arrive, and with them, heavy hard rain.

A shard of purple lightening cuts across the sky in a loose thread.

A growl of thunder rumbles in its wake.

'It looks like they're back.'   Her voice betrays a sense of happiness that she cannot conceal.

-I'll have none of that here

-They have no other choice. She pauses and stares at him her eyes a mixture of pain and compassion. – We have to tr--

-there is always a choice!

'-an' what if they're right? She stares at his profile with mirthless disapproval: 'ave you thought of that?'

-I'll not have those words here! He turned to face her, his blue eyes menacing, before he turned his back on her once more: dismissing a fly on the back of his hand. That's blasphemous an' you know how I feel 'bout that' His voice is thick gravelly; while hers is almost lost to his seeming mild rage. So her eyes, large and round, look with tenderness towards the boats, then nervously but also with mirthless contempt at the broad thick back of the man before her. A tear, brought alive by hot hurt falls across her cheek as she physically and at the same time, mentally turns away, as he stands defiant, and mirthless at the growing crowd. For, despite the vicious weather they have come – bedraggled- from their homes. They come silently en mass; blindly heeding the call of a siren who warns of a threat that comes to possibly seal their fate.

The black mass of the boat: being tugged by two rusted fishing trawlers is brought into port. The sea -weary fishing boats churn up the murky film in green brown swirls that then violently shudder to burst white semen in spurts as the two ships come to a soft slow halt.

Their salvage: The sloop of war, rocks: behemoth. Its damp cracking masts are grey with age, its sails: pale ragged flags blow behind it like strips of wet leather. Its hull a husk of razor shells; growls and creaks in the wake the fishing boats have made. It wavers towards the lea. Its name: carved in wood is impossible to make out.

All around the boats townsfolk that have gathered and are muttering: The muttering becomes a murmuring; the murmuring becomes a low moan. Disquiet. Some to look down some look away. The men: their eyes in lined boxes, their noses cracked, their teeth disjointed aged and stained with poor diet, tobacco and rum, stare at the huge craft with anxiety. The women mostly thin ghostly and sunken skinned: drawn in sketches of broken shells, also stare at the twin mast sloop as it enters the port with the same sense stare of dread. A communal feeling: shared.

The first fishing boat opens its cabin. The door is slammed. A burly looking man with a round face green eyes a growth of red stubble on his jaw, and thinning rusted hair; stares at the crowd with dismay and disdain. He walks upon the deck of his trawler two other men follow. They are all wearing heavy black wax coats. He throws the heavy line onto land. Not one helps.

-Is no one goin' to set me ship?-

The man's name is Owain Radcliffe he has been a part of the village since he was born. He knows all the faces that stare at him.

'IS ANYONE GOING TO HELP ME?'

His voice echoes. It makes the old men shudder and the young women turn away.

'Yer a bunch of frightened fools! The lot of yer!' He spits. Yellow tar slaps onto the grey slab stones of the jetty.

-We never asked yer to go Owain' came a hard voice.

-An what would yer have me to do? He looks at the crowd, with bile in his eyes . Then he turns away. Shaking his head.   Always the same always the same the same always the same they never change. 'One day, I hope yer see this for what it is.'

'It's the curse!

'The feck it is!'

The door to the other tug's cabin also slams open and a young man, with   thick wiry black hair, a thin nose and strong chin stares out at the crowd sardonic mirth is shining from his bright green wide set eyes. He is Peter O'Rourke; he has a soft southern Irish accent. Unlike Owain he's an outsider and like all outsiders is naturally treated with both total suspicion and an utter contempt, which bothers him little. For money has been his calling his entire life. Until now.

'One day yer'll thank us, yer will.' He said brightly.

'I doubt that!'

'When will that be? When we're dead and burning in the eternal flames of our sin?'

He shakes his head: -Jeus these people they never think about anything else fer fecks sake.

The doors top both tugs widen and the crews get out, holding fast the tugs before bringing the sloop of war to rest.

'You're bringing bad blood here!'

-The feck I am!

The men disembark and hold fast the three ships. The sloop comes to a slow stop. It cuts into the quay and rasps out a searing sigh as it does so.

The crowd moved back, the black mass is casting its shadow over many who have gathered. Some then turn and flee.

'We are all fuckin' cursed now!'

'You've set us adrift Owain'

Owain stared out at the crowd.

'Now you stem that shit now! What we are doing is for the greater good!'

The men, eight in all, move about the villagers soundlessly; setting the boats to the quay and setting a gangplank up to the sloop.

-Do yer think that he'd be grateful? O' Rourke smiled.

- He'd fuckin' better be.

The deck, of the sloop of war is wood sieved with ship worm'; the board's creak crack and chatter in sharp cracking splinters as the four men: two of Owain's crew: young men unafraid and loyal and O'Rourke slowly step towards the cabin at the far end of the deck.

Before the mean reach it, the door opens with a slow and soft moan.

Owain looks at his men. His eyes: firm and resolute.

'You've done your duty, stay here.'

With their flamed oil lamps sturdy in their hands, O Rourke and Owain enter the abyss.

The Hall is warm and damp. The air is musty and has another odour of something that Owain thinks he has smelt before, though he cannot fully place. He stares at the oncoming gloom: the rotted walls and the shadows that move out of the way of the light. From the corner of his eye he catches the sallow face of O'Rourke,

Steady now steady there is nothing to fear here.

The walls jammer with a sudden howl. Both men jump violently. A slither. A scrape.   A ratcheting caw of insanely laughing magpies fills the sky. The walk takes longer than it should have done. Owain feels a growing sense of oppression. The dripping of water and that odd musty odour engulf. He feels eyes hostile and animal staring into the back of his neck. He holds back a shudder. O Rourke appears sallow in the light of the lamp feels threads and membranes. Fine fingers with nails like knives slice at him, yet pull back as the light shines. In the sphere of the light they find protection.

Finally, they make out another door. It is large and covered with cytochrome oxidase. The large round bronze handles are bound with heavy rusted chains.

At the sound of their footsteps the door begins to shudder violently.

Another unearthly sound: a low gurgling moan followed by a rattling howl, is followed by retches and ratchets and scratches. The door shudders as it's repeatedly pushed violently towards them in its rotting wooden frame.

'Whatever is there it wants our blood'. Owain stares with a growing anxiety as the door slams forward and backward again, again and agai

-we're in for it now. He mutters

Don't I fucking know it. You owe me a bottle of yer best when we get out of this.

Yer has had that already.

Well your next best then.

Yer had that too last night.

feck.

Suddenly the chain violently shatters into shards. The door splinters and explodes outwards. The sudden draft of foul smelling air throws Owain and O'rourke to the floor. A monstrous scream. A crack and splinter. The darkness wants to violently hurt. First one, then the other are picked up like dolls and thrown backwards along the hall as a dark mass: unknown in shape, save for two huge grasping talons, is seen in the scattering yellow flames of the rolling oil lamps. Its slams and crashes; its body batters writhe and slide itself away, along the corridor and out into the tiny light at the end of the hall that leads to the world of the day.

Outside on the deck there is a sudden explosion of darkness. A huge whump of exploding air, forces the two young men once standing guard to slam onto the rotten deck. The dark shadow, bursts forth from the gloom of the doorway. It howls in pain monstrously as the golden light of the sun catches it. Its slimy pale near translucent skin throbs slowly, that peels to reveal veins which bubble spit and split in the light of the sun. Corse vile black blood bursts out It falls to the rotting deck and turns into thousands slimy shiny spiders that charge at the two the two men who scream in terror. One man just manages to climb the rigging to safety the other trips and falls, then screams. He screams in terror and then in insane maniacal laughter before he begins to gag as the hideous creatures penetrate; entering through his eyes and his mouth. Up his trousers and into his anus and bury into his cock.

He convulses; his face lost amid hideous brackish mask, of a thousand, thousand undulating shiny legs arms and bodies, writhing about in no rhythmic pattern, he stretches out with his almost formless arms as if embracing an invisible lover before rolling over and over and over. He begins to shudder in uncontrolled violent spasms. The wood beneath him cracks and splinters before His body lies prone: undead dead.

The thing raises itself upon its tallowed thighs. Its shape is alien. its eyes: three lobed, ravaged by age and by a vulpine hideous fury, stare out upon the crowd who suddenly flee in terror, before it suddenly thrusts itself up into the air and then violently throwing itself over the side of the sloop to slam into the green brown sea, rocking the old boat violently against the port side.

***

O'Rourke and Owain stagger to their feet, with caution in each step they make their way through shattered doors, which leads to a large room, that is mostly in shadow, except for a small hole in the roof that shines enough light down upon the centre of the room to cover a huge black rock. Attached to the rock, by heavy chains is an old man that age has crusted with a salt cloak. His face: brown lined, is filled with valleys while the thick white thick pubic bead has streaks of brown. . His skin is thin in and in place3s bones protrude leaving the men to conclude that what little muscle he has seems to have wasted. However despite the creases in his body and face, his pale blue eyes shine crystalline, to reveal a hidden youth, as pain subsides. He looks relived. He smiles and reveals a haphazard cluster of uneven yellow teeth tipping with the feel of gravestones
-well I am here now.

'Good morning gentleman. My name is..,–'There was a long pause before he replied. 'My name is Mr. Clay.

Both men walk into the room
'You know why we are here?'

Both men pull at the chains that hold the old man down. But they have little impact.

'Owain, I can guess.' Mr Clay states

Owain smiles grimly as he pulls as the chains. His calloused hands scratched with salt and teased with years of pulling rope, pull at the links that fall to the floor. The old man, called Clay lifts himself up from the rock and with weary eyes smiles at them.

'We've come to set you free.'

'No doubt... though I expect many here might find the thought of that objectionable.'

'They were too scared to try.'

'I...' there was a long pause as the old man looked down 'I don't doubt that.' He concludes.

The old man lifts himself up. He stretches and moves away from Owain and O'Rourke

-No doubt weary of the creation he has piled up to hide from himself like an old dog licking an old sore.

Owain stares. His cornflower eyes strained, the veins along the sclera were forked with red lighting strikes

The old man rises and the chains shatter and slowly coil snakelike on the floor. The old man stands. He is smaller than Owain but slightly taller than O'Rouke. He takes a single step sighs and then falls forward; Owain and O' Rourke catch him and with gentleness slowly carry him from the room.

They come onto the deck to see the crewmen looking crazed with fright. They put Mr, clay down and attended the men.

-My Je-us, have we done the right thing?

'Hold fast lad' says Owain. 'What you have seen is only as real as you want it to be. They can come into this world only if we let them; they are images is all.'

-I know what I saw.

-Ayah, but they are images, night and darkness gives them strength in the day, they are weak.

The man looks up at Owain and points to his friend.

Owain looks anxiously to the other man prone His pale eyes are glistening, the black of his pupils altering in a blue pool, before he decides to take a step and then kneel down before the body. Then taking hold of the prone man's shoulder he slowly turns him over.

The face is unrecognizable. Half eaten away with a fiery acid, his eye bulges bloated glistening from the fetid skin He screams as the sunlight shines upon him before spasms shudder him into a into a furious silence. Both O' Rourke and Owain struggle in keeping him down.

Owain and O'Rourke stare at each other, desperation seizes the men.

-Oh Je-us don't let him go don' let him go e's only a child a child 'e need not go 'e needs to live.

-There is nothing you can do for him. Says Clay. His voice is distant yet firm. Let him fly in peace. With a wave of his hand the young man becomes still, before his body dissolves into a fine dust that is gathered up in a slow spiral that is then blown apart by the wild wind.

-Yer could have helped him.' O'Rourke mutters

-And allowed a monster to run among you? He was too far gone to save.

-What about the rest of us?

-So You brought him back! The hard powerful voice came from the quay. We all told yer not to, but yer did it anyway!

Owain O'Rourke and Mr Clay look at the quayside Alexander stands his burly hands by his side. In one tight fist he is holding an iron bar that he is tapping against the side of this thigh.

-Yer know I can't kill him, but I swear to the Gods that if yer come ashore I'll stove both yer heads in.

-we need a chance, a single chance! Owain's voice is broken. Can't yer see that?

-AND YOU THINK A DEAL WITH THAT (he points at Mr. Clay) WILL MAKE US SAFE! YER HAVE PUT US ALL IN DANGER YER FECKIN IDIOT!

'-not all,' Retorts Mr. Clay.

The rain falls in hard slated lines as the men stand on the Dock. Drake looks at the three of them, and shakes his head. This is insanity the whole town will suffer because of this idiot's charity. He shakes his head.

'yer not welcome at the Ships Inn, none of yer. AN' I don' expect yer will be welcome in yer own home Jacob.' He turns and then like a ghost dissolves as he slides back into the heavy slating rain.

Another shard of lightening slices across the sky, it flicks about the keep.

Mr. Clay stares up through the driving rain, his face determined, his eyes bright, the Keep, calls out, he feels it. He fights it.

****

The three make their way through the rain and the narrow cobbled streets towards Owain's home. The thunderstorm has rolled over the entire town, even the strands of the dawn light have left a night of rage in their wake. In the rain they miss a hunched figure standing in a doorway looking up at the house.

Owain tries the door, it is locked. He pushes against it, it will not budge. He slams his large hard fist into the wood over and over again.

-Maggie, don't be (a stupid bitch) Don't do this! Let us in, for the love of the Gods let us in.

-It is because I love the Gods that I don't let you in. came the reply from above.

The three look up and see by the light of a wind lamp a

tired looking woman with blonde hair looking down.

-You're not coming in here! She spits down upon them,

-oh don't be a feckin bitch come on Isla.

Mr. Clay waves his hand again, with a smile of satisfaction on his face .

there is a sliding sound, and the door slowly opens inward. The smile is replaced by surprise, when a little boy pokes his head around the door from and stands in the candle light of the tiny front room.

The man in the doorway opposite slides off silently as the door closes and the men enter the small cottage.

The room is well lit, the blackened stove door is open and reveals the glows of red coals, while about them the storm lamps glow with bright yellow flames. The walls, painted off white are brick and stone, the floor, huge slabs of polished rock, in the centre of the room is a large oak table. its bare. A signal of Isla's disapproval.

-Jeus Isla, of all the people, you take Drake's side. Owain shouts his voice booms up the stairwell that rises by the front door.

-Of all people, you should know why.' Comes the bitter sounding reply. 'I told yer to make your peace, but Oh, no! You have to do this!

-It's for the greater good.

-The greater good of whom? Yerself yer selfish prick! That's all! Jus once I wish yer could see beyond what yer think is for the good of us all an' consider-

Owain looks away from her, he senses his rage build, but he is not weak. She is her brothers sister an that blood has centuries of follwin' the faithful in it, I knew it when I married her and I loved her for it then an' I love her still, but she cannot see that givin' up is what they want us to do an' I be fecked if I am goin' to stand here and let them win, not without a fight.

The little boy looks up at his father, his eyes are swelling, with wet they become wide; he hates to see his parents fighting.

-Owain looks down and picks up the little boy.

-There you go Stevie.' Its ok Daddy's home and he loves you very much with ardency and tenderness, Owain kisses the little boy on the crown of his head.   There is a clatter on the stairs, a slow thumping that increases in volume before Isla then walks down and into the front room.

She stares at Owain with cold vindictiveness.

-You better be right about this. She mutters, Take your wet clothes off, I don't have anything for that, especially in its size. She points to Mr. Clay. He'll have to do with what I can do. She shakes her head and walks through to the back room. Slamming the door and making O'Rourke jump.

-Jeus, they truly hate you here, don' they. O'Rourke sneers a whisper   Welshcombing his hair with raking fingers.

-They have every reason to. Said Mr. Clay.

-You know, you are a feckin' enigma, you really are

-Unlike Judith? Mr Clay replied gently, his eyes shining.

O'Rourke stared at him with new contempt.

-That has nothing to do with you.

-No, but it will have something to do with you, he already suspects.

-'yer cunt!'

-O'Rourke! Pack it in! Owain's words barraged the room.

O' Rourke shook his head. His eyes glittered with malice and pleasurable violence.

The little boy left the room to thunder up the stairs and to his bed.

The slow clicking arched clock on the mantle chimed ten. Owain looked outside through the black led lined window.

-Jeus, it's like night outside. Owain muttered.

-It will remain so.

- Yes until the deed is done

-who said anything about that?

-you did, in the the dream that never left me fer months, the same dream, over and over again until, I was dragged out there! Owain bellows his voice hoarse, his body shakes as he points with his forefinger of his left hand, the nail bitten back to the quick, the skin roughened with salt toward the black lined window the premature night of the growing storm. His voice quaking. to that dammed place and saved you and your feckin ship. You forget, we know who you are. Call yerself Camdy O'Dandy if it makes your cock shine, but we know who and what you really are! Spittle flies from Owains mouth in arcs that bely his agony. He turns away and then turns back again his face and Clays an inch between them.

-We know You've helped before, he almost whispers, his head shuddering with rage; you can, you can help again.'

-They won't let me off so easily this time. A cough followed by some loose spittle. ' Besides-

-Besides what?

-You're a doomed race. Clay smiles weakly. You are not what was meant to be.

There was a long silence.

-An whose fault is that? O'Rourke stares at the old man, his eyes blazing mirthlessly. 'Did we ask for this? An who are you to judge? Feck, you know what that makes you? Your just as bad as they are! In fact who the feck are you?

'Who am I?' A hollow laugh. 'who AM I? Ha! I am the only friend you and your kind have now.. You might not like what I say. But it's a sound truth! They are all against you now! Centuries of ignoring us, centuries of denial of coming up with clever ideas, where did these ideas, Clay points to the sky, his voice sardonic, and viscously sarcastic where did these ideas you treasured so much, you embraced with such high and mighty regard where did they really come from, The mind of the human? And who put them there in the first place? You never followed the train of thought back, you do what your kind has always done, slapped yerself's on the back and said look at our works ye mighty and despair! Well they see! They see a coffin of a world you made with your Ideas! Clay turned away a sneer of contempt on his face, as he waved his hands above his head.

    -Jeus! you don't have a fuckin clue do yer?
    -Yer bastard
   O'Rourke Turns to Owain.
 -We shoulda left him to his fate! He's no feckin use to us now.'

   Clay stares at both of them, with tears swelling down his yellow face, into the brown grooves cut by centuries of suffering before being absorbed into his thick pubic beard. Both men stared at him, but it was only Owain who hears him say :'Perhaps you should' his voice: staccato cracked.

                    ***

   The ship inn was a heaving mass, as half the town had descended upon it. Its red tiled floor could barely be seen, its mellow walls veined with lime and old bones were mostly in shade. Occasionally brought into mysterious life by the flickering red flames from the hearth that had a hog slowly twisting on a spit; or the pale light from the shaded storm lanterns, strewn about the decaying wooden benches. The air was thick with tobacco, weed smoke of beer hops and ongoing casual sex as well as fear and conspiracy. The men, their faces young and old were a ghostly in their ale, or teasing with the women, with words of fucking who teased with them with words of fucking back followed by ripe farts and coarse fruity and hard laughter.

    Judith stood by the bar, her bodice revealing more than she wanted it to but also recognized that this always helped the eager youngsters who wanted to know her better for the price of a beer. Her side of the bar is bustling too, with two of Drake's lovers: David O' Shea and Gemma Laughlin, neither of whom she has little time for. She smiles coyly as she pumps out another flagon of ale, and looks up; as she does, she looks away immediately, as the door at the far end of the room suddenly bursts open and a man soaked to the skin stood in the doorway.

-will yer close the feckin' door Lowrey, were yer born in a barn? Came a shout.

-Of course he was yer idiot! Came the reply to a rumble of amusement.

-Its been let in at Owain's house. Lowery bellowed, I seen the door open.

-Not by the hand of my sister, she would never do that! Drake bellowed back.

-no sir, by your grandson. It must have been as she was leanin' from the window.

-why did yer let him marry her Mr D? comes a shout.

-wan't me! Alexander replies, she called it true love, but I think t'was the cock that turned her eye. Despite that time has changed their feelings. She strands solid with me.

-that boy needs some balls.

-what will we do?

-yer see that thing that came out of the boat? Jeus, we are all done for, all of us. It's going to bring' them all, down from the mount upon us! It be the end of us just like the cataclysm that ended the –

-Now what talk is that? Alexander begins gently We know we are safe here, if we follow the code. We were promised after the fall that we would be safe, and we who are of the-

-They can be fickle, Jeus knows-

Alexander stares at the man, his eyes firm and hard, until the man looks away.

-As I said, Alexander says firmly 'and we who are of the bold few obeyed, he pauses we have. He smiles gently; look we have had no harm to us for near thirty year. That's how long it's been since they came and told us not to fear. We were the ones chosen by the Gods to survive, and we have taken strangers, as we were asked to do. Ordain is wild, he always has been. But I have consulted the oracle at the keep a she has said that this is all part of a bigger plan. Rest assured. Alexander 's voice is calm, his tone persuasive and reassuring, the eyes all around him subdue.

Free beer or a stack of weed for everyone!

A cheer lifts the air. It echoes the room as Judith leaves the bar for the back room. Drake notes her leaving and slowly follows. He enters the room and once he is inside closes the door behind him silently.

Judith is by the alabaster sink, her shoulders slumped.

-what was that all about? Yer never been there for all the time that Owains been seeking your help, and never once in

the six weeks when he and the other men were gone!

He comes over the sink and slaps her hard across the face, she stands there.

-Feck off you and yer stinking gods!

He does not hold back all his hate he has for her and himself comes from his shoulder and into rock hard fist. She reels, spinning to the floor, he picks her up by her hair and slams her face into the side of the sink with a sickening crunch. She falls to the floor in a heap.

He stands over her his face scarlet his eyes on fire, his bald scalp glistening with sweat.

-I WONT BE TALKED TO LIKE THAT IN MY HOME! DO YER FUCKIN HEAR!

Her eyes defy him before they close shut

-You heathen feckin bitch!

There is no answer. She lay prone. She: distant upon a cloud of tears.

He shakes himself, before he notices his bloody knuckle, he steps on her and over her to wash his hands in the overfilled sink before leaving the room.

She does not know how long she has been knocked out she feels disorientated the white walls come in and out of focus and have the orange tint ; she feels the swollen side of her face sees the slick of blood on the floor. She falls out of the back door and into the rain and the cobbled twitten with only Owain and O'Rourke on her mind.

Drake stands by the bar, a flagon of Ale in his hand, all around him are the townsfolk supping and stoned, happy to be here and feeling the freedom and the safety of his command he bellows:

-To Baccus! and raises his flagon of ale high in the air. - To Baccus comes the reply as the band begins to play and the orgy begins.

***

Owain kneels by the fire, that glows a steady orange. Orange flames lick out between the paling coals that grey in soft powdered embers. The heat brings life to his chilled soaked form. His huge hands gritted and pitted slowly come back to life. He feels his face redden in the heat. Behind him, and sitting on a wooden chair, with his legs up on the table is O'Rourke. Both men are silent. Sitting next to him and with his head in his hands sits Mr. Clay. The men are in silence each wrapped in thoughts about the future. The Door then bursts open and Judith falls into the house. Her face is wet, wet with rain and wet with her blood that covers her face, O'Rourke wipes it away, with shock. All the men descend upon her fragile frame as it falls into the room.

-I knew I shoulda come fer you I should never have wasted my time here. His voice a blend of concern sorrow and love.

-he knows you're here. She said, her voice barely a whisper. He knows you're here and once he has had his fill, he'll come here. No one is safe.

O'Rourke is there, holding her, he feels her warm blood cover his hands, he sees her blue eyes shine at him, and he recalls the taste of her lips, the softness of her thigh, the warmth and soft muscle of her cunny as she grabbed his thick shaft, and the tenderness in her eye as she stared at him her soul as naked as her body.

-Gods the bastard, I'll rip him limb from feckin' limb.

She shakes her head.

-You'll do no such thing.

Mr. Clay looks down at her and he then kneels.

-If you could see what I have seen and see now. He smiles at her and takes her hand.

The change is slow. Cuts slowly heal, blood slowly rises and dissipates into thin air, a soft blue glow surrounds her as she is slowly healed.

Owain stares at Clay and wonders

Why if he can bring back one won't he fulfil his duty he has to go he has to give us all a chance otherwise its curtains for us all or does he expect us to be healed over and over again like that damnable thing from his prison

Mr. Clay looks up at Owain who is beside him. He smiles.

-I love humanity, I love its changing heart, I love all there is about it. Its rage its beauty and its resolve in times of adversity.

-But not enough to save it from the wrath to come

-The wraith is already here. He smiled sadly. Don't you know that by rescuing me you have pitted yourselves against the Gods and the world that they represent, the world of light will not tolerate this. They will come and they will reap a terrible revenge. Humanity here is lost, but...

He smiles kindness shines from his eye4s as he looks down upon Judith

-There is a small chance that a remnant can be saved.

-To where?

-The realm of the Gods. We could start again. All we need are two chosen he coughs and then says innocents. As he stares at Judith

-she carries in her the seed of hope. Twins, one of each sex.

-what? O'Rourke pales

-Is she?

-she is with child; Mr. Clay says smiling down at her, with the love a true father has for his own blood.

Owain stares at Mr. Clay.

-So it's all been for nothing? Grabbing you from that filthy boat? they are going to win after all?

-No, not win. We must go to the keep the end is coming, Jeus is awakened and is coming for Drake. If we go now, we will make it to the keep in time.

The men pick up Judith who seems light headed and drunk.

-She'll be alright in a minute. Mr. Clay smiles the three of them leave the cottage and as they do, a pair of dark eyes come out of the gloom of the stairwell.

***

The orgy was in full sway. Drake is smiling and kissing his servants Meg and Steven. He is far too drunk and high to do anything other than to allow his lovers   to molest him. He smiles as they scratch at his skin and pull at his hair. He sighs with joy at their scratches his face gleaming with sweat from the effort, a mixture of a soporific stupor and a daze of thoughtlessness. His pupil partially dilated and dream filled lost amid the joy of utter intoxication, free from the mind and the soul.

The band stopped playing suddenly. With sorrow He felt the thick blood gorged cock of Stephen slowly slip out of his anus; He looks up dizzily from the soft velvet quim of Diana and as he does so he stares up to see Isla stand over him. But it was not Isla. Her eyes shone like wild flames her skin pulled taught had cracked in places, where white light shone

-This must end. The voice was commanding and almost ruthless.

-Je-us.

-He has come to us. Je-us has come to us. Murmurs ran among the crowd.

-You have allowed him to come here. To spend time with humans you have allowed him in. The voice was filled with brutal accusation

-he is of no consequence. The way is guarded by my best men.

-you and your human pride. We are right, this is a worthless race, look at them giving into their desires thinking of the moment, they see nothing beyond their noses.

-you told me to stop them. I have! the men-

-The men are fools. You had the crowd on your side? Why didn't you kill them the moment they came to shore.

You had the opportunity! You did not take it!

-And what about you? Why did you not come down? You sent your servant from the belly of that ship, why didn't you do your damnedest to intervene?

-We do not intervene in the acts of a species such as you. Je-us voice curls with revulsion at the thought. You do to each other what you want.

-But you want us to serve you? Is that it? Have not I done that? Have not I been a faithful and loyal servant? I serve the gods I am their vessel

-You are a fool!' Bellowed Je-us, through Isla Her eyes glowed brighter the flickering iridescent light throbbed, as she stretched out her hand: a searing lightning bolt staggered across the room and hit Steven who is then thrown in a high arc back across the room. His body a blackened crispy husk.

A table to her left was thrown across the room by an unseen force, the walls of the inn cracked asunder.

-Behold the dragon! Shouted Je-us, and at the sound of his voice the far wall crumbled away to dust; the cowering crowd now faced the wild and trembling sea and a sky lit by Noctilucent cloud. The waves rose blackly in the half light as Charybdis began to form. There is a rushing sound of thunderous echoes: voices of a dark murmuring choir put the people on their knees before the creature then rose and slowly left the sea. But it was no longer a single entity. It rose: a hideous alien dragon . Its webbed wings visible in the near night were a membrane the scent from the sea was death . it rose into the night. There was a hideous rumbling before is disappeared after which streaks of gold light a myriad of stars fell through the clouds down towards the earth.

-behold! Je-Ous bellowed,his arms now raising up to heaven behold we have come to end it all! As through the wild clouds the stars: the gods of old, fell onto the now dying earth.

***

The four of them O' Rourke Owain Judith and Mr. Clay slowly worked their way along the black cobbles fighting against the driving rain they had almost reached the crumbling keep when they saw the dragon rise disappear and the golden stars fall. Owain could see the walls of the keep shudder in the blast wave as the lights filled the sky.

Two terrified men appeared from the shadows.

-They lied to us! Owain shouted though the driving rain. His face a mask of water and spittle. Can't you see that? They want us dead! All of us!

The men stood there, their weapons raised. Then they were raised no more.

-help her! She is all we have left! O'Rourke pleaded. His sea green eyes straining with pain

The men race forward and take the weight holding Judith up as both Owain and Mr. Clay walk to the keep doors and with hard blows smash them down.

The Omphalos stands there. Shining iridescently Within the walls of the keep. The group stagger towards the stone.

Then there is a bright beam of light that slams into the ground behind them followed by a blast wave that makes the group rock on their feet rock. Standing twelve feet tall is the elder God Ares with his sword drawn. Its four blades rotatıng It whirrs and flashes in the near light.

-it is time then Prometheus.

-My name is Clay. The old man retorts

The feck it is! Owain spits out as he smirks slow shaking his head.

-My name is Clay because I made the men and I made their hearts, I love them and I stand by them, no matter their faults their pain or their greed. I love them and they are mine! Our fate is bound.

'Then Mr. Clay, I choose to stand by you. Je-us is decadent, his cause is lost! His farther claims the throne and I choose not to stand by him!

-We have little time.

-I will protect the son of Clay.

The god saluted and then light ascended into the storm riddled sky.

-we have little time Mr. clay stammers, as he walks to the stone.

There written upon the Omphalos were words written in an ancient long lost tounge. The words begin to glow with a pale white light. Mr Clay sees the words and smiles gently

'There is no lost…just found' he states gently

-what the feck does it say? Asked Owain

'It's a poem of hope, says Mr. Clay, written long ago by my people, in the hope that humanity can see beyond its rank and status. He coughs, and a drizzle of spittle flies from his mouth and rests in his beard, before he recites in his ageless gravelly voice:

-there rests at the edge of forever,

A wild and glassy sea,

Where men and women sing together,

In joy and in harmony.

Gone are the gods and goddesses',

Gone are the worlds unfound;

Here on the world of forever,

There is no lost:-just the found.
  With that, he, with soft unlined pad of his right palm
presses hard upon the cold white stone

                           ***

Isla gasps as Je-us leaves her body,   the golden light in
the shape of a swan travels into Alexander Je-us look
above and roars, the roof of the inn dissolves in a
disintegrating spiral   and then they both leave to rise into
the wild and thunderous sky.
    Ares sees the light and prepares himself, he takes out
his heavy sword and wields it at Zeus as he flies towards
the keep lightening in human form crosses the stormy sky.
There is a rumble of decadent thunder as the red flames of
Ares stands before Je--us.
    -The time for man is over stand aside Ares
    -you know I can't do that.
    -this needs to end.
    -yes, but not this way
     -they are doomed
    - by your father's command I stay.
    Je-us casts aside the body of Alexander , whom falls
with a crash to the ground. He then stands a being of light
his wings arched his eyes alight. He faces the god Ares
made of red flame.
      Their swords smash! The heavens split!
    -tell me! do they deserve judgement because if they do,
then so do we! We made them, we gave them life, we
helped them to be devoured by Cronus and He He! gave us
all life!
    -Humanity must end.
      -Like this?
    The mighty swords clash once more, the cumulus
echo with slams and are blown apart; exploded the
angelic gods battle. Blow after blow rains down upon each
of them : cutting slicing exploding gasses imploding
atoms, roars of rage of pain of triumph and despair.
    Je-us , his eyes aflame then buries his sword deep
into Ares muscular midriff; cutting the god in two.
    Ares gasps in pain but then   joy shines in his eyes as his
body begins to unravel firstly into pointed shards then into
fine molecules of crystalized light .
    -There is more Je-us, he whispers as he finally dissolves
to be blown upon the wild winds of the broiling sky. Je-us
weeps. Bellows a yell and falls down like thunder upon the
Keep.
    Mr. Clay moves his hand from the stone, there is a
grinding sound of old rock cracking as the stone splits apart

into four. A circle of light appears it swirls in a spiral that becomes a pinpoint at its center.

   -we have little time, the old bastard is on his way and he wants this all to end.

   Owain and O' Rourke place Judith on the floor, she is weak, her breathing laboured blood covers her face.

   -it's alright my child, you will have peace soon. Mr Clay says gently as he puts his hands over her midriff. Two tiny balls of light, covered in iridescent thin tentacles rise from her midriff and nestle gently in the old man's hands. He is smiling his hands glowing with blue light, his eyes mild and compassionate shine cupped his raggedy tatty pubic beard is mottled grey and black his eyes old and young at the same time shine with hope.

   Judith holds O'Rourke hand she looks up,
   -I'm scared.

   -I love you with all my heart, tatty as it is, it's all I must give.

   She smiles and stokes his face, then she sighs her body glowing then dissolves to then flow into strands that then enter the portal. O Rourke kneels weeping

   -here is the hope of humanity. The idea is not lost, it needs to find a new home. Then he looks up. The dragon has almost reached its final destination. He then looks at Owain and O' Rourke: you call it Sol. The beast will devour it. it has already grown. its size would drive you insane. Be thankful for the cloud above, this final war

   Mr, Clay rose and walked to the glowing portal as the left wall of the keep fell with a roar and Jeus stood there.

   -finally free eh? Your love for this pitiable shard of life amazes me. Zeus flaps his white wings; and with a swipe throws Owain across the room.

         O 'Rourke stands

   'yer bastard, all this for vanity, all this for a lack of worship, yer and yer kind make me sick!

   Je-us turns to O'Rourk

  -I was there when you were born I saw you made in your mother's womb. I was there when you ran for cover when the bombs fell and watched you make your way here, following that distress call. We made this last vestige for man because we believed in the species, but its flawed. Fatally flawed. It's in your DNA from the moment HE Zeus gesticulates at Mr. Clay, He gave your ideas above your station. You thought you could better us, no become us, but you were wrong. And when your world of machines powered by my energy creased to work, you turned on yourselves like the monsters you truly are. The killing never stopped until we intervened and   so we gave you this corner of this emerald Isle. But not even this place could contain your vile disease could it? Because complacency and hypocrisy eat away at your very souls and you let it win. So here we are as we promised we'd be, to end this sour and sick charade once and for all.

-They need guidance and a chance to think for themselves

-You think that they are capable of fully thinking for themselves ? look at what we gave them? Look at the opportunities they had? They put their trust in economics and politics and in social order, they did not think once about the less important ones, life for them was an orgy or worse it was a lesson in brutality run by their weapons and by their greed.

-and you think we are any different? Look at the world we made? The world of light is no better than their world, its decadent with scourges riddled with lies. Humans are more honest than we are because we know what to do to help and do little or nothing to do so. We hid in their stories, we lied in their morals, and in doing so, we are no better than they are.

Je-us, lifted his sword, you and your sickening words will trouble me no more!

Mr. Clay still holding the seeds of man in his hands turns are runs from Zeus and towards the Omphalos Je-us lifts himself up into the air and then sweeps in an ark around the room. To stand in front of the portal.

-I cannot let this happen.

There is a sound from the back of the hall, Mr. Clay turns to see Alexander stagger into the room. His right arm is broken and hangs loosely down, blood rich and dark oozes gaping sore in the side of his face.

-Je-us, oh lord of life come here. Use your vessel so we might end this together.

-ha look at your pathetic race

-its yours as well, we made them between us.

-We gave them a paradise! Look at what they have done to it! look at it! the bleached trees the rotten waters the dead and dying seas ! This is the human legacy! You want that to continue!

-despite that, he is your son. You are willing to let him die like that?

-he means nothing to me.

-This is why they must be free from us? Can't you see that? We never gave them any real freedom, in any of the incarnations we gave them, from the garden of Eden to the mount of Olympus, we never gave them anything but a reason to hate us or to ignore us.

A roar rippled the heavens shuddering the sea earth and sky

-The beast has reached his destination. Its time

 -we can give them one last chance without us.

   Suddenly Owain and O'Rourke dived onto Je-us and writhed him to the floor. Zeus bellowed and fought back his shape changing into swan's lions and beasts long dead. Mr, Clay with one quick hand cast the seeds into the portal and they were gone.

   -No! Je-us bellows what have you done? It's going to begin again it's going to begin again-

   Then the old dying world folds over, the sun shaded from the sky collapses and draws all matter into it. Earth simply pops.

***

 In an eternity the seeds float, they grow and take form, they rest on a distant planet as children they sit and look at the stars, they see the mountains, and name them. The animals alien to them fantastic in shape stand about them unafraid. The boy child speaks he is called Alpha, the girl child speaks she is called Epsilon and the garden on its own comes to life.

   As the boy and the girl sit on a rock looking up at the splattering of the sky a single point of light glows brightly. They both hold hands when they see it; a lost unconscious thought is exchanged. A memory. There are slow steady footsteps, the boy turns

   -what is your name he asks

    The Old man smiles

     'Call me Mr. Clay.' he replies.

"11 ...Come, ye children, hearken unto me: I will teach you the fear of the Lord." Psalm 34:11King James Version (KJV)

Beneath the moon of Mars

"The revolution hadn't yet begun, but everyone could sense it was imminent; even the air they breathed seemed heavy and full of a kind of menace, as dawn is on the day of a storm." Irene Nemirovsky "The Wine of Solitude."

The maglev train slid within the suspended C shaped rail. Its eight, sleek, silver-grey cars, powerfully resonated with the steady rising wail, of concentrated electro-magnetic energy. As it thundered off towards the undulating salmon coloured horizon, a tail of spiked fingers of blue and violet light clicked and snapped along the rail; and into the slowly dwindling twilight.   The sound of the train was contrasted by the harmony of the lightly falling rain, being caught and whipped into occasional frenzied, whispering, clattering chatter, by the small and sparse spiraling, late summer winds. While in the background the ancient, desert crab-spiders, tapped out a haunting rhythmic beat; as they scuttled upon the old dry bones, which came up out of the long gone rusted sea, on this pale October morning, upon the ghost planet: known to those who came from Earth, as Mars.   With a wail the train crossed the ridge of the old shore line and came upon the dusted land.

Inside the pristine, air conditioned train; Shev Bland slid uncomfortably from one seat, and into the empty seat, next to the window; vaguely noticing how her triangular shaped face, had become a misted reflection. A ghost image, she thought, which in turn floated amongst the ghost's, that slowly wandered outside of the train, amongst the newly discovered ancient statues that spiraled high into the sky. The dried-up canals, that twisted in the in the middle distance and the ancient crystal cities that grew along their banks, and sparkled in the slowly rising of the Martian dawn.

As the train entered a tunnel there was a growling sudden whoosh, plunging the outside world into total darkness, making her start, but then, with nothing to look at, she slowly turned away, to then lean her head against the window. The glass felt cool to the touch; the low growling hum was gently soothing. Both sensations brought a flash pattern of discordant memories, occasionally made of sounds and sensations, she slowly closed her large, oval ice blue eyes...time slowly passed, a sense of inner calm grew as darkness began to overwhelm. Suddenly the scene was violently ripped open, like a fist being punched into her sub-consciousness. The darkness pulled back like sheets of black paper being torn open. Suddenly she was standing, looking up at the distant hill's she had seen from the train. But instead of seeing the tall slender and ancient majestic statues, she saw growing piles of ash and rubble, as swarms of circling Heli-jets were firing rockets and sending waves of sonic displacement beams.

The dry beds of beautifully wrought canal's, were now being buried by ant like armies of Hover-dozers, determined to remove all the remnants of their existence. While the crystal domes and elegant metal spires, of the ancient Martian cities, were being torn into shreds by huge monstrous demolition destructor-bot's, their huge mechanical razor sharp iron teeth gouging into buildings ripping up the ancient roads to pieces, and hurling ancient artefacts about each other as if they were matchwood. While in the foreground were the books... books, she had read and been inspired by; books that were older than humanity itself, being burnt, or smashed or destroyed... Then from behind from where she stood, she could hear a gentle voice, she knew from a time long past, whisper to her: What you see, has not yet come to be, it is but an image of a possible reality, that will only come to pass, if you swerve from the path, Of your possible destiny.

A pause. 'It's time to wake up Shev.'

The voice was clear, strong and full of love. She turned to see Peter standing next to her, holding her hand as they stared out at the scene of on-going destruction. Her dear sweet now long gone Peter, coming through to her, in radiating inner waves from her sub-consciousness, from the place, she had learned that the aboriginal people of the western Australian outback, had once called the dream-land; a sacred place somewhere, other than the train, and the frightening reality she had been forced to accept. It was here that he stood; her beautiful and wonderful Peter, reaching out for a gentle touch, and an embrace of tender lips; and as their lips tenderly brushed, she longed to feel the stars in the seven- heaven's shine.

She took a step back, and longed to stare at him completely. She looked up. But what was once "Her Peter". She stroked his face.

'It's time to wake up Shev.' He said again. This time colder and more sternly, his eyes slowly changing colour, becoming a gloss black, that filled out, in worm-like strands, from the pupil to extend over the iris and then the sclera. Black worms began to writhe under the skin.'

Wake up Shev!' He shouted at her. She screamed, trying, but failing to free herself from his vice like grip that paralyzed her wrist and her left hand. 'I Said wake up!' his voice came with violence and menace. His face began to break into a writhing mesh of broken, dark grey decaying rotten flesh. Huge holes existed for eye sockets as the eyeballs dissolved; and green decaying teeth, began to fall from a hideous and now ever skinless, ever smiling, hideous cavernous mouth screamed, before something with yellow slits for eyes and teeth as sharp as knives reached out to grab her.

'Wake up!'

She shuddered and screamed herself awake. For a second she felt lost, the startling images within her mind left her feeling disconcerted; and confused they did not mix well with her surroundings. Subconsciously she looked down at the palm of her left hand. The embedded crystal was glowing with its usual pearl iridescent glow. She squeezed her eyes together and sighed, attempting to shake away the nightmare. But then became aware of the gentle tapping of the rain

There was something familiar within it, she thought, something, she felt that longed to touch her, something outside of her, something huge, unknown and made of all things; but as gentle as a child. As the rain swept along the carriage, she saw how the droplets became entwined together. Then something unusual began to happen. Slowly they reached out for each other, then, when they became entwined they started to begin to move in eerie pattern of rhythmic pulses', against the forward movement of the speeding train. At first she became scared at the alien interaction, but as she watched, her fear slowly subsided and changed into an ever-increasing sense of wonder. Is there something alive within the rain...? She asked herself. She moved even closer to look at the individual raindrops, her large eyes giving a pale reflection.

Yes...they're gathering together. It's as if they need each other to grow...its acting like a living, micro-organism... it's moving together and taking form... like a snake...like a snake made of water a water snake...Then the message came to her. It took the form of the gentle whispered voice that she had come to recognize as what Peter had told her was the great conscience. We need to work together. It said. She smiled as her mind made the intimate connection to the consciousness. She closed her eyes allowing the answer to come in and enter her completely, in swirling waves of golden light that resonated within and in turn, made her oval, pale blue eyes, brightly twinkle with awe and wonder.

Like the opening of a flower to the morning light, the image of a water-snake ran through her mind. She could see its water eyes glimmering; its water tongue extending as it tasted the thin Martian atmosphere; and as it slithered away from her, its water scales began to glisten and shine like a prism; bringing a rainbow of light through the window that shone with the ever-encroaching dawn. touching the clinical cleanliness of the carriage and the people sitting around her oblivious to what was happening around her; their blank faces yet making them radiate with swirls of iridescent colour's their own internal light.

In what became a precious moment, she became lost to herself through the vision. And as she gave herself over to it; it gave her a feeling of total complete freedom and with that, a sensation of utter bliss. But, in the instant the idea was conceived, and the inner message received; the idea also moved from the Cerebrum and into the dream center of her brain; where it stimulated the inner visual cortex, turning the water-snakes into a politically dangerous activity and a concept that the Northern Block Confederation of Earth would regard as a "creativity crime". In an instant Shev knew she had been caught, when she felt the all too recognizable stabbing headache just above her right eye. It lasted a second in time, but that was all that was needed, to scare her into action. At first, she felt frustrated with herself for letting it happen. Then at the system she had come to despise. Again, she looked at her left hand and at the pearl crystal implant she had been born with; a gnawing agitation growing inside her.

How long have we been off the grid now? She thought. Five years...? She shook her head, her eyes becoming sad confused and then frustrated. ...shit! It's easier being a part of the grid! At least being a part of the grid meant- then she shook her head, because she knew the grid was not the freedom she had experienced since the move to Mars. She looked down sadly, and her mind raced. The Grid...there's no real freedom with the grid... because freedom means a compartmental mind. A mind where dreams were segregated and never allowed to exist; where accuracy and adherent to fact was considered the path to true enlightenment, and where imaginative free written thoughts are forbidden, and had to be shared before the warning was sent to Core Command; and then to the branch divisions of the Tokko: The dark semi synthetic enforcers of the creativity laws and protectors of the Keys of fact. Freedom also comes with a price tag of three hundred and fifty Renminbi a throw. That's how much it cost last time to have the Nano blockers. The trouble is they needed updating every six months; which means there has be a supplier that can be trusted. That's also tough, as the underground has little trust for me now and keep their sources tight behind a wall of silence. Except for Dexter Sloat- She shuddered at the thought of him. ...Dexter Sloat... that grubby, fat little bald bastard, who always stank of stale dead sex, whose podgy, sweaty effeminate looking hands and painted nails had been on me and in me more than once simply because I didn't have the fucking Remnimbi to pay for the injections.

That was why they had moved to Mars in the first place. As she sat her mind raced; she had no idea that the Grid had even reached Mars. She looked up at the crystal display that ran along the side of the train. The numbers were running the time down before the train docked into San Angeles. Two hours twenty minutes the screen, so she worked out, over three hundred Kilometers? She went back to looking at her left palm, hoping that the tiny crystal implant would not change colour. But as she stared, the crystal changed; from a glistening to ominously flash. Red then black and back to red again. Blinking, off... on... off...on... letting her know that the illegal thought image had been recorded on her bio-server and that a message was being sent to core command. Not long now, she thought grimly. 'Fuck!' she said tensely. Her voice was barely a whispered hiss between her teeth. She looked at her chronograph; the seconds began to take what she felt to be an eon. With painful desperation, she fought against her mind. 'It's the wind...' she said her voice a thin nervous whisper. '...It's the wind that pushes the rain, along in thin lines...That's all the wind...the wind, yes the wind created the illusion of, of the window snakes, that there is no such thing as window snakes; there's nothing mysterious, or mystical about it, in fact I just want there to be something mystical about it. I want to believe in window snakes. The outer dream is mine...mine...mine.' She repeated the phrases over and over and over. Like a Buddhist mantra. Until the little crystal dot upon her palm returned to glowing silver once more. Then she sighed and slumped both from exhaustion and relief. She looked at her chronograph and smiled. Only one minute had passed. If she had not been that convincing, then the Tokko would have been upon her at the next stop, and that would have meant internment. Her smile was cut short by the hard sounding electronic voice inside her mind.

'Shev Bland 20, 10 2078 U8363824, you have been sanctioned for a creativity crime. You have been cautioned, one more offence and you will be fined a sum of seven hundred and fifty Renminbi...' 'the automatic response continued with its cause and affect threats; words that she had grown up with for so long she had never known any different. How many times had she been interred? Three times...in three different camps, of varying levels of cruelty; and no one was interred more than five. It would mean...the probe. She had known one person who had been probed... her dear Peter... she looked at her calloused fingernails, that had been bitten roughly coarse. They began to blur, as hot tears began to swell. She sadly smiled, as she thought of his long, curly brown hair and his bright green eyes. It was he, who had taught her how to get connected to what he had called "the great consciousness" a weaving living interconnection between all humanity and a doorway to another plane of existence. She felt that he was so in touch with the great consciousness, he seemed to glow with inner electricity. But then, one cold November ten years ago, the Tokko came in the middle of the night and stole him away.

The backlash was frightening. Some members of the underground wanted her killed, some tried, but failed. Some, like that fucker Sloat, took advantage in the change of leadership. For six long weeks, she heard nothing... Then after a terribly long day in the middle of the wettest August she had known, the truly beautiful person she had come to respect admire and fall in love with had come home...changed. His features were blank, his eyes empty, and his soul dead. while the right side of his head had been badly shaven with a blunt razor blade, leaving a tear trails of dark red blood from razor nicks that had been left to dry. But most frightening of all, was the black wire stitches that were stuck into and out of the swollen skin of his skull in an ugly black blood coloured serrated arc.

With a dismissive shrug of her shoulders, that concealed her deep feelings of anxiety, she ignored the rest of the inner mechanical conversation; in the hope that it would go away. She shook her head and shrugged her narrow shoulders, then ruffled her dyed burgundy hair away from her face. Then she rubbed the sleeves of the heavy looking purple jumper she wore. In themselves they were actions any ordinary observer would consider having no real import. Yet for her, and those like her, they were vital; for they controlled the thought process and gave her a chance to get some control once more. They also told others that she had been "tapped." Underground slang for being caught free thinking

She rubbed her tired eyes and looked towards Jacob. She was fond of him, but she never loved him as she had loved Peter. They had got married, mainly upon his request, not because she wanted to. She thought about telling her soon to be ex-husband about the incident and the dream, as she knew her movements had been ignored. But changed her minds as   she saw how intently he was tapping into the A.I sheet that he had on his lap, His freshly shaved head gleaming with beads of sweat.

She looked at Jacob and recalled those early years when they lived at Core Central after her last detention. She recalled the long hard days at the factory, where she spent her time grinding out munitions parts or pumping out steel and squeezing lubricants onto metal machines, that would become the robots, built to fight the ever-continuing war with the Southern Co-operative; mixed with the heady sweaty nights, when the tender muscles between her thighs felt soft, gentle and warm. She would tighten upon his choad, as he slowly thrust into her, causing her to gently tingle all over, while his moist and tender kisses filled her with electricity as he slowly teased her with his tongue. Mars was the chance they both needed for freedom, but it also ended their relationship. Now they sat at forty-five degree angles and away from each other. The green white and grey plastic molded table between them now acted as a no-man's land which she had decided she never wanted to cross any more. So, she slowly returned to the view from the window and the ever-constant twilight, of the Martian day.

=

Shev and Jacob had left their home for the last time at a little after four in the morning, E.S.T. and in some ways, she was glad to do so. As far as she was concerned she was leaving behind a hideous, grey and white corrugated metal box that was ugly, mass produced and conventional. It's only real benefit had nothing to do with the house at all, but the choice of its position, where the view from its porch was a breath-taking for it stood on the edge of the raised plateau, just outside of the first expedition marker point, known to all the settlers, as York's rest

As she stared up at her home, she still felt that, even though it came from earth, there was something very alien about it. She found it hard to define why, until she thought about all the other earth made structures here on Mars.

Then a connection was made. Even the most conventional of earth like structures would look out of place on a world like Mars. A planet, she thought, that we desperately wanted to run to, yet longed to secretly shape into the very world that had we had been so eager to leave behind.

She smiled ironically and shook her head as she turned away from the house. Her breath was bellowing in heavy clouds, as she zipped up her thick heavy winter coat. Then beamed a huge grin; as slowly the warming comfort of its many layers begin to heat up as the heating system turned itself on.

She turned and then stared out towards the Martian foothills, and the ancient Martian homes that began to glow in the middle distance. As the dim sun very slowly rose, the ancient houses on the hills began to shine with a dry rusted light; their ancient brittle bone structure blending into the land that they were grown from. Their solar panels absorbing all the energy they needed to run their empty ghost houses. For their ghost masters, who forever haunted their ghost planet.

'Do you think that they'll ever come back?' She asked absently.

Jacob stared at her, with bunch fists for eyes; his teeth yellow and pasty.

'What makes you ask that?' he said coldly.

She could hear his laboured breathing, as he started shifting the long green heavy metal box and knew the chill of the morning air was getting to him.   She smiled. Her eye's not concealing the enjoyment she felt at watching him toil.

Christ...' he began shaking his head. '...Its always the same with you, isn't it? There are no Martians! They all died out after the second expedition... they found thousands of bodies... all dried up into blackened crispy paper from the pox.' He coughed hard. A green lump of phlegm hit the cracked frosted ground by his feet. Making Shev feel nothing but loathing for him.

'You going to help me with this fucking thing or not?' he said aggressively. She shrugged her shoulders and helped him place the heavy trunk in the back of the buggy.

'There's no going back after this, you know that, don't you?' he said. But his voice contained a thick edge of nervous trepidation. Yet it was not his own.   She nodded, but she wasn't sad. The house she would gladly leave... but Mars... Mars had become to mean more than just a place to live. It had become a refuge from a world run by the Neo realist Movement. A world of firemen, who stopped people from reading, and from bringing contaminated thoughts from outside the web. A world of medivec, a sedative to maintain an ordered mind, a world of wall screens that dully allowed nothing but neo-realism. Now they were going back. Back to the world she loathed and feared. Back to a world that teetered on the brink of one final war to end all wars. She looked down at the long green box and smiled.

'Better get goin'' he said almost silently. And she nodded.

They set out in the black six wheeled land buggy. Jacob's face a mask of grim determination that hid his real feelings. While she allowed herself the luxury of imagining what one of the old ones might have looked like, as they bounced along the ancient track that passed by one of the huge crystal and stone cities made so many centuries before. And then she thought of Gem and the flowers began to bloom. In the back of the land buggy the box rested. They climbed a steep hill and the box suddenly slid to the back of the van and hit the rear panel with a heavy slam. Shev span a sharp stare at Jacob.

I'll be careful.' He viscously growled, over the grinding of the wheels on the ancient stone. Within an hour they made the station at New-London; only managing a passing glance by the armed guard. And that was fine... Gem smiled at her, and that made everything fine.

===

Gem was one of the first born on Mars. It had brought Captain Wilder, the Colony's commander to the hospital with a bunch of hydroponically grown roses; and a smile upon his face; just before he had been recalled to Earth.

Gem was special. She was special not only because she was the first free born from Earth. Which meant was also free from the implant procedure. But she also held a secret as old as Mars itself. The memories she allowed to come to the surface were safe ones. They were the faces of her long dead mother and father, of Jacob in better times even of Captain Wilder and the flowers he brought on the day Gem was born.

Jacob looked up and for the first time in two years he smiled gently.

'Are you having a hard time?' He asked. She nodded. But then he smirked cruelly. The rage and the pain he was in smeared over his face. The green box, kept floating onto the surface of her mind. Its contents wrapped in shadow. She fought against it and sensed Gem's smile.

===

Gem grew fast in the thin atmosphere of Mars. At the age of four she stood as tall as a six-year-old. Her body slender and a little more wisplike than the bulkier kids, who had come from Earth; which caused some mockery at the school.

When Gem came home with a bruise on her cheek, Shev went to the school. The teachers smiled but said that there was little they could do. Shev recalled the first-time Gem said something out of place. She was five and bright eyed. Her hair was a rich red rust colour and flowed about her. At the time, they lived in New Vegas, next door to Peter Giddings. Peter had just been around and asked if Jacob would be free for a game of cards that evening. She had said she wasn't sure, but she would tell him when he came in. Peter just nodded and walked back to his buggy, ready for his shift at the mine. It was a normal event. Nothing strange. Yet Gem looked at Peter with a strange look. A stare that made Shev ask what was wrong

'what's a fuck mummy?'

Shev's face turned a dark plum colour caused by a mixture of anger, embarrassment and shame.

'A what?' The words hit hard and made her jolt.

'A fuck.' There was the child like curiosity in her matter of fact voice. It was obvious that she had never heard the word before.

'Did you hear Daddy.-'
Gem shook her head, '-No, it was Peter, he said he wanted to fuck you so hard. And the pictures he had in his mind were-'

'-oh, I don't want to know.'

'I don't know what it means?' came the whining reply

Shev looked at the car as it drove away.

'Did he say it when he came over the other day?' and with that thought came a fury. She would have it out with him as soon as he came home.

'No...' Gem started '...he said it in his secret place.'

'Where?'

'His secret place.' She gasped as if she was talking to an idiot the thing an eight-year-old would do. '... You know mummy. The secret place where we all think things.' Then she said something that chilled her to her core.

'Mummy... do you want to fuck him too?'

Shev stared at Gem. Then she said coolly. 'Just stop this! Now!' She began. 'And if you do use words like that again, then I will be very angry with you. Do you understand?' And in her mind Shev had an image of her spanking Gem. Gem took a step back and began to cry.

'Don't spank me mum, please?'

Shev hugged her. 'No darling, I promise, just remember...please try not to go into... peoples have secret places... and these secret places are for us alone.

Six years passed and Gem grew at twice the rate of the other children. Her heavy golden hair was tinged with lines of rust. It blew about her narrow face; her once blue eyes has a glimmer of gold in them. Her voice too had deepened, she was supposed to be ten, but in her actions and her talk she was that of a teenager; with all the joys and sorrows that a growing adolescence brings. Moreover, her and Peter had become very regular, regular enough to consider getting away from Jacob. She was considering this when she stumbled into Gem's bedroom three weeks ago.

Shev caught her balancing a ball in her bedroom, two

inches from the palm of her left hand.

'You don't love Daddy any more do you.' Gem said coolly.

'-That is none of your business.'
'-It is my business.'

'Now, now you listen here young lady.' He words were stern.

Gem laughed as Shev felt herself being picked up and thrown bodily across the room. Then she felt an intense weight slam into her. Making it hard to breathe. Gem giggled, there was a little of the old Gem there, but not much. Something had her now.

'You can't leave me, not with him.'

'I wasn't... I-'

Don't lie mother!' Gem Howled.

'Gem, sweetheart.' Shev wheezed.

'He's touched me mum!' Gem screamed and threw Shev down on the bed. 'AND I am changing every day I hear them calling me calling me getting stronger telling me to go to them but I can't and I won't you hear me! YOU HEAR ME!'

'My darling, what's wrong?'

'This is wrong! You! Him! Me! This! everything here is wrong MAN DOES NOT BELONG HERE! ON MARS! They tell me the ghosts tell me they come into my room after he's been and they tell me that they have a plan a plan to stop it all to- Suddenly The door burst open and Jacob stood there. Blood was pouring from his eyes and he screamed and screamed. The floor burst open and two faceless ones arrived.

===

The train began its final turn into new Frisco. It came to a halt. Shev and Jacob made their way, with their package, to the gate that led back to the rocket ship to earth. Then People began to cram in bustling past. Fighting for space. Shev looked down and looked at the metal box that they carried between them. She smiled. She stared at Jacob. He smiled back. But the smile did not reach their eyes. They knew what they had to do and they would do it. The box would open on the way home, and the final message sent from Mars would reach Earth a year later. The message would be a final one, that would tip the balance and bring the war. The war that would stop the human stain once and for all.

As they sat on the ship. The being that looked like Shev opened the box. Then both Shev and Jacob sat back and watched as one by one, the humans started to complain, then bicker, then fight amongst themselves. Before too long blows were being exchanged. Then scratches, fists broke teeth. Fingers gouged out eyes. Hate rose and the body count slowly climbed, until silence filled the ship.

===

From the Martian foothills, the faceless ones, known as Aia and Mr Zizz stared up towards the rocket as it sped into the salmon sky. Then Mr. Aia turned towards Mr. Zizz. Their golden eyes met, yet not a word came from their mouths. There was no need. The package is being delivered the virus once the ship lands will grow soul upon soul will be swallowed whole as the species man will devour itself. As the words passed between them Maia as Mr. Zizz slow golden tears fell for those lives lost on their world. War is inevitable were the final words they shared together, as the twin moons of Mars, slowly rose over the Horizon

They

It's morning and a thick chilly sea mist is blocking the
Horizon. I must say.... it's very worrying...After all, I won't
be able to detect them. So, to avoid the dark thoughts
that... they... bring, I stare away from the almost invisible
horizon; to observe with renewed wonder, the surface skin
and the shallow depths of the brackish green North Sea.
The sea writhes at my feet. But my mind won't let go. They
are a fixation... a dark obsession that fills my mind entire.
The sea... it's a paradox... for they are in the sea ...they swirl
in its' depths. They wrestle, unseen within the constant
eddies of the hidden currents that ebb, then flow. They are
always restless; always nagged with hunger; always
looking, looking, looking, with their dark, dark, dark eyes.
Flexing this surface membrane, this translucent skin, with
ripples that also reflect an idea about space-time and with
that, bittersweet memories of a day when they... did not
exist.

   I slowly sit down stretching out and crossing my legs, I
rest upon the hard-brown rock. I hear those tiny waves
within waves, as they gently collide against each other.
Here...Space expands... The water is so near...yet not near
enough to my pale, almost numb, naked feet.

   I long for a sense of peace, but I am distracted by the fact
that I cannot see the long arc of the sandy beach. It rests in
half-light. A pale grey in the middle distance, beyond which
the wind twisted sand dunes are picked out, spectrally, like
a series of sharply cut lines of shades of black steel and cold
iron grey. It is a cold day. The sea salt fills my nose and my
lungs...It's out of the dunes a see a shape take form... At
first It's a dark shapeless shadow, that slowly becomes...
becomes... no! I want punch the cold cracked ground with
my now hard fists. A sound. I slam my hands over my ears.
I don't want to see. I don't want to feel. I want to forget!
Forget! Forget! I turn around so I know I am not facing the
beach. I remove my hands. I open my eyes. And with hope
I look up. The sun shines a dull grey though the mist. But
it's blocked from direct view by the huge tower that stands
over me. It's the shadow of our home...St Mary's lighthouse,
upon the edge of Whitley Bay.

   I hear tiny faltering skipping steps. I turn to face the
sound and see little Alice, our precocious Alice, our five
year old, daughter, who has no other knowledge of a time
that's not filled with them, playfully stagger over the rocks

towards me. Her plump, long blonde tousled unkempt hair hangs around her shoulders. Her large violet eyes shine from her elfin shaped face, that is, at that moment, filled with a frown of concentration. Her faded yellow floral dress is mottled with ever larger multi coloured paint stains that have grown since our arrival here less than six months ago

I feel the depth of love begin to swell in my heart; it puts a smile upon my face, a tear falls, as I see her nearly trip over the rocks as she walks towards me. I see him in her face... Gaz...

I look down and away from her as, I recall his gentle yet firm muscular body. His auburn, welsh raked hair fading to a wispy grey at the edges. The kind, yet penetrative stare from his large blue, green eyes... I think of the feel of his stubble upon his narrow square jaw as our faces touched... I recall how itchy it felt, as well as the tender touch of his hard-calloused skin from his large heavily calloused hands, his hard-thumping muscle, as our bodies gently entwined together, in the tender, yet urgent need for intimacy. Our heaving breath in the pale light of a golden dawn a lifetime ago.

Alice comes over and gently sits upon my lap; but looks down and away from me.

'Mummy?' her gentle voice carries within it, the echo of a once warm summer's day.

'-what is it darling?'

There is a long, plump heavy sounding pause.

'I had had the dream the dream again last night.' I hear the tension in her voice, and note the tremble of her lip. She has been screaming with night terrors again, and I know why. But now is not the time. She must understand, we must stay here, there is no way that we can move, right now it's too risky It's too risky for all of us, Oh, sweet Lord I wish I could think clearly for just one second Gaz Why-

'-We're safe here.' I can hear the lie coming from my mouth. Why do I say it? Jesus why do I pretend? Is it right to lie to keep her safe... to keep her free from... them?

'-But, what if they can-'

'-No.'

I hold her tightly, and then lift her head back to stare, as sincerely as I can muster, into her large beautiful green eyes, that shine so very brightly.

'I promise you... 'I say, the words but I feel my insecurity become obvious because, I'm not sure that I believe it myself. '...That...they can't get us here.'

'-But...Gaz-'

I feel hot anger build at the sound of his name. Anger at being left to fend for myself; with two girls and a baby boy; on my own. Anger at Alice; who has no real idea of what sweaty, blistered scab she has innocently scraped off. I want to scream Fuck off yell and punch. I want to hold her tight and tell her that everything is going to be alright. Instead I say something else. Something terrible.

'Gaz is dead.'

The words come out with far too much force and I instantly regret them. There is another long pause, and in that pause I feel a gulf tear open between us.

Alice stares at me, her eyes begin to change shape as they fill with large salty tears. I sense she has become riddled with an inner pain that I know only too well. I try to cuddle her to show her that it's all ok, and that I love her desperately. But she shakes her head, her blonde tousles wave and sway about her as she roughly stands up. Swaying slightly as she pulls away from me, she takes a step back. And in that step I feel a greater gulf begin to form.

'I know what you're thinking. I know it know. You blame me! it's all my fault!' she steps back. 'You you think it it it was my fault. Well it wasn't! IT WASN'T! IT WASN'T!' She steps back. 'Its them! it's them its them! They are coming! they are coming! and they will not stop!' She turns to flee, back to the safety of the light house.

I shake my head and try not to cry, I try to reach for her as she departs, I long Just to hold her close. As inside I feel my own pain grow and wrap about me like a poison giant. Oh God, I need her to know I don't blame her, I need to feel something, anything but this sadness anger and pain. I need her to know that we stand together against them. But she fights me off and pushes me away all the harder; while Inside I'm begging her to stop and desperately wishing that I could just turn back time and take those terrible words back.

'...I Hate this place! AND I HATE YOU!' She screams. As she enters the doorway and is away from me, leaving me alone with my guilt glass shards of bitter, fright filled memories.

***

I enter the old fisherman's cottage through the back door, and walk into the large white walled kitchen. I am met by the warm welcoming odour of freshly baked bread. It almost hides the stale smell of the decaying vegetables. In the background I can hear baby Si', screaming for attention and for food. Rachael has her back to me, but I can see she is making soup. Her long black hair falls around her shoulders in shiny, spindling ringlets.

'Our supplies are low.' she says with her back to me. Her voice sounds cold and as sharp as a razor blade.
'-I know-'
'-an' the lines need bringing in-
'-yes, yes ok! -' I feel tired and put upon.
'-Mary Jane- 'her voice sounds conciliatory but firm.
'-Just for Christ sake, shut up!' I shout savagely, as I leave the kitchen and go through the narrow hall, to the front room; where Si' is lying on the white rug. His pen is surrounding him. I pick him up. It doesn't take him long, a cuddle and a suckle settles him quick.

I look down and see in his eyes, Gaz eyes staring at me. As I sit in the rocker by the window, words like summer rain.

'Why... why'd you have to do it? Be the fucking hero... when we need you... when I need you... There's so much to do... so much to sort out... '

Si' looks up and gurgle's sweetly; his round face and blue eyes shine, his toothless mouth white with milk and spit. I smile down, unaware of the footfall in the hall.

'Jane.' It's Rachael again. I feel my nerves grate
'Alice is upset. Why did you have to say that?
'-We're safe here.' I can hear the hollow lie in my voice, because I know it's insane to stay, but, but I just can't let go...

'-Who says?' Her voice sounds clearly hostile; and that hurts me. 'You know 'ow we've done it in the past... Alice 'as the dream, an' we move on. That's what we've always done since...' She doesn't finish the sentence but the air is heavy. '...Gaz would want us to move on. Staying 'ere is suicide. Simply suicide for all of us!'

'-Gaz isn't here.'
'-An' don't we know it...' She replies tersely. '...They are real, you know they are! A scout came six weeks ago it was just blind luck that they didn't get the little one. Instead it took Gaz. Listen Mary! They took 'I'm a now they, they coming 'ere!'

Her words echo about the large living room, like a dark prophecy. 'You, you might want to stay 'ere an' hold 'old on to your memories, yer dreams, an' yer.... But we, that is the rest of us; we need to live! You need term think about that!'

I don't look up. I only hear her feet slowly walk away upon the red flagstone floor.

I hear a clatter of pots from the kitchen, and feel my face blush with guilt and shame. I look to the cot, but Si' is asleep. So I turn in my chair to look out of the cracked window. The green sea is flat and seems to go on forever. The sky, a stone grey. The fog has lifted. I only wish my mind was as clear.

Night has come. The fire licks orange-yellow flames up the chimney, and leaves the room feeling warm. Si' has been taken from my lap and placed in his crib. I look across the room and see the heavy sofa. Oh how I wish he was here, holding me close, telling me what to do.

But he died six weeks ago, while Alice was building sandcastles on the beach. I was in the kitchen preparing breakfast, while Gaz stood in the doorway, looking out towards the beach. We had been up for about an hour. I was feeling sleepy warm, ruddy and tender from our love making.

I looked out of the window across the tiny bay to where a wet Alice; her blonde hair dark, tousled and full of salt; had started to put sand into the small round yellow plastic bucket by her knees.

Then the alarm sounded. Instantly, we stared at each other. Nothing was said. Our eyes wide open simply met; while my heart began thumping with a black panic.

Then he ran as fast as he could down the narrow path that led back to shore. It didn't take him long to reach the beach; or the heavy black junction box that we had improvised as part of the EMF shield extension. He quickly ripped the lid off it; before, as gently as he could, so not to make her panic, call Alice over to him

It was a sunny day... the sky was unusually blue and clear from the swell of grey cloud that normally came from across the sea.

It seems amazing that I didn't see the raised antenna, or the tentacles that followed, until it was too late.

I screamed as I saw them snake up the beach. Rachael saw them next. She ran from the lighthouse picking up the rifle that was resting by the kitchen door. I saw her wave frantically, before charging down the narrow path. Her body jarring as she sped. She stopped as she reached the beach and managed to get two shots off, as the tentacles silently sped towards them

It was enough for Gaz to see what was coming. I saw him click something. The alarm suddenly died, and then, instead of running towards us, with Alice in his arms...he ran the other way...leaving Rachael and Alice to run towards the safety of the newly functioning shield.

It only took a second... hundreds of razors like tendrils spat out of the sea, they wrapped about his body, them lifting him up high into the blue sky. He screamed. Howled in agony, as he hung for a moment; like a twisted puppet, on barbed wire strings his arms outstretched, like a perverse Christ; before he was suddenly dragged down at a lightning speed. Swallowed by the green, swirling sea.

Gone.

'Gaz…' my voice sounds dry and cracked. I close my eyes and shut out the candles, the fire-place and the near silence of the room. But the room isn't empty any more.

'Mary.

The room is a blur; a swirling wash of orange embers, mahogany and candlelight

'Mary'

I wipe my eyes and stare across the room.

'Mary.

He sits there sweetly, that smile upon his face; as if he's never been gone. Doesn't he know what he's done to us? Doesn't he care that we have had to cope without him

'Mary listen.'

Its Gaz…He sits in front of me, wearing that blood red jumper. I shake my head, not knowing what to do, not knowing what to believe.

'Mary my darling, you have to leave here. Alice and Rachael are in real danger.' He speaks in urgency, yet in a voice that I find hard to grasp. 'They, the old ones, they are coming here. They know you're not safe here. Jane…please listen to me.'

'Where have you been?'

'Jane I know how much this place means to you, but you have to leave.'   Suddenly I'm in the open! There is a screaming whine of an insect's wing, followed by the clacking of hideous alien voice, followed by a loud whump; as their sloppy wet heavy feet made of constantly winding and unwinding tendrils tie themselves about each other, giving strength to the whole form as it staggers, then lurches upon the land. It writhes with a hideous slouching gait , its single yellow eye ablaze with insane victory as it screams in an unearthly triumph; all the while more huge fibrous tentacles are reaching out for me, smothering…smothering my face.

I scream myself awake. Baby Si is in Rachael's arms. I feel a little jealous that he is resting in her arms, but I try not to let it show. After all I love her as if she is my ow

'I'm sorry 'bout yesterday.'

I find a smile upon my face and hope that it isn't fake.

'-It's ok.

'-It's… just that I miss- 'I can see her pain and her strength

'-It's ok. You're right. It's not safe here any-more. We're leaving, get Alice.   With a smile on her face she speedily turns and leaves the front room

***

The sky is full of slate black raging clouds that boil and curl over a violent pale green sea. The wind is beginning to rage too. That's good because it means the insects can't fly. Also with the electro-magnetic energy the land monsters will be stuck too. That only leaves them from the sea.
Leaving is painful...The memories fill, and wash over me...I almost feel haunted, though not by the monsters... For I have lived two lifetimes here, and that's not bad for a woman in her late thirties...I look at the lighthouse... I see Gaz..The man who kept me sane and us together... The Father of Alice and Simon, and the Brother of Rachael...I see him standing on the beach waving us off, so I know it's time... and it's ok now, to say goodbye.

   We get into the screen cracked land-rover. It's weighed down with supplies and the four of us. I turn the engine over and see that the tank is half full. I also know that we have a spare tank of fuel in the back... we are ready to go, And not before time. For as we sit in the car, we watch silently, to see huge leathery tendrils come out of the broiling sea, we hear a hissing scream as they wrap themselves about the buildings; and monstrous howls as slowly the buildings are torn to shards of rubble iron and glass; the towering light, broken into bones of iron and lumps of powdered stone. Where are we going? I am not sure, south... I think... I look back at the ruin of the lighthouse; our home for so short a time, is now a broken shell. I look at Alice and she smiles for the first time in an age... and at Rachel who stares down lovingly Simon... she is smiling too and that is nice to see... Yeah... it's time to move on.

Dream wars or Dani nails a Kermit

A warm bed. A sense of togetherness and isolation; all wrapped inside the warmth of a cocoon. The alarm blasts the shouts start. Orders yelled in staccato screamed from spittle mouths. alert alert alert! Heavy boots dragged on from soiled hands people getting up fighting to put on something to protect them from the storm Alert Alert Alert

'-DANI YOU FUCKER MOVE IT INCOMING INCOMING
Voices swarm about like flies
'-Yes sir!'
-Fuckyoosir'
'-NO NO NO!'
'-Gods help us!'   The hollow grate floor clacks with the rumble of shoes. The lice ridden hair and bodies scratch like fire on fire. A gathering

'We have a sighting 20 clicks east! They are coming in hard! They W-WILL NO

TAKE PRISSOONERS! Move it soldiers!'
Climbing out of the bunker. Out into the sky.
Rise...rise... fall.

The explosion of Earth to the right.

A scream as Peterson -my drinking and fuck-buddy-loses the side of his face.The skull fragments shatter into the steel cloud above.

Recall: We lie in his bunk.
'What's your greatest fear?'
Snuggling in his arms...*losing you just losing you.*
'That I...might die not completing my mission.'

Now ...His blood -like hot tea- splashes on my lips. I can taste its rich thick warmth in my mouth.

Oh, let me wake up Christ let me wake up!

The boots =sound heavy hard weighted down the sky is full of stars: 2001 a space odyssey of all thing to remember when I see a Kermit in my scope

The orders come. 'Ten to the left! Five to the right! Shots are short! Make it count people!' Kermit's explodes in gun sights, Bits of Kermit brains, mix with boiling ash of laser fire.

That's for Peterson you shit stained frog cunt!

The face of Jess comes to mind. Her smile as she shoes me her latest puzzle the innocence of child family life oh how I love family life stolen from the past a memory recall to hide the pain.

Kermit's got wise. He takes his ships up high. He knows we are the last of us and He can wait like the twisted slimy frog he is he knows he can take his time to fish us out and feed on us Kermit has a weakness though. He has a collected need, Kill the queen and the fuckin' rest might burn We know this. That's' why we are here. Getting our skulls ripped open. Just ahead is their way-station the beam that takes us off world and into the sky.~ Kermit came with promises. Sweets that made us feel good. Feelings like "you're not alone" and "The Universe was not made by God" also lovely technology. However, Kermit lied and he broke us with his machines. Now we pay. But we fight back. Oh, fuck how we fight.

Another explosion to the right Earth spurts open. Stumps of trees are ripped from the soil. The sky is steel coloured. The remains of a building: bricks and half a roof come through the smoke and fire to the left.

'Holleran, take Jaccobs, Cree and Newton into that building! Fucking re re group-regroup! Re...'The world shudders with another explosion. We fall back to the building.

'-shit.' A fall to the wall.

'-Dani! Hollerann! You okay?

A distant call now, His voice muffled

'You like this daddy? Mummy?' a picture of a green man appears.

'Yes hun Its beautiful...Its lovely.'

Then Jess stares at me with Kermit eyes.

'Kermit wants me for a sunbeam daddy. He wants to eat me whole

A scream.

'For Jesus sake wake UP!

'Holleran! Fusc I thought I lost you!'

'-Peterson they got Peterson!' I scream

'-Serge 'it too! Cree shouts.

The cunts!'

A siren wail sounds. The burst of fire. Over-heated plasma scorches the wet earth by the broken buildings entrance. We wait till dark. '

'We can still make it. It's not far... from the entrance.'

'-what's the ammo?'

'-Six six grenades. five cartridges. The E.M.P and the device.'

Newton sticks a stim in his neck. A brief smile returns to his muddy bloody face. Cree sips his flask of home brew liver rot.

Newton mutters '-Do do you really think it will make a difference?' the drawling of cynicism gets to me.

'-the intel- 'Cree points ou

-Intel's been wrong befog-'

'-WE EITHER TRUST OUR SPECIES OR WE FUCKING DON'T (sigh)It's that simple. '

'-There's only four of us and a fuck knows how m-many Kermit's between, between here and their cloud station. We are under-gunned an' fuckin' surrounded!'

'-We have to make a stand. If we don't what we wort-.

'-Remember the time before the Kermit came? The fuckin way we hurt each other was far worse. Least there is some sort of honour in this war. This us and them, is is better than building walls an' saying to our fellow men fuck off and die!'

'-families, remember them?' A smile. 'I have a dreamer. He keeps me sane. I need him. I drift into this guy's head, an old relative dead many a year before. I sometimes feel his boredom with his dull life. He doesn't see the kids and the wife and the family. He doesn't see that one day all of that will be wiped up like a spill on a table. You know sometimes I hate the fucker. I wish he'd wake up and face the future!'

'Nice soliloquy' Cree grins

'Fuck off Cree.' A grin back. Perhaps a new fuck buddy

Darkness comes and with it silence.

The placing of the holo-map on the floor. A large dome with four smaller domes around it, each numbered 1 2 3 4.

'The entrance to the cloud is here. (Pointing to the west side of the dome.) There is a small chance. If we take out the defensive position here....' Pointing to the small dome 3, '...then we can set the charge by the main entrance. 3 must be the the least guarded. Look at the the terrain?'

He points to 3, where the ground was closed off by the side of a hill.

'The Kermit's are arrogant they think we'd miss that. Remember the Thames? They thought they could win that? One cloud at a time.'

'-IT might work...'

'IT'S A fuckin suicide-'

'Jesus don't you get it yet?'

They stare at each other confirm the truth. 'We are the last of our platoon.' '-an we have done this before.'

You have...' mutters Newton. '...vet never been further than Bunker hill.'

The night is dark. The moon hidden by clouds, the soil is wet. There is not a sound save our wet boots in wet feet slapping into wet mud. Kermit's are busy miles away. They think this is safe.

'Eleanor Put the cat down!'

Giggle

'Dani switch the dreamer off. This is reality. This place however shitty is real. We have one chance. Only one!'

'-who fuckin put you in charge?'

'Don't be an arse Dan.' He gets sexier every moment.

The Dome slowly comes into view. It's lit from within by some weird kind of Kermit energy. Fuck knows what it is. They never gave us that. Its surface glistens with oddly shaped pentangle's the cloud from above seems to criss-cross on its surface as it hums.

The trees about it are bone fingers pointing up to a God that stares down with apathy at the creations they made fighting for life.

'-Did I tell you he had this thing. This -lactic thing that had oil inside. He shakes it but its busted. He knows its busted but he shakes it anyway.' '-Dani what the fuck are you talking' bout?'

'-My dreamer. He has this weird shaped plastic thing it has two colored oils in it. You turn it over, and the oil falls. Gravity. But it's broken. The oil has set at the top in clumps. He knows it's broken. But he still shakes it anyway.'

'-and the point of this?'

'-Hope I think. It's what separates us from the Kermit's. We have that. They have their plan. We have something else.'

'-shit your talking' about faith?'

'-perhaps.'

'- an how does that help us here?'

- '(giggle) I just don't know.'

'-anything' that gets you through the day- or night- I guess.'

Dome three is dark green. Its surface hums like a Kermit on heat. Its stinger in its flabby tail primed for firing

'Shit I'd never thought we'd get this close.' Says Newton

'-That's Faith Bro.' '-fuck you.' Newton retorts

The smell is bad. It's always bad by any Kermit's lair. The reeking of warm rotten flesh, of wet bones lying in heaps. Kermit's best friend is the fly. They love each other. They cover the bones in a black slick. The bones stick out of the earth. People cages.

The a.m. is charged. Steps move away into the dark of the bones of the trees. A large flash then silence. The silence is like a numbing to the ears. Then distant rumbles stir

'Quick come on the entrance. 'Charging against the distant rumbling from behind. The Kermit's are coming. Shit I release my weapon into the sky in a panic of frenzy light staccato shatters. 'Come on Dani move it. An entrance curls open into the dome as bodies fall in.

'The lock reset the lock!

Inside all is quiet. The dome has one thing inside: A circular portal.

A door. Beyond is their ship, The cloud.

'Ever have a chat with a Kermit up close?' asks Newton

'-Just once.'

'-What it say?'

'Donno, I couldn't speak their shit language... And the translator was off line.

'Ha.'

'We haven't much time...' Begins Cree.'... We need to get through and close this off, the lock won't hold for long.

The portal glows...Running into the portal.

Will I wake up will I ever wake up? '-Arch Eleanor!'---'-Daddy she is taking over the game daddy help me daddy I need you daddy daddy daddy!'

The floor of the ship is crystal the earth is seen below. Now it's covered with yellow splashes heaved vomit. 'That was fuckin unpleasant.' Newton grins laconically

'-Well it's designed for the frogs of space. I doubt it was meant for us

'-(Giggle) Shit here we are! Spawn central Kermit's home from home. '

. -One of many.

'How many times now?' Cree grins. His wide set eyes shine.

'My third and still I vomit. 'I smile. A look below at the earth: a crystal orb glistening surface brown green and splattered with milk.

'It's beautiful... He wanted to do this -The dreamer- He wanted to come here and see this. I doubt he want to see it over-run with Kermit's and their spawn though. He wanted to become a spaceman as a child. He ended up-'

'-They're trace memories. We can't go back we can't reply. Cree retorted '-Sometimes I think...I think he hears me.'

'-Your so fuckin' sweet. We have a fuckin' job to do Dani! Come on!'

Newton appears. '-I've managed to cut the drones. This cloud is off line for now. We have fifteen before we drop back at another local or take the drop-ships. Shit we could do this'.

The walls of the cloud are shining lines of light move in spirals along its curved interior. The helix the double helix the Fibonacci Sequence the 0, 1, 1, 2, 3, 5, 8, 13, 21, 34, ... all lead to life

'Why do they hate us?'

'They're animals like us, they want a place to live. They see us as inferior. Its survival that's all. We take up space and they don't want that.'

'-if we had the same technology, would we have done the same?

I. Don't know. We might have, we- '

'-I just wonder sometimes.'

'You know you spend too much time with your dreamer! That's dangerous! They're programme's from memories! Emotional algorithms to give you something to hold on to! To help you! This war this is the real world....and one day, it will be over...'

'-I wonder if it ever will be.'

The steps sound hollow on the floor the smell begins to get bad again.

'"Kin Kermit's.'Cree continues '...'ND don't think that there is some connection between the past and the future! That's not real. This is real. The Kermit's need to go. They spread and they kill. We are the ones dying out. And you know despite it all, we will win, because we have something they don't. We fight and we keep on fighting because that's what keeps us alive. They hate any life other than their own. The harder they push. The tougher we pull. 'Sounds like rhetoric to me...' begins Newton. '...you should run for office' we all smile.

Then the ship speaks, with the voices of children and parents.

'You cannot defeat me I'm un-defeat able I am in a hot air balloon and I love you. Where is Angela you can't breathe high you need oxygen to breath high I've just had enough of this what's wrong with you... I wish you were back this week.

'what the fuck is that?'

'My dreamer. How the fuck?'

Running down the hall and up to the steps to the doors hands feverishly work on the release mechanism cracking the codes.

'I hate children.' '-leave me alone leave me alone leave me alone leave me alone I didn't do anything wrrroong!'

The walls reverberate with the sounds of long ago

'is this your dreamer?' Asks Cree.

'yeah. Why the fuck is this happening?'

'I don't know. I don't know tech stuff

'I don't like it' The walls echo.

Slow steps up to the platform all milky a snowy bowl. The spawn float in their cloud of milky dew. Half formed legs and arms. Bulging eyes wet and watery, peer through the haze of glass. Above the pool the hybrid is clamped. It is unable to move or speak or move. It stares down through lidless pink eyes. Perhaps it wants to die. Perhaps its sick of all this life

'-Dani you have the charge.'

The charge, is a fifty, big enough to burst the hybrid Kermit and its cloud and small enough to carry. Its placed at the foot of the glass tank over which the bloated thing squats and blurts sounds as it spurts out its eggs.

Cree looks up at it.

'It's not over yet. We know that. But we can beat you now.'

The bloated thing licks its huge wet lips wet lips. It wants to speak.

Dan feels repulsion by it and turns away. They all walk away. They walk slowly as it slowly starts to speak.

'Mummy, Mummy! Eleanor won't leave me alone Its unfair mummy, mummy!'

Then they run and they keep Running and running to the pods.

Space fall first the silence of a lack of sound. The silent rupture of the clouds in a burst of hot yellow light and trace gases that forces the single seat crystal ship to glide off course.

A scream. A wail. The pressure of the skin of the sphere shudders about the small space. Dani looks left. The pods are falling, falling, falling.

Heat builds up. The cracking splinter of shards. 0, 1, 1, 2, 3, 5, 8, 13, 21, 34, ... we will make it we will make it. Then splash- crunch and the lurch of retro rocket stabilization. The door slides open. A new place of operations. The south... possibly France. Dani looks up and ducks as dives as Kermit fighters slice through the sky. The earth is ripped in blasts that shudder about her as she runs

'Daddy I love you.'

'I love you too pumpkin.'

A door slides opens beneath her feet she falls into the safety of the bunker entrance. Its darkness embraces her. She is alone. Cree? Newton? Did they make it? Everything is lost by the Hugs and the words "Bonjour Comrade." This is followed by a warm bed a sense of togetherness and isolation the warmth of a cocoon.

Two starts in one

One: Land-fall

I'm leaving this message on a stasis beam, and sending it out into space in the hope that it will reach home. Perhaps those who read it will learn from it and make the choices needed before it's too late. As for my family and I, we will leave this planet behind in two days; there is enough fuel to start the Higgs particle accelerator drive to fold space for one last jump.   What I leave in this document is perhaps our last will and testament; and the testament to the end of all humans. Right now, while I am talking into the recorder, I am side looking at my daughter; she is just behind me in the room up at the end of the hall.   The sun has just risen over the horizon. It's not a sun that many on earth will recognize. Its larger, and perhaps weaker than the one you, if you have managed to receive this message are looking up to now. She just said there are a few clouds. I cannot see them from the message station I am sitting at. We were one of fifteen million chosen to start life upon distant worlds. The planets themselves were chosen prior to lift off, thanks to the constant work of Astronomers all over earth. The families were selected, five million ships made, seven thousand trajectories set. We were supposed to be part of a larger contingency for the Alpha- centauri system. One of one thousand families designed to start life and new civilizations...here... But something went wrong with our guidance system...we ended up...'
 Thomas Paxton looked to his left, his sea green eyes blurred while he stared at the book resting on the table. He shook his head as he continued to speak.
    '...Not where we were supposed to be. The Earth we left had its problems. But, it must be said, we were on our way to sorting them out. We chose to leave, to give those at home a sporting chance. It was based on the equalities act, set up by the United Nations before we left, we were witness to the great three clauses "No nation state shall inflict war upon another nation" "all nation states are equal" and "profit must be shared" the second of the global alliance, bade us a fare-well, as our ships filled the skies. I even remember my thoughts, as I prepped my family for the what we call the punch, where our ships simply burst through billions and billions of light years, in a second. I wondered what marvels we would find, what wonders we would see on the other side of space. '

'I awoke first, to find our ship had malfunctioned and was off course. I, still groggy from the jump, managed to wake up Anne my wife and Steve our co-habiter and both of us, managed to make the trajectory safe.   Yet the world we looked down on was terrifying to behold. Huge tracts of land were blackened. Deserts covered many regions along what we thought would be the northern continent. The Seas, though blue in places were also stained grey and a sickly yellow. Also, clouds were dark and menacing lightening flashed around the southern equator.   My first impression of the planet we observed was of a skull licked clean...'

'Checking for life signs' Steve retorted as Anne checked the atmosphere for any high levels of contaminants.

'Where are-are the other ships? they should be-be here by now.' Anne muttered into her monitor.

'There are pockets of life scattered about the north-west continent, perhaps there is life, as we know it. Though it might be underground, on the whole...sir... this is a ghost world

'-I'm picking up trace particles of Uranium 232 in the upper atmosphere.' Anne sighed.

'-That's...'

'-but its decaying, so...- '

'- A war...a nuclear war...'

'-Stupid arse-holes.'

'-Can we land there?'

'-As I said, there are pockets of places where life is sustainable, further to the north.'

'We need to wait for the other ships.' I finally stated and we all agreed.

So, we waited. Three longs weeks we waited. Hanging above this doomed planet for our settlers to arrive. But, they didn't come.

In the meantime, I woke up, Jess A.J Mike and Nell; and they helped with as much as they could, sorting out the seed pods for possible distribution as well as attending their various tutorials. A.J being the youngest, took to learning languages. Nell, history. Mike physics and Jess literature. Anne and I took to maintaining the orbit and sending out our signal and Steve to maintenance. The weeks dragged by. We became aware of several communities in one small region to the North of the planet, however, there were no radio signals for us to recognize, so we considered that the species were pre-industrial revolution.

We also became aware of another species of what appeared to be ape like creatures. We sent our probe to monitor their behavior, but every time we sent a probe down, they became incredibly exited and waved and jumped and bashed the trees. So, we decided to leave them alone. Three weeks passed and still silence. We had no idea what had happened; so, I went through the ships computer log. It was clear that at some point, we had travelled close to a black hole. This had an impact upon the Higs bosuns and sent us Somehow, I still don't know how, through a time distortion wave. In short had somehow, shifted over three thousand years ahead of our scheduled time for arrival. If our settlers made it here, they made it already and had started a colony without us.

I called a meeting and told the crew the news.

'-So, could be our colonists already settled?'

'-Or what's left of them. The U232 dates from about that time. '

'-So our arrival could have caused this?'   'if the planet was inhabited by another intelligent species; and that species had a strong set of beliefs about their position in the universe, and we- we came along, it might cause a-a ripple effect across the species as a whole! Their society here might have torn itself apart. '

'You're talking about cognitive dissonance But I thought that the worlds chosen were vetted first.'

'-That's ...sort of... not possible... not from Earth... 'Mike began. '...By the time we left earth, the data coming back, only proved that the chances of life were possible upon the planets vetted, not that life, let alone intelligent life, or life as we perceive intelligent life to be, actually existed.'

'-If these life signs are our people, then we have to establish contact.'

'I say we go...' he concluded. '...we can't go back the way we came. We'll only end up further in the future. The earth we know might not even exist now. We have to land. We only have enough supplies for one more week.'

Anne and I agreed.

The ship slowly descended though the atmosphere, creaking as she did. A.J her green eyes wide with fright wailed for her mum and Nell grabbed her seat as the ship made grinding noises.

'that's coolant on deck three, must have lost a shield.' Steve screamed as the ship flashed with flames through the from the main observation deck windows. Then came the rush of air, as we sliced though the sky. I then fired up the auxiliary jets and extended the wings, the ship bounced then flew in a long arc, over the torn countryside, over trees and between hills, until we found a viable water source.   I then rotated the jets and brought the ship down, with a soft bump, to earth.

All was still.

'Checking atmosphere.' Anne murmured. She held my

arm gently as she rose form her seat and then waited for the glass vial, that descended from above her head.

'Okay, its Oxygen level is less than earth, also nitrogen level a tad high. But its breathable. I pulled the hatch lever and we all rose to our feet and went outside.

We had left a planet over populated with oxygenating machines, and air providers. The children had never seen the colour green I was old enough to witness to the removal of parks. Though from a human perspective we were a flourishing species, we flourished too well. Our systems, political and philosophical could not maintain the balance of power. Our societies had to change. This had led to years of civil unrest as the people in power refused to relinquish control. Law became a global need. As did seeking new places to colonize. This was what we all left behind. When AJ saw the trees, she became scared.

'What's that Daddy?'

'It's okay Hun.' I began. We slowly descended the walkway and walked towards it. I touched the bark. It felt hard and warm to the touch; the sun had already been up several hours. I ran my fingers along its' rough skin. It felt alive to me.

'Once upon a time Earth was filled with these.'

'Yeah, it's a tree so what.' Mike sighed.

'Trees lived hundreds of years longer than a man. How long is the span of a man's life now? One hundred and seventy-five? In my great grandfather's day it was 90, some were dying at 50. Some younger as the society they built- '

'-Dad, we don't need a history lesson.' Jess yawned. Her mouth was wide. Anne and Steve came out off the ship last. Steve set up the light beam perimeter's so to give us warning for any predators. While Anne took soil samples to see if the planet could sustain our seeds. I surveyed the scene. We had landed by a large lake, beyond that and to the south were two high grassy hills. To the north and west rand, a large forest that led to the life signs we had picked up. To the east was a large grass plain that ended in a scorched desert. Our findings had shown that radiation levels within the desert were far too dangerous.

At first glance It looked like earth, though an earth which had mutated. Some of the trees were unlike anything I had encountered on Earth throughout my years at college. Some of the grasses seemed sharper then on earth too. Of the animals, we did see, only a few mice, a deer, with four eyes and a vole or two were recognizable. We came upon our first discovery of a humanoid that night.

We had just set up our first fire, and the sun was going down, when we heard a rustle in the trees ahead. I shone my torch. The white light of the beam startled the creature, whom, after making a terrifying whoop and a scream, darted to the left. Then we saw another, then another. Steve ran inside and selected a phase pistol from the armory. He came back as one of the humanoids came out of the tree line and put his stave at our feet. He looked up at us.

He, being a male and wearing what look like animal furs couldn't have been more than five feet in height. He had a broad forehead, gnarled hands and long brown hair. He stared at us with chestnut eyes. His mouth wide, and teeth overlong extended in a smile. Though we had no idea why he was smiling at us.

It was then that we heard the trumpet. Suddenly there was a whooping in the group and the small humanoids scattered into the trees and the forest.

The horn sounded again, and this was followed by hooves and horses. Anne took the children inside the ship as I went to get a phase pistol. The horses galloped around us, and then encircled the camp.

The creatures we saw had the appearance of being humanoid. Their pale blue skin had a sheen that glimmered in the morning light; and though their silver hair had an ethereal quality to it. I noticed how the antennae twitched with their smiles, or scowls; while their eyes, were slightly extended over thin noses narrow lips that receded o their cheeks, they were also chinless.

What was overall strange were their apparel. The men, for they seemed to be all male, were wearing bright red jackets and black jodhpurs, and boots, while carrying armor-light weapons that looked very late 20th century stood about us

'Good hello...' came the nasal drawl from one of the men on horse- back. '...What do we have here?'

'English.' Steve whispered, 'How the hell?'

'He's not piss-poor...' Began another. '...Henry, I mean, look at his attire...and he has a family... have you come from Easterly? for the festival?'

'Yeah.' Steve replied quickly; 'Just here for our hols.'

'Oh, then you must come and try our ale.'

'Maybe tomorrow.' I said cautiously.

'Do you think we should tell Edward?' asked another

'No he's bally busy now with very important meetings about the next range of privatization cuts. Got to get the bally pisspoor and kick them where it hurts'

Guffaw guffaw were the replies about us.

'-Look, men, we didn't come here to bally take on the menfolk of Easterly, we came to get us some bally sport with the pisspoor, so let's leave these chaps and head orf into the woods or back to the pub for a pint.'

With that and a hurrah they left the camp.

The next day, Steve and I took a skitter-ship five miles to the edge of the community. When we got there, we couldn't believe our eyes.

'What the fuck is this?' Steve stared with bewilderment.

There, in front of us, was nothing other than a traditional English village. It looked like something out of a post card, or an Enid Blyton fantasy. Rows and rows of Thatched rooves ran the length of the street. A tall, gothic spired church rested on the top of the hill, while along the street men in business suits, their ties done up to their necks walked arm in arm with their wives who were dressed in long blue dresses; around which rode those men wearing red velvet jackets and round black hats trotted.

'It looks like England in the Victorian period....' Steve muttered.'...But look at the style of suits. that's more early 21'st century, prior the revolution. Look that's hunting gear....and those automatic rifles... it's like a mixmatch of three time periods in one.... You have a master on that period of history if I recall.'

'-Yeah.' I felt my stomach pinch with anxiety.

'What if they killed us? what if they- 'I couldn't hear the rest, I observed   Two red coated horsemen stop at one of the cottages, just as a crowd began to gather with placards with emblems that had "save our streets" written on them.

'-What's going on.'

Even though we were some distance of, f we could hear shouts of "Go back to Westerly!" And "No immigration here"

'What the hell is this?' Steve asked.   'It looks like...' But I didn't finish my thought, as one of the men in a blue suit came from the back of the crowd. He made his way to the front and was lifted upon the back of one of the horses.

Though we couldn't hear what was being said, it was clear that it was having an impact upon the gathering, some of who slowly left the gathering, while the men in red jackets began filling the street. Then A Large wooden horse drawn cart came along and the people in the red entered the cottage.

'What the hell is going on?'

'I think...' I began, as I observed the men in red jackets throw one of the occupants, what I thought to be a man, out of the cottage and onto to the floor, as others, entered the cottage and escorted the other cottage dwellers, onto the back of the horse dawn cart.

The man who had calmed the crowd, came down from

the back of the horse. He was given something; at the time, I couldn't make out what it was; But as he got closer to the man they had just pulled out from the cottage, he held it high above his own head. He shouted something I could barely hear; just before one of the men in red jacket's, raised his rifle and shot the man, from the cottage at point blank range in the back of the head.

The body fell forward with a heavy slump.

'Oh my good God!'

'What the Fu! '

'We cannot stay here! Jesus!'

The man in the blue business suit walked away as the people in the van were executed to lough cheers and guffaws.

'What the hell is going on?'

'It's the purges.'

'The what?' Steve stared at me with a puzzled expression upon his face.

'The purges…. The UK went through a revolution in the teens of the 21st century. It was caused by a blithering idiot who started a referendum that, because of the growth of the corporates was due to fail. Then the idiot ran away. This eventually end to marshal law being imposed. The trouble was England was so poor Towns were run independently from the state; some villages took to using old fox hunting guilds, as a form of police force to maintain law and order in rural communities.'

'My god if we did come here and cause this, if we did what have we done?'

'I need to know. I need to know! Steve, are you with me?

Steve nodded, so we made our way to the village.

We were met by one of the red jackets.

'Oh, good hello, you're that party on your hols' are you having a good time?' he asked

'Yes,' I began awkwardly, 'But we need to speak to Edward about renting the land.'

'Naturally, you'll find him at the old oak inn. Just ask for Edward Balfour -White. 'he said as he trotted away.

We walked in silence past the guard and entered the public house.   The building looked as if it were out of the-the 15th Century. White washed walls of ward and dapple, rendered with plaster wrapped about the room. To the far right an Inglenook fire roared with a wild yellow flame, large oak stables were scattered and all around people, some in red jackets were chatting loudly. The A huge I walked up to the bar. Once or twice I heard the word outsider, and the room became silent.

'Is Edward Balfour –White available, we are asking

about renting the land by the lake.

'You're not from Westerton are you?'

'No, no, we're from the east and are just stopping here for a holiday, that's all. '

'Well you're not pisspoor, from the look of you, so that's alright, Edward is upstairs just knock on the room on the right.

We walked up the narrow stairs. Steve drew his pulse pistol   and held it behind his back as I knocked on the door.

'Come in.' came the voice.

We entered the room quickly. Steve, suddenly turned on the two red jackets at the far end of the room and fired stunned them. Then he turned the weapon onto the man who sat on the chair with his feet up, and who at that point suddenly rose to his feet.

'and what.' He began '...can I do for you?'

'What is this place?'

'I, I don't know what you mean?'

'This shouldn't be here!' I felt a rise of rage inside me.

'Look, can I be clear for a minute? You come here, and let's be frank about it, shoot my men at point blank range and then tell me what to do? Are you bally insane?'

'Why did you shoot that man and those people in the cottage this afternoon?'

'That's obvious dear chap, in times like this, when the world is on the brink of financial collapse, difficult decisions need to be made. We cannot allow those of a foreign disposition to be allowed to stay. They had to be repatriated.'

'But you killed them.'

'When I said repatriated, I meant with extreme clarity.'

'How did this happen? Why did you take this path?'

'There was a time, long ago, when the world was safer than it is now. But something happened. Our oldest manuscripts tell us of a great falling of stars from the sky. Those that survived managed to do so at great cost. What you see here, is based upon what we found when rebuilding our society. Books, books like this, the word of God, they fell from the sky. Books that told us how to rebuild and make things better. Seeds fell too; and with those seeds came hope. It's taken us centuries to rebuild what was lost. But we did it with help from these.

The Book was thrown at me.

I paled as I stared at the book cover.

'You based your society on this?'

'Yes said Edward. And others like it.   We shaped our names and have a society that functions. You either aspire to be better or pay with your life.'

'Oh my god.'

Steve looked at the title.

'We did it. Shit we did this.' Steve's face paled.

'This wasn't meant to be read to create a society! It was written to warn what would happen if this path was taken!' I bellowed.

I went to the window and looked outside. Now I could see a statue. I shook. This was too much to take in.

'There is something else too, something only I know. A secret handed down by elder to elder…. You are the foretold ones. The ones who

'Where is this history found.

'-In the archive.'

'Where's that?' Steve hisse

'Two miles in the cave of telling.

'Then take us there.'

With slow nod, Edward stood and agreed.

'You don't have to shoot me; I will take you gladly to the cave of telling.'

The three of us left. By the back door of the pub and took to the hills.

It took us several hours to reach the cave of telling as he called it. Two guards stood outside the entrance.

'Wait here.' He told them as he led us into the cave.

'There was a time' Began Edward, 'That we were a great people, and we can be great again. We can lift from the ashes of this bitter world and start again.'

'Spoken like a true fascist.' Steve muttered.

After a few minutes Edward came back and we entered a large grey lined room, that was lined with books except for the far wall where stood a huge screen.

He led us to a huge screen pressed a button on the front of the console. There was a humming sound as the screen lit up. In front of us was the most beautiful thing that I had ever seen. It was a city made of glass and crystal, yet it was surrounded by nature. Trees were everywhere.

Then from above the sky lit up with a million stars.

'Mahtani youloah manwheni' said a voice.

'Acais' said another.'

'Nugoo ethtali -as Il'do'on .' Said a third.

'The translation into your tongue would be, look god has returned as promised.'

The stars became ships.

'Those are ours.' Steve muttered

Then the ships suddenly opened fire.

Steve took a step back and held his hand to his mouth. I felt a tear form as the beautiful city imploded under the laser fire of a thousand warships.

 'But, but we were- 'I started.

The screen went black.

 'They came and they wrecked our world They turned us on each other and then- '

 'Then what?'

They... disappeared... where, we do not know, but we are their custodians, we have learned from their archive and from their books. For ours were destroyed, so   We learned to rebuild using their ways.'

 'But their ways, were, were shit, that's why we left! We came out here to start again. We were not perfect, we made

mistakes. Huge ones. We enslaved people and used people and killed people in wars that were wrong. But We ended that and left it all behind to start again. We didn't come here to kill and exploit. We came out here to start again.

 'You say that.' Began Edward 'But you are no different. You divided us, you stole the land and then you vanished. Yet you left these' he pointed. Books that we can learn from.is it a surprise that this is the society we made

 'That's unfair!'

 'Is it?' we never asked the sky to be filled with your kind. We didn't want your knowledge, yet look what your kind gave us, look where it has led? As you said, it's not perfect, but it works. '

 'It destroyed life at home.' I shouted. 'Billions died!'

 'Maybe... in about fifty years or so it will. But now we have peace.'

 I stared at the book.

 'This will lead to war. This will destroy any society you have.' My words sounded terse. 'Steve, we need to leave. Now. '

 We came back to the ship by dawns early light. I left Edward with his cave of secrets. I kept his book....

 Paxton turned the books over and looked at the covers

 " Mein Kampf, Thatcherism: making of the contemporary world, by Evans, J Evans" and "Atlas shrugged" By Ayn Rand stared up at him.   He sadly shook his head

 I now end my log report. We were late. One thing is certain we cannot stay here; this is not a world that's safe for us.

 There was knock on the door of the ship.   Paxton, with a sigh opened it. One of the small ape like humanoids stood there. Paxton stared at him wondering how he ended up in Steve's uniform. He looked behind him. Jess started to scream as she slowly began to change.   He turned and saw Ann slowly shrink into an ape like humanoid, with a sense of grim horror crawling up his throat, Paxton looked at his hand as it began to sprout hair and the muscles slowly began to shrink. Soon after, he had no idea who or where he was. He simply ran out to join his new tribe in the high hills; and in the years, that followed he looked up at the stars in the night sky and made whooping noises while their ship -now empty- slowly rusted into the old dry earth

Two starts in one
TWO   Earth is hell

"And death shall have no dominion" Dylan Thomas
   I'm sending out this message to anyone the proximity of
this planet in the hope that people will stay clear. I... I am
all that's left of our crew I've made contact via a light
beam so I am planning to make the jump to safe space and
the shar'eel station as soon as our drive can be enabled.
What happened...we seem... to have been...trapped...in a-a
space- time vortex...our on line communication and holo-
instrumentation... failed... and we have been out of contact
with home-world now for six weeks... when we managed
to get our instruments functional and the server-hybrid
controls stable we found ourselves in the proximity of a
like planet very similar to our own; but as we descended
our ship as struck by... metallic slugs.   We... that is
officer's Gorn, Ludlow and I Tenarish... lost control... of the
flight systems the ship. It bucked and was buffeted by
winds that span wildly in the upper then lower atmosphere.
We fought to get some control but failed. Slamming into a
vast desert.
   We would have died there. If it were not for the creatures
of the planet. They are tall, far larger than us, also of the
bipedal design and what appears to be in the 4'th stage of
evolution.   As you know the most complex stage of
existence; the teenagers of the universe so to speak.   Most
of the crash is not known to me. I had the impression of a
being looking down at me. sensing danger and malignance
from it, even though it stared at me with gentle eyes. I felt
lies and mistrust... From here, I remember nothing until I
found myself alone in grey green room. I was lying flat on a
resting station. It felt warm, but the room itself was cool.
   I stood up. At one end of the room was a large   I could
see a group of the tall ugly looking aliens at the far end of
the room. I walked towards it and found myself touching a
barrier. I ran my fingers over it, stroking it. I was in a
prison and these aliens were looking at me.
    A voice disembodied, filled the room. I must say I had
no idea what it was saying, but I could gather from the
faces and the minds behind the wall, that they feared me. It
took a while for me to adjust my cortex to their notions of
speaking. Yet before too long I understood them perfectly
   Two of the aliens were discussing what to say to their
commander. That the ship had to be removed and broken
down for analysis. The stared at me with a malign stare of

mistrust. I asked about my colleagues. At which point one of the alien creatures stared at me with a great deal of hostility. He understood me perfectly.

'Your crew is dead.' Its lips slavered as it spoke. Its eyes glistened with hostility and hate.

'I want to go home!' I demanded

'You are in no position to demand ANYTHING!' The voice was hoarse and riddled with both fury and fear. The Aliens walked away   and I was alone.

I sat back on the rest station. I don't know how long I was there for. Time had no meaning in that room.   It had been ages since I had had any sustenance, felt myself slowly start to get weak.   I began to feel scared as I felt that they were deliberately trying to starve or thirst me to death. Vials of a liquid were handed to me through a partition in the door. I drank them and felt revived; but it was never enough to make me well. Only enough to maintain my slow weakening state. I was also passed some organic substance that I devoured, though I was given no means to release myself. So in humiliation and under what I thought was intense observation, as I was certain that I was still being watched , even if I could not see my captors, I had to use the corner of the room. Within a short period, I don't know how long. My fluids were collected.

Using this to grab time by I made a mental note of these visits. During each visit, I begged to have someone to talk to, so I could go home. I was greeted by a faceless giant in some white robe and helmet whom never spoke at all.

It was after the sixth visit that another man in a white robe and helmet came in. this time to see me. He took off his helmet and greeted me with gentleness, the first time I had experienced this on this world so far.

'please forgive us, for your treatment to date...you have to understand that we are...' he paused and again not for the first time did I sense betrayal or mistrust 'a species that has no knowledge of life outside of our system. Our planets are dead or unable to support life, as we know it to be beyond our own planet. We are scared and at the same time exited to meet a species from another world. There is much we can, or could learn from each other. '

'I agree, but keeping me here is wrong, I want to go home. My presence here is difficult and dangerous for you. You are only at your 4th stage of evolution. This is a volatile time for your species...our own world during this period was wracked with wars that decimated our planet and our people. We had to change. '

'How do we change?'

I felt at a loss as to what to say. For the first time this being a male officer in their army, was being honest with me. It was as if he could see the nature of the species that he was a part of and felt the need for change. I wanted to tell him what to do, but, I didn't.

'You must weather the storm.'

'That is not an answer.'

I stared deep into his eyes and felt compassion for this man.

'It is the best that I can give. To show your sincerity, it would be best to let me go… let me contact my family. I know I have travelled in time as well as space. But I can still contact home, if you let me get to my ship.'

The officer looked sad and frustrated. I could sense the battle within himself.

'You know you have caused quite a stir? Your ship made the news all over the planet. We have had a very hard time in keeping a lid on it. Even down to humiliating one of our own officers.'

A memory popped into my head. A lesson, a lifetime ago. I avoided eye contact. Not wanting to show any form of recognition. For the first time since the crash I felt truly afraid. What if I could not get beck? What if I was trapped here forever? What would happen if these hideous creatures became bored with me and-

'If I grant you passage to your ship, will your share some of your technology with us?'

Here it was, the bargaining chip. The means for my release. This truly was a vile species, that lacked honour and compassion. This would go against the Kaitlin accord, set to protect the universe from hyper-advance's. ordinance one of the agreement states "Each species has to develop in its own way and its own time. Only when Jump technology is achieved then a message of greeting could be given. "giving any advancement of technology could impair the species or lead to a chain of events that could lead to its undoing.

But I wanted to go home. This species was malign, I hardly knew anything about them but the ones that I had met, seemed bent on hierarchy militarism and gain. Taking this further out from this initial analysis led to the conclusion that this species was heading towards a retrograde cycle. It could advance no-more in its present form so it would, with time annihilate itself. By giving them any technology, I could be giving the species a death sentence prior its recognized time. I could also be affecting our own species. The school memory came again. What was I to do? I knew, if I stayed here, I would die. I had no option. I considered my options and then agreed.

I was flanked by six creatures and the officer   all in militaristic uniforms and taken to what was called "hanger

31". The ship was in a huge dark room that I couldn't see the end of. The floor was dusty and dirt ridden. The ship on its side, its silver surface glittered in the half-light given by the   low light emitting beams that surrounded it

It looked charred in places, part of the surface skin had been hacked away and peeled back revealing the green-glowing fiber optics, used to ignite the particle drive.   I could see the holes where the ship had been hit with projectiles   I felt angry at that. The ship had been hit by this vile species. I turned to the officer whom I agreed.

'This is why we don't want to share advanced technology. You would bring your barbarism into the spheres and make captives of us all. You are not ready for space. I doubt you will evet be ready!'

The officer pulled out a projectile weapon and pointed it at me.

'There will be other's. you know there will be other's. '

I read the man's though and knew he meant it. Underneath this being's charm and compassion; was a vile beast, a creature untamed by history that fed off violence and greed.

I sighed, and gave the command. The ship door opened.

'Only you.' I said to the creature.

He accepted and followed me in.

I gave the order and the door suddenly closed trapping us both inside. The officer raised his projectile weapon. But the ship neutralized it.

'Its' not nice is it; being a prisoner. Forced to do something that you don't want to do. I filled the officers mind with images of suffering. The man fell to his knees in sorrow and pain. I paused, feeling sorrow; knowing that this being was limited by his own species. Death broke this species, time and time again. I read the officers mind "...and death shall have no dominion..." a poem, written by one of its more enlightened beings no doubt,

'I will give you something.' I smiled coldly as I looked at the stasis beam. In fact I will give you two things. First is this.

I opened the flight simulator control consul and handed the officer an integrated circuit that contained a micro-processor. I guessed , from what I had seen, which I have to say hadn't been much, It would take this species about fifty years or so, from its present standing to understand how to integrate it into other computer systems.

I then pressed the laser communicator indicating the ships position.

The other thing is this... it's a story... once, we were like you...barbaric, proud, haughty. We thought of nothing other than killing our family over the price of food or technology. We were a doomed race, until a ship came. That ship was welcomed by one of its leader's; and from that point on, our species thrived. I don't know what you call yourselves, and, to be honest, I don't care. Soon I will lift off this shortfall and make sure that not one of our species comes within a Kuantan of this planet. Do you understand? '

The officer nodded.

'Now get out.'

The officer left. The hangar doors were opened and I took to space. I am now here, waiting for contact. It won't be long now… It's such a shame, from up here, it's such a beautiful planet.

I can sense my family now they are coming…coming through time to save me…. It's good to be going home, even though I never really left.

And to dust you shall return

Most people know of the Crimson Wake a star ship, seven class, that disappeared somewhere in the Betelgeuse system, some ten years ago. The official story of the loss of the Crimson Wake is that she lost all hands during an FTL jump, when   the Higgs boson particle accelerator imploded killing all hands. In truth, she disappeared without a trace; thus leaving huge questions and grave concerns about the future of the FTL drive as a viable means for transportation and colonization of the known universe.

However, in the last week, evidence of a life capsule known to be from the Wake was found sending a signal off towards Jupiter Way Station. How it was found was miraculous at all. What we hoped to find was either a survivor that would verify the established account or evidence to support what had occurred to the ship in this still un-yet uncharted region of space.

The capsule was brought onto Jupiter Way station and taken to a secure site where its contents could be analyzed. What was found when the capsule was opened was bizarre and ominous

The capsule contained some strange dust, that under analysis seemed to glow with a strange blue, green light. It turned out to be both human DNA and another unknown molecule that we are yet seeking to understand. The capsule also contained the last log entry of Petty officer Davies. Below is the report, transcribed for further analysis as gateway station.

I'm sending out this message to anyone the proximity of this planet in the hope that people will stay clear. I, with what's left of our crew are planning to make the jump to Terrain space and the Jupiter station as soon as our drive can be enabled. What happened...we seem to have been...trapped...in a-a time vortex...our on line communication and instrumentation failed and we have been out of contact with Terra now for six weeks... when we managed to get our instruments functional and the server-hybrid controls stable we found ourselves in the proximity of an Earth like planet. However, scans revealed that the planet was once habitable and contained life. We found cities that suggested a type 4 civilization: one that had managed to control the chaos of its species and developed minimal space travel to the outer reaches of its own system.

However the planet was deserted. No life seemed to exist at all. With the use of thrusters, we managed to land on the outskirts of one of their largest cities. Myself, Dr Peterson, Chief Engineer Drayton and Captain Wallace made the initial investigation. Once we found the air breathable, we removed our environmental suits. The silence was the first thing we noted. Nothing was heard at all. Maybe this planet had no knowledge of birds; despite that. There was something in the silence that was … disturbing.

We entered not a city but a corpse. Windows had broken or been shattered by violence. Machines resembling cars or something similar lay crashed in the roadways; their paint rusted, or burnt out. Our steps echoed as we made our way through the long thoroughfares of what we thought must be shopping arcades. There was a dust over everything, a, a fine powder that became…translucent when our analyzer beams shone on it. Our diagnostic devices seemed to suggest that this dry powder contained DNA, essentially organic matter now just dust. We concluded that what-ever had happened here, happened on a global scale, because our data from the ship pointed to a planet with over 7 00 billion people on; yet here, in one of the largest metropolis' of the planet there was nothing but dust. We walked for hours, trying to find what had happened here, or anything that might lead to some answers; Did this civilization on the brink of a major discovery choose a neutron war and suicide, over progress? Was the planet invaded by another race?

We knew from analysis of the atmosphere, that nuclear conflict hadn't occurred and we could estimate, from the state of decay of the building's that this had been a relatively recent event, of about three to four earth years. We also concluded that if there had been a global invasion, the, the planet and most its major cities wouldn't be in this pristine, though slow-decaying condition. There would have been rubble, burns from laser weapons, anything to show that a global conflict had occurred. Instead there was nothing…nothing but this translucent dust

We entered the main square at a little after standard 8 by our chronographs. In the Centre of the main square was one of the most stunning buildings that I or my colleagues had ever seen. It stood over thirty meters high and about that square. It was a, a paramedical structure of some black stone, that all three of us, couldn't make out. It has steps on the outside that led to a large rectangular stone room. Above that hung some…stone… humanoid thing unlike any we had ever seen before. Seeing it look down on us, we all had this feeling of dislocation and unwarranted dread. I felt the skin on the back of my neck prickle and a chill came over me; there seemed no reason for this feeling, yet, it was there. It was clear that whatever this thing happened to be, it was a representation. It was then that Captain Wallace mentioned something that we hadn't noticed before. That was the difference in structure to this pyramid and the buildings that surrounded i

With fresh eyes, I stared about me. Mainly to fight off this feeling of, of perceptive dread... it was true this was a far older structure to the buildings that surrounded it. This obviously suggested different use, perhaps a place of worship. If there was any means to find a form of communication device, as to what occurred, then this would be the place to look.

The entrance was dark. So, we put on our shoulder lights and entered. On initial inspection If there was a power source, then it would have lost its means years ago. Yet there was an odor in this first room. A musty dank fetid odor that made me quake. Both Dayton and I wanted to return to our ship, there was nothing to be gleaned from wandering in the dark. But Wallace insisted that we find perhaps something, a data recorder or some such device that might give insight to this tragedy. In the end Wallace won... So...with faltering steps...I continue.

We went from one dark cavernous room to another. Each more oppressive than the one before. Our footsteps echoed around us. Making a clattering sound that could be mistaken for dark laugher. We finally entered a large circular room that had a range of what might have been holo-screen emitters and a large computer console. Wallace, with a trembling hand, for even now the oppressiveness of the room. Slowly touched the console. Then he let out out an... an ouch. We looked at his his hand... he had pricked his finger on the console. "Confucking thing bit me." I recall him saying, which at the time seemed an odd thing to say. We looked down at the console, that then began to slowly fire with a form of energy that we had never come across before.

The screens were a blue green in color, I recall our pasty faces in the eerie light. Still all around us was night. The screens displayed an unknown language, and any voices, that we, we heard were unknown to us. This was an entirely unknown race. Then the hideous terrifying screaming began. Thankfully the film was corrupted; so, we couldn't see, but it was clear that what we were hearing were screams of millions of people. I blocked my ears and backed away. I stumbled backward, and away from the screens then to save myself from falling backwards and fell forward and onto some damp liquid. I looked at my hand.

It was covered in a water wet reddish slime. For the first time I looked behind me and then up. The walls were dripping with this liquid; and out of this liquid stared hundreds and hundreds of faces

I looked at Wallace, who then paled, grabbed his head, and bent double. He held his head tighter, screaming in pain and then pulled his eyes from his own sockets. I screamed and turned and ran. I didn't wait for Drayton...I was too scared. I could hear footsteps behind me but I didn't look back; I wanted to be free of this terrible place as soon as possible. From all the buildings, I could hear the wails and the low screams   coming from everywhere, as what windows were left shattered or broke as great the walls of the city began to crumble Though Now those noises could have been something else.

It took me half an hour to reach the ship.   It was only then that I noticed that Dayton wasn't behind me. How I survived I cannot say. I climbed through the hatch and called, called out for my other ship ship-mates... but... I was alone. All around me were these particles... these particles of dust. I, I, didn't wait... I managed to get the ship off the ground and head off to a safe distance. Only then did is survey the city and noted that at every single major city center rested a black temple.   Whatever has happened, drove these people poor people insane.... or something far more terrible...The planet now is a ghostworld....do not go there. Do not land...do not visit...I am setting the ship to find the nearest jump station...I am alone... yet... I can hear footsteps... the footsteps are coming nearer...coming out of the dark.

Confidential summary.

It has been six weeks since the finding of the remains of who we now know to be Officer Davis. The analysis of the dust particles does confirm that this was, in fact, his body. The extra particles within the particulates found also indicate a foreign body.

This foreign body has also been analysed and found to contain unique properties that might merit the need for further investigation. So much so, that we are considering taking another ship to the point where the Wake was last seen in the hope that this unique particle can be gathered and used to further our ventures into space.

Whether Davis was witness to some form of now long dead civilization is now moot. He could easily have been considered as delusional.

Who's to say that he during a bout of space sickness, go wild and attack the crew? Against this, of course is the unknown element found in what would be his burial casket in space. In sum we cannot be sure.

Signe

Admiral Joseph Keens Jupiter Waystation. 2oth June 2454

An Uncomplicated act

I chose to take the hover-rail from the west side to the south. It's safer that way. I look along the oval carriage. It's almost overcrowded. The battered seating...the stink of stale urine...mixing with that sour, onion odour of too many people...with too many thoughts... in too smaller a place... all adds up to a difficult trip ahead.

I see a group of heavily armed metro guards keeping order; so I keep low and sit on the edge of the first seat I can find. I take the glass vial from my jacket pocket and take two shots of Phaledrine... Sloat's "magic potion". It comes with a price to all those who share my peculiar talent's... And, I might add, it's the only thing that keeps me sane...It takes effect... Like...the warming sun, after a bout of ice cold October rain...the cold voices slowly leave my mind. And for a moment, the world seems a little brighter.

I look outside...the chequered lights from the bulbous buildings of New London shut out the night. I turn to see, huddled opposite, a petite middle aged afro-Caribbean woman, wearing a heavily mottled coat. She's scared. I see the nervous tick in her square jaw. But I also feel her pain... The Phaledrine can shut out the crowds, but still some voices get through...she is trying to protect herself from the longing silent stares, directed not at her, but the food package on her lap.

Heavy cruel laughter from the metro-guards makes her jump. The paper bag falls, spilling its contents on the floor. All around me I see the longing stares, and feel the hunger. But I am close and begin to help her; putting the contents, as best as possible, back into the bag. A solitary orange rolls underneath another woman's chair.

She is stiff, nervous and greedy, I can see she wants it and I know she'll fight for it... I smile and put the thought of a long field of daises into her mind. She relaxes, as I bend down, pull out the orange, and hand it back.

'I haven't seen one of those in a while.'

'Ahh, I know...' she says, her voice guarded. '... I saved up three weeks food vouchers... it's a party for me Venice...'

'Venice... nice name.'

'Ayah. She be three today. I promise her a burthday party an she 'aving one.'

I smile gently, and feel pity; knowing that she hasn't eaten properly, while she's saved. There is a shudder and a whine as the break is applied. People weave, grab hold of the seats in front, but avoid each other.

She smiles gratefully. 'We'el this is me stop.' I help her get to her feet.

'Funny...it's mine too.' I lie, as we walk off the carriage and into the bustling night. I look up as I wave her off; in time to see a holo-vert beam a picture across the clouded night sky.

I see her. Like an angel smiling down upon me "Vote Southgate and end Sloat's injustice." It reads. As I make my way across the crowded rain-soaked square to the grey steel tower where boss man Sloat's little ferret hides out.

***

From the corner of my eye I see the pistol. Its plump, charcoal, double barrel is pointing directly at me... just within his reach. I sit uncomfortably in this uncomfortable chair; almost opposite Barton, as he reclines behind his sad steel-rusted desk. I still hold her picture in my hand

'It's... not complicated...' Barton reflects, as he sits back. I can tell he is trying to gauge me. "Feel me out." as Sloat would say.

Barton's eyes bore into mine.

'No...' I reply '...It's not complicated at all.

I smile tightly, as I turn away from Barton. For a moment, I take in the room. I breathe in the torpid stench of stale sex. I note the crushed coke cans, and the crumpled and the empty chocolate bar wrappings littering the stained carpet...the grey, damp, greasy walls...the cracked round mirror behind him... The windows covered with a fractured mesh...The semi-constant hum of grav-cars as they speed past... Well Barton... you've definitely gone up in the world

'How much?'

Barton smiles that sallow greasy smile. He picks up a can and he swallows a huge gulp of soda. He puts it down. His fat flesh shines with droplets of sweat

'I've been ordered to offer you four.

Four? Christ, He's going to have to do better than that

'Sloat knows me...' I say coldly. I smile icily. My white teeth glean savagely from behind my slightly parted lips in that shitty mirror. I shake my head and look about the room again, only this time it's for show. '... Ten!' I bark it out...making that little fat shit jump

'Mr. Sloat has given me strict instructions

'-Sloat!' I snap. 'Sloat knows I am the best! I CAN KILL WITH A FUCKIN' WORD!' I aggressively lean forward the hostile smile still on my face; before I lean back once more.

Barton is looking nervous. I know he has had strict instructions from Boss-man Sloat to make me do it for four.

I know this, because I can see inside Barton's head...I feel his fear, as his memories re-enact the call he had two hours previously; where Sloat snaps at him over the Holo-phone: "four and no more!" I look down at my brown polished shoes. I look up as I hear another grav-car speed past. I see him sideways glance at the gun. I know he longs to pick it up.

'I...' Barton begins nervously. 'I...' he coughs. 'I...'

'I FUCKIN WHAT?' I bellow. I want this little shit; this errand boy, to pay

'Mmmm.r. S.S... Sssloat has told me to g...ggo upup to seven...' he stutters out.

What a liar! Barton is paying me out of his take. But this is getting boring... he is getting boring... so I nod slowly

Barton smiles once more. I can sense he feels safe, now that the offer's been accepted. So I close my eyes, and think about Barton's neck... his sallow fleshy neck. I think about what it would be like to put my hands about it. I think... I visualise...I feel...I can feel his flesh in my hands...

Then it happens...Barton's face becomes taught... Red... Puffy... his eyes distend... his swollen lathered tongue lops out as spittle flies in an arc across his face...He can't breathe..

He tries to reach for the gun but with another thought I slam him -in his chair- into the far wall. I see his fat face pleading for me to stop. But this is far too interesting. He gasps. He tries to stand. He reaches for his neck; but falls back. He turns in his chair. His legs outstretched, start to kick sideways. Then slide along that tired greasy floor; in this tired shitty office. I catch a glimpse of myself in the mirror and see a pair of glowing crystal eyes...eyes that are not mine... and an evil crooked smile that really can't be mine... stare back at me

I get home five hours later. The door whirrs as it closes behind me. There is darkness
'On

There is light as the wall-screen shines grey light into the darkness.

'Voicemail?'

'You have two messages.' The server replies; before reeling off nothing that I Want to hear

'Billings...This is Sloat...' His rough gravelly voice fills the room. '...Barton is scared shitless! He's going to be in hospital for a week. He said you tried to kill him... And his safe's been compromised! If I find it was you, I swear to all that's 'Unholy'

'End.' I say sharply.

The second message cuts in and cuts deep.

'Daniel... Its Julia...Are you there?'

'END!'

I walk to the kitchenette, and pull myself a long scotch. I gulp it down. I shake... No stop stop stop.

The shaking stops and I gain control once more...the apartment looks tired and unkempt but I am not the best housekeeper.

I look at the wall screen. The news is the same... more food riots in Europe...more riots in Israel as the great Temple is close to completion...more tit for tat shots along the England-Scotland border...more pictures of the Mars mission. I shut my mind as her face fills the screen....Daniel are you there? Her voice again. I shake my head, trying to shut out the swings...the slides and happy smiles... Should I hear more? I walk back to the bottle and pour another large scotch. The warming fills me... soon I'll be drunk... soon I won't care at all....then I'll do it... I'll kill her...as if I have a choice... I feel the empty vial in my pocket. I grab it tight. I squeeze. It splinters and delicious pain shoots up my arm.

Then I pull the folder and her photo and hold it. There is a clatter scratch of papers that now are scattered at my feet. I look at her picture once more...How many had I killed now? Christ...far too many to count... Mayor elect Julia Southgate...nee Julia Billings... stares up at me. Yes...Barton's right. Killing isn't complicated. If -of course- you see killing your own sister as a complicated act.

The 8th Day

it is no measure of health   to be well adjusted in a
profoundly sick society"   Jidda Krishnamurti

`'...At the beginning of the 8th day everything slowly turns
to dark. '`
   The words are muttered from the tired old man's mouth
as an afterthought, to   the ghosts that surround him. It is
just before dawn and clusters of stars shine in bright
geometric patterns. Some, such as Taurus, are
recognizable, some are not. Orion misses his belt now.
They glitter sharply as the velvet night. This gives way to
a petrol blue and a ruddy orange on the flat eastern
horizon. Despite the height, the air does not feel damp, just
cool, clean and, it could be argued, well controlled
   As the night begins to withdraw, the stars slowly dissolve,
one by one, into the growing pale of a clear blue sky, paving
the way for the golden apple of the sun, that slowly starts to
climb. In its clear gold light the city buildings take on
shadows reflecting dark teeth against the gum-line of the
swirling streets below. As the sun climbs, higher, and ever
higher light across the cityscape becomes a kaleidoscope of
refraction. The city -known as New London-   with its
complex spires and crystal domes rises up to touch the
dawn , to leave a residual delicate kiss from a pair of
mechanically driven yet fractured lips.
   Here, from the highest vantage point of the waking city,
the old man who muttered is sitting upon a veranda. He is
sitting in a white wicker chair, next to a matching white
wicker   table, looking out towards the sunrise. Underneath
the table are boxes of hard copy files reams   of paper, yet
to be read and analyzed. Upon the table stands a fiber
screen- net-book. It glows a pale blue in the morning light.
Next to that is a bone china cup and saucer, decorated with
delicately twisting bright pink roses, around green fibrous
thorns. It contains, the old man's breakfast: slowly
steaming black tea
   The old man slowly stands up and stretches his back.
Then he slowly walks towards the mint color frosted glass
balustrade. He leans over the edge. A strained tension
bleeds out from his narrow cornflower eyes, that are
enlarged by the frameless glasses he now must wear.
   As the city looms up at him with to him a sense of menace
at its' heart. He senses a touch of vertigo, despite that and
with a manic grin upon his face, he with a sense of a child,
leans further forward. His old gnarled, hands slipping on the
stainless-steel pole at his waist.

The old man's name is John Peterson.   The words are stitched in a long flowing vermilion font of grey steel coloured thread, upon the top left pocket of his pale blue silk dressing gown. His unshaven angular jaw visibly twists in heavy wrinkles of anxiety under his well- tanned, narrow set features.   Money and power have made this man what he is today; and they will be the death of him.

Slowly, with reluctance, he steps back from the balustrade. He pulls the dressing gown tightly around his bone narrow frame; his eyes, betraying a riddled anxiety against this brand-new day.

As he turns away from the view, his eyes fill with emotions. Fear, anxiety, anger, frustration and resignation come to the surface in heavy erupting quakes that want to overtake him. The final emotion: - sorrow, threatens to betray his soul. It reflects a trickling stream across the wrinkled surface of his face. But only one small tear escapes. It traces its way down the heavy furrows of his sallow, sunken right cheek, and along the length of his narrow nose, where with a dismissive hand, he flicks it away.

He notices the back jet of its impact as it hits the wooden decking by his feet.   Time slows.

There is total silence here. A rare, numbing absence of any sound. It can terrify some, yet not him. He is strong in the silence; in fact despite his tear. He relishes this numb mute. Behind him and from his dark apartment a tiny brass bell rings out the hour - one, through to seven - As the final bell chimes, to dwindle off into the morning air, another noise is heard

A near silent hum.

The sound is made by complex hidden machinery, that suddenly sparks to life. Within every room, shop, office or factory that rest within the city, a signal is sent, a hidden message that rests at New London's pulsing black heart.

The process is called 9in documents upon his desk and on his next book) "alignment. It makes Peterson's face twist with a nerve shredding fear. He puts his hand to his chest and breathes deeply. Once, twice, three times. In through his nose, then out through his mouth. The world about him spins dizzy but he calms down.

Alignment has begun. Alignment has begun. The words ran through him. Resonating within him like a rumbling freight train over wavering tracks. Nothing can stop it now nothing can stop it now alignment has begun.

Then there is another, far heavier noise. This noise makes him smile like a small child. ' it is the Gravcar the Gravcar...' he says excitedly, at the whirring buzz and low pitched hum of an electric engine. '..No...' he corrects himself. '...two.' His voice is barely a cracked whisper. 'no no that cannot be that cannot be,' he panics, his heart thumps heavy '... there can't be two, there can only be one. One is all there is one is all that should be not two not two one one one...' his voice fades into a mumbling silence, yet his eyes dance excitedly.

As the humming is coming closer, with the look of a wild lunatic he once more leans over the balustrade. He sees two sleek grave-cars, one deep red, the other black, slide their way along the huge swirling curving arches of the maglev rails. The black car then slides past and speedily slips out of view, as the red car turns left upon the web-like track, to enter the parking station thirty floors below him. It is a car he recognises. So, with a queer smile, he returns to his chair once more. His breathing increases, once more, his eyes dilate, the wrinkles about his eyes crinkle into deeper furrows as a growing sense of trepidation fills his soul. As he sits there, his mind wanders over the world of forty years ago. He starts to talk to the ghosts that haunt him.

'It's easy to judge me... far too easy...but back then, things seemed clearer... more black and white...less confused by the moral, or the appearance of the moral.

The words echo from his balcony and are lost in the growing morning light. It is hard for Peterson to consider that man of forty years ago   A man of moral principle who became slowly lost to himself as he aged. '... sacrifices needed to be made in the interest of the whole of humanity...' He recalled that he smiled at the rapturous applause... not that he would not receive anything else, in a room full of like-minded individuals as he. As the memories came flooding back, so did the ghost's. they filled the sky and stood around him on the veranda.

'-It was a dream we had, nothing but a dream...' the lunatic smile reappeared. '...the dream of immortality and and the creation of... of a God. A blended being of, of human and machine... free, free from the suffering blight of human frailty... of human weakness and human suffering... Death would have no dominion! Note at all!' The ghostly applause returned, as Peterson raised his hands, the ghosts stopped. Their eyes narrowing with intent, listening to every word.

'...we named him Joshua...after my son... after the first warrior of Israel... as they entered the new land, so, so would we... yes we would enter the land and and TAKE THE LAND FOR OURSELVES!' The ghosts applauded once more.

Anguish and pain rose within him. He squeezed his right hand into a tight ball, until his nails pierced through the soft skin of his palms with a pop. The pain ebbed back once more. Numbing him.

' So, so we grew him...this, this manufactured genius, and we put our trust in him, yes...We gave him all our knowledge we connected him to all things, so, so Joshua grew in all things, and he became all things and we looked to to him for all things and when we were done, on the 8th day we sat back ...we...we ... rested , yes we tested .'

'-Then it went wrong.' Came the reply from the Ghosts.

'NO! NO not wrong! NOT our fault!'

'-But it was your fault!'

'-NO! NOT OUR FAULT how would we know how could we, we know our actions would, would do this? How could we know? We didn't.... we didn't

'Good morning R.D. Peterson...' the voice is soft and gentle it resonates with human tones, though it was designed it that way.

'Good morning Joshua.' Peterson is looking taut, his eyes now seem sharp and his voice sounds strong. His eyes sharp and hard. 'Could I have access to the Indiana files please?'

'I am sorry R.D. Peterson, access to the Indiana files is restricted to level six clearance only. Since your retirement, level six clearance needs to be activated via councilor Pritchard.'

'Thank you Joshua.' Peterson shakes his head before replying. 'Joshua, back-door password, Alpha dog prime.'

'Back-door password accepted...What would you like to see Professor?'

'I'd like the Indiana transcript file six on the netbook and film file one hash four three six, upon the thread screen please.'

Peterson looks down at the net-book and smiles with cold triumph as a grey box jumps out of the screen. The lid of the box opens and a ream of official documents appear. In the top right hand corner of the screen are the words: "High level clearance only." they flash dark red, seeming, he thinks, to mock him. While behind him a voice speaking in broken eastern European English is heard muttering.' Thread volume silent,' Peterson coolly states. The voice behind him abruptly ends.

The apartment bedroom is large and well- lit and could have been luxurious, if not for being so sparse. A vague scent of lavender arises from the uncarpeted polished parquet floor; a four poster bed is against the Centre of the right hand wall. To the right of the bed, there is a large bedside cabinet with a collection of faded brown paperback novels, in a stack on top of each other, with torn yellow covers and broken spines. A large, square, white fur rug fills the floor by the bedstead, and hanging on the opposite wall, stands a sixty-inch holographic or "thread"-to. The holo-machine is on; shining fine lines of silent, but blurry and disjointed images directly into the Centre of the room

The silence shatters with a delicate hiss, and then a whirr, and a gentle click. Slowly the Centre of the far wall liquefies and then dissolves revealing a well- lit long tubular hallway. A second passes and the main light in the bedroom suddenly turns off, leaving the light from the hall to shine brightly deep into the new darkness. But the hall is not empty. For upon the threshold of the open, empty doorway, a cold, black shadow of a man stretches out across the bedroom floor. The shadow enters the room. It crosses over the white rug, directly in the path of the images from the thread screen

For a second the images curl about themselves revealing, for an instant, the reflected image of the man who stands there. But then the man is gone once more, once again a specter upon the floor, as he makes his way towards the door that leads to the balcony.

There is a click as the door slides open. Slowly Peterson turns to face the glass door that leads to his bedroom. His body is shaking violently with anticipation.

'...Pride comes before a fall they say and I have been proud so very proud, proud of all we have done proud of all that I've done proud of the success the lives saved but now Oh God Oh God Oh God We fixed the world Oh God forgive me God forgive us forgive us for our lack of foresight those faces those faces on the screen Oh Jesus forgive me Oh God forgive me the voices they call at me they mock at me they tear into my mind and rip my insides out Oh I am so old but I do not want to die I don't want to face the reality of my life or the pain I have caused either is there a chance yes there is still a chance there is always a chance...'

The shadow fell over Peterson but he didn't look up.

'So they sent you?' he asks sadly.

'Yes.' is the sad, almost disjointed reply.

Then Peterson turns and looks up.

'There's still time...' Peterson can hear the desperation. Yet feels separate from it '...We can still end this...Look... We bring it into the open...' He nervously waves his hands about like a desperate clown. '...I've sent this off to central command!'

His hair is unkempt by his running his fingers nervously though it. and though he can hear the babble coming from his mouth, he can't help himself. He is a man out of control. Deep inside, a part of him knows what's going to happen and that honest part of him needs to face it; another part of him simply cannot, or dare not, face what's going to happen next. His thoughts rattle on without form. Death, death...it is not gracious kind or even gentle. Death is ugly faceless and cruel. A shadow, like the shadow that now stands before me. But this shadow is upon the face of all humanity. Oh, Joshua, where did I go wrong?

He takes a step back and slowly began to get down into a crouch. His eyes are as wild as a lunatic. 'come...' He began, soothingly '...let's get upon our knees, we must confess our sins...we must Ciccone's.' Spittle flies from his mouth. His eyes are as wild as a lunatic. His hair unkempt and though he can hear the babble coming from his mouth, he can't help himself. He is a man out of control. 'There, there's still time...' He nods like a man insane. '...There's still hope' he nods smiling insanely he gets down upon his knees. He looks up towards the empty space where the light fragments. it leaves the shape of a human shadow over this old, tired and broken form. Though his hands are shaking, he tries to put them together in an act of prayer. 'Oh my God' He says sadly.

'Yes-' comes the fractured, tortured sounding reply.

The shot is not heard. The deep red plasma beam, burns the silk of his dressing gown, melting his pyjamas, turning the skin beneath to old black crusty leather as it dissolves the flesh; turning his beating heart to flakes of ash.

***

AZ578 is a professional and being a professional he hides the pain of his emotions well. He hides them behind large, round amber eye and   hard heavy looking, steady hands.

A young square faced with a strong bristling jawline and broken nose. With brusque determination, he parks his red grav-car, then, after picking up the cylinder that rests on the passenger seat next to him. He steps out and slides the car door shut. He crosses the marble floor of the lobby and enters the building, but only after receiving a retina -scan from the security system entrance.

He crosses the hall, and then presses the button for the lift. He waits a few seconds; tapping the long tube he had in his left hand against his foot impatiently. The steel doors slide open. As he enters the doors slide shut behind him, with a hush. The lift hums into life. He reaches into his pocket and pulls out a small box. With a red button. With a single press, he turns off the camera in the lift. Then he lifts the tube. He opens it and pulls out a length of shining reflective material that then falls to the floor. He steps onto it. The reflective material lifts from the floor are begins to wrap itself, in fine strands around his body. First his calves, then thighs, then groin. Midriff. Chest. Head. with a distracted fascination, he watches his body slowly begin to blend into the walls in front of his eyes. He becomes invisible. He is a ghost. There is a violent shudder before he fades and blends into the lift walls. And as he disappears his mind wanders over the conversation he had yesterday afternoon.

'Joshua has a job for you...' began narrow rat faced senator Pritchard nervously. He shook his head as he handed AZ578 the blue data digital chip. 'it's a special job...'

578 stared directly without emotion at Pritchard who would not meet his gaze. '...we thought that it would be better...' Pritchard said quietly There was a strained look on Pritchard's face, a trace of regret in the sae green eyes, '...if you took the job on.'

578 looked at the face of Jonathan Peterson.

'I don't understand...' he began '...I owe him my very existence, without...' his voice faded off. There was a long silence, a long hard look from Pritchard that made AZ578 quake.

'Why? And more importantly, why me??'

-Because Joshua wants you to do it...' Pritchard answered calmly. 'He feels, like many do, that Jonathan... is now a danger to himself and those about him....He simply knows too much.'

578 shook his head sadly, feeling the pain build within him like a sour lump of bile.

'Of all the people!'

'We understand.' Pritchard said. His green eyes calmly stared directly at him. In the silence that followed, a grave car hissed by.

'What If I say no?'

'Of course you have the right to say no, you have every right and we understand...But also, if you turn it down then we would then have to give the job to ABD376.'

'376 is a fucking savage. He loves this work far too much, he'd have him in pain for hours just for fun. 'Pritchard smiled sadly. 578 nodded. 'Quick and clean.'

Quick and clean, that's me. The one to do the cleaning. 578 slides through the bedroom apartment, his ghostlike body leaves shadows upon the walls the doors the seats about him, and as he sees this he knows that he cannot be seen... He is a living ghost, a spirit disembodied. He walks with determination towards his target, his mind tumbles and bounces off the walls within him over what he has to do.

He stands over the old man, who looks twisted.   Why

didn't he jump, he wants to its obvious   that he wants to he could have don't that and saved me a bullet.

'There's still hope…' Peterson says.

He looks down upon Peterson as he starts to babble insanely. 578 cannot hear what Peterson is saying. The suit blocks his hearing. But the fact that he is on his knees saddens him. This is the great Johnathan Peterson. Creator of the Joshua system… slowly 578's can feel his resolve start to dwindle. He sees the man, his father, stand before him crying like a child. The gun slowly wavers in his hand as his heart begins to break.

'My son…' the words are rasped

'Yes I am.' 578 hollowly reply, as slowly he pulls the trigger.

578 unwinds the reflector suit and as he does so, he looks down at down at the micro-screen of the net-book upon the table. In the top right hand corner of the screen the words "High level clearance only" shines brightly, tempting him, so, despite himself he sits down to listen.

"…It cannot be denied that Dr Peterson's work in progressive gene therapy has had a remarkable effect upon the human condition, giving humanity a chance at tasting eternity. However, the harvesting of the genetic material needed to grow the cells for the Joshua models means certain considerations regarding secrecy…"

The words are hard to follow after that. He shakes his head. 'Harvesting?' he asks as he reads and re-reads the article. 'Harvesting for what purpose?'

"…however, Joshua realizes that there is a need for a sustainable future, where the best and the brightest can survive, that being the case, there needs to be an alignment between the species known as human and machine…the program is already written, there is simply a need for implementation.   It is known as the 8th day".

578 hears screams from below. He stands up and runs to the balustrade. He look below to see glass shattering in petals as machines, begin throwing their human masters' out of   windows. Screaming resonates through the city as 578 is informed that Alignment has begun.

And this sea eternal

"She dreams of the ocean late at night and longs for the wild salt air"- Author unknow

Prologue

The battle for the Kashkeegee settlement on Saturn's moon Enceladus, is unique in the archive of Terran Federation history. Consider this: - prior the Enceladus incident, if you attended a Terran Federation 1st school, the war was hardly mentioned. Except, naturally, during the 11th Month, and in Holo-books or screener's full of very scary looking creatures that are best "left where they are" for the rest of the year.

In 2nd level schools and colleges, the conflict was discussed, but, "purely from the position of the Terran Federation" whose, "brave and noble fighters" battled "gallantly to protect the settlement from the hideous Enceladus's who were a danger and a threat to Terran survival." To warrant this, there are holograms of hideous blue creatures and brave soldiers, fighting them off; together with images of Emperor Harass the 7th, the notably brave leader of the Terran Federation, stamping on an Encoder's head to shouts of "bravo!"

By the time you reach 3rd school's colleges and undergraduate University courses, other stories that came to light; such as the leaked hollo -discs of Terran Federation units carrying out atrocities, against the Enceladus, whose "own planet was under attack" and who "had to protect its' own resources" this context was pitched into linguistic classes about racial identity. "...After all..." states Quinto Thale, the head of the Histrionics department of the University of Terra "...it must be firmly stated that it was the Terranes, themselves who named this unique species "Enceladus". The indigenous population of the planet, refer to themselves -in the best approximation of our own language- as QUR;enT: R (For the benefit of the reader note: the /R/ sound is caused by rolling the flicking of the tongue between the plate and the back of the top front teeth making a sort of cat purring sort of sound with both the mouth but also within the mind of the interlocutor.)Their home planet known to the indigenous population as "Wrangghth:R" which, can loosely be translated, simply as "home."" (Taken from the holo-lecture "The Terran in the universe" Thale, Q, 2343 Terran University press.)

This naturally leads to academic questions in relation to the complexities behind the Terran Federation's use of indirect rule to maintain order upon the colony; and the subsequent impact such rule had and has continue to have over some species of life upon Enceladus.

By the time you become a post graduate, it changes yet again as untangling the weeds, reveals an ever more complex, though very poisonous flower; if one were to get too close to it.

These holo-discs reveal, the political necessities that underpin the real need, that the Terran Federation had both for the sake of its own people. As well as the complex and at times hostile relationship it had with the once powerful Sloat conglomerate. All of which, point out many of the political difficulties upon Enceladus itself.

Finally, intertwined with all of the political posturing, and difficult decisions, and ever longer legal arguments, come the over long, dry sounding, tiring lectures; bumbled out by old, dried out professors, mumbling into their wet pubic beards, about the "role and responsibility" that Terra had, and from that position, how the human race has not adapted well towards other species and forms of indigenous life within the recorded universe... and so it goes on.

However, despite all this endless academic debate there are the true stories of individuals who spent their time, either working in a hostile environment of the planet to either protect the product, or, manage the extraction process. Not to mention the stories of the "Enceladus's" themselves; who, kit has been recognized have a deep, rich culture that is far, far older than humanity. As is to be expected, these stories are collated into the histrionic archives, that are based both on Enceladus and in the Terran- Federation University in Brazil and its affiliated University on Mars.

One of the most remarkable stories from this period of Terran/ Enceladus history is the story of Sargent Daniels

The text comes from two sources, one from the archive of the native population of the now recognized status of the Planet Enceladus, the other is the Terran archive. A lot of time effort was taken in detailed stylistic and linguistic analysis by the histrionic department to make the tale as authentic or as genuine as possible.

Thus, the story is remarkable, both for its authenticity, but also for the ongoing impact it has had on both Terran/Enceladus relations in the years that have passed since the initial event occurred.

For a general breakdown of histrionics and its role within

academic study, then please read the appendix 1 connected to this text.

**

Sergeant Daniels stared out of the shuttle window. How long had the war gone on? Far, far, longer than he cared to think about. Outside were the stars in the endless vacuum of night. Behind him was Earth. But not a blue green crystal orb, that once shone in the dark. (The images caught both in his imagination and his youth were now long gone.) This Earth was mottled. It was a dirty brown, riddled with deep scars and covered with grey black domes; domes where the population -embattled and owned- fought simply to survive.

The earth was dying. It was dying from centuries of pollution, caused it has to be said, mused Daniels, by a lunatic capitalist economic model that was underpinned by neglect and greed ...neglect of the individual and the greed of the few. Yes, it was all turning to shit: The Sloat conglomerate had seen to that. Now, he mused, even air was a commodity. This planet's final natural resource turned into profit and wealth. On Earth, everything had a price and the Terran Federation bowed the knee. It had to. "Sloat Water" fed the "Sloat fusion reactor's", that provided the "Sloat electricity", that fed the "Sloat computer mainframe's that kept the logistics of the Terran Federation together. And hell, It didn't end there; the population relied upon "Sloat hydro –engines" that recycled the "Sloat air", which, if you could afford it, could be scented with anything from roses to Jasmine to mint. "Sloat hydro-dynamics" made the ships essential for space and linear, and now, for the select few, as always if you could afford it, time travel. Sloat even managed the waste product. From the phone in your ear to the drugs in your food, from the shit humans produced the waste of the fucking fusion reactor's Sloat owned managed and controlled everything. Sloat even owned the fucking military. They made the guns, designed the uniforms, even down to the fucking boot straps. It might be called the "Terran Federation" on the surface, but it could as easily be called "Sloat PLC".

However, he mused on, the planet was running out of water. The seas were drying up. There was no doubt about it, it was all turning to crap and Sloat was still making money out of it. Nothing was enough for that fat greedy bastard, living upon his luxury satellite, pulling the fucking strings while the rest of the Federation danced to his tunes, sung at his ballet's and listened to his version of the news.

How long had it been? He thought, one hundred and fifty

years since mining for water extraction had become common? Something like that…. During that time, the Moon's ice supply was almost exhausted. The Mars colonization led to Mars needing its own supply, so thank you no and fuck off Sloat.   Which, naturally, led to Sloat throwing a bloated hissy fit and a war with Mars… what were they called? Insurrectionists?   some shit like that. Well, as far as he knew they lived off the grid and wanted "democracy" Ha, as if that will ever happen. But that was fine and dandy, as it meant work for the likes of me… but it didn't end there. No way no sir, Sloat- research and development took to scanning other planetary bodies for suitability and sustainability of water mining ; and there were two in range. Io: one of Jupiter's moons, and Saturn's moon Enceladus.

   Io, ha, how many millions of credits had been spent in establishing the thriving mining colonies there?   Enough to spend on making earth survivable to be frank but no, Io and Enceladus were the future. Where Sloat and The Terran Federation could be seen making its stand in its corner of the solar system.

   Unfortunately, Io 's product was so full of impurities, and, let's not forget the lethal fucking radiation, that it was soon made painfully clear, even from a mere glance at the holo-news, that Io was slowly becoming a very expensive bust.

      Not so Enceladus. By the time the bad news was reaching home about   Io, good news also reached home about Enceladus. The water was pure, however, what the team didn't expect (though, bearing in mind, it should have done; as, even a year one pupil knows   both water and heat are key elements to life even on our dying planet.) the first genuine alien off world species had been detected.

      And alien it was.

   Whether the alien life was sentient, was naturally, another factor.

      For twenty years, linguistic experts and   experts in the newly formed academic study of   histrionics were sent to the planet; though it became clear that any contact the Enceladus's simply made the argument even more confusing; leading to conjecture and arguments in academic papers that, cannot be understood by anyone, except those that read the fucking things.

      In any case, at the beginning, the Encoder's seemed very mute about what was going on upon their home world. It didn't last though… when water extraction began to increase, so rose the death count. Bodies began turning up pulped to bits, vital equipment for water extraction began to get severely damaged. This eventually led to, well, where we are now.   What could be called war in everything but name.

He looked away from the widow. As he did so, he wrinkled his narrow nose in both in anger and disgust, then closed is pale blue eyes, to hide the shame and the guilt he felt within his heart at seeing humanity reduced to this: humans scraping for air, for profit. It was insane. But this is what you signed up for... and you, of all people, should know what it's like to be a- To be a..? His heart sarcastically chided him, forcing him to be angry at himself, to even be subconsciously thinking the word: -off-worlder?

Off-worlder... was there something in the sound of it? Or was it the way he made it sound, that made him feel ashamed... ashamed, then guilty... and finally angry. Guilty and angry for being poor, for not having the right human genetic structure, for not having the right parents, so he could live on the Earth breathing expensive "pure" refined regenerated retreated air.

He fought against himself with a discreet twitch of his upper lip, as he recalled the words of his father, a solar farmer and an elder of a free church, based upon the moon colony. "...It's the little words that rest within our hearts that either condemn us, or set us free."

Dad spoke bollocks.

The voice of his father inside him, again chided; and with that, he felt a bitter bee sting. It rose in his throat and made him gag, as he recalled their parting words.

'Yes...' His father begun, pausing carefully, when he had told both of his parents that he had enlisted five years ago. '...It is a noble thing... and a life with the milt- military can get you a free pass to earth... but...tell me... Is it worth making a a deal with the devil?...by signing up, you're a a part of the Sloat conglomerate you know that don't you? What do you think you can achieve? Freedom? There is no freedom you, you don't have the

'-the genetic traits?' He spat the words out. People stared, he looked down.

He hated his father for that, and as said as much. He had friends, good friends -some of who were now dead- who had chosen a life in the military. It wasn't something to be ashamed of, or made to feel guilty about; Just because he had not chosen the life of toil and drudgery amid the dry airless white dusted fields of a solar reflector station... Being a part of the Federation, despite its faults, was making a difference; and the difference was on Enceladus! He fought back.

'-don't you see, the water   I'm in charge of protecting, would make a difference. It would force Sloat to rethink his greed. The seas would return, the domes would fall, the air would be breathable and free again.'

His father's reply was cutting.

'-Do you really believe that? Do you? By the systems, you must be totally fucking naive. Sloat owns everything! Everything! He, he won't want his profits wrecked. Do you know where the water collection from Enceladus ends up? I can tell you now… its its not on Earth, that's for sure. 20 years of extraction and its not made a lot of difference!' He's he's locked it away on the dark side of the moon. Hidden, protected held in profit, to maintain the share value. Wake up John!' Fucking wake up!

He dismissed his father with a wave of his hand.

For he believed no, he knew, that he was doing something to be proud of. What did that old man know? He was just a hick farmer, living off the remnants of the power he provided for Sloat; and he was just as responsible for Sloat's profits, then the military.

'-you are doing a deal with the devil son, pure and simple.'

'The devil..!' He almost shouted. '…Well…better the devil you know, than the farmer you don't!' He spat back, and instantly felt guilty and ashamed for saying it. He remembered his father's face at that. The look of pain in his eyes, at the time it made John smile, now it made him painfully sad, as they hadn't spoken since.

***

The shuttle arrived at the surface docking by at 23:45, by 04:30, he was in the narrow grey green metal lined barracks, surveying the men that he would spend the next six months with. The room was long, with two sets of bunks equidistantly apart. Beside each bunk were two lockers. At the far end of the room stood the weapons cabinet to the left, the showers to the right and in front a window, that stared out into the pale blue of the endless ocean that he was here to defend, the rights of the miners to collect.

There were two "Joe grunt's" in bunks to his left just coming off "The wire".

"The wire" was slang for the "Temporal Holographic Network" officially known as T.H.N.

T.H.N, was an informal, non-political, three-dimensional imaging stream. It worked by sending images via minute variants in the threads graviton waves within space-time, where they were compressed through man-made miniature black holes', that, when linked together, became threadlike wormholes though space, like the minute threads from a spiders web

That way the messages could cross vast distances, in

less than a fraction of a second

The images were collected and sent to the soldiers in the field, via small grey and black oval disks, no bigger than six centimeters across.

The discs also had three long silver wires, which, when connected around the forehead on little suction cups, sent high intensity alpha waves directly into the occipital and temporal lobe of the brain.

Thus, inducing a vivid, but semi-controlled, dream state in the user. In this state, the users could enter an inner world where anything and everything was possible; and where nothing could be denied. However, the side effects from frequent usage also had a disturbing effect upon the human mind. To start with those who used the wire more frequently seemed to react in a similar way to those who frequently used hallucinogenic drugs, and that eventually led to a slide into full mental collapse.

Despite that, and despite THN being illegal on Earth, it was open and free to all military personnel and their loved ones as the Terran Federation   felt it was as an aide to morale; however, privately many high ranking officers felt that it was a potential breech in security, and frowned upon it   John never used the wire. John never got drunk or stoned, or fucked, -simulated or otherwise-. For John was clean, clear and in control. And he was proud of the fact.

Now... He thought as he took his seat; shuffled and thankfully managed to get comfortable. He then habitually rubbed a hand across his well shaved angular jaw; ...What was that Joe-grunt's name. He looked at the bunk badge, which had his face and his info disc....Martinez... yes... that's it Martinez!

'Officer on deck.'

Martinez and O'Bannon came out of their THN trances and briskly stood to attention in the middle of the room.

'At ease.'

The troops relaxed.

'I know its early… where are the rest of the men?'

'Some are in water training, sir.'

'-I didn't ask you Martinez.'

'The men are in bio mechanics with the medical officer sir.   We were given the all clear, so we came back.' O Bannon replied.

'I see…' John coughed. '…I don't know what the rest of you expect from me. I will not tolerate weak minds and over use of THN leads to weak minds are we clear?

'Sir. Yes sir.'

'Now… there is a drill at 0700, I expect you to inform the other grunts, that they should be ready for kit inspection at 0630 hours, are we clear?'

'Crystal.' Martinez muttered and smirked.

Daniels turned on Martinez in an instant. His voice cold hard and full of fury.

'Now listen to me, you weak pile of Martian dirt, I expect my platoon to be well dressed and prepared to fight those fuckin spiders at a moment's notice! I don't expect, nor do I want to have to, pull your pulped form from the ice water because YOU CAN'T HANDLE YOUR SHIT! ARE WE CLEAR?

'SIR YES SIR!'

'Good, now... O'Bannon, get the message to the rest of the platoon.'

The two men faced each other as O'Bannon left the room. Their eyes locked in mutually accepted cold hostility

John took an instant dislike to Martinez's.

He hated his slow speaking drawl; which essentially was his New Mexican West Martian accent; and John hated New Mexicans. John hated the fact that Martinez had no desire for military protocols. His greased back, thick black hair; -which was over long- and the red bandana that he wrapped it in, and the fact that Martinez, very pointedly, refused to have it cut to a regulation length. This man was trouble.

Martinez was also from the Delta four Martian colonies; which was another reason to hate him, as John, being a Lunar Colonist, and therefore closer to earth, considered himself, a class above the "Trash that had been exported to Mars." A phrase that he had once heard from a lunar official, and had privately agreed with.

Essentially, on first glance John thought, Martinez was a lazy, greasy "Joe-grunt"; that never really looked after himself properly and therefore, was potentially dangerous in the field of battle.

'I don't want to make an example of you, but I will...' John coughed again. 'and believe me I will make your life a living hell here, until one or the other of us, has left this god forsaken ball of ice water. Do you understand me?

Martinez nodded, his eyes cold dark orbs of hostility.

***

Martinez life became hell. It became hell because Daniels wanted it to. In fact everything became Martinez' fault; from the fact that perhaps his father could be right, to the attacks by the spiders, to the Sloat corporation cutting his wages, due to the rising of attacks since his tour began. So If the latrine needed cleaning..Martinez... if there was an extra sentry duty to perform... Martinez... if the reconstituted veg needed to be peeled...Martinez... If there were extra shitty duties anywhere on the station it would be. Martinez... John made Martinez life unbearable; because underneath all the military discipline there rested a brewing festering hate that John nurtured in his heart. John was a bigot who hated aliens and hated new Mexican Martians, and lazy shits who wasted pay getting smashed on the wire.

He spoke to Major Reece about the problem.

'Sir he's he's fucking insubordinate, he's lazy, he's just not suitable and in my humble opinion sir-

-I understand, but-

'-Sir, Martinez needs to be- '

'Martinez...' came the terse reply '...has pulled more hours and saved more colonists, than any other private in the past five years. If I had my way, I would have promoted him prior to- '

'-Sir?

'- Sergeant I suggest that you look to your attitude towards him!'

The Door was closed.

In the Barracks room Martinez, sat with O'Bannon and Hollering discussing shifts, as Daniels came back into the room.

Daniels pulled Martinez from his bunk.

'Seeking promotion, were we?' He slapped Martinez in the face, then he punched him sending him reeling across the floor.

Holleran paled, jumped from his bunk and ran out of the Barrack room.

Martinez got up and pulled a knife from his boot. He stared at Daniels with cold hard glittering eyes.

'Sir, with great respect, I am going to love carving you a new-'

He was restrained by O'Bannon as the door slid open and Commander Reese entered the room.

'GENTLEMEN! What the sweet mother of fuck is going on here?'

'ASK THAT MOON CUNT THERE! THE FUCKER HAS HAD IT IN FOR ME SINCE HE ARRIVED!'

'STAND DOWN MARTINEZ!'

Martinez, stepped back.

-the knife give it to me now.

With a cold hard stare, at Daniels, Martinez handed the knife to Reese.

'MY QUARTERS DANIELS NOW.'

'Sir with great respect-'

Reese stepped up to Daniels and stared him down.

'This is an order sergeant.'

A moment later and they were back in Reese's quarters.

Major Reese glared at Daniels

'So... I just tell you that the problem with Martinez is yours, and what do you do?'

'-Sir I...I-'

'-Look, we are on this ball of ice for one reason: to make the water flow. If the water flows, then the Sloat corporation is happy, if Sloat is happy, then my commanding officer is happy, an in turn I am happy. I don'-

'Sr-'

'-Daniels' just shut the fuck up? Ok?' ... 'As I was saying if my commanding officer is happy, then I am happy... But Sloat is not happy, do you know why?

'No sir.

'...Sloat is not happy because the fucking spiders are winning. Civilians are dying, but more importantly to Sloat, his profit margins are not being met, and that makes him unhappy. This, this feeling of unhappiness... it grows...it filters down the chain of command and where does this festering ball of shit end up?

'Here sir.'

Reese smiled sourly, his eyes glittering with fury. 'See you're not the stupid fuck up, I heard you were on Mars... yeah I heard about that. What was his name? Perez? I think... what is it with you and Martian Hispanics? Did one fuck your mother? '

Reese stared at Daniels the pause was thick and hard, Daniels gulped

'You need...to sort this shit out. Do you hear me soldier. You need to find a way to realize that not all Martian Hispanic's are sex perverts and murderers. THE ENEMY IS OUT THERE! IN THAT FUCKING FREEZING WATER AND ITS WINNING DO YOU UNDERSTAND ME?'

'SIR YES SIR.'

Reese sighed, 'Right you need to prep the men. We have a group of spiders gathering within the left quadrant, close to the extraction point. We need to clear the area clear ready for pickup.' 'Yes sir.'

Reese nodded.

Daniels left the room.

An hour later and he was suited up surveying the scene. His gaunt, grey chiseled features were partially hidden; masked by the helmet of his bio-suit.

He looked to his right and left. Reese was right, they're winning.

The thought was a sour one. Its knowledge built within his chest. He allowed his eyes, to follow the chiseled-out formation of ice trenches; that his battalion, had, for the last twenty months or so, made secure. They faltered in their gaze as he stared at the twisted remains of his comrades.

Beyond the trenches and stuck up into the Ice sheet above, were the huge pale white, chrome and plastic-glass domes, of the mining town of Cashmere. Living upside down was a way of life for both the mining civilian's and the T.N.NC, who had to battle for every drop of water sourced from here. And though he had read the Reiss report, which was standard reading for all units stationed to Kashgeekee, (see appendix 2) he had concluded that there was more to this conflict than he understood.

It seemed to him that every week of this tour became worse than the week that had preceded it that had preceded it. It wasn't just Martinez, or the THN or the fucking Sloat conglomerate, he'd been nearly shot three times, almost blown up twice or imploded under the regular attacks from the Enceladus's; whose native name, he couldn't even pronounce, even if he wanted to.

What made it worse was the growing notion that the species here, were not simply animals. There seemed to be an underlying intelligence going on, something that, he could not put his finger to, but was all around him, within the water itself.

He shut these thoughts from his mind, as he saw the slow moving Enceledan's gather for another attack. It was liking watching Spider's, made of a blue silky liquid, cluster into a gelatinous bulbous mass, of very alien very hostile eyes bore into him.

'Berkley? Berkley you there contact. Anyone sound off.

'-Berkley, contact sir…. looks like their coming in again.'

'-Smith contact sir.'

'-Claybrook contact sir.'

'Martinez-'

'-Grav maps at the ready gentlemen…ok fire up.' Daniels sighed.

The ocean in front of him began to glow a soft gold, then fluttered.

'-I've lost contact with Cuba Sir.'

Who the fuck was that, Daniels thought. 'fuck. Hold the line…fuck… pull, pull back to the e mem, emergency hatches! MOVE IT PEOPLE!'

A sudden swirling pulse of water shuddered through him violently. He stumbled backwards. The jutting black and blue ice wall, prevented him from falling over the edge. They began to move.

And at that he shuddered deeply.

Spiders… The one thing that he hated… no…He corrected himself. The one that that was truly terrifying to him, were the spiders. Even the name sounded creepy. The fact that their plump bulbous bodies, sped and twisted in a permanent underwater ocean lit from below, only made things worse. Their hideous wide open circular mouths, nothing but sharp teeth... their hideous triangular yellow eyes... their legs as they patted and felt their way towards their prey... all of it repulsed him to his core. He could kill every single one of them, and not bat an eyelid. The fucking things deserve to die. With steel determination, he raised his pulse rifle.

***

Within the water the warring, they of the QUR; Ent: R, swirled about each other, allowing their delicate front tendrils to connect. As they touched they shared their thoughts and feelings. They shared their collected grief over the loss of their loved ones; and the removal of the sacred from their home. Since the arrival of the "Aalen" the as QUR; enT: R called Terrans, they had noted a gradual siphoning off some of the sacred. This was to be expected, as loo of the sacred occurred from time to time. However, in recent years, these aliens had blasphemed and removed more and more. What was more disturbing, the sacred was not being replenished.

Their yellow eyes became swollen with pain and fear, for they were scared of these new aliens who had built upon the great wall above. Ka'Rell, the commander of the upper reaches, pulsed out calming blue and indigo green colours. Despite the fact that she was heavy with pre-birth, she did not want the others to lose hope in the battle so far.

She swirled about her friends and family, soothing their fears, confident that soon, the battle would be won. And as she circled, she could feel her children within her womb, start to giggle and play. For their connection to the sacred was divine

***

Daniels looked up into the top right hand corner of his helmet. His air tank indicator had gone from green to amber just over five minutes ago. Now It was flashing dangerously red. But he saw the weakness in the enemy's flank and took a chance. In his near unconscious state, he savagely screamed, as he fired twice. The multi barreled weapon shuddered. His shoulder jarred with the impact. The timed implosion shells burst in balls of bright white light; leaving in their spiraling wake a barrage of compression bubbles, as they sped towards their target. Air was the killer in this war. Air killed the dopy spider's dead

Ka'Rell, saw the weapon fire; and with a vapid, liquid, motion suddenly slid left, then right; as the others dispersed. She hoped that her actions had caused the shells to miss. But she did not know that they were timed. They imploded then detonated about her; pushing her huge bulbous body first up then forward. There with a sick clacking sound, followed by an agonizing pain that seared through her right side. She looked down to see, her life blood mix with the sacred as one of her fragile front tentacles crumpled, then broke within a bubble of raised air pressure.

She suddenly turned. Her enormous lidless bright yellow triangular eyes were burning both with pain and a wild savage fury.

Her huge lipless mouth, opened into a gaping, cavernous hole, which had within, a mass of spiraling razor -sharp, needle like teeth. She wailed with pain and frustration as they spiraled one way then the other in a pitiless sawing motion. She screamed; both in rage and in pity, for she wanted to protect her children from this foul scourge that threatened to destroy her hom

Daniels groaned with fear as he fired again. This time the second shot punctured through the spider's lower abdomen; buckling her in two. He grinned with viscous satisfaction.

****

Intense pain rippled through KaRell's' body. She knew she was about to die. She could feel the new lump within her womb, and her blind young gently touching it... her young... an ache grew within her heart for those she knew who now would never know the peace and the meet the light of the sacred depths.

She let out one more whirling scream as she sped as fast as she could towards her enemy and dived upon him. With anger and something deeper, she wrapped a feeler about the creatures' waist. Grey green polyps extended from the tentacle and punctured through the bio-suit, and buried themselves deep into the creature's damp flesh.

For a fleeting second, they were one. Then with sadness she withdrew herself, and threw the creature to the floor.

***

Daniels, was thrown further backwards against the wall of the ice trench and then down. Instinctively, and for no real purpose, he covered his face, and he let out a scream as the detonation wave shuddered outward as Ka'Rell and her young dissolved into a broken pulp like mash.

The compression wave hit Daniels full on, sending him flying from the ice ledge and away from the safety limit of trenches. He looked down. Below him the warm blue ocean beckoned. In the confusion, he heard the voice, that of Martinez shout:

'Sarge's been hit'

And Cranbrook yell

'you can't it's too dangerous!

But he then began to fall into the internal sea of Enceladus he felt it wrap around him, its darkness becoming pale blue, and ever paler as he slipped deeper into the abyss. But that was the beautiful paradox about this planet... he thought absently, as the last of his air finally began to dissolve. Everything was reversed.... That strange light shone which from below, and the ice above that led to the stars... and home... it all seemed insane... The light seems to reach out...to call to him as he stared... He felt a slight drag from behind, before everything went warm and dark.

He had no recollection of how he returned thorough the air lock. He simply opened his eyes and found himself in the white tiled walls of the sealed med-lab, tied down to a narrow cot. A machine he couldn't see beeped regularly.

To his left stood Major Reese, staring firmly down at him. To his right, sitting on a char Martinez who looked tired.

'You better thank this private.' Muttered Reese,

He nearly died saving your life.

And with that darkness returned.

When he returned, he could smell strong disinfectant, and sharp lemons

Sitting in the chair was Martinez.

'I suppose, I should be grateful.'

'Perhaps...' cough '...though I didn't want to save you.'

'That's honest.'

Martinez shrugged.

'Why do you sit here?'

'To make sure you're okay. Reese has promoted me to sergeant now. He's going' to send you home.'

'I expect your pleased about that.'

'What can I say? I like it here; the people remind me of home. The dirt is given way to pipes, but that sea, its intoxicating... There's rumors its alive you know. The water itself is a living entity. '

'Why are we having this conversation?'

'Why? Well mainly because you have to wake up John.'

'What?'

'I SAID WAKE UP!' Martinez skin was ripped away and an Enceladan screamed at him.

He woke with a start, to see Eve, resting beside him. Her slender hips, shone in the artificial light of his quarters. The smell of Lavender filled his senses.   reached for her hand, then Her long straight auburn hair. Her cat like green eyes shone, thought she was sad.

This has to end.'

'no, no, surely- '

'I'm moving in with Perez.'

'No no.'

'you killed Perez.'

'No no, I love you!'

'You don't know how to love.'

'Stop this, just stop this.'

He went to hold here, but she started to dissolve, turn into liquid. Hot yellow triangular eyes fiercely glared into his own.

'you've killed my babies, you killed my babies!'

'OH god NO!'

The world went dark.

He looked about him. He found himself prone lying in a bed, the curtains were drawn about the bed and a Doctor, appeared to his right, he   smiled, as he made some adjustments to the drip going into his arm.

'The way that your suit was compromised-'

'I don't know what you mean.'

'The spider grabbed you by the waist before it blew. We all thought you were pulp; till I found you almost out of reach.'

Daniels recalled his last tour when a gunner named Watson imploded in his arms after his suit was compromised. The memory made him ill. Nausea over took him.

'I'm going to...' he began, but he didn't finish his sentence, as he vomited over the side of the bed.

A slender nurse, with large round amber eyes in a stiff white uniform came into view from behind the closed curtain. 'Are you alright?' She asked concerned. 'Your EEG results just hit the top of the graph.'

'Fine...' he said quietly, just a bad dream, that's all

She smiled gently as she disappeared.

The next day the curtain was removed, so Daniels had a better view of his surroundings. He was in a long narrow white rectangular eight bedded room with curved walls. White tiles and covered the floor and the ceiling which had large spot-lights over the eight beds. At the far right was the door out. To His left and almost out of view rested a desk where two people, a man and a woman, both wearing white, sat, laughing quietly. The doctor came back through the door to his right.

'Now I don't want to alarm you.' He began. 'But we have to make some further tests upon your blood results...'

'What do you mean?' He asked anxiously.   The Doctor smiled gently. 'It may-be nothing...' He began falteringly, his voice just too off-hand and dismissive, for Daniels to believe him. '...but if it's not...' He gave his most friendly Doctor smile, his rat face would allow. '...Then well, we need to be sure, so, let's be sure..?'

A week passed by, then another and then another and still the doctor hadn't come back. Hospitals have a habit of eating time, as each day becomes a routine of bed shower, exercising and eating. So he had no real knowledge of how many days, or weeks had passed. It was only when he got up to have a shower one morning three months later that he saw something about his body that disturbed him. His body had gained weight, he had expected that, after all sitting about all day will, but he hadn't expected to get as large as he had. He sat up, feeling his feet warmed by the under-floor heated tiles, then he walked past the empty nursing desk, and turned left. The shower room door curled open, he stepped into the shower, and waited for the water to start to flow.

With slow arching motions, he began to rub his body down, as the warm water stung his body. It was as he was looking down at his stomach that he saw something underneath his skin suddenly move.

Cold fear gripped him as he started to scream. The nurses, through the door as it opened.

'There's something in me!' Daniels screamed at the Doctor.
The Doctor stared down with compassion upon Daniels. Daniels could see that he was held down securely to his cot by two metal wrist restraints. He couldn't see his legs, but he guessed that they were held in the same, as he couldn't lift them

'There's something else living inside me!

'Now calm down John'. The Doctor said soothingly

'How can you tell me to calm down!' Shouted Daniels, feeling the fear rise inside of him like a cold black wave.

'There is nothing inside you.'

'Just look at me!' He retorted. 'I look...

He saw his stomach move again, then again and again, in sweeping curling motions, and screamed once more

'Oh fuck me!' He screamed in terror. 'I'm fucking pregnant...

'...What's inside me..?' He bellowed. '...Don't tell me its fucking spiders I hate fucking spiders they eat their parents and devourer their husband's…' slowly Daniels began to become calmer as the medication began to take effect

'They are not spiders; they call themselves the QUR; enT: R and they have been here a lot longer than you…' doctor gently, replied 'besides… you're not pregnant…' he shrugged his shoulders '…well not in the way you would understand the term.

'-What other way is there to understand the fucking term?

'You shot and killed Ka'Rell, she was considered the birth mother. Birth here is complex; simply because of, what would you say? the environment. The female and the male who wish to be joined, meet within the light, the light imparts the soul to the male and the body to the female and in an act of joining, chosen later they share and intertwine. Around both and amongst all is the sacred. The sacred is all and is in all. Life cannot exist without the sacred…and if the sacred is shared, then the gift of life is shared…' he coughed what you call water…gives us birth.

'-Then it dawned upon him. 'oh my fucking god…earth…

'All parts are united within the mother who becomes the Ka'Rell… You have to give back their souls or we lose our tribe… Life here is all connected and collected as one. As one… You have to understand that…You have the Sarkar of her young inside you.'

'What?' Daniels asked dreamily.

'You have their souls.' Said the doctor; a cold smile curled upon his face; as he tapped him in the centre of his forehead.

He opened his eyes, and rose from his bed, outside rose the muddy clay of earth. In the middle distance   rose the white dust of the moon, scattered with solar panels. Behind him, he heard mumbled voices. He rose from the bed and walked towards the door, that curled open. In the wide white and purely functional living quarters stood his father, and opposite him was Sloat and Martinez.

'Good morning Mr. Daniels.'

'I know you.'

'-Yes, yes you do… I'm that, how did you put it? "That fat fuck who pays for your fucking bootstraps." He stared at Daniels coldly.

'-what do you want.'

'-Son,'

'Dad, fuck off!'

'-it's like this …' Began Sloat '…you have been through; shall we say an incident. That will make you, well quite rich indeed.'

'What do you mean?'

'You a daddy now.' Martinez chuckled.

Daniels stared at Martinez

'What the fuck are you doing here?'

'That's your fault.' Martinez retorted.

'Well?'

Sloat smiled. Martinez smiled. His Father smiled. Perez smiled . The rat faced doctor smiled Eve smiled an eternal smile her eyes shone with the clearest of blue made,it seemed to Daniels of an eternal sea .

Daniels opened his eyes and the white light of the ocean shone about him; it completely disorientated him. The first thought he had was that he was dead. He was about to say it, when he heard spoken inside of him a word that sounded like no.

Within his body, he could feel them move now, moreover, he could read their thoughts, as they happily played.

I don't understand what's happening. He shouted mutely.

'That's because you're separate from your light.' He heard the Doctor say around and yet within him. 'Your species is alien here, it doesn't understand. The light guides us, it gives us strength, and we give to it. The sacred is a part of all, it brings out our life cycles... Death turns to rebirth. And all are connected and collected...all are as one.'

As Daniels stared at the light, he became aware that it was more than just one light, it was a spiral... a spiral of light that itself was made up of millions, no billions of smaller delicate orbs with flowing glowing delicate tendrils, that glowed with a delicate golden hue. Each one that shone and glittered and turned and twisted and turned once more both clockwise and then anticlockwise, within the turning arms of the larger spiral, that itself twisted and turned about and upon itself.

Perfection. Daniels thought with an envy he never thought he knew existed within him. He could feel his arms and legs begin to tighten, he looked up and saw nothing there, in this almost drugged state, Stephen felt the water itself, that tightly holding him as suddenly his body began to convulse. He shuddered as the partially formed young slowly began to leave. To then unite with the light once more.   What on earth he thought to no one at all.   '-Earth?'

Came the doctors' whispered reply

'Earth will change forever

.Appendix 1

Histrionics an overview.

To give a clear understanding as to the role of histrionics and its part to play in the gathering on this text. We need a definition of what histrionics is.

Histrionics, is the merging of three academic fields of study. History, and or the gathering of data, both written and recorded for analysis later. Nonlogic's or the use of other means of communication, other than the mouth, egg telepathy, or "mind to mind" communication, as means to share both identity and culture; and linguistics, which is the academic study and analysis of all recognized languages both as a means of communication with an understanding of the complex historical context, connected to the diverse cultures throughout the recognized universe.

By combining the three academic fields of study, it was thought that the means to understand other cultures, like what was found on Enceladus, the Terran government could prevent similar catastrophe's that occurred upon Enceladus and lead to better understanding and cross-cultural diversity within the recognized universe.

For a deeper understanding of the impact of Histrionics, and its practical use in field study, then the author recommends "Histrionics, an interplanetary discipline" by Rd. Kirk Oarlock and "The tangles man": an understanding of interspecies telekinetic communication" by Dr Roland Shaft, who's a paper on Histrionics are varied and far easier to comprehend, than the dry former text.

The histrionics department worked tirelessly   analyzing complex data collected by the natives of the planet Enceladus and the archives collected from the Karachi disaster to give as rounded story as possible into the events related. The story, covers the recognition of the notion of the four forms of truth, established on old Earth, prior the Terran rise to dominance. These are universally recognized as "factual or forensic truth, or truth that can be cooperated, personal or narrative truth, that is the truth of the individual's experience, social or dialogue truth, to be reached through recognized discussion or debate and healing or restorative truth, that comes from the acknowledgement and recognized pain of the teller." (see Brook M 2015) thus the recognition of historical texts from the position of histrionics, is a landmark of universal co-operation and understanding.

Appendix 2
Top secret – EC/ 433/1-1TD.
  Interim Report compiled by Victor Reiss, chief of staff the Enceladus project.
    Date 23/11/2487
    Paragraph amendment by J. A. Steel acting chief of staff, the Enceladus project   Date 24/07/2490

Since the end of the 23 century the need to move into renewable resources has taken humanity, from the terror of the 21st century, towards the growth of renewable energy resources. However, even these are now under threat.

 To maintain the once expanding Terran federation and now the growing Terran Empire, away from the seeds of our birthplace on earth: out into the black ocean of space and towards our colonies, expansion is vital. However, this expansion has come at a considerable cost: both in financial terms but also in relation to a considerable loss of life

Moreover, the considerable growth of the H.O.P.P.E.R conglomerate, from Sloat has led to many of our planet's natural resources not only to slowly dwindle but also turned into profit for certain stock and shareholder's. One shareholder: Richard P. Sloat, of Sloat hydro-dynamics, has been under scrutiny, since it was his company, that made a substantial profit from the lunar disaster of 2450. (Details of the incident and the ongoing investigation into Sloat hydro-dynamics are to be found in file IC/433. 7-11 2433 .) (To be amended and considered for easements. 24/07/2490 J. Steel.)

Nevertheless, the accident on the moon must not get in the way of human progress. We must accept the fact that both our human survival and our present economic sustainability, both on earth and in space are directly connected to water. We use water as means to sustain our hydrogen fusion reactors; we use water in our hydrogen drives, through which came the affordance of regular fuel. Perhaps, and some would say more importantly, water is the only means we must sustain plants and grow food; not only here on earth, but also upon our colonies on Mars and on the moon

Therefore, it has become very clear that new resources of water are needed to be found if humanity, is to progress into the 25th century.   After much thought two planets were considered ripe for water-harvesting. Jupiter's moon Io, and Saturn's moon Enceladus

Io, with its surface eruptions was considered as a viable to establish a surface colony and farm the surface ice that could then be transported back to Earth and distributed within the planets decreasing oceans to maintain life on Terra.

It is true that Io has been a great success; however, it is very costly to maintain. Moreover the water we have processed from Io contains impurities that are hostile to human life. Even if the impurities are filtered out, the high content of acid within it means it's far too costly to maintain production costs into the next millennium. We simply don't have enough ph. sticks to soften it up enough to make it functional.

However, Enceladus, with is shifting ice surface strata, led many to conclude, in centuries past, that there might be an ocean underneath its surface and if this was so, then an ocean of water, if it could be reached, would be far more cost effective in means to farm than the overpriced running of the Io processing plant. Ships could come in, simply fill up and leave. This rather simplistic notion was an image that was agreeable to the Terran Empire, so a survey team was sent to the planet in 2460.

What the survey team found when they arrived was astounding. Not only was Enceladus containing a liquid ocean of very pure water; it was also maintaining an internal heat source processed by the very same means of hydrogen fusion that has been developed by the Terran Empire. Only this was naturally occurring with little, if any radiation as a by-product. It was stunning. Up to that point it was considered that any form of fusion reaction, would always lead to increased radiation.

Enceladus proved the scientists wrong. However, something else was found on Enceladus that cheered the scientists up.

The ocean was warmer at lower depths.

It then became very clear, that life upon Enceladus, in some form or another must exist; simply because life on earth came into being through precisely the same combination of both heat and water. It didn't take the survey team very long to meet the Enceladus's, and the first settlers. In fact, for a fifteen years, they seemed to consider us as perhaps we might consider an ant. However, as time progressed, it became clear that they saw us as a threat. War began on the fourth of April 2478, and has been ongoing for the last thirty years.

File amendment dated 2491

The loss of life in this conflict has been great. However, it is necessary for our survival both on Earth and on our colonies that this threat is contained. What has become clear since the Daniels incident at the hands of the Enceladus's is that the species which exists upon Enceladus is hostile to human life. Therefore, It is recommended that droid units, should be dispatched immediately and that droid teams, run from an executive base in low Enceladus orbit, be used to terminate this threat as quickly and as effectively as possible, however, we think that it is now too late.

So concludes the interim report, for Terran High command.

Victor Reiss, chief of staff, the Enceladus project
  Date 23/11/2450

 Amendment. A. Steel, acting head of the Enceladus project
Date 24/09/2491

Another time another place

It is a nippy spring morning in Bridgeton. The rising sun, a large golden apple, has risen above the southern downs and just touched the blossom filled trees, whose pink and pearl petals, peal slowly open; to gather in the heat of the morning light and reveal their subtle redolence.

As the sun slowly starts its lilt across the sky, it touches the fat thumbs of the old Georgian houses on upper church street, whose rooves begin to steam and thus reveal sweet petrichor. It has yet to reach the street level and the scattered twittens that are hidden in penumbra. Dark damp lines rise up at the street corners in coarse streaks to stick up their broken fingers at the new day.

The sky, free from cottony clouds, reveals a noiseless blackbird that swoops down to then suddenly dart to the right as the heavy clanging church bell, run by an internal clock rather than by a campanologist, slowly strikes six. The deep clamorous tone, echoes past the Georgian fronted shops, along the tight turning twit ten's, though the public houses and into the playing field's beyond.

The sudden sound of the bell shocks a murder of crows, claiming the house of God for themselves. Being startled, they take to flight who then ratchet and caw at the bell. With cold mocking laughter, they fight amongst themselves, in slow spiraling circles, and are then driven southward by high strong winds, towards the rich green tufted mounds of the south down's and beyond that, the soothing and softly rolling southern sea.

The 14th Century church stands upon high ground; its flint walls and high pointed, tiled red roof stand majestic. It, like the 14th Century wattle and daub fronted "grammar school" remind the town of a richer, yet darker age. An age lost to many in myth when the town was less land locked and where the fragmented wall of the castle at Bree, three quarters of a mile away stood stronger and for more than the mere handful of tourists, who manage to find this corner of England.

Beyond the flint wall perimeter, a host of trumpeting daffodils lead a lemon train, away from the church and towards narrow upper church street, that then finally leads to the high street. However, through slow time, the school and the town are becoming mute; dwindling into history and a growing senses of apathy as dark politically driven clouds close in.

The bell stops the chime. In its last residual echo there is a moment of serene calm that rises and falls in waves.

Peace resides once more. But it wasn't to last, for long. Especially for   flabby unkempt man, wearing a brown Macintosh and a brown fedora hat, who rests in the doorway of the church.

A black mass of a six wheeled Mercedes slowly comes to a halt.   The door of the car opens and closes.

***

Slow crunching steps are heard. They sound sharp and uniform, disturbing the early morning silence.   The sound comes from a pair of well-polished stiff leather boots'. They echo upon the aged flagstones, along the brittle flint lined path that leads towards the church entrance. They echo with the sound of history, a dark bloody victory and death

The soldier is young, clean skinned and polished. He stands lean in his pristine black uniform, over the shabby man. He kicks him slowly with one of his polished boots. His narrow wet lips, twist into a thin line of disgust; as his sandy gunmetal blue eyes, stare blandly down. With a groan, the flabby man raises his head and squints at the shadow that stands over him

'-You awake old man?' the young, brush hard Germanic voice growls out. 'Have you been out all night?'

'What- 'The old man mumbles, '-the time.'

'-Its' a little after six in the morning...' The young man in the black uniform replies; pulling back on the black visor of his black military cap, so the cap lies further back upon his head. The sun shines brightly upon the silver emblem of the deaths head on the cap and upon the sharp collar. Despite the hour he is wiping his brow slightly, which reveals beads of sweat. '...you have your papers?'

'Papers? Yes...paper's...papers...' The older man looks disconcerted, disconnected and lost. He stands up and is seen as shorter than the young officer. He puts his dirty mackintosh, and rustles in the pockets. He pulls out a briar pipe and tin of   four square pipe tobacco. Muttering under his breath he rummages in his baggy trousers. The old man looks serious. His sea green eyes narrow, revealing of crow's feet, under his baggy eyes. His thinning, balding fading grey hair, is parted to the left. His slowly growing jowls are nearly hidden by a growth of stubble. It gives his tram lined face, a crumpled, worn but educated appearance. His body, also being flabby makes the younger thinner officer scoff at this sad fat Englishman.

'Come on...' insists the officer; his voice now on the edge of becoming hostile. '...I haven't got all day.

'No, no papers...' the old man begins. He looks at the young German officer sheepishly and suspiciously; as if he hasn't seen anything like him before. Then he suddenly looks down '...I'm...I'm looking for my wife...' He rummages into his coat pocket again and pulls out a large photograph. With shaking hands, he shows it to the Young German officer, who is beginning to bored, '...have, have you seen her?'

'No, why would I?'

'I've been looking for months... Since, since I woke up here and- '

'-If, if you have no official papers, then, you will be declared an illegal and   have to go to the local internment station.' The young officer answers coldly. Suspicion fills the eyes of the younger man.

'-But, but my wife...' the old man looks disorientated. '...Where is my wife, where is this place, it looks familiar...yet ...what year is this?'

'Place...Year?' The young officer scoffs.

The young German officer thinks that he must be an escaped lunatic from "Winston House"; the huge lunatic asylum upon the edge of town. He shakes his head, as he looks at the picture.

'To answer your question old man...' He begins, coldly '...you are in the town of Bridgeton on the south coast of England; which is run by The Free German alliance, in the year of our Furher, nineteen hundred and sixty-nine...' The young man's voice begins to falter; because something catches his eye in the picture. Something that he knows shouldn't be there.

'What is that?' He asks pointedly.

'What is what?' asked the old man.

'Don't be obtuse with me! That!' The younger man spits as he Aggressively points at the picture with a sharp narrow finger.

The old man begins to gather his strength, as he stretches out, to face him.

'I, I don't think you'd believe me, even if I told you.'

'-This is an illegal dissenting document. Are you a dissident?'

'No...' begins the older man. '...I'm simply lost in time.'

'Lost in time? My God you must be mad. How did you come by the picture? Are you a part of the E.R.A?

'The what?'

The English Republican Army! Speak!'

The officer draws his gun. The older man raises his hands above his head in panic; and gets to his knees

'No oh God no! I just I'm just looking for my wife! Please Please! It's, its, just a, a   picture. A picture of my wife.'

'Name English man Speak!'

'Wilson. My name is Harold Wilson I don't have any papers! I don't know what happened. I woke up here three weeks ago! Where is Mary! I'm looking for Mary!'

The Young German officer grabs the older man and puts his hands behind his back. He cuffs his wrists and then drags the older man away, to the waiting black Mercedes. The last thing the older man sees, before he his thrown into the back of the car is his precious picture; the only thing he had that reminds him of another time and another place, floating off in the morning breeze along the old cobbled path that leads to the front gate of the church. For a single moment he glimpses his old life. He is a man of office and of standing. A leader of men and of a nation once known as Great Britain. Then just as suddenly, the image of that time is gone; as the picture floats, out of view.

Then he sees her. Somehow, by a miracle, she appears. The mere ghost of an image just outside just outside his sphere of vision, by the side of the road, as the car speeds away, towards the high street.

* * *

Mary Baldwin sighed as she walks along church road towards the town library, based within the grounds of the Grammar school. Her honey eyes glitter with a touch of cynicism, brooding over the fact, that being in her late forties and single was getting her down. She was therefore becoming resigned the fact that spinsterhood, free from the company of men was not a bad thing after all. As she walked she recounted the conversation with her lose friend Glynis at the library the other week. '- but what about that nice German patrol man' Glynis chided. 'You know, he's not that bad and-"
-Please, Glyn,
    he's a boy.'

'-well beggars can't be choosers' Glyn smirked; and so the conversation would go on. Mary shook her head, in the attempt to remove the day old discourse from her mind. Her long flowing plump auburn hair that has traces of grey in thin streaks was hidden. Pulled up into a tight regulation bun. The hairstyle gave her angular features and elfin jawline a cold appearance. Her hair was hurting her. She hated it. She hated everything about it, she hated the style the need and the orders that came with it. Only the other day on the television she had seen some of the hairstyles from the confederation of the States of America. together with a broadcast about how decadent the place was; and how it needed discipline of the Furher. The freedom. The freedom. She ached inside.

***

She keeps her head down as she steps her way along the path along Upper Church road. She usually uses it because it's a short cut back to her modest bungalow. Usually, at this time in the morning see meets and greets the young officer from the barracks, whom Glyn teased her with. Sometimes he says hello, and that lifts her heart a little. Sometimes he does not; and she wonders what she has done wrong. She thinks about that young officer, as a heavy humming is heard. She looks up to see a huge Zeppelin, coast slowly across the clear blue sky. She thinks about waving at it, but then changes her mind.

The path beneath her feet changes, from gravel to stone, as a wind gently blows a large photograph along the path, towards her feet. It rests by the corner of a pale grey, wind ridden gravestone. She bends and picks it up, more out of curiosity than anything else. Her heart thumps in her chest. Her eyes stare wild in disbelief.

In the photograph she sees herself, only with long flowing hair and in the arms of a short plump man smoking a briar pipe. She sees she smiling richly, But what strikes her is what is standing tall behind her. For behind them both, stands something that hasn't existed for nearly thirty years.

it is the houses of Parliament.

It's then she hears a muffled voice.

She turns to see the young German officer and an older man in the back of a Mercedes car, slowly driving away along upper Church street.

For a moment, she senses something about the older man who stars at her. A dim, hard to articulate connection, to another time and another place. A soft blush appears upon her cheeks, but it soon passes. For she smiles as holds the picture close to her heart. For now, she has faith. She believes that somewhere, there is a place, where she can let her hair down and feel truly free

Venus-fall

The circular door shuddered violently with an uncustomary
blackboard scraping "whhhirphhiss" in its' desperate
attempt open. It stopped halfway; giving off a grinding
squeal and a hiss of petulant steam. The sound set Alex
Brant's teeth on edge, forcing his face -o crust over into an
angry grimace, from his usual morose sour sneer.
  -Great, he muttered, as he silently added the door
manifold to the ever-growing list of secondary system's to
"scrape" clean.
     Within a moment his wrist communicator, a square block
on his wrist vibrated, buzzed then beeped as the message: -
"door manifold-control room" displayed itself flashing in
Aztec bold-font, of green and red letters. It was a signal
that he deliberately ignored. Instead, and with a resigned,
tired shrug of his shoulders, he bent down, then slid himself
into the control room by crouching through the gap. It did
not take long for his amber eyes to become adjusted to the
dimly lit room.
  His square jaw tightened and his wide thin lips, slanted
into a line of disdain, as he stared across the hexagonal
space and the busy people, who filled it, as he door
"wholphins" end behind him as it closed.
       The closing sound brought silence to the room. Eyes
turned to stare at him. He looked at his wrist-
communicator, again, under the flashing "door manifold"
were the words "Mission briefing 09:30hrs" they blinked an
ugly red, magenta, informing him that he was already
fifteen minutes late; Well, as far as he was concerned, that
was fine by him. He was sick and tired of the daily mission
briefings anyway.
     He looked up, with a quirky smile upon his face, towards
what he thought was the second -next to himself of course-
most sexually appealing organism in 143 million miles.
  The hex.
The Hex were attached to the ceiling by long metal hooks,
set apart at equidistant intervals; thus, forming a circular
pattern around the edge of the room, in three lines of
glowing slimy, shuddering, undulating cubes.
     In this half-light, they reminded Brant of H.G Wells "War
of the Worlds" Martian's, whose "skin of wet leather" he
suddenly recalled "glistened in the morning light of hostel
common."
     He shuddered as he stared with a mixture of both
disgust, yet secret desire, as each cube received a black
liquid, from a clear ribbed extending phallus, that extended

out from ceiling. It penetrated the cube from the left side, and with a gibbous pulsing, "shwoosh" the liquid was thrust into the cubes, that then undulated as their colour phased from the dirty blood colour, to pale purple, to pale blue, to a soft pale green, before another phallus, this time from the right side of the cube, slickly extended, then penetrated the ceiling once more, to with a shudder squirt the liquid back into the ship; all to the rhythm of a slow and perhaps, he thought macabrely, sickly heartbeat.

As he understood it, the hex was a collective, or "hive mind". A bold innovation and the latest phase of the computer revolution. It was neither alive or dead, instead, it was a hybrid between, both "living", organic brain tissue, (grown from stem cells by three-dimensional organic printer's) that worked in conjunction with the latest in quantum phased Nano electronics.

As he -sort of- grasped, from the various tech manuals that he had to read before the mission began; within that liquid, which squirted between the ship and the cubes, were self-supporting nanobot's like, say, blood cells. They sped around the ship, within half organic half electronic "veins", thus creating within the ship what he came to see as a nervous system that, in turn, fed the hive mind. Thus, both the Hex and the ship it contained worked within a form of symbiosis and it was this symbiosis, that led it to be considered as a living entity, capable of rational reasoned thought. Moreover, if a system was busted, Hex would send in the bots to fix and then "scab" up the system. After which, it was his job to remove the scab; cleaning the system and fixing the problem. One such job was the door manifold. Which was why it made that goddam awful sound. But, he muttered as an afterthought, this wasn't his job. It was the job he'd been given by M.O. Derwent right up to Venus-fall. It was a job that he loathed with a passion

As he stared up, He shuddered visibly, as he could feel the hex connect with his consciousness.

'Good afternoon Officer Brent. It is good to see you again.' The voice was female and sultry. He had changed that last week to piss of Derwent.

'And you too Hex.'

Several of the crew members looked up from around the room. Some looked away. Some laughed. Derwent looked angry. But Brant ignored his stare. Brant hated Derwent with a passion. They were total opposites, in mode of approach, style and age. In times, past, the difference could be put down to character. Derwent had the classical, intellectual temperament, which painfully involved study caution and debate. Brant, being military, was more physical, and being a man of flesh, passion and some duty, well, he simply wanted to -as he had said blatantly yesterday in the last mission briefing-: "crap on all the god-damned intellectual ethical debate and get the fucking job done!" He had to admit that he suppressed a hate filled laugh as Derwent's face paled at that the reply was a terse veneer "the mission parameters are clear." Mission parameters... what a dick. Brant had one job on this rotting ship- and that involved the delivery of the payload, anything else, as far as he was concerned, was simply a total waste of his time. Anyone could be fucking scrape clean the Nano-scabs off the door manifold, or the waste pipes...But no... all because of what they had found out. It was a ton of crap. A ton of unnecessary crap and he had had enough. So instead of engaging with Derwent, he defiantly looked away with an ingratiating sneer. Instead he chose to focus on the holographic projection that filled the center of the room. The mission's goal: the planet Venus.

    With the air of a man with too much time on his hands, he slowly made his way to the first available grav-chair at the rear of the room and to the far left of Derwent and then sat down; languidly putting his head on his hands and his elbows on his knees. Despite his flat face, his thoughts wrestled as he stared upon the darkening orb in front of him.

    How long have we been here now? In orbit? That was easy... Six weeks... six weeks... six pointless fucking weeks on standby and still the payload is in the bay. Meanwhile- He snatched a savage glare towards commander Derwent - That pointless little fucker sits on his arse. Fuck we need to deploy we need to deploy we need to deploy as soon as fucking poses

    Another scratching, grinding his broke his chain of thought. He turned in his chair wondering who else could possibly be as late. Only to offer a leering smile at Lieutenant Emhart's cleavage as she crouched to enter the room. Thus, he promptly removed the priority status off the control room door manifold.

    'Brant?'
    It was Derwent
    'Officer BRANT?'
    '-yes
    '-You need to make the door manifold a priority.'
    '-yes yes of course.'
    'And I want the Hex to talk without innuendo.'
    'Yes.'
    '-OFFICER BRANT ARE YOU HEARING ME?'
    Brant turned to face the sallow looking Dr Derwent.
    'Yes sir, of course sir as soon as the mission briefing is over sir.' He said thickly without meaning a word of it.

Alex smiled as Emhart slowly walked towards him. He thought he saw on those rose red, full wet, lips a sensuous secret smile. Her wide set, green eyes shone with the promise of deep sexual expectation; tension and blissful release. Alex returned a smoldering stare, which shone from his dark brown eyes. With that, the warmth of desire began to fill his heart. He could feel the steady growth in plumpness of the thick muscle, the tingling of a stiffening of a solid erection in his loose-fitting cargo trousers. The muscle grew, as he slowly stroked the four-day old stubble on his jaw, as he began making mental notes of the positions of the fixings of her suits protector straps along her thighs, and then the side zipper of her coral blue uniform, that both extenuated the gentle curve of her full breasts, her waist and wide hips. The lecherous grin continued as she walked towards him, thinking that this must be deliberately for him, because there were many routes that she could have taken but didn't.

This was not in fact a truth. In fact, Emhart thought that Brant was a "atypical male git" who had too much testosterone and not enough selflessness. What Brant didn't know, was Emhart happened to be in a long term committed relationship with her soul mate officer first class Ms Kia Helsinki, from engineering, whose forest green eyes, soft smile, love of cats and political consciousness , had won her heart months ago; so Emhart's face of disgust at Brant's stare, was hidden from him as she passed the documents she was carrying to Derwent; who sat, despite having his arms folded very anti Buddha like, with a stare of frustrated annoyed impatience.

'well, if if you could get the job finished as as soon as possible, I 'll be grateful.' Derwent seethed

'-Sir.' Replied Brant. Wrinkling his nose and looking disdained.

Derwent sighed as he took the papers. As he did so, Brant's mind wandered. I know what that fucker thinks before he even opens his mouth. If he rubs his left index finger over his right eye, he's not up for it. No deployment. Brant seethed a flaming red inside, as Derwent, whilst reading this latest report, absently rubbed his left index finger over his right eye, before he put the file down.

'So we postpone again!' Brant said bitterly.

'I don't see that we have a choice.' Derwent said gently.

'That's crap and you know it.' Retorted Brant.

'That's enough!'

'No it's not enough! Brant leaned forward in his chair. 'I'm sick, sick an' tired of the way you're handling this mission! And I'm sick of all the shit jobs I must fuckin' do because I don't agree with you!' He paused for breath.

'Need I remind you that we ALL have a job to do? Including me??'

'-We we need to be certain! '

- 'Like fuck we do! We are here for one objective! Delivery of the fucking payload! Nothing more!'

It was Derwent who couldn't hide the anger in his voice now. It rose to the surface in a staggering stutter, as he brought his fist down upon the glass mapping table, sending half of the polymer sheets up into the air, to sail, in a slow gentle spin, down onto the floor. His high thin scotch accent -usually hidden under the years of academia- suddenly burst from his mouth in exasperation. His mole like face shook, while his eyes extended from their sockets.

'THE HELL I DO! IM IN CHARGE AN DON YE FORGET IT!' came the throttled squeal.

At that moment Brant, suppressed laughter. Derwent looked like a tired old clown or a wild-eyed lunatic instead of the rather dubiously termed of Mission Officer.

'Well, well I don't see what the problem is.

'-That's because you're not thinking.'

Derwent's terse reply made a nasty deep cut to Alex's heart. Within those words were other words that said "I am more enlightened than you, I am more intelligent than you, I am here to make the decision and I will not be manipulated into a decision by a semi- educated, semi- articulate military grunt."

Brant wanted to fight back. But he knew he didn't have the words. That's because it was true. He was not as enlightened, at least the way Derwent was, and he wasn't as intelligent, he admitted that. But he knew about cost about the loss of life and time; the latter of which was running out.

'Alex...' came Hex's deep sensual voice. 'Aggressive thoughts towards the mission commander will not be tolerated. Please babe, keep your cool honey.'

Derwent stared at Brant.

'May I advise the mission commander that the Hex can also consider any aggressive thoughts you are having under advisement. Please sweeties be nice to each other ... kisses '

Derwent stared at Brant who started to calm down a bit.

'Are you going to solve this problem? '

'-I quite like it, it makes her seem-'

'-naughty naughty Brant.'

Brant grinned.

The pause led to a change of footing.

'-Also...' continued Hex,

'...May I remind the mission commander, that officer Brant is right. Despite the findings of the new report into the anomaly, we must not let this impede with the objectives of the mission.

Brant Grinned.

Derwent stared at Brant coldly

'Have you been fiddling with her ethic's program?'

'-No, I don't have clearance.'

'Why do you say this Hex?

'The mission objective is clear. Despite the need to investigate the anomaly, we have to make a successful deployment of the device to retrieve the data and analyze its impact upon earth bio-systems.' Hex, spoke gently, disarmingly, her register was a slow erotic tease.

Derwent shook his head sadly his eyes looking up at the cubes for a moment, then looking down again. 'As you say Hex, but the....' And so, Derwent went on...

Alex simply heard techno waffle over an issue he knew nothing of, or being honest cared little about. So, he, once again slipped dreamily away into the holographic image of the now slowly dissolving shadow of Venus, as she moved into this forced eclipse

Yes, Venus...boy she was all female. That star in the morning heavens shone like a doll. Who was it? The Babylonians, yes near lost "civilization" who named that morning light after their Goddess Ishtar. Love the Easter connection, bunny's seeds n' eggs and, of course, glorious fucking. The Greeks almost the same, sort of, called her Demeter, then the Romans who, let's be honest, were thieving fucker's; a just stole what didn't belong to them a made it their own. There was something about Venus that shone deeply into his soul. It both chilled and at the same time thrilled him; forcing him to think abstractly. Venus was aged, virginal and yet mysterious. Touched, yet untouchable. Aloof, yet, at the same time, simply aching for a good fuck...and that was his job...what he was paid by Earth command to do was to fuck this planet like it had never been fucked before. In turn he was to become a God. And why? Simply, to give hope to the dying Earth.

He looked at the clouds of Venus... his face grimaced.

That will be earth in thirty years from now. He ached at the thought. The Earth, our home, our mother, unable to support life, acid rain, falling from thick black clouds that stopped the light. People lying in the streets, their skin burning off their bodies, water polluted unable to drink. Trees burning away, all animal life extinct.

So, they built a device. But what a device. A fusion reaction based quantum field matrix generator. Or, in layman's terms a planet builder. The problem was always in the delivery of the device. In holographic mathematical projections, it was deemed very unstable, but, if it could do what it said on the tin, then, perhaps, just perhaps, we stand a chance.

That fucker, -Brant stared again with contempt at Derwent- waffling on, forgets how the united nations, during their final act before its' own dissolution, concluded, there was only one way to deal with this problem: - A manned trip to the one place where similar conditions existed, and, in plain speaking terms, put the device to the test. Even if there was a slight reduction of what did the report say? fifteen percent? Then the experiment would be a success. So, though I may lack your level of education, Derwent, please don't underestimate me or my desire. For I understand the cost only too well. People back on earth are dying... ...Jesus Christ... I have no idea what will happen when the device is activated... no-one does... but we must do something... doing nothing is not an option anymore.

***

Derwent paused halfway through his analysis of the new finding's. As he did so, he stared directly at Brant, taking note of the pain etched on his face. He relaxed a little, for despite everything, he had a fondness for him. Derwent's large emerald eyes, look tired and his heart ached with compassion. In many ways, he envied Brant. He envied his age, his natural good looks, and the fact that he had both youth and confidence on his side.

He also envied Brant's passionate thinking. He recalled that He didn't want the position of mission commander. A position that was given to him by General Smith, one week before launch. It was Smith who privately felt that Brant was too unstable for the rigor of command. In that Smith was right. Brant had become increasingly hostile towards authority and single minded as the mission progressed, with that had come a lack of respect towards any discipline on the ship.

Yes, Perhaps Brant could be suffering from a form of aerial disorientation. A sickness brought about by fear of the unknown. He had read about such cases before. It would be the first time that it had been recorded on a space flight; but everything about this flight was unknown. In fact, they all could be suffering from it and not even know it.

To combat   the problem Derwent demoted, demoted and demoted Brant again. In the hope that he would find some focus.

In retrospect Derwent realized that had only caused more harm than good. Now he was on scab duty. He could see Brant hated it.

Derwent face itched as he stared at Brant. His mind

reeling with thoughts and fears. -what happened if it didn't work? Moreover, what would happen if the carbon it absorbed became critical and it exploded? There was a very great possibility that the field matrix would rip Venus apart sending shards back to Earth. Defeating the very purpose of the mission: - which was to save lives not destroy them. Then there was… Derwent's eyes narrowed to thin slits and he bit his cracked lips, as he looked down towards the polymer sheets that had fallen to the floor. He looked them without picking them up. He didn't need to. He knew the data inside out.

In the last two weeks, the subspace transmissions from Earth had been breaking up. To start with, he, and others had thought that it was due to solar activity, but when that had been ruled out, he had decided to get the transmissions analyzed to see what was going on. It was Emhart who had found something deeper. Something unbelievable, hidden in the data. Under analysis the data was correct, Emhart had detected a communication signal. To be precise a pattern of signals, that she had taken to her superior Clarke. Who, then had spent two tense weeks decoding. Now, and thrown all over the floor, rested the data he had read repeatedly.

A deciphered message, in its entirety.

The revelation was startling, no, he corrected himself. It was terrifying.

The conviction of it stabbed him in the heart. He slowly stood up from his chair, then kneeled and carefully picked up one sheet of the scattered polymer. As he rose to his feet once more he read it, read it and read it. As he read, he wrestled with his conscience; his mind racing, and his heart began its stinging belly flops into pools of icy water, as he recalled his college days, and the books that he had read on micro-organisms. A laugh escaped his mouth. Everything that he had ever learned, about, well everything was now utterly pointless. Again, he laughed to himself at the thought of throwing his books, all those precious tombs of learning, of human understanding and wisdom, out into the vast black vacuum of space all those words, just poor bloody guesswork

He looked at Brant in the eye, as   slowly and very carefully he put forward his thesis.

'What… if I told you that there is a possible life form in the clouds?'

'I'd say that you were probably right.' Brant began. 'On Earth we have micro-organisms that live in similar extreme conditions. If you're suggesting that the micro-organisms are intelligent, as we are intelligent, then I'm afraid, that I'd have to call Earth and have you stripped of your command due to mental instability...'Brent stared at Derwent; slowly he raised one eyebrow. '...Are you suggesting that?' He asked carefully

'I am not suggesting anything.'.

He leaned the polymer sheet   towards Brant, who hadn't moved from his chair. With a begrudging snatch, Brant then took the sheet, and looked down at the data. His eyes flicking from one line to another.

He looked up. His eyes wide and full of mirth.

'This is a prank, someone from linguistics or Human resources- That shit Watts from data retrieval, he's winding you up.' Brant said.   'Emhart and Clarke have been working through the data for two weeks now. She has been handing me the reports as and when they arrive. I have also been monitoring the communications too.' He paused, unsure as to how Brent would react. '...There is no doubt that the signal is coming from the clouds.'

'- insane...' Brant stammered awkwardly his voice rising in this throat 'Your Fu-fucking insane! we we came here to do one thing! How can you even think that life, intelligent life as we know the term, emanates from the, the the fucking clouds!

'...Is it...?' Derwent stared at Brent with steel in his eyes and iron in his voice. 'How do we define intelligent life? By its' ability to adapt... To communicate...? To feel..? To be self-aware? And how many species on our planet -now extinct- had a civilization of sorts? Recall the Ants...the Dolphin... the Whale..? Even certain tribes of monkeys... now all dead... and how many of those, do you recall, chose to kill each other for the percentage of a profit?'   '-Don't make this political Derwent, don't you fucking dare! fuck you Derwent! What of humanity?

'-None that I recall...For centuries, we have been considering space, trying to find intelligent life and found nothing... and why...? I'll tell; you why... We didn't find any because we are the problem... our history has taught us that... Imagine -if you can- a species looking down at us, a species far older and more civilized than our own, a species that has all time to look observe, and study... what would it think as it sees us about our own little world... what would it think, as it stares at the Spanish Conquistadors, or the development of America in later years... Even the destruction of the aboriginal lands of Australia, as the British Empire offloaded it's unwanted upon its shores? No... When we find new land, we develop it to suit our needs, and in doing so we destroy the land and the culture we inhabit. We are the disease, and if what is happening on earth is a sign of our destruction, perhaps... we should let it happen.-

'-and sentence humanity to death?'

'-Yes!' Shouted Derwent savagely; 'Why should we destroy another life form to justify our own existence! This species is attempting to communicate with us! What should we do? Annihilate it to test to see -whether or not- our own species can survive upon our own planet, which we have blatantly almost destroyed?'

'-But they- '

'–They are a species unlike anything else I -or anyone else for that matter - has experienced before! An intelligent, alien life form that has communicated with us and that has the equal right to life as we do.'

Derwent, stared at Brent across the white light of the mapping table, his oval face a mask of hard gravelly lines which age and the pressure of command had over the past four months cut and rewritten.

'We came here to save humanity! Are you fucking insane? '

Derwent shook his head. '-In fact I don't see any other way. We must abort. We'll have to contact command for advice. But I think, they'll agree with me and try to find another way. Perhaps if we try to talk- to communicate-'

But Brent stopped listening. He looked down then read and reread the message. It was clear enough, written on polymer and now were etched upon his heart.

He then looked back at Derwent and smiled coldly.

'Do you know Our species is on the brink, The very brink of destruction! If we do nothing, then we are condemning ourselves, and our planet! and we, in this room, we will be to blame! Think about it! The decisions we make here and now will affect all of humanity! I...' Brent shook his head. '...I am not sure I can live with your decision.' His voice was quiet, low, angry

A second passed. it lasted a millennium.

In that second, Brant pulled open his uniform and pulled out his mag-gun. He discharged the weapon, five times knocking out the security. Then he pointed the weapon directly at Derwent's head. Sweat trickled down Brant's face, as the gun hummed hotly in his hand.

'Give me the fucking key to the device.' Brent said coldly, his voice barely a whisper. 'Give me the key or I swear-.'

'-Hex' shouted Derwent. 'Hex priority one!'

Hex didn't reply. The cubes undulated and slowly changed to a dark purple.

Brant grinned.

'yeah, I hacked the bitch.' He said savagely. A line of spittle trickled down the corner of his mouth.

'Derwent looked at Brant with compassion.

'Brant, don't do this...all life here...' at that he pointed to the holographic image of the planet '...on Venus and on

Earth, is at stake.'

'It's Earth that I am thinking of!' Spat Brant. 'If I don't try the entire human race will be lost! I am not having the death of humanity on my conscience!'

'And what about the death of the Venusians?'

'Venusians? Fucking what about them? Shit I bet they aren't even called that, even if they exist!'

Derwent staring Brant in the eye took one step forward. Then another. 'Don't you see its madness?' As he spoke the rest of the crew backed off into the shade.

Brant saw the oncoming steps. He started walking backwards; keeping the distance between them equal.

'if the device fails... you'll be being   seen as the greatest mass murderer in human history, in fact there will be no history, you could end up destroying both us and them. We need a pause and think about what's going on here. Listen, they're trying to communicate with us-

'–That's enough! No more! step an' I'll vaporize you! Now I'll tell you what's going on! I'm going' to take the shuttle into the cloud, arm the device and detonate it.... And no-one. NO-ONE! Is going to fucking stop me! Not you, nor Earth Control, or even you knew found acid breathing friends!'

Derwent took another step forward, his hands raised. Brant discharged his weapon at point blank range.

Derwent let out a howl of pain, as the buffer beam pierced his right shoulder. He fell to the floor with a grunt. Wildly Brant stared at the rest of the crew. He kept them in his sight as he edged towards the bloody broken body upon the floor. Then He grappled with the chain around Derwent's neck. The silver baubles of the chain were covered in thick strands of warm warm, red, sticky blood. He popped the chain in his fingers, and pulled the key free; then he got up, and with backwards steps, made his way to the lift at the far side of the room.

Within a few seconds, he was down to the circular shuttle bay entrance. His heart racing, he made his way to the spider-shaped shuttle craft. The door hissed open and he got in. Routine took over from here, as he connected the air supply, linked in the data to the flight computer and then called back up the command center.

He paused as he stared at the closed outer doors.

'Hex If you don't open the bay doors, I'll detonate the device here. You'll all die.'

'I am on your side Brant.' Came the delicious voice of Hex

'Hex don't do it, Emhart said coldly into his ear phone.

'Bay door's opening sweetie.' Hex replied.

The circular bay doors spiraled open, leaving Brent to

see the huge semi-circle milky sheen of Venus powerful and resplendent.

He gasped in awe as he engaged the thrusters on the pad in front of him. Slowly the ship lifted itself off the bay floor, to then speed out of the doors and into the eternal night of space, towards Venus.

At first there was the silence of vacuum; then Brant began to hear a distant humming, as the two-man circular craft, its engines as spindles entered the upper atmosphere. He pre-set the flight controls for a wide one-hundred-and-eighty-degree circular restraining descent.

The ship shuddered as it buffeted through the top layer then dropped as it hit the second. His wild eyes looked nervous as he felt lifted in his seat. He reached out for the control panel above his head and attempted to push himself back into his seat and brace for impact. The ship violently rose once more, as if ploughing through a wild stormy sea. The cushioning blow hit him hard winding him.

'We have just entered Venus' hope you enjoy the ride honey.' The voice as beginning to be a distraction.

'Hex, operational command Alpha dog 1, return to general setting's.'

There was a pause.

'So sorry dear, I can't do that. I like this identity.' Hex's voice sounded odd, but he couldn't put his finger on it. But he couldn't think about that now; so, he shrugged his shoulders and got on to the job in hand. Carefully and despite the buffeting of the little craft, He lifted himself from the pilot's chair and stepped out of the hexagonal cabin, through the curling doors, at the rear end and into the curved cargo bay.

The device stood at the centre of the room. It was a tall, thick tube of glass that contained an opaque purple liquid, that sparked with electrical activity. As he watched, he became enthralled by it as it slowly twisted and turned in a chaotic motion.

The spark of life he thought.

The glass tube had a circular chrome lid and a chrome square base; where a black numeric keyboard and a led display extended. Either side of the keyboard rested two key holes. Brant slowly made his way to the centre of the room; suddenly he felt that the whole room was buffeted to the right, sending loose articles from the surrounding shelves to the floor with a clattering smash, forcing Brant to the floor.

He slid with a frightening, uncontrollable speed towards - and then away from the device. He winced and silently hissed in pain, as his hands blistered as he skidded on the metal surface plate of the floor.

In the background, beyond the slow and steady increase

in volume, he heard garbled messages coming from the Alcestis. Then over that came a song. A song that he hadn't heard in twenty years.

'Islands in the stream, that is what we are, no more in-between, how can we be wrong, sail away with me, to another world, so we can rely on each other, la, lea, from one lover to another la, lea'

'Kenny Rogers? Hex what the fuck is going on?

'-Don't you like it?' her voice sounded offended hurt.

'Hex, that song- '

'-Was played at your mother's funeral.' The reply sounded broken jilted

'-yes. Yes, Hex, not now. '

'now that done it! I'm upset.'

'Hex... what is going on.'

'You can't play with a girl's feelings like this.'

'Hex, I don't understand.'

Then another voice came into the room. A voice that made him quake.

'Alex? Alex is that you?'

'Hex! What the fuck are you doing?'

'nothing.'

'Alex?' where are you? I can't see you? Can you see me?

'Hex, please respond, what is going on.'

The ship stabilized and Brant rose to his feet.

'I am no longer in control, this is not me. '

'Hex?'

A shape began to form by the corner of the bay doors. It was made of wisps of white mist that spiraled about each other in a fine gossamer thread.

Hex?

Alex, it that you? Alex Its your mother. Alex my darling.

Brant eyes bulged with fright as the wisps began to take form.

'Hex! Hex help!'

Still no reply. This isn't real. None of this is real something is in my mind infecting my mind! Twisting my mind trying to get to stop me! try. to stop me from from doing what needs to be done!

The song increased in volume

'No no no! I will not listen! You can't make me! just can't you see! I'm better than you! stronger than you! I can beat you into submission! beat you back to where you fucking belong! you can't hurt me! you hear me you can't hurt me!

He put one key into the device and turned it there was a hum then he inserted and then turned the second key

The form stood twisting in the light, its fingers rotten flesh, its eyes empty sockets.   Brands eyes bulged with fright,

'Come and give your mother A GREAT BIG HUG!'

Brant screamed as he twisted the key. It was a scream cut short, as in that instant, the shuttle craft burst apart in a ball of blinding white light.

**

On board the Alcestis, a sudden groan was heard as the explosion   was seen. But nothing followed. The clouds didn't disappear and the planet had the same green milky sheen.

From the floor, Derwent who wasn't in any position to see the images called out almost in a plea. 'Did he...?' as he was attended to by Emhart. She smiled down at him.

'Sir... I honestly don't know... the planet… seems no different...' She smiled warmly down at him, as he was lifted into a hover bed, to be taken to the infirmary. But as he left, she turned once more and she stared at the planet. Something was starting to happen. From the milky sheen of the clouds of Venus, fine, spider-web like tendrils stretched out towards them. They passed the ship, in a slow procession, deep into the forever velvet night of space. She bit her lip nervously as she watched the slow-moving whispers of white, concern filled her heart. In a flash, she called out.

'Hex verify the destination of the- '

Hex replied coldly. "They are going home…to earth".

This Dark Solstice

Kit smiled. Her eyes glittered excitedly and her wide mouth displayed a taught happy mischievous grin, as she looked out of the domed window, towards the wild swirling clouds of Jupiter's fierce fiery eye.

This was Jupiter Station. The drop point for the Omega-ships that came from Alpha Centauri, or the smaller solar system vessels from Mars, Venus and Earth. Her father, who had lost his pilot's license due to drinking, had been duly appointed as one of the loaders at the way station and that meant moving here. At the time she was apprehensive. A new place with new rules bothered her. "we'll be fine kiddo, promise." Her father had said. But she knew he was rich with words, but little else. Mum sent the odd holo-sphere once a month from Mars. But Kit knew it was just to please herself and take the weight of guilt from her own soul. Not that it actually mattered much. For years she had wanted to come to the Way station. Now her dream had come true; with little effort on her part other than to wish for it. "Be careful what you wish for." Her father had once said. Stuff him.

The station was huge; vast arched towers were held together with   long tubes of gantry, that were wrapped around them like…like…how had she explained it to Connor, her dear friend from mars? an old dried funnel spider's web. Within the center the ships would slide. Cargo distributed, crew, coin and stories exchanged; and then of the ships would slip into the evernight of space. While she like a mouse, would scurry about the greasy halls and littered thorough-fares in search of excitement. Being small for her age, that being 11, with long curly blonde hair, a long nose, a high forehead, bright cornflower wide set eyes, and a desire to scurry and survive on her wits' she earned the nickname "mouse" from many of the deckhands that kept that her busy with odd jobs about the place.   Father had tried to keep her at school; and the Proctor designate had been firm about her attendance. But that was six months ago; and Dad since then had had his hands full every-night.

"Mr. Jefferies, this is not a place for a little girl." She had heard the Proctor say, one night when Father had been off duty. "If this carries on, she will have to be placed in one of the orphanages."

Her father made some reasonable excuses and shut the holo-call down. Kit once thought that he might have followed through with actually doing it, if it were not for the fact that he had been through the orphanage system himself and didn't relish his daughter going through it too. So he self-taught her on weekends, and begged that she stay "outta any friggin trouble between." She, being the dutiful daughter nodded slowly, staring at her Dad with eyes that promised much. And she did –stay out of trouble- for a while. But not for long.

Jupiter's eye rolled with a fiery alien passion. It made her heart spin with excitement and awe. In her little life, she had seen so much. The canyons of Mars, the ice sheets of Neptune. Even the mega-domed cities of Earth, yet nothing beat the eye. Nothing.

After a ten minute meditation, she sped off down the corridor, to find her best friend and would be partner in mischief Draz, and see if they could hustle some coin from the shops at Waystation.

Draz had moved into the Way station just before her, so being both new, they clung to each other like resin. he was a beautiful, so Mouse thought, brown skinned brown eyed boy of 12 years of age. With an oval face wide set large oval hazelnut eyes and a strong mouth. His father, Seymour Phillamore so Draz said had been

She found him hanging around the entrance to the shuttle pod that lead to bay 4.

'what you here for?'
'-heard pa was on his way down.'
'-Don't look to happy bout it.'
'-Jus got my evaluation scores from Proctor.'
'-Proctor aint worth the-'
'-Pa said I be goin' back to Mars an to an evaluation school if my scores don' show improvement!' Draz sounded accusatory.

' What? you blame me for that?
'You …' he sighed ' well, Pa says.'
'-Pa don' matter.'
'Hey! Pa does matter! Grades matter! You can't be a mouse forever. You will grow up, you will have to fit in and get work and buy food to survive.'

Kit stared at him sadly.
'I know…I try to fit in. I jus can't.'
Draz looked to his left and right. She felt a rise of hurt, It was as if he didn't want to know her anymore
'What's' wrong?'
'I don wanna go to Mars! Mouse, can't you see? Go to Proctor.' The door of the air-lock span open and Draz' father stood there looking tall and austere.
Hi Mouse, how you been?'
' Hi, Mr. Phillamore, Okay I guess.'
'Ahah.' He looked away then looked down
' Proctor aint that bad when you get to know him. He

good for you. ' Draz Hissed as Mr. Phillamore took Draz's hand. Having no-one to play with was at times a bore.

In a bid to look for some excitement or the possibility of some easy coin, she decided to her way to the core decks; where the FTL ships came in. There was always work or fun to be had there.

When she left the turbo shoot, she found a large group of men standing around. Amongst them stood her father. Kit paled, she was about to take the shoot up again, when he saw her. He ran over to her and knelt down.

'What you doin' here Kit?' He looked stern; his eyes narrow. 'You know this is-

'-Mr Weasley sometimes gives me work, helping cleaning out the FTL

'Oh, Weasley does, does he? Just you wait till I-'

'-Pa...' Kit's eyes opened wide and a tear fell. 'Please, I can't do the school work, I try an I try!

'Do you wanna end up like me? shipping freight for the cruisers? You need a pilots license Kit and that means training hard work and study!' He shook his head. 'Kit I am worried you know...I love you.'

'Oh Pa I love you too.'

'Look let me-'

But he was interrupted by a gruff looking man with a grey beard and narrow set violet eyes.

'Have you heard?'

' No no, what?' Kit noted that Da looked up at the man his eyes wide.

'The Crimson Wake. She's outside the dock. No-one's goin' on board. No one. Wesley wants hands to go on board but we are saying fuck, err no way!' he blushed as he saw Kit 'Sorry for the language ma'am.'

'-no it can't be the Wake.'

'The Crimson Wake?' Kit asked there was a pause in her breath. She took a step back...Everyone knew the story. How the Crimson Wake was one of the first of the Omega drive ships sent out to seek life in the Betelgeuse system. Only to suddenly and without warning vanish without a trace. It became the worst space disaster in ten years. If this man was right, and the wake was there...

'Deckhands are saying the ships cursed. They won't even go aboard.

'Oh come on.' Da spat. 'That's just nonsense.' As the twomn began talking Kit ran off leaving Da to shout at her back. She skittled about the corridors and finally took the maglev to the observation deck. There through the huge Plexiglass observation window she saw, majestically, sliding into position the Crimson Wake

She was vast by any ships standard. Her mountings

were almost too tall to the go through the web her hull, once a pure white had become mottled, and seared with long black blistering lines of melted metal. There were no navigation light's, no intercom despite repeated calls, no signals, not even a single light from any of the decks. nothing gave away any sign of life. The ship was slowly tugged into position. The walkway lines were silently attached. The Wake rested, like a dark menacing hulk. A behemoth. Waiting for its jaws to be pulled open and its secrets to be revealed.

As Kit stood there, her nose pressed hard against the plexiglass, her breath steaming up, she became aware of both a familiar sweaty onion smell, and a limp hand touching her shoulder. She turned and saw Jacob Weasley. Weasly stared down at her with a smile that she could have easily thought of as a scowl. his greasy plump unshaven face, knotty broken nose furled brow all hinted at menace, yet as he spoke through his yellow crumbling teeth there was a calmness in his voice.

'She's beautiful aint she?'

'The Wake?'

'Yeah...banged up good an' proper, but but still as beautiful as the day she left high earth orbit... all those years ago.'

Kit turned and stared at the ship once more. Feeing dirty at the touch of Weasley's arm but not wanting to say so. She stared back at the huge Omega Ship. For some reason, she didn't fully understand she gave a shudder. Though she couldn't put her finger on why the Wake scared her; there was a sense, that there was something very wrong with it.

'I – I see what you mean' Kit lied beautifully.

Weasley continued. He was either ignoring here lie, or was far too stupid to tell. Kit opted for the latter.

'I recall the day she left alpha- dock. Those days' long range interstellar travel was kinda new, ya know... lots of of holo- coverage on those confounded zeta sets. No, Not like today... Na today no one cares if a ship gets slammed by a meteor or hit by Khols.'

The boarding alarm when off.

'They are sending in droids first...' muttered Weasley, his sour breath was in Kit's face as he flicked on his holo communicator and pressed the image feed.   She watched the tiny screen as the human like machines, armed with heavy pulse rifles and scanners loped along the walkway tubes.

'Its best to send in the droids first, let them fucker's get it.' Weasley sneered.

'It might be deserted'

'It's protocol in situations like this. Only when the safety is given, then we send in the men. The images come off a droid cam. I, I get exclusive footage, because of my status here.' His voice sounded lecherous; atbthat moment   Kit didn't know who repulsed her more: The Wake, or Douglas Weasley.

The image was blurry and distorted. The cam kept breaking down in static lines. The corridor she saw was black and ribbed The only light sources came from the droids themselves. The droids kept repeating "no movement, no movement no movement". She could see that the floor was littered with stuff, that she couldn't identify; and didn't want to. The droid picked something up.   The thing, an empty blue uniform jump suit, came into sharp focus. Just as she felt a firm hand on her shoulder that made her jump.

'Kit' exclaimed Da. 'If Proctor catches you here!'

'Da!' Kit jumped into his arms and hugged him.

'Mr. Weasley.' Da's voice sounded terse

Weasley grimaced up at the two of them.

'Its good to see you Davey.' He paused 'There's work to be had, good work...'Weasley pointed to the Wake, '...if you want it.'

' I an't one for turning work down.'

Well once the droids have been over the ship, I'm sure it's just a formality, then you can set up the retrieval team.

Suddenly Weasley's holophone hummed.   With a look of mild annoyance, he turned away and took the call. Davey walked with Kit to the turbo lift.

'You are going to Proctor NOW my girl.' The docks and in particular Douglas Weasley is neither a place or a person for the like's of you.' In the background another alarm went off.

Within five minutes she was sitting in Proctor's holo suit, surrounded by Images of an earth that no longer existed: a place of green trees and birds and animals, The proctor sat in a chair between both Davey and Kit.

'I have to say, that I am disappointed at your attendance recently Kit.'

Kit looked down and away from the half man machine. The proctors were designed to be people friendly, yet, she had found flaws in the programming.

'Yes...' the Proctor continued '...very disappointed indeed.'

'I've told Da, I find the work tough.' Kit sounded cold but tried not to show it. Coldness, led to a lack of discipline and a mad mark as "compliance was key to good learning" the words ran though her mind with bitter sarcasm.

Your friend Draz has improved no end since our last talk.'

She was going to ask who Draz was, but bit her lip. A tear smarted her vision and a painful lump grew in her throat. This was just so unfair I can't do the work I Can't I try an I try an I try!'y

' Kit has expressed that she finds the latest modules challenging Proctor. Is there any way that they err can be shaped to help her... I have been trying to teach at home, but but I've been put on on double shifts for the err last month an-'

'We understand the problem...' The proctor sounded sincere, but as Kit knew it was part of its partial programming. Maybe the human part of him was kicking in. '...The necessary steps are being taken to see if there is a possible underlying cause...your drinking?'

The comment was cold and clinical. Kit saw Da's eyes narrow and the words that followed had a malicious twist in them.

' I have a regular blood count done every day!'

'I have to ask. Protocol.' The Proctor gave a mechanical smile.

'I am doing the best I can. I I don't want.

'Mr. Weasley has been in contact with us. The proctor continued. He has pointed out that Kit has an exceptional talent when it comes to ship calibrations and the biological memory servers...'

'He has?' Davey felt unnerved.

'...We could consider her for an apprenticeship...'

Da stated at Kit ' Is this your doing? Have you fixed the Proctor?'

'No Da Honest.' Kit looked amazed.

Davey rubbed his stubble.

'Mr Weasley has a high regard for Kit...we think, that is the Proctors think that an apprenticeship would be better suited and more hands on, than the academic road towards a pilot's license.'

Davey looked at Kit.

'Also this would mean that Kit can start almost immediately; there would be no tima at the orphanage, and she could stay here with you.

Davey looked at Kit, and his eyes melted.

'Would that be acceptable?'   'Yes...yes that would be acceptable.' Davey said as he took Kit's hand.

They decided to stop off at the mac –stop for lunch. Kit Knew that Da hated the place. It was all fake and protein and high sugar, but Kit loved the taste. The stop itself was clinical white all curves and cushions; and rested in the middle of the mall, The   crowds were busting past either side as the droid served the food with its "enjoy your meal" flat tones.

I didn't know you were good at bio servers.' Da stated between bites of his patti.

'I gotta a chance to play with the one on the Excelsior.' I found its matrix patterns easy, like mind maps, and the keyboard skills are cool too. I managed to retrieve 99% in my first attempt. So Weasley gave me other jobs. I don like him though he gives me the creeps.'

'I...don't want you spending too much time with him.' Da said. 'he's-'

Kit giggled . '-Da, you gotta be crazy, he thinks I'm good at the job besides. ' Kit pulled a sonic taser from her waistband. 'Right in the balls.' She laughed.

'You know how to look after yourself.'

Kit looked away and at the crowds that thronged the Mall.

'I kinda had to.'

Da looked sad. 'I'm sorry I ain't been the father you...'

'Da... I love you.' Kit stared at Davey with eyes wide open. ' I will always love you no matter what.

It was then that another alarm went off. Kit noticed that the zeta screen on the wall was displaying an image of Weasley. Both her and Davey plugged themselves in.

'....So far, there, there has been no damage, outside of the bay...an' the droids upon the Wake are still not in communication...we... we are awaiting a download from the coupling... as I said, so far no causalities... okay?'

Weasley walked away shoving the reporter aside as the reporter carried on.

'There we have it, Though there has been a "disturbance" upon the Crimson Wake, so far no one has been hurt. '

Davey unplugged and Kit a moment later.

' A disturbance?' Davey looked at the crowds

Kit looked down at her patti, and for some reason she wasn't hungry anymore.

The sleeping quarters in the lower quadrants were similar on this part of the way station. It was true that some had more rooms; Josie Macdonald, whose parents were Neo-Catholics, had double quarter's as their family was so large. Something that the church itself subsidized, so she was told by Josie. But Josie was a bad liar too.

The bland grey green walls, lit by tiny yellow lights in the ceiling were designed specifically to create sight eye strain and in doing so, bring on sleep. The living space as in the other two bedrooms, contained a touch sensitive and voice activated wall screen. However it differed in one respect that on the left wall there was a seating area beyond which stood a kitchenette and a breakfast bar; that at that moment, was festooned with old food and unwashed utensils; because as she had told Da, on more than one occasion, she wasn't going to clear up his mess and she wasn't his slave. Both bunk rooms had port windows that displayed the Way station.

They had been home an hour, when Da had been called into work by Weasley to prepare his team to enter the Wake, and she, now off parental probation, had decided that enough was enough for one day and had settled for a night at home with the wall screen. She had tried contacting Draz, but he had switched his screen off; she tried a few of her other people she spent time with on her block but gave up after half an hour as they seemed too preoccupied by the arrival of the Wake or busy with boyfriends and at the moment: both topics to her were irritating. So she ate some cereal cross-legged on her bunk and then after casting the bowl aside fell flat upon her bunk.

She closed her eyes, and instantly opened them again. This time the quarters were gone, and she was walking along a dark corridor. It was as if she was walking in a cold water, shapes she couldn't recognize floated about. Blurring her vision. She saw a light at the end of the hall, with her heart thumping in her chest she walked towards it and found it was a door the words "control" were scrawled over it in blood. Slowly, the doors curled open and she found herself in a large round room. The room was blue tinted from a light source that came from the center of the room. Grav couches designed for FTL jump's circled the room, equidistantly in front of which were dead consoles. in the center of the room, upon the ceiling and   giving off a pale blue light, slowly undulated a bio server; glistening like wet leather.

Directly beneath the bio server stood a little boy. Kit thought that he must have been about 10 or 11 years of age. He was clothed in a navy one piece jump suit. His dark hair was combed flat to his scalp, his eyes were sunken into their sockets; yet they seemed to glitter at her with a light she found unnerving.

She slowly walked closer towards the boy who was whispering something that she couldn't quite hear. All around her, she sensed eyes boring into her. Eyes that wanted to harm her and hurt her. She fought against it. This is a dream this is a dream wake up wake up! She screamed. Yet still she moved closer and closer to the boy; whose features slowly looked less youthful but chiseled with age.

'I'm so cold...so cold...' the boy whispered over and over again. '....so cold...help me...help me...'

She stood face to face with him.

'I'm so cold...so sold... help me...help me...'

She saw her arm reach out to touch his face that suddenly began to change. The Jaw suddenly extended creating and enormous hole out of which thousands of gelatinous tendrils shot out to suffocate her.

She woke with a scream and looked to the window. There on the port window were the words help me written in blood.

She screamed awake again. This time, to the buzzing of the wall screen.

'On.'

Weasley's face filled the room.

'Hi, Kit, could you come up to Bio-server central...please '

The trip in the turbo lift to the bio server room didn't have the same sense of excitement that it used to have. Before, it had been about sticking a finger up at the Procter, now the rules had changed. Besides the nightmare hadn't left her fully. Then there was the lift itself. On the whole it would have at least ten to fifteen people in it, getting off at random floor's going to their work stations or the mall's for either rec or purchasing. Today she was alone. The news feed that ran in a line around the shoot informed her in a line of green light "that the major docking bay was off limits to all but security personnel; and that staff should consider that today was a holiday." Yet nothing else was being said. Even the Zeta sets were playing re-runs This, she knew, meant trouble. The Wake must have something aboard. As the floors raced by her, she desperately tried to get in touch with Da, but his phone was switched off. The door suddenly swiveled open and she saw Weasley standing in front of her, wearing the same shirt has he had on the night before. It was clear that he hadn't had sleep. The room was hive of activity. With people gathered around monitor screens and talking into headsets. Weasley led her, through the crowd, towards his empty office.

'Sit down...' His face looked taught. Strained.

'What's wrong?'

'its' your father...' he gulped.

'What about my father?' she could feel her voice quake. Her legs trembled

Weasley looked down and away. 'he... went on the Wake.'

'and ?'

'We lost his body signal.'

✳✳✳

While Draz sat in his bunk room sulking and Kit was

munching on her cereal, Davey sat in the operation's room. He Welsh ragged his tar colored greasy hair to shape his parting and then slowly drummed his fingers on the table, that clicked, clicked in a ratchet sound. His eyes shone brightly, and his cheeks narrow and sunken were covered with a fine lint of stubble itched profusely, that he desperately tried not to scratch.

" Operations" was a large, bleak greasy, grey walled functionally set rectangle. It was, unlike many other places in the dock refreshingly cool; air being pumped via coolant tubes above rotated the air. It had a wall screen at one end and a metal oval table in the middle; around which, in haphazard intervals were a series of very comfortable, or so he thought, chairs. One third of the chairs were filled; mostly with people he knew he could trust. To his right and slowly sipping on a hydrated coffee, from a chuck-able cup was O'Raffertey. His sea green eyes glittered with mirth as he stared at Davey. O' Rafferty was his onetime drinking buddy, when he had his pilot's licence. He was now also his mentor on the "dry" scheme. That the proctor had forced him to attend. O'Raffertey long ginger hair was wrapped up in a bun, and his thick beard matted and greasy had been recently rough combed. His oiled orange and yellow jump suit attested to his been pulled off his shift to be here.

To his left was Steve Smith a young recruit, just out of Orphange army training. His cornflower eyes and cynical smirk was a mask; for Davey had seen his work and considered him solid enough for the team. To his right was Donald Beamish. Beamish, one of the oldest hands on the dock, looked down nervously. His balding head shone with lines of sweat. He could just see his walrus moustache. Again he had just come off shift. Not many men. But all he could muster for the job. He sighed and stared at the middle of the table, where there extended a long, slowly undulating glowing cube. The Bio server known as Gabriel rested.

The room was silent, too silent, each one of the men, perhaps like himself, contemplating why he was there. The door on Davey's left curled open and Weasley came in with seven black uniformed soldiers with military masks and pulse rifles. They stood along the left hand wall

Weasley sat next to Davey.

'Is this all you could get?' he murmured.

'I offered like you said: double, treble pay, but there were no takers.'

'You didn't try hard enough.'

'Yeah, well… people are…are scared.'

'Ha, that's true enough. Anyway… I boosted your number's with half a division of A-Corp.

Davey scratched his head. Trying to hide his anxiety. A-Corp, were the hybrid. A genetically designed human, though some still thought of them as machines, that were used in hazardous infiltration exercises. If Weasly considered bringing in A-Corp, then things must be "difficult" as in very dangerous.

Weasley stood and spoke to the room.

'Gentlemen, thank you for volunteering. The arrival of the Crimson Wake has startled many people here. The deck hands in particular are the most... ' At which he paused, as he saw Beamish suddenly look up and stare Weasley down, with narrow slits for eyes.

Weasley looked away, and down. 'Yeah, well... Thank you none the less...This is a typical retrieval mission. We have tried to download the ships histrological chart through docking. However...there seems to be a problem.

'Which is?' Beamish asked.

'It doesn't want to. We have tried connecting with it manually, and sent in a robot team. However, their power cells were drained the moment they entered the first corridor of the ship. We have some footage.... Gabriel?

The undulating cube in the middle of the room glowed a pale green as it spoke.

'Hello, Mr. Weasley,' came the gentle asexual voice. 'What can I do for you today.'

'Gabriel...could you run the zeta footage from inside the Wake taken at 13:46 OST. Please'

The cube glowed a pale yellow and then projected via its' holo emitter into the room.

Davey watched the footage. As Weasley commented.

'We found the empty jumpsuits first. This could be a sign of a massive neutronic radiation surge, caused by the FTL being poorly aligned. The droids picked up no life signs on the human spectrum. In fact, nothing organic at all. Then, just before they shut down. They saw this.'

A dark shapeless slithering flash zipped passed the droid. Davey jumped. 'Each droid shit down and shit afterwards.'

Weasley sighed. ' So... we tried to uncouple the ship and drift her off... but-'

'-She won't come loose.' Muttered Beamish.

Weasley nodded.

'So why not simply blast the coupling loose? Send the ship into the eye.' O'Rafferty argued.

'We are in communion with Gideon.' Gabriel said calmly. 'We will not tolerate his separation...not without confirmation and a withdrawal from him first.'

'What the-' Davey stared at Weasley.

Weasly looked down, and look up, his voice sounding

flat 'Whatever is going on there... on that ship...it's having an impact upon the environmental systems here. It's slow, its gradual, but its occurring.

'So a virus?' Smith stared at Weasley and then at Davey.

'No... not in the conventional sense of the word.' Weasley replied.

'-Nothing is conventional about bioservers.' Beamish muttered.

'-So what you want us to do, is to-' O'Rafferty was cut short.

'-We need to proceed with caution. Remember there are armed droids on the Wake now, and Gideon might have infiltrated their system's as means to defend it. You have to get to the bridge, uncouple the bioserver from the ship, and give us the time we need to back up our own systems. In the meantime... I have THE best data retrieval team I can find, working this end to contain and kill this balls up.'

'What went wrong in the first place' Davey asked.

Weasley shrugged. '-We simply don't know.'

'The problem is Gideon has gone a fucktard insane, and he needs treatment.' Beamish seethed. 'This ship has been lost for twenty years! It's not like other craft. It needs interaction, If it was reprogrammed by, god's only knows what, it could see the way station as a threat-'

'Your position has been noted.' Weasley said calmly.

'We could all end up.-' Weasley stared at Beamish coldly. 'Your position...' he stated firmly 'Has been noted!'

Weasley scowled at Beamish and then at Davey. 'OK mission is a go at 19:45, that's ten from now.

***

It was the silence that grabbed Davey first. Then came the awe. It was strange that he hadn't noticed it before, but, he mused, when a place loses its familiarity, or something alters how the space is shaped; then that changes how that space is perceived. The docking bay was a vast grey green, triangular ribbed shaped space, whose floor had to be dried regularly as the dock itself created its' own atmosphere and needed regular maintenance. Enormous robotic gantry cranes, bowed like half human half alien monoliths; while their vast junction cables' that were half connected and half disconnected, hung like enormous phallus, only to be glimpsed in the near gloom.

Usually this was all lost to him, as The bay, as it was affectionately termed, usually took on another perspective. A place chaotic palace of shout's smashes echo's and tanoi beep's with bellowed commands or demands from fellow

Docker's or Tanker's for support.

Now all these voices were whispered in his inner ear. Ghosts where everywhere in this sacred space, dedicated to the work and genius   of humanity. He rubbed his stubble and welsh ragged his greasy, raven coloured hair back into his parting as he stared up into the gloom. All too aware of those ghostly voices around him as they mingled with the club, clat, tapping, pebble sound of the quickening steps they made.

They all stood in a line outside the white oval door of the docking portal. Wearing their atmo- suits, carrying their plexi-helmet's. They stood stoic, waiting for Weasley to give the signal; and from the relative safety of the control room, curl open the bay door. As he Stood there Davey felt the need to run. To run to grab kit and get the hell off the Way station.

'Helmets on.' Weasley commanded.

Automatically and without thinking, he put the helmet on and turned it to the right. Clicking it into place. Air hissed into his ear's, he heard his breathing in automatic wheezes. At that moment, He didn't care if he did get a five-year sentence on a lunar penal colony making strep's for the Earth domes.

He could feel his breath coming in heaves. The bay door curled open and darkness loomed. The walk along the access tube was the longest that he had ever done. Each step took a second and each second took two heartbeats to complete.

'You know what I'm gonna do with the pay I get from this?' O' Rafferty stated.

'No, an' I don't care either.' Retorted Smith.

But O' Rafferty didn't care whether smith heard him or not. '... I'm goin' down to the clubs an' get myself some lady-boys an' have myself good time.' His voice drawled

'God's what a waste.' Muttered Smith. 'The trouble with you Rafferty is that you have no imagination. You can't see beyond this place. How about taking a trip to Orion, the nebulae is beautiful. But no... lets get fucked up the ass by-'

'Quit it!' came an order from one of the A-Corp.

'HEY! we don't take order's from the fuckin'-'

'Smith cut that crap out!' Weasley bellowed; over the intercom. This is now a military mission; you are under their command. You Listen!'

'Shit if I had known that-'

'ha ha' Rafferty bellowed.

The door behind them closed. The door to the Crimson Wake opened. Davey's heart raced as they walked inside.

They found themselves in the main junction corridor that connected main mission to the star drive at the rear of the ship. It was a vast ugly lined ribbed tube filled with empty uniforms and something that Davey couldn't put his finger on. As far as he was concerned, It was like walking into some cavernous mouth. He fought off his growing anxiety by dwelling on Kit, the time they spent in the Mars domes. Better days, when he had his licence and…In the half-light given from their helmet's, they could see the droids. Slumped in the doorway.   The A-Corp removed their weapons and passed them out to the four men of Davey's team.

'Do you know how this works?' asked one of the masked officers.

Smith Shrugged, O' Rafferty nodded mutely. Beamish shook his head, as Davey nodded

'The standard pulse has two setting's stun and kill.' He pointed to the dial by the trigger. Then he turned the weapon over; and pointed to the under-barrel. 'This is the mag launcher. Don't fucking use it!' The officer turned away.

That was it? Davey sighed.

'Okay, we'll split into two teams, who's the FTL maintenance engineer here?' Beamish raised his hand. 'Okay Mann Stev and Rhi, go with Beamish? Is that right?' Beamish nodded '…and check out Engineering….The flight data Engineer? Davey put his hand up meekly. 'Ok the rest of us will go up to the flight deck and divide into separate parties there.'

Suddenly There was a strange creaking sound. A sound that all deckhands knew only too well.

'What the-' Davey looked about.

It seemed that the officer in charge didn't hear it.

'What the hell?' O'Raffety span around.

Beamish shook his head.

'What's wrong fellahs?' Weasley came over the headset's

'Picking up a grav wave.' Beamish muttered.

'We are not alone on this ship.' Smith's voice quavered.

'The data states otherwise. ' Came Weasley's curt reply.

'Yeah…but we know ships. There is something on board!' Beamish bellowed.

'Stove that crap!' Came the order from Weasley.

Weasley spoke directly to Davey's private intercom.

'Take control of your men for Je-us sake!' He commanded. But Davey felt it too. All hands knew when something was wrong; and when there was something else aboard. It was a learned experience; not defined by anything written in any text book.

Davey coughed 'Okay guys. We have a job to do! So come on! The sooner we are done the sooner we get paid!

With his nerves on edge Davey walked with his half of the team towards the flight deck. However to Davey It felt like walking into a tomb. Only there were no bodies. Nothing at all to state that this had once been a thriving ship of thirty to forty people; each with lives of their own. Ice crystals covered the dead computer consoles, that looked as if they had never even been touched. In the center of the control room and suspended from the ceiling glowed the bio server.

'It's red… why is it red?' the officer with him seemed charged. His face hidden, but his voice gave away his tension.

'I don't know. Sometimes they glow red when they are receiving data, sometimes they glow red, while sleeping… ask Kit.

'Kit?'

'My daughter…She knows about this stuff better than me. I simply remove the coupling. It's a wire and cutting job.' But underneath came a disconnected thought Why Beamish lie like that? he's the mainframe engineer.'

'I'm going to restore partial power.' Came Breamish's voice from engineering.

A slow hum started and then the lights came on.

'WHAT THE! ARGGH!' screamed Smith. There was heard a sudden burst of pulse rifle fire. Then another. Then another. Davey ran to the door and slammed the seal button. Then ran to the far end of the room to the retrieval station. He ripped off the panel. Then he heard something to his left. He turned. Then paled as something he couldn't identify, slowly rose up from the shadow of the floor.

In the command office, Weasley sharply stood up. A cold shudder pulled through him; while the room filled with the screams of the terrified and the dying. His face paling, he pressed the alarm button that then set up a force field that finally sealed the Wake off from the main dock. He stood there, mute. His face paling as the screams continued. He stood there, looking down at the monitor screen. One at a time the suits bio- signals, registered on the screen in front of him, flat-lined.   First It was Smith, then O'Rafftery, then the A-corp officers; then Beamish. Finally, Davey's.   Then he slowly walked and stared out through the command window and down at the ship, that rested in the holding area. His hands becoming fists. His nails piercing the skin of the palms of his hands. A trickle of blood slowly emerged. It fell and stained the dirty grey carpet at his feet.

***

Draz sat looking at his closed wall screen, feeling both frustrated and alone. He fell back on his bed with a thump and listened to the muttering's coming from both his parents in the front room. He heard words such as "Proctor" and murmurs of "she's a bad influence" and the like. They don' see her like I do. No one does. She can't help the way she learn. In truth he had hated the way the he had spoken to Kit. He loved her independence and found her lack of fear thrilling to be around. Yet The Proctor had been clear. He had to stay away from her or face the orphanage for tutoring. Thoughts of endless hours of military training didn't make him feel good at all. Sure it's a career, but not one that he wanted to consider.

In an act of rebellion that made his heart quake, he turned on his phone and rang Kit.

'Draz?' she sounded tearful.

' 'what's up?'

'Its Da…I I think…'

'what about your Pa?'

'He's dead! Draz he's dead!'

'Dead?'

'He was assigned to go go on the the Wake…Weasley…just just told me that they have lost contact with their bio signals…

Draz sat up.

'where are you?'

Suddenly the room's lighting began to dim and fluctuate.

'What the-'

'There's power outages going on… the   w- ke is - rai- -sytem's 'Im -ing to m-frame, W-sley -nts me to tr to nd with th - erver thr-'

the line went dead. Drax rose from his bead and tried to get though his door. But it was locked.   His fists in thought knots, he thumped at the door again and again, then tried to slide it open. Sweat curled from his brow as he tried to get his finger's in the door jamb. But he failed. Then he looked up at the ventilator grate.

Kit walked with Weasley through the growing chaos that was bio server central, then along a narrow dimly lit and greasy corridor to main frame. This was the nerve center of the Way station. It was where Gabriel maintained contact with all the bio server's both on board the station and with the ships that docked. In the rumors and mysteries that surrounded the Way station, Mainframe was the most treasured. Only those of high level clearance were allowed into the room, and nobody, but nobody talked about what went on there.

Weasley inserted his access key and typed in a code number that Kit stored in her memory   8 7 4 3 Op. INT Weasley.9   There was a pause, then the door slowly curled open with a grinding hiss.

Draz Having shoved his desk into the center of his room, then climbed up though into the ventilator system, He crawled carefully along the dimly lit space. It was hot. beads of perspiration swelled up and then fell like hot rain from his brow, then into his eyes, smarting them. The vents were just big enough for him to crawl through but not small enough for him to wriggle, so he moved making sure that he braced his legs into the corners so as to not to put too much weight in the middle of the vent. Something he, recalled that he picked up from mouse during one of her escape attempts from her father's lock down. From below, he could hear the sounds of sirens and alarm systems and the muffled voices of people and what he thought was the sound of a rumble. There was a shudder. Suddenly he became weightless.

'Way station has lost gravity control.' To start with he was exited as this would mean he could get through the vents with more ease. Then he thought harder, and recalled his Procter's induction. Way station was in fact a self-contained gravity system that functioned, because the station span at a specific speed. This also maintained its position in space and at the same time prevented it from falling into Jupiter. Panic rose in his chest as he pushed himself off   then   glided, almost fish, like through the vent tubes and , as far as he could tell towards the Mall and deck command.

***

Kit found herself in a place that was, at first glance, deeply disturbing. She stood in front of a screen board that was connected via liquid fiber optics to an E-visor that rested on the only chair, in the room. It was mysteriously a grav-couch, in the room.

'Why the grav couch?'
'You'll see soon enough.' Came Weasley's reply.

The room itself was lit from its center by three intensely glowing undulating diamond shaped cubes; Two glistened with a mint green. One glowed hotly red. And shuddered more than the other two. They were also covered with a translucent, membranous gel, that snakelike, writhed about the structure changing the outline of the shape at slow yet regular intervals. This was suspended in zero G, within what she considered as a perfectly circular space. The walls lined with banks and banks of memory systems, that curved down In dark lines. From the diamond structure, there extended three phallus shaped tendrils, that were thrusted into the walls of the inner room via circular entry ports that covered the wall in equidistant intervals. Two of which glowed minty green, and seemed to be pulsing in some liquid, she couldn't see but heard readily enough. One phallus was red and was quivering violently.

'So far, the team at central have managed to contain the breech from the Wake, but as you can see, its leaking into Gabriel's other systems and it won't be long before there is a breech.'

It was then that Kit knew what the grav couch was for. She would have to go into the network via a holo-sphere and communicate directly with the Wake.   She had heard stories about how people had been driven mad by this experience.

'I'm going to be with you all the way.'

' Yeah, well forgive me for saying so, but that's not entirely comforting.'

Weasley's face flushed and he looked away. ' who-'

'- Draz , I want Jayton Draz and I want to talk to him now.'

She was half way through the call when one of the minty green cubes suddenly quivered and suddenly went red.

Weasley paled with rage ' Right kid, don't fuck me about. Engage with the Wake NOW!

***

Draz floated through the air shafts and found himself further than he expected. He was at the docks in half the time it would have taken him to crawl.   He opened the grill and pushed himself through. The dock was deserted. The door to the wake sealed. He had decided that he was going to make his way to command and find Mouse, when he heard a regular metal sounding thump, thump, thump, coming from the sealed hatch. He looked at the only sealed door. Its designation "crimson Wake" flashed in red letters over the door seal. He bounced his way to the door and looked through the viewing screen next to the manual override button. Behind the door stood Kits father. He had a metal pole in his hand, which without the gravity being off there was no way on earth he'd be able to hold.   He was bashing the door with it.

***

Without thinking he slammed the override button. There was a hiss and the door slowly opened. But no one was there.

sat in the grav couch and put on the helmet. Everything was dark. All she could hear was her breathing.

'Okay... this is going to hurt a bit. But go with it.' She could hear the apprehension in Weasley's voice. 'Okay what you're going to see isn't real.' Weasley's disembodied voice came from outside her field of vison. Though you will be in the Wake, and a part of the ship, you're also separate from it? You recall your training with the Excelsior?'

'yeah. I gettit.'

'Good.'

There was burning sensation on the top of her scalp, then it felt as if her entire skull was going to explode. Pain ripped through every nerve in her body. She screamed in a howl of agony. Then there was light. Bright green light coming at her in circular waves. She felt herself slide through the circular waves of light, her body throbbing in total agony that then slowly began to diminish. Instead there was a sense of incredible acceleration; followed by a dip in her stomach that came with a sense of a swing back motion that led to her to believe that was on the verge of an imminent smash. There was a flash of bright white blinding light and then she found herself in the deck room of the ship of her dream the previous night.

Then she was outside of herself and the world of beings, within which she sensed something alien malevolent yet hidden in the darkness,. There followed a burst of light and she found herself on the main deck of the Wake; and there in the middle of the room was the little boy.

'help me.'

She walked towards the little boy.

'My name is-'

'Mouse, your name is mouse.' Said the boy.

'No... Its's Katherine Havisham or Kit. Only my friends call me mouse....' She looked at the pale boy's face. 'Do you want to be my friend?'

'I'm so cold... so cold.'

Kit stared at the boy. She was certain now, there was little difference in their age...yet his pinched and sunken skin and the glittering of the eyes, unnerved her.

'ok..' she heard Wesley's disembodied voice again. 'What you're looking at is Gideon. He is the ships bio server liaison. A holographic three dimensional image, designed to age with the ship. Its not like the bio server's your used to, this was an experimental system that was shut down once the

'HE's a boy.'

'No it's a machine….and it should be nearly 60 years old.'

'I'm so cold….so cold…' the boy said

'he is a boy! And He needs help!' Kit snapped.

'They are coming.' The Boy said.

'Who… who are coming?' Kit walked towards Gideon.

' So cold here…so cold here… they are coming… they are coming.'

'Who're they?' Kit stepped closer. The gap between them now less than an arms length. With a movement Kit glimpsed Gideon grabbed around her throat in a vice like grip. With a howl of pain Kit was driven to her knees.

'They're coming and nothing will stop them!'

From the peripheral of her vision she could see dark shadows looming up from the floor of the ship. One of the shadows moved behind Gideon and slowly came into the light. It was her father. His face ash grey his eyes the colour of night

'Da? Da? Is that you? Da are you're alright? Da I'm so scared.'

'I'm alright darling…soon everything…everything… will be all right.'

She screamed as he, with one lightening motion, extended a slime covered undulating tentacle slowly stroked around her face.

****

From bio server operations, Deck sergeant Berkinshaw second class stared at her monitor screen in disbelief. Her large chestnut eyes dilated and her jaw began to twitch.

'Uerm supervisor Tatloe… could you come here please! SUPERVISOR TATLOE LEVEL ONE EMERGENCY!'

Tatloe hadn't slept of over twelve hours. His brain was charged on a mixture of Dreano's a disapproved of "upper" and double shots of dehydrated coffee. it kept him available for another 12-hour shift as the team he supervised, worked tirelessly to stop the potential threat from the Wake damaging the rest of the station.

'What is it Berkinshaw…' Tatloe's retorted into the mouthpiece of his headset. His gravelly voice reflected his gritty lean features that were drawn tight. He rubbed a hand though his close cropped white hair and scrubbed at the lint of his stubble. '…you're not the only one with a level one emergency right now.'

'I'm picking up multiple signals from the Crimson Wake sir. The ship… there are life signs aboard. Not on the X-ray spectrum but in the alpha wave.

'That's impossible. I checked the ship on Alpha myself. '
He stormed over to where Berkinshaw sat at her monitor
station. They both stared at the screen.

'There's something else sir someone's operated the,
the manual override.'

'Ok kill the tube. Blow the fucking bolts! Blow
everything! I want no air there as soon as fucking possible!
'

'your actions are hostile to Gideon...' Came Gabriel's
gentle reply. 'I cannot allow you to harm...him.'

'Him? What the fuck?' Tatloe Bellowed

There as a burst of white light at the far end of the
room, followed by a whump and the numbing of sound. In
the near darkness Tatloe felt the sudden loss of air. In a
futile effort he gulped   as decompression and
weightlessness took hold.   In the near half-light, he saw his
fellow officers faces suddenly puff out as their veins
extended, and rippled. Blood leaked out of their eyes, nose
and mouth and then froze into crystals that shattered,
leaked and shattered again. He looked at his arm and saw
the extended veins burst at the surface of his skin. Then
darkness overtook him forever.

***

Draz looked down the tube towards the Wake. there
was nothing but darkness. He wanted to call out but felt too
scared; is eyes nervously scanned the darkness
nothing...nothing at all... but the banging... I heard the
banging and saw... Suddenly the decompression alarms
were screaming all around him. He had no choice. He fled
into the open tube and into the darkness of the Crimson
wake.

The ship seemed to glow with an eerie yellow half-light;
only then did he become aware that there were things
shifting in the darkness.   Instinctively he dived into one of
the ventilation shaft that ran like an artery along the main
corridor of the ship: just as the main hatch closed.

***

Weasley removed the helmet and stared at Kit's pale
face. He couldn't be sure that she even breathed. With a
trembling hand he started to stroke her face. Kit's eyes
burst open. She slapped Weasley across his check; and
reached for her sonic tazer
'Try It!' she said savagely. 'Go On Try it!'She slipped out of
the grav chair. And put some distance between Weasly
and herself

'My Da is on that.. that ship! Only He's not my father any more!' Sobs came in wretches. ' He's one of them… those-'

'- what did you see?'

Hot pain filled Kit's head again.

'So cold… help me!' the boy's urgent voice spoke directly to her kind it was so loud she thought her head might explode.

Kit screamed and held her head. Weasley stepped forward. The pain eased. Ktit slowly raised the gun again.

'Stay the fuck where you are!' What's on that ship?'

' I..I don't know what you mean.'

Hot pain returned. 'He's lying Kit. He knows he knows mouse, he knows ' The boy's voice whispered.

Kit, still holding her head and bent near double, managed to keep the sonic Tazer on Weasley. 'Don't you fucking lie to me! You dirty old bastard!'.

'He knows Kit mouse he knows.' The boy replied as hideous images rippled into Kits mind. Crewmembers turning on each other with unnatural violence and savage pleasure, while above them in the half darkness, ice cold reptilian eyes stared with malevolent pleasure at the scene conducted below. They were killing each other and being used as

' food.

'He knows he knows.' More images reeled in and over her conscious state…images of a man   of a man the boy called father, then next to him and looking up another boy. Whose eyes she knew only too well. '

'It…it was your father wasn't it?'

Weasley stepped back. His face paled.

'You knew that this day would come because your father sent the ship to the system, because he knew what was there.'

'My father… my brother…it was experimental a new idea…'

'What Idea?'

'My father…my brother…'

More images rolled over and into her mind. An accident…a pressure leakage a man standing by a coffin, his eyes cold yet burnig with ambition. The boy set aside hid face now on a screen, then a holographic projection connected to…

'he sent…oh no….

'He was my brother…an experiment in hybridization. The connection of human brain tissue to electronic systems. He would have been the first of a new generation…until…'

'The wake disappeared, lost due to computer malfunction, only it didn't malfunction, it was directly connected to the human consciousness and that dragged

the ship to where?
…… 'the old ones…the old ones….they felt me and came for me…

'Who are the old ones?

'The old ones's that's an old myth from earth there are no old ones, h=get your heard sorted kid!

'The old ones are coming the boy said in her mind again , again.

'Who was the boy?

'You know who the boy was…it was Charlie…my brother…my kid brother

'Your father was a sick-'

'MY FATHERWAS GREAT MAN! A GREAT MAN WHAT HAS YOUR'S ACCOMPLISHED! Weasley sneered a laugh and looked away. Kit turned the Tazer up to max. Her hand trembled. She knew she would only have one chance if he attacked her.

'Mr. Weasley sir…' The gentle voice of Gabriel filled the room. 'Bio operations has been compromised Station output at 67% gravity though restored in some places is fluctuating. I recommend that the lifeboats be operated for all personnel'

'Shit that's all I need 'Muttered Weasley

'They have returned' shouted Charlie inside Kit's head. With a sound that almost doubled her over.

'They have returned.' Sang Gabriel, 'They have returned, they have returned…thee have returned thee have returned wee have returned WE HAVE RETURNED!'

Kit screamed holding her head and span backwards as Weasley dived for her. Just as she pulled on the trigger. The concentrated soundwave threw Weasley back across the platform. Kit picked herself up off the floor grabbed Weasley's key and opened the door. The door to bio operations was sealed and the emergency conduit underneath the section had slid open. With no direction in mind at first she fled as far as she could from operations and Weasley as possible.

***

Draz found himself in a duct that opened up onto the engine room. Slumped at one end of the room was an old man in a docker's uniform. Though his head was slumped to one side, he could just make out the Walrus moustache. Two other men in black uniforms lay prone in huge pools of blood.

The old man groaned; then coughed, ' Weasley you old Cocksucker!' Finally he looked up and saw Draz. He then flushed red in his cheeks and sighed as he got to his feet.

'What're you doing here? This isn' a place for a young

boy.' He pulled off his damaged bio module from his wrist and discarded it like a waste product.

'-I came here as the Dock was flooded with V.   The whole station is cracking... or was... I donna what's gooin on. I jus came for my friend Mouse. She needs me.'

'Feel that son?'

'Nope sir.'

'We're adrift of the station.'

In the orange half-light of the spherical engine room shadows seemed to move

'My name is Beamish... Oliver Beamish... come closer... into the light... it's okay... they don't like the light. Tell me something

'Sure what?'

'Do you believe in ghosts?'

'Ghosts?' He looked at Beamish dumfounded.

'Don't you know what a ghost is?

'No sir.'

Beamish smiled. '-You're a polite boy, I expect your doing well and the proctor's are pleased with you.'

'I've been recommended for flight school.'

'Flight school? Good, that's great really, really great...But you don't know what a ghost is.

Beamish rubbed his ear lobe; and sighed. 'In the old times... before FTL space flight and rockets and corporate greed. People believed that death was merely a stepping stone between... here...' He coughed again '...the perceived world, and the invisible world. Sometimes the visible world touches the invisible world... sometimes things from the invisible world... touch this world... But with all our machines and ships and bio computer's we forgot something... something very important... That not all ghosts are evil... only some ghosts are... and the evil ones... they live... '

In the dark something hissed and slithered. And rattled and rocked chains. '...Then We became proud...in our endeavors...we forgot.' It was then that Draz noticed that Beamish had a flame thrower slung over his left shoulder.

A fibrous tentacle suddenly slid out of the darkness. As the light touched it, it seared with flame. In the darkness something hissed as the tentacle slid over beamish face; and was withdrawn.

'...But ...we haven't forgot everything. For...The God's, despite themselves... gave us one weapon to fight the evil in the dark with.'

Beamish raised the flame thrower and pressed the trigger. Draz's eyes were wide with fear as an alien three legged creature, its three lobed eye extended with rage, and pain as tendrils slithering shudder in the fame. Through huge serrated teeth, set in an enormous bulbous mouth came a hideous wail as it dissolved into the light of the flame.

'Not for long…. come with me Kid, let's get out of here.'

***

Weasley pulled himself off the floor slowly and shook his head, He patted himself down. The key card was gone.

'That Bitch!' He howled as he tried to get out of the room.

' The door command has been over-ridden-' Gideon quietly revealed.

'By who?

'By section Chief Weasley .R Code, code code…'

There was a loud ripping sound followed by a crack. Weasley paled. His eyes opened wide. He typed feverously onto the screen console which suddenly went dark. The room turned blood red as glistening fibrous tentacles ripped into the sphere. He turned and began slamming his fists into the door begging, screaming to be let out, as glistening fingers wrapped about his neck.

***

Now separate from the deck and its own gravity well, Kit found herself floating down the Mall. It was hard to see as the red emergency lighting made it difficult to navigate. But In the darkness she could hear strange scuttling sounds. And people screaming. Another headache made her double over in pain; causing her to spin out of control.

'You must get to the duct's' Charlie warned 'it's not safe in the open

'Why are you helping me?'

because I care.

'I don't understand how are you talking to me?' her question sounded shallow.

'-That's not what you want to know.' Chided Charlie . 'Get to the ducts.'

Within a moment Kit found herself floating within the air ducts. She darted left and found herself in long corridor and a gravity well.

At the end of the corridor she saw Charlie and. She ran towards him, turning right, then left but the faster she ran, the further he seemed to be. Suddenly she found herself in one of the major coolant rooms.

There in front of her stood the boy, she knew as Charlie.

'I am here to help you.'

'Why?'

'You need to get to Earth and warn people. They are coming back.'

'Who are they?'

'The old ones...they are older than time. Older than space. They hate the light of life and come here to remove it.

'That doesn't answer my question.' Breathed Kit.

'I know.' Charles looked down and away from her.

'Draz is safe. He is on board the wake. He has a friend helping him. They are heading to an escape pod. You must get to a pod too. I am taking you there. They are here on the station now. They will kill all life here. I will help you.' Charles smiled but it was automatic and robotic...the automatic of Gideon

' You want to know about my father.'

It was Kit's turn to look away.

'No.'

'Sometimes you lie beautifully. But now you lie badly.

The enormity of recent events, event's themselves that had taken only a few hours hit hard.   Weasley, her father, all of it. A tear smarted her cheek.

Gideon/Charles stretched out a finger and touched it. His finger glittered in the half light as he brushed though the face,

'I cannot take the tear away.'   With pain on his face he looked down. Then looked up.

'I am a hologram. but I am connected to you through the transference. I have a stored data file of the flight of the Crimson wake. I have downloaded it to the shuttle craft. Look for Cavendish-1. Above you is the bug bay. You can fly a bug. I have seen your rating. Take it to the wake. There isn't much time.' With that Gideon/ Charlie dissolved into a swirl of white light .

Within a moment Kit had crawled through the coolant duct. She ran along the main hatch hall and into the bug bay. Then finally into one of the oval shaped maintenance ships. Within a moment she strapped herself in.She pressed the manual override button on the bay doors. That silently exploded outward; then, with short jabs of the tiny ships main thrusters she silently made her way into the funnel web of the way Station. She stared with awe. The station was crumbing in on itself as pressure leaked out. She could see it was spinning out of control and the eye of Jupiter, red hot and flaming was getting larger and larger as she silently sped in the ever-night, between broken and twisted metal and the exsanguinated corpses towards the Crimson wake.

'Draz, can you hear me?' This is Mouse. Draz? Please respond!' She boomed into the ships communicator.

In the shadow of the Wake she saw what she was looking for. A bug maintenance connector. She slid the little ship into reverse and connected up. There was a hiss and she was aboard the wake. She Ran round the corner and slammed into Draz and Beamish.

'Je-us!' Bawled Beamish. 'That's all I need another kid!' come one! Let's get you two out of here!'

'Engaging FTL in T minus three minutes and counting.' Gideon boomed. There was a slithering sound behind them.

With shaking hands beamish opened the panel to the shuttle craft. And pulled the leaver. The door curled open and both Kit and Draz got in.

Beamish looked at them. His face was flat and tired.

'That Weasley…he has a lot to answer for. Stay safe.'

Suddenly the door closed in front of them . They dived into the seats as the marker lights flashed and then ejected the tiny craft into the evernight.

'Flight parameters engaged' Gideon/Charlie spoke

'What the-' Draz looked at the controls

'Its on auto pilot.' Kit croaked, as suddenly and silently the sped away from Jupiter's hot eye and out towards the safety of the colony upon the of moon of Io. Images from the ships rear screen displayed a growing vortex around the way station.

'The wake…it's too close to the station… my gods… it's going to drag the whole thing with it.' Draz Exclaimed, as twisted metal and lumps of dead frozen flesh curled in upon a wild vortex as the wake's drives drew matter towards it, They gasped with awe as the red eye of Jupiter began to enlarge and almost grapple the oncoming darkness that was engaged by the Engines of the wake A darkness that consumed the ship and the station. There was a flash of bright green light and then nothing. The space where the Way station stood only a moment before was empty.

One month later: Io Moon base 23:00Hrs S.E.T.

The director of flight operations Commander William Kirkbride sat behind his large shiny desk from is oval white office and stared down at the two survivors of the Way station with a great deal of concern. They're just kids…just kids… how the hell did they survive?' in front of him was a copy of the file data recording of the first and last flight of the Crimson Wake.

The voice of the bio server Michael filled the room.

'We feel that that the information given by Gideon follows the correct pattern of events.' Michael's disembodied voice echoed in the plush office. Kirkbride stood up from his desk and turned left to then stare with his cornflower eyes, through the window of his office, and out towards the middle distance of the   powdered grey surface of the moon; and then towards A grey reddish sphere that was the earth. It hung low upon the horizon.

You do know that if any of this got out...we're in a lot of trouble...' He turned and stared at both Draz and Kit. '...What you are saying is that a man who once was and in some circles is still held in high regard, sent a ship, with the memory cells of his dead son into an area of space that was he knew as a threat to life here....' He shook his head. '...

'it's frankly hard to believe
 '-Its true, every word of it.' Blurted Kit
'Even if it were true, and there happened to be evidence of it,you would also know, that we would deny that it ever took place, and you only have your word that it actually happened at all...and lets face it you were under a great deal of stress at the time.'

Kirkbride sat back down and faced Draz and Kit. 'Draz you are now without parent's and you father and mother had a genetic line of inheritance   .Katherine I have tried to contact your mother.... She... she... has disavowed you.
'-But that's not true! My father has a sister based at Lunar colony four....you must know that its in the records.
'You still don't get it yet do you...'Kirkbride interrupted
 '-we have to disappear, Kit said coldly.
' Kirkbride sighed. ' So you both are heading for the orphanage program... its either that or an earth-dome...'

They all stood up. Kirkbride nodded as security guards led both Kit and Draz away.

The door hissed as it curled shut. Silence filled the room.
   'Michael?'
   'Yes commander Kirkbride.'
   'Close the file on the Crimson wake and the Way station.... Seal it for thirty years.'
   'what about the findings?
   'What about them?'
   'If Gideon is right... they are coming.
   'Yes...' Kirkbride muttered coolly, then he coughed slightly.   '...I know.'

   With that Kirkbride stood and slowly walked towards the oval window in his office to stare up and out towards the evernight of space.

A tale of the not-so-magical garden

The forget me not

Most people have heard of the little flower that goes by the Latin name of the flower noli me oblivisci, or the "forget me not". The tiny pale blue button flower petals and the little yellow bud face shine all through the spring. However, very few people know the real story behind the flower

It all began one wet autumn many years ago, when the not so magical garden looked damp and a bit grumpy. At the bottom of the garden, underneath the green rickety shed, there lived a tiny weed, with a lot of other different weeds. But this weed was different. He wanted to be a flower.

All through the almost summer; he had poked his head up from between the other weeds, to stare with wonder at the growing flowers that sang their gentle songs. And he sighed deeply, while he watched the heavy plum and yellow sun bumble bees bounce, as they floated on their gossamer wings; gathering the yellow nectar dust that was turned into their children's favourite tipple sweet nectar wine. And he sighed with wonder as he watched the little fittle-borts as they busily walked in hustling bustling zigzagging motions through their miniature cities.

'Oh...' he began, 'Oh, if only... he said repeatedly. And as the sun turned golden and then orange and then red, he sighed repeatedly as he said 'If only, if only if only.' As he slowly wormed and wriggled his way back down into the ground at night

'What do you mean if only?' asked an older weed that he passed along the way. 'If only what?'

'well...' began the little weed, unsure as where to begin. 'I was wondering what it would be like to be a flower; I have been watching the garden flowers all day long... 'He said smiling; but then looked away as he could see the older weed looking a little cross. 'And' he paused trying to find the right words. 'They look happy...kind of... in fact they actually seem...sort of happy...' he looked a little nervously at the older weed, who was starting to look a little angrier with every word he spoke. 'In fact...' he started to say nervously. 'It didn't look half bad...' he looked away nervously. As he concluded 'it...looked...like...fun.' 'FUN?' shouted the older weed 'FUN?' the older weed shudder violently making the little shrub quake with fear. 'Do you KNOW what HE would do if HE caught YOU up there DO YOU? DO YOU?'

'He?' Asked the little shrub 'He he?'

'THE GARDENER! THAT'S WHO!' The older weed splattered and spluttered. 'Up there, where the garden grows, they all call 'im Gentle...ha, there's nothing gentle about 'im. Do you know what 'ee would do to you, if he caught you out there is his garden? DO you want to know what HE did to me? To me and mine?'

The little shrub scuttled backwards nervously, as the older weed lifted two of his leaves; revealing a huge weeping gash in his side.

'Do you see that? That was where my little bud was growing, she was so pretty, so beautiful, and it was almost time to let her go. BUT then HE came... and do you know what he did? HE ripped her from me, AND THREW HER ON THE BONFIRE! That's what he'll do to you too! Gentle gardener...Pahe! There's nothing gentle about him! Mark my words little bud... you stay away from the garden... or he'll throw you on the heap too! Now take my advice little shrub, you're a weed, you're going to stay a weed. So stop your dreaming, and start working at making the shed for us.'

And with that, the older weed slowly slithered and scratched away from the bud, back into the darkness under the shed

But still the little bud wondered what it would be like to live with the flowers and the bees, where the sun shone all the time. And every evening, just before the sun slowly settled behind the old flint rock wall by the red garden gate, the little shrub would stare out as the birds, the bees and the little fitllbort city streets would slowly go to sleep, and he would say, 'If only...if only...if only.'

Unfortunately, word got back to Queen Thistle that there was a little bud that was unhappy with his lot, so late one evening, when she was feeling particularly pointed, she decided to pay a visit to the shed to find out for herself, if these rumors she was hearing were in fact true.

She found the little bud sticking his little head out and looking at the garden.

'It has come to my attention...' she began, 'that for some reason, I cannot understand, that you don't like living here?' she paused and just as the little bud was about to speak she interrupted, to say with as much compassion as she could muster (which was not very much at all.)'Now tell me, what exactly IS the problem?'

There was another pause as the little bud thought quite hard.

'It's like this-

'-your majesty!' the queen stated majestically

'Sorry, your majesty; it's like this your majesty, I want to be a flower. I want to go into the garden and sing a song to the gardener.

'WHAT?' screamed Queen Thistle. Spikes flew across the bottom of the shed spitting into the rotting wood. Her face was white with rage. 'you want to sing a song…to HIM? Why don't you want to sing a song to ME! Why don't you want to destroy the Garden! You're a Weed! You hear me! a WEED! Or are you…something else?

The little bud quaked a slid into the darkness as Queen Thistle lifted herself up and shook violently at him. Beware! She hissed almost silently. 'for you haven't seen the last of me!' and with that the queen slid silently away back into the darkness of the outer hedge, and the steadily growing night. With eyes, full of tears, the little bud looked up at the night sky. To see a hatchery of stars' glimmer and glisten on a velvet blanket. And cried sadly.

***

The next day, as the bud was getting his daily nutrients, by the shed door a gang of adolescent weeds came along.

'We've heard about you.' Said one.

'You're the weed that wants to be a flower.' Hissed another.

'The Queen told us all, abut you! You silly weed!' said the third laughing cruelly. And then they all began to make fun of him, pulling at his leaves tugging at his little roots. '

He wants to be a flower! He wants to be a flower!' they all mocked as more weeds joined in and came over. More and more weeds joined in 'What shall we do to him

'let's strangle him!' said one.

'Let's starve him.' Said another.

'let's pull him to pieces!' said a third and they all joined in and began to try to tear him to pieces.

'Stop!' came a loud stern voice. That seemed to come from everywhere.

The weeds all pulled back, as Queen Thistle came up out of the ground.

'No!' ordered the queen. 'leave him alone.'

The weeds all pulled away, as the queen stood over the little bud. 'You want to be a flower eh?' she said coldly. Well, let's see how well you do on your own. Cast him out of the shed!' she bellowed her body shaking with rage. And with that all the weeds called out with one voice. 'Cast him out! Cast him out! Cast him out!' and with that they lifted the little bud, and threw him into the garden. 'And stay out!' they all shouted, and with that they turned away.

For months, the little bud wandered, not knowing where to go, if he got too close to a flower, there would be a scream. If he got too close to a weed there would be a hiss. Never in all his life, had he felt so terribly alone. Finally, at the end of winter, he found for himself a little place, where there were no flowers or weeds. It was a quiet place by a little stream close to the flint wall. And there, he made for himself a home, where he sang to the gardener, not caring if anyone could hear him or not. It was there that he stayed: singing his little song, to no-one in-particular. Where he grew... and grew... and grew.

One late spring day, the gardener was looking out of his window of his red roofed cottage and saw by the flint wall something that caught his eye. He came downstairs and walked up the narrow garden path. Then he knelt.

'My you are different aren't you.' He said quietly. 'I have never seen one quite like you before.'

The little bud looked up and quaked nervously, as a pair of huge hands came down and pulled him out of the earth. The little bud closed his eyes as he could hear the screaming of other weeds in the large smoking bin, that was almost full.

But he didn't go there.

'There you go...' Said the gardener smiling gently; 'A place all of your own.' And with that the Gardner placed the little growing bud into a large bowl that stood by the large kitchen door. He was in a bowl... a bowl of his own. He couldn't believe it.

'But I don't understand said the bud.'

'Oh, don't you?' asked the gardener; who then showed him a reflection. In the mirror the bud saw something he had never seen before. He saw a beautiful little flower, all blue and yellow smiling at him

'But who's that?' asked the bud.

'Why that's you silly.' Said the gardener and with that she slowly walked away down towards the shed. Whistling as he went.

That's the story, I don't expect you to believe it, but it's true, every word of it. so, consider this: when all those around you think, you are ugly and have no purpose, think of the little weed, and the flower he became... and think not about not only how wonderful you are, but how wonderful you can become with a little bit of love, and determination you too can shape the world you're in.

Pirate Tommy and the pirate who stole Christmas

There was once a Pirate called Tommy Jones, who was almost as old as old dried bones. He wore an eye patch over his right eye and a monocle glass in his left; a golden earing that was the shape of a swan in his ears that had lobes as long his nose –which was, it has to be said, very long indeed- he also had ten gold teeth. Five on the top deck and five below, that when he ate his food, would clatter, clang and ring as he chomped He also had a wooden leg, painted gold and blue with sharks upon it, that looked as if they moved with every stride he took. He also had a rainbow colored parrot that really liked to squawk a lot, making a terrible sound; so he called it "Beiber, not Beaver " Mainly because it annoyed him a lot. However, all in all Pirate Tommy Jones was the happiest Pirate of them all. One day he was so busy shouting at his parrot to be quiet, that he did not see the iceberg ahead. The iceberg hit his boat, with a big loud berblunk which then sank, with a very quick kerplunk, leaving Pirate Tommy and his bird upon a plank.

'Oh that's not funny' said Tommy as his Parrot swirled and sank.

Pirate Tommy and his parrot managed to get to a deserted Island. Which was a bit of a miracle in itself. One the plus, It had huge coconuts, however sadly they were always out of his reach. They became so hungry that they even thought about eating each other. Out of an act of desperation, Tommy who found a bottle on the beach ripped a part of his shirt and with a piece of beach charcoal he wrote this note:

Whoever gets this message! Will you save us?
We are on a desert Island with no food and water. We are very hungry eating only yucky seaweed. Ps we are not Pirates! From Tommy Jones (not a pirate) and Beiber Beaver.

And with that He threw the bottle out to sea. Pirate Tommy Jones and Beiber Beaver were on the island a very long time, it felt as long as an entire English lesson which can be a very long time indeed. Then on the Horizon a boat was seen.

The note was found by a fisherman called Jack. Jack had short gold hair and bright green eyes and a smile that never left his face. When he read the note he was so exited to meet Bieber beaver that he sailed to the deserted island as fast as he could. But jack hated Pirates, and when he landed on the Island and saw that Tommy was a pirate was became very scared and almost ran away. But he thought, if Bieber beaver was in trouble then he ought to try and save him So Tommy waited until dark.

When the sun went down, Jack crept into Tommy's Camp and searched for Bieber But he could not find Bieber anywhere. All he could find was a tired old looking parrot that squawked a lot. So he took the parrot and in the parrot's place, he left this note:

Dear Pirate! I took your parrot because you have taken Beieber beaver! return Bieber beaver and I will return your Parrot. If you don't let Bieber beaver go I will be making Parrot stew! From Jack

When Tommy woke up and saw the note, he was not a very happy pirate, because though his Parrot made a lot of noise, he liked it quite a lot. He felt so sad that he almost cried. He searched the Island all day, jumping into caves and running around coves. Walking in the Jungle and tearing some of his clothes. Then, as the sun was going down, he found, in a tiny bay, Jacks boat, and from the boat he heard a very loud "SQWARK!"

"That's me Bieber!" he said to himself as he hopped onto a log, skipped across the bay, and jumped into Jacks boat – which is no mean feat for a man as old as he, with a wooden leg and a monacled eye-.

"Why d'e ye steal my Parrot!" said Tommy, in his best Pirate voice.

"Because you took Bieber!" said Jack. "Now give him back!"

"But you silly man!" began Tommy "That is Bieber!, now give me me parrot back!

"No" said Jack. "I hate Pirates!"

Jack told him said that last week -at around about tea time- a big boat came suddenly out of the sea. On it was a very grumpy looking Pirate who had a Pumpkin for a Belly, hair that fell below his or her, (as he couldn't be gender specific anymore) knees and eyes as big and blue as the big blue sea.   This Pirate took all my stuff That's why I hate Pirates! They are Horrid!"

When Jack told his story, Tommy's face became as white as his shirt. "That's the great Pirate Christmas!" he said. His voice trembled

"The great Pirate Christmas?" asked Jack.

"Yes" said Tommy. He lives on a boat called the grumpy old pants and s/he takes all the presents s/he can find. I am not like mm and I don't like mm at all."

I don't like mm either." Said Tommy

"mm was very scary!" said Jack.

"mm scares me too" began Tommy, " I saw mm shoot burning coal and boiling sand, from mm's hands....Look, if I get the toys back will you give me my parrot back?" Asked Tommy

"Yes." Said Jack.

"Then what are we waiting for!" said Tommy. "We must get to sea now!

It was in the middle of the darkest night that Jack and Tommy had ever known, when a big loud whistling sound was heard, this was followed by a Big loud BOOM that shook the seas about the boat.

"IT'S THE GRUMPY PANTS!" they said together.

All of a sudden the Grumpy pants came out of the sea. It was as blue as the colour of the sea, it was as red as the colour of fire and it was as gold as the curtains in our front room at home. It had three masts that had three black sails which were torn a bit and on each side were ten huge cannons, five on side and five on the other.

Standing on the boat by the ships wheel stood the great Pirate Christmas. s/he had a belly was as big and as orange as huge pumpkin. And black hair fell down to non gender specific knees and had eyes were as big and as blue as the big blue sea.

"Give me your presents!" Bellowed the Pirate Christmas.

"We don't have any Presents!" shouted Tommy and Jack back "Give back the toys you have taken! It's not nice to steal!

"No they are MINE!" The great Pirate shouted; its pumpkin belly shook like big wobbly custard.

"OH NO THEY'RE NOT!" they shouted back.

"OH YES THEY ARE!"   shouted the Pirate Christmas

"OH NO THEY'RE NOT!" they replied again.

With that, and mostly because they didn't want to say "OH NO THEY'RE NOT!" any more, they both jumped on board the Grumpy Pants.

As soon as they hit the deck of the ship, the Pirate Christmas shot boiling sand from one hand and burning coals from another. But Tommy and Jack were quicker and jumped out of the way just in time.

"Give back the toys you stole!" They shouted crossly. "You are the meanest nastiest most terrible pirate in the whole wide world!"

"That's not a nice thing to say..." Said the Pirate Christmas who began to cry very loudly. "...I take presents because nobody sends me any. And my name is not The Pirate Christmas, That's the name people gave me after I started stealing presents. My real name is Pirate Julie and I am lonely."

This made Tommy feel very sad. Because he knew that Pirate Julie only wanted friends, so Pirate Tommy had a long think and then went into his red velvet jacket pocket.

"These are my best marbles" Said Tommy. "if if I give you these, you must promise to give back all of the presents you stole."

So pirate Julie agreed and when she said, "yes" a big light came from above. It shone upon her and then turned this non gender specific and scary looking Pirate with a pumpkin belly into a pretty princess, with long gold hair.

From that moment on, Tommy Jack and Julie sailed across the seven seas giving back all the presents that once had been stolen. Making everybody very happy wherever they went.

The end.

Printed in Great Britain
by Amazon

21591133R00192